BUSTED IN BOLLYWOOD

Busted in Bollywood

Nicola Marsh

Entangled Publishing, LLC
2614 South Timberline Road
Suite 109
Fort Collins, CO 80525
Visit our website at www.entangledpublishing.com.

Edited by Libby Murphy and Stacy Abrams
Cover design by Liz Pelletier

Ebook ISBN   978-1-62061-122-7
Print ISBN   978-1-62061-121-0

Manufactured in the United States of America

First Edition June 2012

The author acknowledges the copyrighted or trademarked status and trademark owners of the following wordmarks mentioned in this work of fiction: Titanic, Monsoon Wedding, Bride & Prejudice, Slumdog Millionaire, How to Lose a Guy in 10 Days, Maid in Manhattan, When Harry Met Sally, An Affair to Remember, Sleepless in Seattle, Shall We Dance?, Runaway Bride, You've Got Mail, Two Weeks Notice, Saturday Night Fever, Casablanca, Bananarama, Stetson, Bergdorf's, Donna Karan, Aladdin, Saks, New York Post, Brut 33, Davidoff's Cool Water, Nike, 7UP, Ben & Jerry's, Chunky Monkey, Versace, Gucci, Valentino, Manolo Blahnik, Jimmy Choo, Prada, Chanel, Chanel No. 5, Old Spice, Starbucks, Gloria Jean, Revlon, Doritos, Remington, Lancome, Estee Lauder, M.A.C., L'Oreal, Maybelline, Sky High Curl, Glam Shine, Doritos, Giorgio Armani, 007, U.S. Postal Service, Buffy the Vampire Slayer, Coke, Elle Magazine, Angry Birds, TAG Heuer, TV Soap, The Young and the Restless, Bold and the Beautiful, UNESCO World Heritage, Glee, True Blood, CSI, AMEX, Mills & Boon, McDonald's, GQ, Pantene, Villeroy & Boch, Universal Studios, Sony, Rolex, Hugo Boss, Yankees, Disneyland, Charlie's Angels, Grease, Miss Universe, Fendi, Visa, Happy Days, Calvin Klein, Perrier, Tiffany & Co., Bill & Ted's Excellent Adventure, Christian Louboutin, Elizabeth Arden Red Door, Dirty Dancing, Burberry, Ralph Lauren, Learjet, Subway, Hermes, Nobu, Bobbie Brown Professional Cosmetics, Inside Style, Netflix, Colgate, The Plaza Hotel, Google, Facebook, Seinfeld, Friends, BBC, Birkin, Vogue, Christian Dior, Valium, The Russian Tea Room, Stella McCartney, Waldorf Astoria, Dolce & Gabanna, and Moet.

For the new kids on the publishing block: Liz Pelletier, Heather Howland, Libby Murphy, and the fab folk at Entangled. Thanks for loving this book as much as I do.

CHAPTER ONE

Look up *stupid* in the dictionary and you'll find my picture.

Along with revealing stats: Shari Jones, twenty-nine, five-seven, black hair, hazel eyes, New Yorker. Addicted to toxic men like my ex, cheesecake, and mojitos (not necessarily in that order), and willing to do anything for a friend, including travel to India and impersonate aforementioned friend in an outlandish plot to ditch her fiancé.

See? Stupid.

"You're the best." Amrita Muthu, my zany best friend who devised this escapade, cut a wedge of chocolate cheesecake and plopped it on my plate. "Have another piece to celebrate."

I loved how she always had cheesecake stocked in her apartment freezer but as I stared at my favorite dessert I knew I couldn't afford the extra calories. Not with my destination of Mumbai—land of food hospitality—where I'd be bombarded with rich, sugar-laden treats that I'd have to eat to be polite.

Despite my Indo-American heritage, *jalebis, gulab jamuns,* and *rasmalai* are not my idea of heaven. The sickly sweet morsels were a testament to years as a fat kid, courtesy of an Indian mother who wasn't satisfied until my eyes—as well as my waistline—were bulging from too much food.

"Eat up, my girl," Mom used to say, shoveling another mini Mount Everest of rice and *dahl* onto my plate. "Lentils are strengthening. They'll make you big and strong."

She'd been right about the *big* part. Still waiting for my muscles to kick in.

But hey, I survived the food fest, and thanks to hours in the gym, smaller portions of *dahl* (yeah, I'd actually become hooked on the stuff), and moving away from home, I now had a shape that didn't resemble a blimp.

"Shari? You going to eat or meditate?"

"Shut up." I glared at Amrita—Rita to me—then picked up my fork and toyed with the cheesecake. "Too early for celebrations." *Commiserations* were more likely if this wacky plot imploded. "You're not the one spending two weeks in Mumbai with a bunch of strangers, pretending to like them."

"But you don't have to pretend. That's the whole point. I want you to be yourself and convince the Ramas I'm not worthy of their son." Rita stuck two fingers down her throat and made gagging noises. "Bet he's a real prince. Probably expects the prospective good little Hindu wife he's never seen to bow, kiss his ass, and bear him a dozen brats. Like that's going to happen."

She rolled her perfectly kohled eyes and cut herself another generous slab of cheesecake. Curves are revered in India and Rita does her heritage proud with an enviable hourglass figure.

"You think my naturally obnoxious personality will drive this prince away, huh? Nice."

Rita grinned and topped off our glasses from the mojito pitcher sitting half-empty between us. "You know what I mean.

You're flamboyant, assertive, eloquent. Except when it came to your ex." She made a thumbs-down sign. "I'm a wimp when it comes to defying my folks. If anyone can get me out of this mess, you can."

Debatable, considering the mess I'd made of my life lately.

"No way would I marry some stooge and leave NYC to live in Mumbai. Not happening."

She took a healthy slurp of mojito and ran a crimson-tipped fingernail around the rim of the glass. "Besides, you score a free trip. Not to mention the added bonus of putting Tate behind you once and for all."

That did it. I pushed my plate away and sculled my mojito. The mention of Tate Embley, my ex-boyfriend, ex-landlord, and ex-boss turned my stomach. Rita was right—I *was* assertive, which made what happened with him all the more unpalatable. I'd been a fool, falling for a slick, suave lawyer who'd courted me with a practiced flair I'd found lacking in the guys I'd dated previously.

I'd succumbed to the romance, the glamour, the thrill. Tate had been attentive and complimentary and generous. And I'd tumbled headfirst into love, making the fact he'd played me from start to finish harder to accept. Maybe I'd been naïve to believe his lavish promises. Maybe I should've known if something's too good to be true it usually is. Maybe I'd been smitten at the time, blinded to the reality of the situation: an unscrupulous jerk had charmed me into believing his lies to the point I'd lowered my streetwise defenses and toppled into an ill-fated relationship from the beginning.

"Oops, I forgot." Rita's hand flew to her mouth, a mischievous glint in her black eyes. "Wasn't supposed to mention the T-word."

I smirked. "Bitch."

"It's therapeutic to talk about it."

Morose, I stared into my empty glass, knowing a stint in India couldn't be as bad as this. If there's one thing I hate, it's rehashing the mess I'd made of my love life. "What's there to talk about? We're over."

"Over, schmover. If he came groveling on his Armani knees you'd reconsider." She jabbed a finger at me. "If he comes sniffing around you again I'll kick his sorry ass to the curb."

"I already tried kicking him to the curb and now I'm homeless and unemployed."

Three months later, I couldn't believe he'd played me, thrown me out of his swank Park Avenue apartment, and fired me all on the same day. So what if I'd called him a lying, sleazy bastard with the morals of a rabid alley cat? If the Gucci loafer fit…

Rita refilled my glass, her stern glare nothing I hadn't seen before. "He'd reduced you to ho status. He paid your salary, your rent, and left you the odd tip when he felt like it."

She stared at the princess-cut ruby edged in beveled diamonds on the third finger of my right hand and I blushed, remembering the exact moment Tate had slipped it on. We'd been holed up in his apartment for a long weekend and in the midst of our sex-a-thon he'd given me the ring. Maybe I'd felt like Julia Roberts getting a bonus from Richard Gere for all of two seconds, but hey, it'd been different. I loved the guy. He loved me.

Yeah, right.

Tate had strung me along for a year, feeding me all the right lines: his wife didn't love him, platonic marriage, they never had sex, they stayed together for appearances, he'd leave her soon, blah, blah, blah.

Stupidly, I believed him until that fateful day three months ago when someone at Embley Associates, one of New York's premier law firms, revealed the latest juicy snippet: Tate, the firm's founding partner, was going to be a daddy. After years of trying with his gorgeous wife, nudge, nudge, wink, wink.

Say no more.

Unfortunately, Tate had tried some schmoozy winking with me to gloss over his *'I was drunk, she took advantage of me, it won't change a thing between us'* spiel. I'd nudged him right where it hurt and things had spiraled downhill from there.

Hence, my homeless, unemployed, and dumped status.

I folded my arms to hide the offending bauble—which was so damn pretty I couldn't part with it despite being tempted to pay rent. "Your point?"

"Forget him. Forget your problems. Go to India, live it up."

"And save your ass in the process?"

Rita grinned and clinked glasses with mine. "Now you're on the right track."

"I must be crazy."

"Or desperate."

"That, too." I shook my head. "Have you really thought this through? Word travels fast in your family."

"We've been planning this for a month. It'll work." Rita lowered her glass, an uncharacteristic frown slashing her brows. "You've been living here. You've seen my mom in action. You know why I have to do this."

She had a point. While every aspect of Rita's Hinduism fascinated an atheist like me, her double life was exhausting. Her folks would be scandalized if they knew she drank alcohol and ate beef, forbidden in her religion. But according to my inventive friend, who liked to stretch boundaries, cows in New York weren't holy and the alcohol helped her assimilate. Likely excuses, but living beneath the burden of her family's expectations— including an arranged marriage to a guy halfway around the world—had taken its toll. She needed to tell her folks the truth, but for now she'd settled on this crazy scheme to buy herself time to build up the courage.

I could've persuaded her to come clean, but I went along with it because I owed Rita. Big-time. She'd let me crash here, she'd listened to my sob story repeatedly, she'd waived rent while I fruitlessly job-searched. Apparently out-of-work legal secretaries were as common in job interviews as rats were in the subway. Didn't help that the low-key, detail-oriented job bored me to tears in my last year at Embley Associates, and I'd been wistfully contemplating a change. Therein lay the problem. I needed to work for living expenses and bills and rent but my personal fulfillment well was dry and in serious need of a refill.

Another reason I was doing this: I hoped traveling to Mumbai would give me a fresh perspective. Besides, I could always add actress/impersonator to my résumé to jazz it up when I returned.

"Telling your family would be easier." On both of us, especially me, the main stooge about to perpetuate this insanity. "What if I mess up? It'll be a disaster."

Oblivious to my increasing nerves, Rita's frown cleared. "It'll be a cinch. My aunt Anjali's in on the plan, and she'll meet you at the airport and guide you through the Rama rigmarole. She's a riot and you'll love staying with her. Consider it a well-earned vacation." She clicked her fingers and grinned. "A vacation that includes giving the Ramas' dweeby son the cold shoulder so he can't stand the thought of marrying me. Capish?"

"Uh-huh."

Could I really pull this off? Posing as an arranged fiancée, using a smattering of my rusty Hindi, immersing in a culture I hadn't been a part of since my family had moved to the States when I was three. Though I was half Indian, spending the bulk of my life in New York had erased my childhood memories of the exotic continent that held little fascination for me. Sure, Mom told stories about her homeland and continued to whip up Indian feasts that would do a maharajah proud, yet it all seemed so remote, so distant.

It hadn't been until I'd become friends with Rita, who worked at Bergdorf's in accounts—and who gave me a healthy discount once we'd established a friendship—that my latent interest in my heritage had been reawakened.

Rita had intrigued me from the start, her sultry beauty, her pride in her culture, her lilting singsong accent. She encapsulated everything Indian, and though my life had temporarily fallen apart thanks to the Toad—my penchant for nicknames resonated in this instance, considering Tate *was* cold and slimy—the opportunity to travel to India and help Rita in the process had been too tempting to refuse.

"You sure this Rakesh guy doesn't know what you look like?"

"I'm sure." Her smug smile didn't reassure me. "I'm not on Facebook and I Googled myself three times to make sure there were no pics. You'll be pleased to know I'm decidedly un-Google-worthy. As for the photo my parents sent before they left… well, let's just say there was a little problem in transit."

"Tell me you didn't interfere with the U.S. Postal Service."

"'Course not." Her grin widened. "I tampered with the Muthu Postal Service."

"Which means?"

"Mom gave Dad a stack of mail to send. He was giving me a ride, and when he stopped to pick up his favorite tamarind chutney I pilfered the envelope out of the bunch."

"Slick."

"I think so." She blew on her nails and polished them against her top, her 'I'm beyond cool' action making me laugh. "Besides, we look enough alike that even if he caught a sneak peek at some photo, it shouldn't be a problem."

Luckily, I had cosmopolitan features that could pass for any number of backgrounds: Spanish, Italian, Portuguese, or Mexican. Few people pegged me for half Indian, not that I'd played it down or anything. In a country as diverse as the U.S., an exotic appearance was as common as a Starbucks on every corner.

"I like your confidence," I said, my droll response garnering a shrug.

"You'll be fine."

"Easy for you to say." I twirled the stem of my cocktail glass, increasingly edgy. "Even if this works, won't your folks fix you up with another guy?"

"Leave my parents' future matchmaking propositions to me." She snapped her fingers, her self-assurance admirable. "If they try this again, I'll pull the 'I'm your only child and you'll never see me again' trick. That'll scare them. I would've done it now but they've planned this Grand Canyon trip for a decade and I would've hated seeing them cancel it, and lose a small fortune, over me."

She paused, tapped her bottom lip, thinking, as I inwardly shuddered at what she'd come up with next. "Though I do feel sorry for them, what with Anjali being their only living relative, which is why I pretended to go along with this farce of marrying

Rakesh in the first place."

"You're all heart."

She punched me lightly on the upper arm. "You can do this."

"I guess." My lack of enthusiasm elicited a frown.

"Here's the info dossier. Keep it safe."

She handed me a slim manila folder, the beige blandly discreet. Welcome to my life as a 007 sidekick. Halle Berry? Nah, I'm not that vain. Miss Moneypenny? Not that old, though considering the time I'd wasted on Tate, I was starting to feel it.

"My future as a single woman able to make her own life choices depends on it."

I rolled my eyes but took the folder. "I know everything there is to know about the Rama family. You've drilled me for a month straight."

"Okay, wiseass. Who's the father and what does he do?"

I sipped at my mojito and cleared my throat, trying not to chuckle at Rita's obvious impatience as she drummed her fingernails against the armrest. "Too easy. Senthil Rama, musician, plays tabla for Bollywood movies."

"The mother?"

"Anu. Bossy cow."

A smile tugged at the corners of Rita's crimson-glossed mouth. "Sisters?"

"Three. Pooja, Divya, and Shruti. Watch them. If the mom's a cow, they're the calves."

Rita's smile turned into a full-fledged grin. "And last but not least?"

"Rakesh Rama. Betrothed to Amrita Muthu, New York City girl shirking her familial responsibility, besmirching her Hindu heritage, shaming her mother, disappointing her father, embroiling her best friend in deception—"

"Smartass."

Rita threw a silk-covered cushion at my head, and thanks to the four mojitos I'd consumed my reaction time slowed and it hit me right between the eyes. Reminiscent of the lapis lazuli paperweight I'd thrown at Tate as I slammed out of his office that last time. Pity my aim wasn't as good as Rita's.

Her scheme might be crazy but I knew I was doing the right thing. India would buy me some thinking time about what I wanted to do with my life.

I dribbled the last precious drops from the mojito jug into our glasses and raised mine in Rita's direction. "To Bollywood and back. Bottoms up."

• • •

"Oh. My. *God.*"

Shielding my eyes from the scorching glare of Mumbai's midday sun, I ran across the tarmac like a novice on hot coals, seeking shade in the terminal yet terrified by the sea of faces confronting me. How many people were meeting this flight?

A guy jostled me as I neared the terminal, my filthy glare wasted when he patted my arm, mumbled an apology, and slid into the crowd. I wouldn't have given the incident a second thought if not for the way his hand had lingered on my arm, almost possessively. Creep.

I picked up the pace, ignoring the stares prickling between my shoulder blades. Were the hordes ogling me, or was that my latent paranoia flaring already? *There's the imposter—expose her.*

I battled customs and fought my way through the seething mass of humanity to grab my luggage from the carousel. Caught up in a surge toward the arrival hall, *culture shock* took on new meaning as men, women, and children screeched and waved and hugged. On the outskirts I spotted a woman holding aloft a miniature Statue of Liberty, like Buffy brandishing a cross to ward off the vamps.

I'd laughed when Rita told me what her aunt would use to identify herself at Mumbai airport; now that I'd been smothered by a blanket of heat and aromas I didn't dare identify, jostled by pointy elbows, and sweated until my peasant top clung to my back, it wasn't so funny.

I used my case as a battering ram as I pushed through the crowd toward the Statue of Liberty. I'd never been so relieved to see that lovely Lady and her spiked halo.

"*Namaste*, Auntie," I said, unsure whether to press my palms together in the traditional Hindi greeting with a slight bow, hug her, or reel back from the garlic odor clinging to her voluminous cobalt sari.

She took the dilemma out of my hands by dropping the statue into her bag and wrapping her arms around me in a bear hug. "Shari, my child. Welcome. We talk English, yes?"

Holding my breath against the garlic fumes, I managed a nod as she pulled away and held me at arm's length.

"That naughty girl Amrita didn't tell me how beautiful you are. Why aren't you married?"

Great. I'd escaped my mom's Gestapo-like interrogations only to have Anjali pick up the slack. I mumbled something indecipherable, like 'mind your own business,' and smiled demurely. No use alienating the one woman who was my ally for the next two weeks.

"Never mind. Once this Rama rubbish is taken care of, maybe you'll fall in love with a nice Indian boy, yes?" Anjali cocked her head to one side, her beady black eyes taking on a decidedly matchmaking gleam.

I don't think so! I thought.

"Pleasure to meet you, Auntie," I said.

Rather than quiz me about my lack of marriage prospects she beamed, tucked her arm through mine, and dragged me toward the exit where another throng waited to get in. "Come, I have a car waiting. You must be exhausted after your flight. A good cup of *chai* and a few *ladoos* will revive you."

Uh-oh. The sweet-stuffing tradition had begun. *Ladoos* were lentil-laden balls packed with *ghee*, Indian clarified butter designed to add a few fat rolls in that fleshy gap between the sari and the *choli*, the short top worn beneath. Mom's favorite was *besan ladoos* and I remembered their smooth, nutty texture melting in my mouth. Despite my vow to stay clear of the sweets, saliva pooled and I swallowed, hoping I could resist.

Exiting the terminal equated with walking into a furnace and I dabbed at the perspiration beading on my top lip as Anjali signaled to a battered Beamer. "My driver will have us home shortly."

I didn't care if her driver beamed me up to the moon, as long as the car had air-conditioning.

While Anjali maintained a steady stream of conversation on the way to her house, I developed a mild case of whiplash as my head snapped every which way, taking in the sights of downtown Mumbai.

Cars, diesel-streaming buses, motorbikes, bicycles, and auto-rickshaws battled with a swarming horde of people on the clogged roads in a frightening free-for-all where it was every man, woman, and rickshaw driver for themselves.

The subway on a bad day had nothing on this.

Anjali—immune to the near-death experiences occurring

before our eyes—prattled on about *parathas*, my favorite whole-meal flatbread, and her Punjabi neighbors, while I gripped the closest door handle until my fingers ached. Our driver, Buddy (Anjali had a thing for Buddy Holly and thus dubbed her man-about-the-house Buddy, thanks to his Coke-bottle glasses), maintained a steady stream of Hindi abuse—at least I assumed it was abuse, judging by his volume and hand actions—while his other hand remained planted on the horn.

Pity I hadn't held onto those earplugs from the flight. Would've been handy to mute the Mumbai melodies. I squeezed my eyes shut for the hundredth time as a small child darted out after a mangy dog right in front of our car. On the upside, every time I reopened my eyes, something new captured my attention. Fresh flowers on street corners, roadside vendors frying snacks in giant woks, long, orderly lines at bus stops. Bustling markets and sprawling malls nestled between ancient monuments.

Amazing contrasts—boutiques and five-star restaurants alongside abject poverty, beggars sharing the sidewalks with immaculately coiffed women who belonged on the cover of *Elle*, smog-filled streets while the Arabian Sea stretched as far as the eye could see on the city's doorstep.

When Buddy slowed and turned into a tiny driveway squeezed between a row of faded whitewashed flats, I almost missed the frenetic Mumbai energy that held me enthralled already.

"We're home." Anjali clapped her hands. "Leave your luggage to Buddy. Time to eat."

As I followed Anjali into the blessed coolness of her house, my hands shaking from the adrenaline surging through my system, I had an idea. Maybe soaking *ladoos* in white rum and lime juice would counteract the calories?

My very own Mumbai Mojitos.

Take a bite, get happy.

Eat two, get ecstatic.

Eat a dozen, get catatonic and forget every stupid reason why I'd traveled thousands of miles to pretend to be someone else.

Great, perpetuating this scheme had affected my sense of humor, along with my perspective.

Hoping my duty-free liquor had survived the road trip from hell, I perked up at the thought of my favorite drink (to be consumed on the sly as Rita reminded me a hundred times, in case I forgot I wasn't supposed to drink while impersonating her) and climbed the stairs behind Anjali, trying not to focus on her cracked heels or the silk sari straining over her ample ass.

"Hurry up, child. The *ayah* has outdone herself in preparing a welcome meal for you."

Wishing I had a housemaid-cum-cook back home, I fixed a polite smile on my face as Anjali launched into another nonstop monologue, this time about the joys of grinding spices on a stone over store-bought curry powders. While she chatted I surreptitiously loosened the top button on my jeans in preparation for my initiation into India's national pastime — after cricket, that is.

"I hope you enjoy your curries hot, Shari. Nothing like chili to put pep in your step." Anjali bustled me into a dining room featuring a table covered with enough food to feed the multitudes I'd seen teaming the streets earlier. "Eat up, child. Men like some flesh on their women. Perhaps that's your problem?"

With an ear-jarring cackle, she proceeded to show me exactly how attractive men must find her by heaping a plate with rice, Goan fish curry rich in spices and coconut milk, *baigan aloo* (eggplant and potato), *chana dahl* (lentils), *pappadums* (deep-fried, wafer-thin lentil flour accompaniments resembling giant crisps), and *raita* (a delicious yoghurt chutney).

Had she noticed I hadn't said more than two words since I arrived? If so, she didn't let on, happily maintaining a steady flow of conversation while making a sizeable dent in the food laid out before us. With constant urging, I managed to eat a reasonable portion of rice and curry, leaving room for the inevitable barrage of sweets, wondering if I could sneak up to my room for a fortifying rum.

However, like most of my dreams in this world, it wasn't to be.

"Excuse me, Missy." Buddy shuffled into the room, his dusty bare feet leaving faint footprints on the polished white tiles. "There's been an accident."

Rather than looking at Anjali, Buddy darted glances at me with frightened doe eyes.

"Spit it out, man. What's happened?" Anjali spoiled her attempt at playing the imperious master standing over her servant by stuffing another ball of rice into her mouth with her curry-covered fingers and smacking her lips.

Buddy stared at me, panic-stricken. "It's the missy's bottles. They broke. Leak everywhere."

"Bottles? What bottles?" Anjali paused mid-chew, her plucked eyebrows shooting skyward.

I rarely swore. In fact, the F-word made me cringe. However, with my stomach rebelling against the onslaught of food, my nerves shot by the drive here, and my secret duty-free mojito stash now in ruins, all I could think was *fuuuuuck.*

· · ·

I wanted to sleep in the next morning but Anjali didn't believe in jet lag. She believed in breakfast at the crack of dawn.

"Eat more, my girl. *Idlis* will give you strength for the day ahead." She pushed the tray of steamed rice cakes toward me along with the *sambhar*, a lentil soup thick with vegetables.

Not wanting to appear impolite on my first morning here, I spooned another *idli* onto my plate and ladled a sparrow's serving of *sambhar* over it. "What's on for today?"

"I've planned a grand tour of Mumbai especially for you." She held up a hand, fingers extended. "First stop, the Gateway of India."

One finger bent.

"Second, a boat cruise on the harbor."

Another finger lowered.

"Third, Chhatrapati Shivaji Terminus. Then Mani Bhavan, at the home of Mahatma Ghandi."

She waved her pinkie and I hoped our last stop included shopping.

"And finally, we eat at my favorite restaurant."

The thought of more food turned the *idlis* to lead in my stomach, and I edged my plate away. She didn't notice, her face glowing with pride, like a kid who nailed a test. I didn't have the heart to tell her I was more interested in Mumbai's malls than cultural icons.

"Sounds good." I injected enthusiasm into my voice, but it wasn't enough to distract Anjali as she eyed my plate and untouched *idli* with a frown.

Thankfully, Buddy entered the dining room and Anjali clapped her hands. "Time to go."

Relieved, I followed her to the car, thanking Buddy for holding open my door as I slid onto the back seat. He shuffled his feet in embarrassment but I caught the flicker of a bashful smile before he slipped behind the steering wheel. He'd been mortified over the duty-free bottle breakage, but what could I do? Confess to a secret alcohol stash? I'd brushed over the incident last night, citing special clear coconut juice I'd brought from the States before hiding the broken glass and condemning labels deeply in the trash. That's all I needed, for some nosy neighbor to out Anjali for secretly swigging alcohol.

As Buddy tested his Angry Birds skills—people were like the game app birds, seemingly flinging themselves at our car—I swallowed a curse. Oblivious to my morbid fear of inadvertently killing one of the many pedestrians jamming the sidewalks and spilling onto the road, Anjali stared at my hands, where I clutched at the worn leather.

"That's a lovely ring." She pointed at the ruby. "From someone special?"

"No." I released my grip on the seat to twist the ring around, wishing I didn't love it so much. Definitely not from someone special.

She didn't probe, her curiosity snagged by my watch. The gold link and diamond TAG had been a gift to myself with my first paycheck at Tate's law firm, a splurge I'd justified at the time by saying I needed to look the part at an upmarket practice, when in reality I'd wanted to impress the boss who'd already made a pass at me during the first two weeks.

"That a gift, too?"

Jeez, who was she, the jewelry police?

"A gift to myself."

Needing a change of topic fast, I pointed out the window.

"That's the third cinema we've passed in a few blocks."

She craned her neck for a better look. "Nothing unusual. We're the movie capital of India, so there's a multiplex cinema on every street."

She had to be exaggerating, but as Buddy weaved in and out of the road chaos, I spotted five more.

"Personally, I prefer cable." Anjali rummaged around in her giant handbag and pulled out a *TV Soap* magazine. "Hundreds of channels, better viewing."

She flicked it open to a double-page spread of buffed guys with bare chests and brooding expressions. Not bad, if you liked that fake chiseled look. By the twinkle in Anjali's eye as she shoved the magazine my way, she did. "Bill Spencer is my favorite."

Clueless, I shrugged.

Horrified, she stabbed at a photo of a dark-haired, dark-eyed Adonis with rippling pecs and a serious six-pack. "Don Diamont. You've never heard of him? *The Young and the Restless*? Dollar Bill Spencer in *Bold and the Beautiful*?"

"Uh, no, I'm more of a rom-com gal."

Shaking her head, she snapped the magazine shut and thrust it into her bag, casting me a disbelieving glare. "I'm thinking Amrita did you a favor sending you here."

I didn't want to ask, but there was something cutesy and lovable about Anjali, and I couldn't resist. "Why, Auntie?"

"So I can educate you."

I stifled a snort. "About soap operas?"

"About *men*." She rattled her bag for emphasis. "These are the men you must aspire to. Handsome, tall, broad shoulders, rich."

"Fictional," I muttered, earning a click of her tongue.

She crossed her arms, hugging the bag and magazine to her chest. "You'll see. Once you ditch Anu's son, we can concentrate on finding you another boy."

I refrained from adding, "I want a *man*." No point encouraging her.

Buddy swerved into a narrow parking space between a cart and an auto-rickshaw. I didn't know what was worse: the promise of Anjali's matchmaking me with a soap-idol lookalike or the ensured whiplash every time I sat in a car.

"Good, we're here." She gathered the folds of her sari like a queen as she stepped from the car. "Where every tourist to Mumbai starts exploring." She threw her arms wide. "The Gateway of India."

I might not be a cultural chick but I had to admit the huge archway on the water's edge was impressive. Roughly sixty feet, it had four turrets and intricate latticework carved into the yellow stone. "What's this made from?"

"Basalt stone, very strong." Anjali linked her elbow through mine and drew me down the steps behind the arch to the water's edge. "Come, we'll take a short cruise on a motor launch."

I eyed the small, bobbing boats dubiously, hoping the captains steered more sedately than the drivers on the roads.

Anjali didn't give me a chance to refuse, slipping a launch operator some rupees and hustling me into a boat before I could feign seasickness. The motor launch shot off at a great speed and I clung onto the seat. Good thing I'd skipped the manicure before I met the Ramas. It'd be shredded by the end of today.

Anjali hadn't prepped me for the upcoming Rama meeting. Not to worry. Rita had more than made up for it. "The Rama welcoming party should be interesting."

"Coming face to face with Rakesh might be interesting."

Anjali screwed up her nose. "Meeting that witch Anu?" She muttered a stream of Hindi, her tone vitriolic.

Witch? Intrigued, I waited for a pause. "So you know Anu?"

"You could say that." She folded her arms, her expression thunderous.

O-kay. Untold saga alert. Surprising Rita hadn't mentioned any history between her aunt and prospective mother-in-law. "Is there a problem between you—"

"Look." Anjali nudged me with her elbow and gestured toward the arch. Nice change of topic.

I conceded for now. "You were right—the view from here is fantastic."

The corners of her eyes crinkled with pride, as if she'd constructed the archway by hand. "It was built to commemorate the first-ever visit by a British monarch, King George V and Queen Mary in 1911."

"Interesting." She was distracting me with a tour guide spiel. I'd play along, lulling her into a false sense of security before resuming my interrogation. I pointed at a beautiful white-turreted, pink-domed building behind the arch. "What's that?"

"The Taj Mahal Palace." She touched the tip of her nose and raised it. "Very posh hotel."

"Maybe Rakesh will take me there?"

"Probably, if he's anything like his bragging mother." Anjali snorted. "I wouldn't know, I haven't been invited to the house yet to meet him, despite being the aunt of his betrothed." She made a disgusted clicking sound with her tongue. "Bet that's Anu's doing, too."

Fascinated by her obvious dislike for Rakesh's mom, I probed further.

"Hope she won't have to chaperone." I subtly sided with

Anjali, hoping she'd elaborate.

Her lips thinned. "Don't worry about Anu. I'll deal with her; you take care of breaking the betrothal."

I scrutinized her, mulling her blatant antagonism. Why would a woman who'd been raised to accept arranged marriages be hell-bent on ruining one?

"Why are you helping Rita break her arrangement?"

Startled, Anjali shifted and the boat tipped alarmingly before righting. "Amrita is like a daughter to me. She deserves to choose her happiness."

Deep.

"Not all of us are so lucky." Anjali shrugged, the sadness tightening her mouth, making me wish I hadn't probed.

"What about Senthil? What's he like?" I hoped switching from marriage back to the Ramas would divert her attention.

"Very fine musician." Her lips clamped into a thin, unimpressed line before she turned away.

Guess discussing the Ramas hit a sore spot.

I pointed at a nearby island. "Is that temple significant?"

While Anjali prattled on about nearby Elephanta Island where the Temple Cave of Lord Shiva could be found, I pondered her revelations. She knew next to nothing about Rakesh, admired Senthil's musical skills, and despised Anu. It shouldn't have mattered, but her dislike for Rakesh's mom made me uneasy. If Anjali had another agenda, one I knew nothing about, it could jeopardize our entire scheme. Like I wasn't anxious enough.

I focused on the Mumbai skyline, captured by the complexity of this cosmopolitan city. I'd been here a day and barely scratched the surface, but from what I'd seen on Anjali's grand tour so far I was starting to get a feel for the place.

"You're awfully quiet," Anjali said as the boat docked and I helped her step onto land.

"Just taking it all in." The sights, and the mysterious disclosures.

She patted my arm. "Don't worry about meeting the Ramas. If Rakesh is anything like his father, you'll be fine."

"What's Senthil like?"

"Nice enough." She shrugged, her blasé response belied by a quick look-away.

"Shame I'll be dealing more with Anu and not him."

Anjali frowned. "Be careful with her. She's astute and devious." She made a slitting sign across her throat. "Cunning as a rat. Dangerous when confronted."

Uh-oh. The last thing I needed: a perceptive psycho. My nervousness morphed into full-blown terror.

Before I could discover more, Buddy pulled up and we piled back into the car, his presence effectively ending further communication about the Rama plot. When Anjali started rummaging in her bag, I braced for another hottie fix-up. Instead, she pulled out a snack bag. "*Sev?*"

"No thanks." The refusal was barely out of my mouth before she popped the fine, crunchy, deep-fried strands of chickpea dough into hers. By the time she finished the bag we'd arrived at our next stop, the biggest train station I'd ever seen.

I should stop pestering her and drop the subject of the Ramas, but the tidbits she'd revealed had only served to rattle me and I needed reassurance.

As we left the car, I tapped her on the shoulder. "Auntie, I'm a little concerned."

"About?"

"Meeting the Ramas." How to phrase this without getting her riled? "If Anu's so shrewd, won't she see through me?" And worse, reenact some of that throat-slitting action Anjali had .

mimed.

"We won't fail." Anjali squared her shoulders, ready for battle. "If she tries to intimidate you or harass you, she'll have me to deal with, the sneaky snake. She's a ghastly, horrid—"

"This place is still functional, Auntie?" I'd had enough of Anjali's adjectives. I got it. She hated Anu's guts and further questioning would only contribute to her blood pressure skyrocketing if the ugly puce staining her cheeks and sweat beads rolling down her forehead were any indication. Besides, the more wound up she got, the more I wondered what the hell I'd become embroiled in. If Anu discovered my treachery… I suppressed a shudder.

Anjali took a deep breath and exhaled, hopefully purging her angst. "Yes. Very busy place and the second UNESCO World Heritage site." She dabbed at the corners of her mouth and dusted off her hands. "Chhatrapati Shivaji Terminus was formerly known as Victoria Terminal."

My very own walking, talking encyclopedia. Goody.

"It's amazing," I said, unsure where to look first as we bid farewell to a patient Buddy again and joined the throng surging toward the station.

Grand Central in NYC might be impressive but this place was something else entirely. A staggering feat of architecture, the station had countless archways and spires and domes and clocks that were an astounding combination of neo-Gothic, early Victorian, and traditional Indian.

As we entered, Anjali pointed to a platform. "Over one thousand trains pass through here daily. Efficient, yes?"

I nodded. "How many passengers?"

"About three million." She said it so casually, I could've mistaken it for 3,000.

"Wow, this place is incredible."

We strolled through the station, admiring the architecture, the wood carvings, brass railings, ornamental iron, and precise detail engraved into every stone.

As we neared the entrance, Anjali touched an archway with reverence. "So sad, the smog and acid rain is damaging this beauty."

I had to agree.

"Next stop, my favorite restaurant." Anjali rubbed her hands together in glee while my stomach rolled over in revolt.

I didn't dare ask why we'd skipped seeing Ghandi's home. I knew. She'd been so rattled by my less-than-subtle harping about Anu, she needed to comfort eat. Besides, getting into a car here was living dangerously. Getting between Anjali and her apparent love of food? I wasn't that brave. "Restaurant?"

"No tour is complete without a stop at Chowpatty Beach."

A beach? Good, maybe I could walk off the inevitable gormandizing.

We made small-talk as Buddy commandeered the streets, dodging buses belching diesel fume and carts and people, so many people. Interestingly, my death grip on the seat had loosened considerably by the time we reached the beach. I must've been growing accustomed to the chaos.

Anjali gestured toward the shore. "Now we eat."

We abandoned Buddy and headed for the sand, the lack of restaurants confusing me.

Reading my mind, Anjali pointed to a row of street vendors lining the beach. "The best *bhel-puri* ever."

I'd never tried the renowned *chaat*, fast-food. With Anjali dragging me toward the nearest stall, it looked like I was about to.

She ordered and I watched, fascinated, as the young guy manning the stall dexterously laid out a neat row of *papadi* (small, crisp fried *puris*—flatbreads) and filled them with a mix of puffed rice, *sev*, onions, potatoes, green chilies, and an array of chutneys.

I may not have been hungry but the tantalizing aromas of tamarind, mango, and coriander made my mouth water.

"My treat." I paid the vendor, who gawked at Anjali as she popped three *bhel-puris* in her mouth in quick succession.

I laughed, loving her exuberance for food, more accustomed to it—even after a day—than the vendor.

"What's so funny?" she mumbled, eyeing the remaining three.

"I'm just happy to be here." I took one and shoved the other two in her direction.

"You sure?"

I nodded. "Positive."

She didn't wait, tossing the *bhel puris* in her mouth and sighing with pleasure.

That good, huh? I nibbled at mine, the instant sweet/sour/spicy explosion on my tastebuds making me want to demolish it as fast as Anjali. Maybe I shouldn't have been so quick to pass on the others…

Anjali grinned at what I assumed was my orgasmic expression. "We'll come back here one evening. You'll be amazed."

"By more food?"

She gestured toward the sand. "By everything. The beach is transformed with ferry and pony rides, balloon sellers, astrologers, contortionists, snake charmers, monkey-trainers, masseurs." She snapped her fingers. "You name it, this place has it. Very entertaining to people-watch."

Glancing at the smallish crowd, most of them dozing in the shade of trees, I couldn't imagine the carnival atmosphere she described. Would be well worth another visit.

Yeah, for the *bhel-puri,* too.

"Sounds great. What about tonight?"

She shook her head. "No can do. *Glee* finale."

I stifled a grin at her addiction to TV, along with food.

She rubbed her belly and winced—no great surprise considering what she'd stuffed in there. "Time to head home and rest."

Good. My mind spun with all I'd seen, and I couldn't wait to fill Rita in on the gossip.

Plus I needed to steel my nerves to meet the Ramas. My rapidly dwindling confidence had taken a hit following Anjali's disclosures about Anu.

This could get messy.

CHAPTER TWO

To: Amrita.M@hotmail.com
From: Shari.J@yahoo.com
Subject: Mumbai mayhem

You owe me.

Not just a year's supply of cheesecake. Not ten year's worth of mojitos. But big-time!

We're talking a date with Leonardo di Caprio, new apartment on Fifth, a Valentino original. Twenty pairs of Manolos. Get the picture?

Nothing, and I mean nothing, could've prepared me for this. And I haven't even met your lover boy yet. This place is crazy! But I guess you already knew that, huh?

Went touring yesterday, fab fun. But hair-raising! The traffic? Seriously scary. Crashed for the afternoon. Had planned on emailing you but got waylaid by Anjali and her unforgiving addiction to Glee, CSI, and True Blood. Today, I've walked around the local area, exploring, but jet lag and the heat have caught up with me and now I'm laying around.

On the upside, your aunt is sweet. She's killing me with kindness and raising my cholesterol to staggering highs with her force-feeding habits. Don't worry about my personality scaring Rakesh away. He'll take one look at the lard-ass he's supposed to marry and run all the way to Delhi.

Speaking of your betrothed, the big welcoming party for me/you is set for tomorrow. Apparently, the Ramas can't wait to meet me/you, though Anjali has held them off for my first two days here, thank God. Your aunt has some serious issues when it comes to Anu. 'Hates her guts' would be putting it mildly.

Have you heard from your parents? Better brace yourself for the heavens to fall in when they return from the Canyon. If we succeed in getting rid of Rakesh, guaranteed they'll fix you up with someone else, only child or not.

Anyway, will do my best to repel Lover Boy at the party tomorrow. Anjali gave me a special outfit to wear, an amazing green salwar kameez I'm sure inspired Versace's spring collection last year. The flowing pants make my legs look like Gisele's and the tunic is mid-thigh, embroidered in crystals and utterly fab. I actually look Indian! Mom would be proud.

That's about it. Anjali's about to twist my ear and drag me away from the computer for dinner. Can someone overdose on halwa?

Missing you.

Missing Mojito Mondays more.

Hugs,

Shari xoxo

(PS. Is it a coincidence my name rhymes with sari? Maybe I was fated to be a stand-in fiancée all along. See, I'm hallucinating from the heat already.)

"Shari, come and eat. You need to put some flesh on your

bones." Anjali's screech drifted upstairs and I glanced around the room, wistfully contemplating a getaway.

I darted to the window and peered at the drop to the dirty concrete below, wishing an escape route would miraculously appear. If I saw another *pakora, bonda,* or *vada*—heavenly deep-fried lentil and veggie snacks—I wouldn't be responsible for my actions.

"Shari."

I sighed and cast a final, tempted look out the window. "Coming, Auntie."

Before I let the gauze-like curtains slide back into place, a movement in the semi-darkness across the street captured my attention. Someone leaned against the shop front opposite, *Punjab Sweets*—where else would Anjali live, but opposite a sweetshop?—smoking a cigarette, staring at my window.

He kicked at an empty soda can and I noticed fancy steel-capped snakeskin cowboy boots poking out beneath his jeans. A devoted shoe aficionado, I always noticed footwear before faces. Tate had discovered my weakness, taking note of my 'matching shoes, matching outfit' motto at work, and homed in for the kill accordingly by taking me on a shopping spree for our memorable third date. His hand cupping my heel as his thumb caressed my instep had been seductive. His platinum AMEX, impressive. His consideration in carrying four boxes of the most exquisite shoes I'd ever seen all the way back to his apartment had sealed the deal. I'd shown my gratitude by donning strappy red-sequined sandals with a three-inch heel, knowing they perfectly matched the satin bra and thong I wore beneath my T and jeans. Yeah, he got to see everything, lingerie and all.

Come to think of it, my inherent stupidity probably started around that time.

Back to the Mumbai cowboy. A slow spiral of smoke from his cigarette wafted skyward, the only indication of movement. What happened to the teeming hordes that swarmed the street all day? And where was the usual line outside the sweetshop? Everyone had vanished, leaving me locked in a staring comp with a stranger.

"What's keeping you, child? I'll starve to death waiting for you." Anjali's shriek had reached ear-splitting levels and I grinned, knowing if she were to die it sure as hell wouldn't be from starvation.

Curious, I peered at the international man of mystery before facing another interminable meal with Anjali. Yeah, I know, pretty pathetic way to get kicks, but hey, there wasn't much else going on. I let the curtain drop and he moved, stepping away from the shadows to stare directly at my window.

Jeez-us. Broad shoulders, bulging biceps on full display in a cut-off denim shirt stretched across his chest, trim waist, and long legs. Impressive. Tate had worked out, but this guy had *muscles.* I couldn't see much of his face thanks to his hat, a Stetson.

I giggled. First the boots, now the hat. The Lone Ranger, surrounded by a million Indians. By the size of his biceps, bet this cowboy could bench-press a thousand Tontos without breaking a sweat. Humming "The William Tell Overture" under my breath I snuck another peek, glad for the anonymity the curtain provided.

As if sensing my stare, he tipped his hat—freaky—before sauntering down the street. *Nice ass, too.*

Note to self: must not perv on stalker-ish guys. Though I'd always had a thing for cowboys.

"Mom and her *Mills & Boon* novels," I muttered, vowing

to steer clear of rugged cowboys and move on to reading about dashing tycoons and charming billionaires instead.

Maybe I should buy a stack tomorrow and share with Anjali. Reading risqué romance would surely distract her from fattening me up. I could live in hope.

• • •

To: Shari.J@yahoo.com
From: Amrita.M@hotmail.com
Subject: Mumbai makeover

Hey girlfriend,

You sound like a new woman, embracing all Mumbai has to offer: the food, the people, the clothes. Wish I could see you in that salwar kameez.

About Auntie, she's had this vendetta with Anu Rama for as long as I can remember. When I've spent time with her she's called her everything from a thieving slut to the Bombay Bitch but she's never said much beyond the name-calling. No surprise she agreed to help me pull this stunt.

Good luck at the party. Bet it'll be a blast. NOT!

As for your stipulations regarding payment, Leo says his calendar's full 'til 2015 but he'll squeeze you in after that. (Stop watching Titanic endlessly with Anjali. I forgot she's a fellow Leo aficionado!) The Fifth Avenue apartment might be a toughie but I'll see what I can do. The Valentino dress and the Manolos? Too easy. Increase your demands next time, why don't you?

Why the mojito withdrawal? What happened to the duty-free stash? Our Mojito Mondays are a tradition. In fact, I'm raising a glass to you as we speak (shh... don't tell Mom).

To Mojito Mondays in Mumbai!

Thinking of you.

Love you.

Rita xx

P.S. I know India is a bit of a culture shock at first, but when in India, do as the Indians do... Eat a few *jalebis* for me!

I chuckled at Rita's email the next evening and tried not to salivate at the thought of a mojito being raised in my direction. Of all the cultures I chose to impersonate, I had to choose an alcohol-free one.

Don't get me wrong, I'm no lush, but Rita was right about one thing: Mojito Mondays had become a tradition. Men had come and gone, friends had drifted in and out of our circle, but nothing and no one came between us and our mojitos. Until now.

Slicking a final coat of gloss over my cherry-coated lips, I pouted at the mirror, ran a fingertip along my eyebrows, and stared at my reflection. With my hair in an elaborate bun, enough borrowed gold dripping from my ears, wrists, and fingers to rival Fort Knox, and the emerald *salwar kameez* skimming my curves, I looked like an authentic Indian. Being here, surrounded by the bamboozling culture, I actually felt my Indian roots reaching out and anchoring me to the soil of my birthplace.

I descended the stairs, smiling at Anjali's wide-eyed surprise when she first caught sight of me. "Come here, child. You look positively… positively—"

"Indian?" I braced when she threw her arms around me and squeezed the air out of my lungs, sniffling into my *kameez*.

"Oh my. Stunning." Her head wobbled from side to side, which had me wondering if she was agreeing or disagreeing.

"Shouldn't we get going?" I glanced at my watch, wanting

to get this ordeal over and done with. In particular, facing my ridiculous fear that Anu would flay me alive if she discovered my deception. The sooner I met the Rama clan and scared off their son, the happier I'd be.

"Of course." Anjali clapped her hands twice, her usual sign to summon Buddy. Amazingly, he always came running, no matter in which part of the house he was hiding from her ladyship. "Let's wait on the veranda while Buddy starts the car."

I smothered a smile at Anjali's reference to the 'veranda,' a dirty, two-foot square of cracked concrete stained red from years of servants spitting *paan* juice, the tobacco stuff they chewed here for kicks.

We'd been in the car on the way to the Rama roost less than five minutes when she cast me a sly glance. "You're beautiful, my girl. Perhaps you'll find a nice Indian boy here and get married?"

Uh-oh, here she goes again. My fingers flexed, creasing the chiffon of my pants and I deliberately relaxed, taking several calming breaths before responding, not wanting my voice to come out an indignant yelp.

"I'm supposed to be betrothed, remember? Besides, I'm not interested in marriage right now, Auntie." I'd wished a pox on the entire male species three months ago. Now my new, improved motto was 'Like, lust, leave 'em for dust.'

"Ah-ya-ya." Anjali's hands flew to her mouth while her eyes widened in shock. "Don't say such rubbish. Every woman needs a good man."

"When you find one, let me know." Poor comeback. For Indian moms, matchmaking ranked right up there with force-feeding their kids.

"I can make some inquiries?" She rubbed her hands together at the prospect of finding me a boyfriend.

I didn't like the cunning glint in Anjali's eyes, not one bit.
"No."

"No?"

"No." I waggled my finger under her nose for emphasis and
she batted it away.

"Silly girl."

Thankfully, the car slowed at that moment and I craned my
neck for the first glimpse of the Rama place. Between Anjali's
sniping at the family and Rita's dossier, I gathered the Ramas
were rich. Very rich. And by the size of their newly whitewashed
two-story house, they were loaded. In a country where real
estate was at a premium, these guys had a monopoly on space,
their house taking up a quarter of the block.

"Nice place," I said, smoothing the chiffon of my *kameez*
and hoping all the drama training at high school would count
for something in the hours ahead.

"All pomp and show." Anjali's glare at the house would've
exploded bricks if she'd had superhuman powers. "A fat cow
needs a big barn."

Smothering a laugh in case Anjali's evil eye turned on me,
I followed her toward the front door, which flew open as we
approached.

"Greetings, Anjali. And this must be our little Amrita." A
tall guy in his fifties wearing what looked like white PJs opened
his arms to us. I gritted my teeth, smiled, and stepped to the
plate, wishing I could pick up my bat and ball and go home.

"Senthil, lovely to see you." I watched, transfixed as she
turned on the charm like a coquette. Probably to annoy Anu
more than anything. "You're looking younger every time I
see you. How's the music business? Have those nearsighted
producers snapped you up to act rather than play tabla?"

Senthil twirled the ends of his ludicrous black handlebar moustache and grinned. "Still the sweet talker, Anjali. Just seeing you again makes my heart beat faster than any tabla I could play."

Give me a break.

If Rakesh was anything like his father, I was in for an absolute treat—yeah, right.

Anjali giggled like a schoolgirl. "You're incorrigible."

Bracing myself for another corny line from Suave Senthil, he surprised me by winking at Anjali and turning to me. "Come, child. Step into the light. Let me see you."

Taking a steadying breath, I did as he instructed, wondering if this sham would fall apart right then, confused as to why everyone over here kept calling me child. And a tad annoyed. Being involved with a married man who happened to be my boss *had* been immature, but I'd grown up since then. Impersonating my best friend, playing dress-up in fancy Indian gear, and about to tell a host of fabulous lies. See? Totally grown up.

The extent of the charade I had to perpetuate sunk in and the insecurities niggled. What if someone had snuck a pic of Amrita to Rakesh? What if I was banished from old Bombay in disgrace? What if I made a mess of this the same way I'd mucked up with Tate?

"Beautiful." Senthil sighed, and I could've sworn his bulging black eyes misted over.

Rita, you are soooo going to pay for this…

"Nice to meet you." I dropped my eyes in the show of respect Rita had advised and pressed my palms together. "*Namaste.*"

No amount of rehearsing with Rita could've prepared me for the sight when I raised my eyes.

Unbe-freaking-lievable.

The guy standing behind Senthil's left shoulder had melted

chocolate eyes, chiseled cheekbones, a cut-glass jaw, and a smile that could make a nun reevaluate her vocation. He stepped around his father and held out a hand, his smile sincere rather than sleazy. "Hi, I'm Rakesh."

Shit. This was going to be hard. Very hard.

I had a radar for judging people straight up—in my defense, it developed *after* I'd met Tate—and right now I suspected Rakesh was a good guy.

And I was the one who had to dump him.

I'd been all psyched up to despise him, to pity him, to laugh at him. A spineless guy being shoved into an arranged marriage with a total stranger. Didn't he have any balls?

Bedazzled by his smile, I couldn't tear my eyes away long enough to look down and check.

"Nice to meet you." I shook his hand, half expecting a little zing from a hottie like him, yet relieved there were no sparks. That's all I needed, to fall for my best friend's soon-to-be-ex-arranged-husband. Rakesh might be a babe to look at—a babe in freaky white PJs that matched his dad's—but that's where it ended.

I couldn't fathom his odd glance as he dropped my hand and stepped back. "Welcome to our home."

Trepidation tiptoed down my spine. Why had Rakesh stared at me like that? Like he *knew*. Impossible, according to Rita, but she wasn't the one about to step into a houseful of Ramas and their hundred closest friends, judging by the rising decibel levels spilling from behind the door. Too late to balk now; I had to go through with it. But I hesitated, my hands trembling. Fearing they'd set my gold bangles jingling, I clasped them behind my back and silently wished I'd get through tonight unscathed. I'd had enough drama in my life—no way did I want to add to it.

Anjali gripped my arm and strode forward, her verdigris shot-gold sari billowing in her wake as I stepped into the house and stifled a gasp. There were people *everywhere*. Filling the foyer, spilling out of rooms, draped over the elaborate staircase, and every pair of eyes was trained on me.

My mouth went dry as I tried a polite smile that must've come across as inane considering my rigid facial muscles bordered on rigor mortis.

Silence reigned for five seconds before the cacophony resumed, as a rotund woman waddled toward me dressed in an ornate silver sari resembling floating space debris.

"Amrita!" she shouted, and I resisted the urge to cover my ears with my hands lest it offend—though wasn't that my aim here tonight? "Give your new mommy a hug."

Anu. Anjali's archenemy. And by Auntie's death grip on my arm, I was about to get caught in the crossfire.

"Leave the poor girl alone, Anu. Can't you see she's shell-shocked?" Anjali placed a protective arm around my shoulder and I flexed the arm she must've bruised.

"Shut up, Anjali. She may be your niece but she's going to be my new daughter!" Another ear-piercing shout. Anu was seriously scary.

Anjali stiffened. "You dare tell me to shut up? You vile, stupid—"

"These must be your daughters." I raised my voice, desperate to avoid becoming a referee between these two.

Anu's attention diverted, though she managed one last evil glare in Anjali's direction. "Yes, these are my beautiful girls. Come meet your sisters."

Anu latched onto my arm, and with Anjali's protectively draped around my shoulders, I'd become a human tug-o-war rope. By some slick maneuvering I'd honed to a fine art at the annual Saks sale, I stepped forward and shrugged off both ladies—and I use the term loosely—to meet Anu's daughters.

"Hi, I'm Pooja." The eldest, a miniature rotund Anu, had a shy smile and my predilection for nicknames instantly dubbed her Pooh: round, soft-spoken, cuddly.

"Divya." The middle one flicked a dismissive glance over me and gave an imperceptible shrug, more intent on patting her sleek hair and studying her nails. Definitely Diva.

The youngest enveloped me in a brief hug. "I'm so thrilled to meet you, Sister. I'm Shruti and if there's anything you need during your stay here, don't hesitate to ask."

I might've been impressed by such an effusive welcome if I hadn't caught the furtive glance she shot her mother, seeking approval. Her expression begged 'have I done well, Mommy?' Shrewd Shruti, knowing who controlled the family and how to stay on her good side: she became Shrew.

I'd met the three stepsisters and the fairy godmother—of my nightmares. Before I could beg a drink from the nearest servant, who moved among the guests with a fancy gold tray bearing goblets filled with fresh lime juice, Rakesh appeared and I blinked at his beauty all over again.

"Could we talk?" His soulful brown eyes reminded me of a beagle puppy I'd once found as a kid: docile, trusting, and eager to find a good home. In this case, I hoped Rakesh didn't have his sights set on the Big Apple. New York wasn't big enough for the both of us, considering one of us was a big, fat phony.

I glanced around, wondering about protocol. Could the betrothed slip away?

Damn, why hadn't Rita drilled me on every last detail? If I botched it now, she'd be the one to pay, though it'd serve her right.

Amazingly, both Anjali and Anu nodded in agreement and I followed Rakesh down several polished marble steps into a separate foyer. A hundred pairs of eyes stared as we left the room, the eerie hush soon broken by raucous shouts, cheers, and laughter as he closed the door.

"Guess you're glad that's over." He leaned against the wall and folded his arms, drawing my attention to a great set of biceps. Did Rita know what she was doing? Arranged marriages had been happening for centuries. Surely a hot bod and sensational smile could be grounds for 'I do.'

Aiming for cool, I nodded. "When Anjali said there'd be a welcoming party, I didn't expect so many people."

He shrugged. "This is India. Get used to it."

I don't think so, Lover Boy. "About that—"

"I know."

Huh?

"You're not Amrita."

The *dhosai* I'd snacked on before arriving roiled in my stomach and I would've staggered without the wall behind me.

I could've bluffed, uhmed and ahed and generally made more of an ass of myself than I already had, but there didn't seem to be anything sinister about Rakesh, so I opted for honesty. "How'd you know?"

A glimmer of a smile tugged at the corners of his mouth— this guy was seriously sexy. "Contrary to what you may think, I'm not some Indian hick waiting to be shoved into marriage with a woman I've never seen or met. This is the twenty-first century. I value my parents' opinion and respect their choices but that doesn't make me an idiot."

No, *I* was idiot enough for both of us, thinking I could pull off this ridiculous charade as I belatedly wondered if the crowd waiting beyond the door would stone me on the way out.

"I'm sorry," I said, ready to tear off my fake finery and grovel at his feet.

No mojitos, no cheesecake, and the proverbial egg all over my face—what ever happened to the hip NY girl I used to be?

"Who are you?"

I sighed. "Shari Jones. Amrita's best friend."

"Where are you from?"

"New York City." Duh, maybe he wasn't so bright after all.

"Originally, I meant." He rolled his eyes. "You look like Amrita so you must be part Indian."

"My mom's Indian. I was born in Arnala."

He nodded, satisfied. "Knew you had to be from these parts."

I expected his interrogation to continue. Instead, he frowned as if mulling this disastrous situation. The silence unnerved me more than his disapproving stare.

I tried not to squirm. "This is kind of weird for me, so if you skip to where I can get out of here and nurse my humiliation in peace, I'd be eternally grateful."

"How grateful?" He hadn't come across as sleazy, but maybe I'd misjudged him. Maybe he had only half a brain like the rest of the Neanderthals in his species.

"Not that grateful."

"I didn't mean it like that." I braced myself for whatever punishment he dished out. As long as it didn't involve more food, I figured I could handle anything. "Heard of Eye-on-I?"

"Uh-uh."

The name sounded vaguely familiar as an image of a full-page glossy ad from the in-flight magazine sprung to mind.

Something had grabbed me: cute kids posing with cuter animals? Half-naked men doing housework? It'd come to me eventually.

He raised an eyebrow and stared at me like I came from another planet. Which I did, and I had every intention of getting back to Planet New York as soon as humanly possible. My cover was blown and there was no way this Bond Girl was staying around to face the fallout.

"Eye-on-I is India's number one Internet provider. We do it all. Hosting, domain stuff, IT bundling, the works."

Uh-oh. Top IT guys would have loads of resources available to their spying, prying eyes. No guessing how he'd sprung our scheme.

I plucked at the hem of my tunic, fiddling with the embroidered crystals, worrying about the punishment dished out to fiancée imposters.

"We?"

"My partner, Drew Lansford, and I. Graduated with MBAs from Oxford, went into business soon after. India's IT industry was about to take off and we jumped on for the ride."

Fascinating trivia, but I had no idea of its relevance to my penance. I managed a tight smile. Get it over with already.

"I have the world's top IT resources at my fingertips, including online PIs and experts able to infiltrate any site, which is how I found a picture of Amrita and information about her."

He'd used a private investigator and a hacker? Desperate, and so far ahead of Rita's scheme it made us look like schmucks.

Anger slashed through my nerves. What right did he have to invade Rita's privacy? "Aren't you a clever dick?"

He grinned like a naughty schoolboy caught with his hand in the *ladoo* jar, and I couldn't help but like him. Damn, he had class. He could've made a fool of me in front of his family and the assembled hordes but he hadn't. Perhaps I should be grateful rather than abusive.

His brow creased as he pretended to ponder, before snapping his fingers under my nose. "Yeah, my IQ isn't bad, which brings me to my proposition."

I envisioned nasty connotations when guys said the P-word, yet when Rakesh stared at me with a mischievous glint in his eyes, I almost laughed. "Why don't you fill me in? You're going to anyway."

"My plan's simple. I keep my mouth shut about your deception, you score me an introduction to Amrita."

"What?"

"I want to meet Amrita. In person."

"Why?" Call me thick, but I didn't understand.

"I'm intrigued by a woman who'd go to such lengths to ditch me." He shrugged and took three steps, which constituted pacing in the small foyer. "Any woman with that much daring is worth meeting."

His face lit up and I thought, *Wow. Here's a smart, funny, understanding, gorgeous guy who's into my best friend.*

Closely followed by, *What's the catch?*

I'd learned from my mistakes. No way would I dismiss or justify suspicious behavior from a guy ever again. "Why don't you jump on a plane and go meet her? Why perpetuate this sham?"

His eyebrows shot up like I'd proposed he scale the Taj Mahal in his underwear.

"Because if this gets out, her parents lose face, Amrita's marriage prospects are irrevocably damaged, and, worst, she'll be ostracized from the Indian community." He shook his head and crossed his arms. "I refuse to be responsible for that, even though she sent an imposter in her stead to dump me."

I'd better add Upstanding and Moral to his growing list of attributes.

"Not to mention my family will bear the brunt of gossip and scandal." For a moment his mutinous expression relaxed and I glimpsed vulnerability. "My dad's got a heart condition. Nothing serious, but he could do without the stress."

I sighed and stopped plucking at the crystals embroidered on my tunic's hem. "I can't fault your motivations but I feel like I'm a bit player in a sweeping Bollywood saga."

He made a fake movie clapboard with his forearms and snapped it shut, an action I'd seen a hundred times while watching the extras on DVDs. "You're not a bit player; you're the star attraction, *Amrita*."

The thought of continuing this charade left me cold, but his reasons made sense. I couldn't stand the thought of my best friend being dragged through a scandal that might taint her reputation in her community—something she should've thought of *before* we started down deception road—so I'd do this. So much for our foolproof scheme. Rather than ditching Rakesh as planned, I now had to play the devoted fiancée during my stay. And arrange a meeting between Rakesh and Rita. Fun. *Not*.

"Okay, I'm in."

We shook on it, co-conspirators in a game I hoped wouldn't end in tears.

CHAPTER THREE

After I agreed to Rakesh's plan, he became my new best Bombay buddy. He stuck by my side during the party from hell (a hundred of the Ramas' closest relatives and friends each wanting a piece of me), fended off his mom, charmed Anjali, and generally made me like him more.

Then I met Drew.

I'd exchanged air-kisses and empty hugs with Pooh, Diva, and Shrew for the required two minutes. I'd fake-smiled for camera flashes coming from all directions, and bade farewell to the rest of the family, including my new mommy. After telling Anjali I'd meet her outside, I sighed in relief I'd made it through the evening relatively unscathed—discounting Rita's betrothed blackmailing me—when a tall figure stepped from the shadows of the Ramas' sprawling veranda while I waited for Buddy to bring the car around.

"Hey, Drew. You're late. Come meet Amrita." Rakesh didn't stumble at my name, earning him further brownie points.

He'd been the consummate performer all night, the adoring

fiancé without crossing boundaries. I'd been a mess. My jaws ached from smiling, my head ached from my hair pulled into a tight bun, and I couldn't wait to drop the charade and head back to Anjali's, but I fixed one more polite, fake smile on my face and turned to meet Rakesh's business partner.

"I've heard so much about you." Drew Lansford moved into the light and my smile faltered as I stepped back in time.

High School. Brad Stoddard, first love. The guy had stolen my heart at the cafeteria checkout and proceeded to toy with it for months. He'd teased me, sleazed me, and almost pleased me, but I'd chickened out before he could round third base and our one brief, passionate night had ended there. Brad had never spoken to me again.

Facing his adult doppelganger transported me back to that night in Manhattan. We'd made out in the back of Brad's grungy wagon, surrounded by McDonald's wrappers and Coke cans. I'd been high on the fumes of his dad's Old Spice he'd slathered on, oblivious to the stale pizza crusts lying in scrunched boxes on the floor. The joys of youth.

"Hi." One syllable more than I thought I'd manage considering Drew's uncanny resemblance to Brad, while registering the intelligent blue eyes, the messy brown hair tumbling over his forehead, and the slight dimple in his right cheek.

He had a serious Hugh Grant thing going on, complete with British accent. Super hot. I'd sat through *Four Weddings and a Funeral; Notting Hill; Bridget Jones's Diary;* and *Love, Actually* several times, wondering why the oddly foppish guy who talked with a plum in his mouth had me salivating.

"Congratulations." He thrust his hands into designer denim pockets while I tried not to ogle the charcoal T-shirt clinging to a chest that could hold its own in a roomful of GQ models.

I gaped at him like an idiot—blame it on my recall, which had me almost sniffing for a hint of Old Spice—wondering what I'd done to deserve congrats.

"Yeah, Amrita is thrilled about our *engagement*." Rakesh's pointed glare reminded me of our bizarre pact. The fake engagement to limit his dad's stress and keep the Indian community grapevine happy until he visited New York in a few weeks and met his real fiancée. Riiiight…

He wasn't asking much, to continue what I'd set out to do without dumping him or alienating his family. I'd asked him what would happen if the unthinkable happened, and he hit it off with Rita and they fell for each other. He'd glossed over it with a 'my folks will be so thrilled to see their only son married they won't worry. Besides, I'll say you were Amrita's lovesick friend who went behind her back and tried to win me over for yourself.' All very logical, except for what Anu would do to me if she believed her golden boy's little white lie. I had a feeling Mama Rama wouldn't take kindly to thieving best friends or the deception I'd tried to perpetuate.

I did a 'right back at you, Rakesh,' complete with faux smile. "Thanks. Are you coming to the wedding?"

"Wouldn't miss it for the world." Drew sounded genuine but the way he stared at me, intense, brooding, like I'd make off with the Rama valuables, set my spidey senses on high alert. Why did I get the feeling he wasn't entirely happy with his friend's pending nuptials? Or worse, the reason behind his reluctance had something to do with me?

It might've been the lack of warmth behind his smile, the lack of emotion in his eyes, but I knew I'd have to watch him. Or he'd be watching me.

I hated being painted as a deceiving desperado but Rakesh

was so glib, so assured, I didn't want to rattle his confidence. Besides, what were the odds Rita would fall for him? Slim-to-none. I was worrying about nothing.

The way I saw it, Rakesh would make my remaining stay in Mumbai a lot easier. I had another ally now and could relax without having to pretend to be the Bitch of Bombay for his family.

Increasingly uncomfortable with Drew's intense stare, I blurted, "I wonder what's keeping Auntie."

My plan for Drew to head into the house failed when Rakesh craned his neck to look inside. "I'll go check." His affectionate tweak on my cheek earned a glare from Drew that Rakesh missed as he headed inside.

"So." Drew leaned against the wall, arms folded, expression grim.

"So." I straightened my shoulders and did a Pantene commercial hair-toss to show I didn't give a damn. It bombed, considering I'd worn my hair in a bun.

By the groove slashing his brows, he wouldn't have been impressed even with my hair loose. This guy didn't like me.

His frown deepened. "Are you a Robbie Williams fan?"

Huh?

I could blame the late hour, delayed jet lag, or the sheer lunacy of what I was doing but I had a hankering to flip Drew the finger and run after my fake fiancé.

"You've heard of Robbie Williams?" He spoke slower, like I couldn't keep up.

Jeez, what was it with English people? Did they think no one on the other side of the Atlantic had a brain? "I saw him live at Carnegie Hall. He's awesome."

Awesome? *Awesome?* Sheesh, memories of Brad must've

resurrected my scintillating vocab from back then, too.

"You're familiar with all his songs? Even the swing ones?"

Duh. Hadn't I said as much? Where was Rakesh? I'd kill him for leaving me here with the equivalent of the British Gestapo. After protecting me all night he'd left me in small-talk hell when all I wanted to do was crawl under my mosquito net and hide for the next ten hours.

I darted frantic glances at the door, wishing for Rakesh, Anjali, or even the dreaded stepsisters to save me from this. "Yeah, I'm one of Robbie's biggest fans."

"You'd know my favorite song, then? 'Have You Met Miss Jones?'"

I choked and covered it by a combined cough and fake sneeze.

He grinned, and in the wan light I could've sworn his eyes glittered with triumph.

Rakesh had confirmed the importance of utmost secrecy: one leak and the fiasco could blow up in our faces. Yet something about Drew's cocky expression screamed he knew I was a fraud and was enjoying taunting me way too much.

"Not a bad choice. Personally, I prefer 'Something Stupid' from that CD." Could be the theme song to my life lately. "Though Nicole Kidman singing that duet with Robbie? Debatable. She should stick to acting. Her singing career taking off is as likely as a reunion with Tom. I mean, Tom Cruise and Nicole Kidman married? There's a mismatched couple. Inevitable split. The height difference, you know. He has to be at least a foot shorter than her."

I blathered, hoping he'd get tired and leave me the hell alone.

No such luck.

"I'm onto you." He spoke so softly I almost missed it as he took a step toward me, invading my personal space, a lot more personal with him in it.

"Onto me?"

"Quite the little actress." His head jerked toward the house. "So you fooled the hordes in there, including the usually astute Anu? What I want to know is why."

And what I wanted to know was where the hell did this guy get off, thinking I'd explain myself to him? He might be used to snapping his fingers and having minions jump to his tune at work but the bossy, demanding thing he had going on? Left me cold.

I'd love to tell him where to stick his questions, but alienating Rakesh's business partner probably wasn't the smartest thing to do.

That's when it hit me.

Why not have a little fun at Drew's expense? Rakesh knew the truth, and what Drew didn't know wouldn't hurt him. Let him postulate in that posh English way of his, and when I'd had my fun, I'd casually tell him the truth and watch him squirm.

My plan could be shot down any second if he actually confronted Rakesh but I didn't think Drew would do that. With that stiff upper lip, I seriously doubted he'd risk losing face with his business partner by prying into personal stuff.

Me, on the other hand, he seemed content to grill. I didn't like him delving into a situation that didn't concern him. In reality, my plan was less about fun and more about teaching Mr. Inquisitive a lesson.

I bit back a grin. "You're onto me." I snapped my fingers. "Better stay away in case you become embroiled in my devious plot."

Buddy screeched to a halt in front of us at that moment, and

I heard Anjali shrieking her good-byes to all and sundry.

Drew stared at me through narrowed eyes and I wiggled my fingers in a taunting wave. "See you around."

"This isn't over." He stepped back as Anjali descended on us in a flurry of sari, smiling at Drew and whisking me down the steps before I had a chance to reply.

Breathing a sigh of relief as I slid onto the worn leather seat of Anjali's battered Beamer, I slammed the door, shutting out Drew's tuneful whistling rendition of "Have You Met Miss Jones?" and wondering what the hell I'd got myself into this time.

• • •

An hour later, in the comfort of her lounge room, I filled Anjali in on the new plan. Pensive, she sipped her *chai* and popped another *ladoo* into her mouth. "All things considered, the evening went well, don't you think?"

I'd rather not. Think, that is. The more I did, the more convinced I became I was starring in a Bollywood extravaganza where the lying heroine gets her just desserts—no pun intended—in the end, and I'd muck up my lines any moment.

"Mmm," I mumbled, sipping the *ayah's* special *masala chai*, a mouthwatering concoction featuring cardamom and cinnamon and cloves, vowing to try Gloria Jean's *chai* when I returned to New York—in ten days, twenty-three hours, and thirty minutes, exactly. Who's counting?

"You fooled that upstart Anu good and proper." Anjali chortled into her cup like a witch peering over her cauldron. "Stupid cow."

"She didn't seem too bad."

I hoped this would get a reaction and reveal her vendetta

against the Rama woman.

She didn't disappoint.

"Not bad?" Anjali shoved away a plate of half-eaten sweets in distress. "Not *bad*? The woman's a curse. She's a lying, thieving slut and I'll not have you say one good word about her, not in my house."

"Did she steal from you, Auntie?"

"Steal? *Steal*?"

By now, Anjali's voice had reached record levels and I doubted the neighbors appreciated the ear-splitting symphony at two in the morning.

"I'll never forgive her. Ever!"

O-kay. Curiosity urged me to discover the rest but her eyes misted over and I couldn't do it. Not when her lower lip wobbled, too.

I patted her hand. "I'm sorry."

Inadequate, but I had to say something to soothe the wildness in her eyes. "She'll be sorry, too, once we pull this scam over her." Anjali's maniacal laughter made me shrink into my chair. Everything in this city involved noise and it would take months for my eardrums to recover.

Now that she'd mentioned it, that's something else I'd been dying to know. Her real reason for helping Rita perpetuate this sham, beyond the brush-off answer she'd given me during our tour. "You mentioned supporting our scheme so Rita can choose her own happiness. What did you mean by that?"

She wrinkled her nose, her mouth twisted in disgust. "Because I don't want my darling Amrita ending up trapped like me."

Clueless, I raised a brow and she cast an evil eye at the photos on the mantle behind me. "My arranged marriage was a disaster. My husband?" She made a horrific hawking noise in the back of her throat. "We argued day and night. Totally incompatible. My parents made a terrible mistake in arranging my marriage."

She tore her bitter gaze away from the photos. "I don't blame Amrita wanting to make her own choices, and I'll do whatever it takes to support her."

Wow, for a Hindu woman I had pegged as traditional, Anjali sure knew how to surprise.

Smiling, I nodded. "I think it's great you're helping her."

"You too, my dear." Her gaze flitted to the photos again and I stood, eager to make an exit before I heard any more tales of her dreadful marriage.

"I'm tired, Auntie. Think I'll head to bed."

"Good night." Anjali said, though I could tell her mind was elsewhere, lost in memories best left forgotten.

I slipped from the room and padded upstairs, craving a mojito. After the night I'd had I deserved a drink. Hell, I deserved a whole damn bar.

I settled for a cyber drink with my long lost pal, the same one I'd personally kill when I returned to New York for inviting me into this mess in the first place. Though that wasn't entirely true. I'd made my clichéd bed. I had to lie in it. Complete with geckos falling from the ceiling, mosquitoes eating me alive, and the five a.m. wake-up call from the sitar-playing beggar next door.

The mail icon blinked as I powered up the computer. I clicked on Outlook, eager to get a taste of New York via my ex-best friend, but as I registered the sender, my heart sank.

TO: Shari.J@yahoo.com
FROM: DrewLansford@Eye-on-I.com
Subject: Robbie

Dear Ms. Jones,

Who knew I'd have the honor of meeting another star in the making tonight? You would do justice to a role in the next Bollywood movie I'm backing so if you'd like to audition for a part, please present yourself at the studios tomorrow at three sharp. I'll send a car for you, and feel free to invite your 'fiancé.'

I'm positive we'll have much to talk about, what with our mutual regard for Robbie Williams and his music.

We have another thing in common and that's my friend, Rakesh. I don't like game-playing so make sure you turn up at the studio.

We need to talk.

At your service,
Drew Lansford

I read the email twice before stabbing at the *delete* key, breaking a nail in the process.

Who the hell did this guy think he was? *At your service,* my ass. Considering his business resources, made sense he'd figured out my identity and email address.

First Rakesh, now Drew. Regular Sherlock and Watson, those two.

Drew thought I was actress material?

Come tomorrow at three, I'd give him a performance he'd never forget.

CHAPTER FOUR

I woke to the sounds of the Punjabi sweetshop owner abusing a customer in rapid Hindi, a squawking rooster losing a fight with a rabid dog, and Anjali berating Buddy for missing a spot while polishing the car. Gotta love Mumbai mornings.

I stretched and rolled out of bed, tangled in the mosquito net like every morning since I'd arrived. Damn useless thing if the number of angry red splotches on my legs were any indication. Like Anjali, the mosquitoes had a tendency toward feeding frenzies, too.

Heading for the computer, I sat and typed as fast as my fingers could fly before I changed my mind. Last night I'd contemplated giving Rita an edited version or blurting the truth.

I decided on the latter.

TO: Amrita.M@hotmail.com
FROM: Shari.J@yahoo.com
SUBJECT: Mix up a batch

Hey Rita,

Guess you're dying to hear how last night went, huh?

Before we get to that, I suggest you mix up a batch in that exquisite Villaroy & Boch pitcher I bought for your b-day last year, take a seat, and pour yourself a large glass. You're going to need it.

Okay, where to start? Firstly, Rakesh is a nice guy. I know, I know, sounds corny but it's true. He's gorgeous, funny, sweet, and blackmailing me. Oops! Did I actually write that last part?

Now it's out, I may as well explain.

Your fiancé knows. Everything.

He cornered me not long after I arrived at the party. (I forgot to add intelligent to the list.) Apparently, he's some hotshot IT guy and has access to all sorts of 'Net data, including an online PI who investigated you. Knows everything, especially what you look like, so no prizes for guessing he noticed I wasn't you.

Being a good sport, he didn't out me. Nuh-uh. Being the all-around great guy he is, he's blackmailing me instead: he'll keep our little secret (and save your family's reputation) if I orchestrate a real face-to-face meeting between the two of you.

Isn't that sweet? Ain't love grand?

Looks like you've made quite an impression on Romeo Rama.

Had a healthy swig of mojito? Good. See? It's not so bad. I keep up the charade for the remainder of my time here, your family saves face, and all you have to do is meet with Romeo once. Easy-peasy.

Did I mention how gorgeous and funny and sexy he is?

One more thing. Romeo's business partner may be a problem. The guy's invited me to a Bollywood studio today and I'll probably go to get out of the house, but he's got some strange power-trip thing happening so I better check him out. (Oh, did I mention he knows I'm not you, too?)

OK, gotta dash.
Have an extra slurp on me!
Hugs,
Shari xoxo

I'd debated not telling Rita about Drew discovering my identity—the poor girl would probably jump on the next plane out here—but thought better of it. I needed to offload to someone and I had a feeling following my outing this afternoon I was going to need it.

By the time I'd showered and dressed, Rita had sent a response.

TO: Shari.J@yahoo.com
FROM: Amrita.M@hotmail.com
SUBJECT: WTF?

Shari,
WHAT THE FUCK is going on?????????????
He KNOWS? Rakesh Rama KNOWS?
I'm dead.
My dad will kill me, my mom will help pile the wood on the funeral pyre and light the first match, while the entire Indian community in NYC will pelt me with stones as the fire toasts my tootsies.
I can't believe this. Freaking Internet! Freaking men! Freaking Indians and their arranged marriages!
Ahhhhhhhh!!!!!!!!
Mmmmmm..............
OK, I've screamed, I've vented, I've downed a glass of the sweetest

minty mojito ever put on this earth (hope you're drooling!) and I've calmed down.

Guess it isn't so bad. I'll meet Romeo whenever he pops up in New York. Who knows, it might never happen, right? RIGHT?

As for this other guy knowing, what's the story there? Can he keep his mouth shut? What does he want in exchange for silence?

Shit, a taste of real Bombay bribery at its best.

Keep me posted.

Your friend indebted to you forever,

With lots of love and a cherry on top,

Rita xx

(PS. Did you talk up Romeo to cushion the blow or is he really a hottie? Just curious.)

Smiling, I closed Rita's message. All in all, she took the news pretty well.

If only my afternoon could go accordingly.

• • •

My trip to the studio known as Film City to the locals was taking on similar importance to Ivana attending the Red Door for a spa treatment, complete with entourage in tow.

Rakesh and Anjali accompanied me, Anjali relishing her role as the dutiful chaperone—I thought I was a movie buff but Anjali put me to shame—and Rakesh going all-out to impress his parents with his devotion to his bride-to-be. Whatever their reasons, I was grateful for the company. Meeting Devious Drew had my insides tied up in knots—or was that the fiery *vindaloo* I'd toyed with for lunch?

"Are you into movies?" Rakesh turned his head to peer at me, smirking when he noticed my position.

I huddled in a corner of the backseat, trying to put as much distance possible between me and the garlic-infused folds of Anjali's sari.

"Love them," I said, excited at the prospect of seeing how real films were made. Bollywood was mega business over here, producing about a thousand films a year, grossing close to $4 billion. And with releases like *Monsoon Wedding, Bride and Prejudice,* and *Slumdog Millionaire* in the States, the whole world had woken up to the razzle-dazzle of Bollywood at its best. (Despite Anjali chastising me those weren't strictly Bollywood movies considering they were made by Westerners.).

I adored the three-hour-long musical extravaganzas complete with songs, dances, love triangles, comedy, melodrama, and daredevil thrills.

"What's your favorite movie?"

"Too many." I deliberately kept my answer vague, knowing he'd laugh his head off if I told him. He'd been playing the devoted fiancé to extremes ever since we got in the car, pretending to know all kinds of crazy stuff about me and it'd started to grate.

He wanted to know my favorite movie? Let him sweat.

"I'll guess, then. *Pretty Woman?*"

"No."

"*Titanic?*"

I adored Leo and cried buckets every time I watched *Titanic* but "No."

"*How to Lose a Guy in 10 Days?*"

"Nope."

"*Maid in Manhattan?*"

"No. JLO's butt just doesn't do it for me."

Anjali chirped up at this point. "Children, please. You're giving me a headache with this bickering."

Rakesh gave me a thumbs-up sign of approval, thinking we were impressing her with our faux closeness. I hadn't told him she was in on the original plan, too, and was enjoying having the upper hand for once.

"*When Harry Met Sally?*"

"No. I don't fake it."

He raised an eyebrow as if to say 'oh yeah? Then what the hell are you doing here?' before continuing.

"*Sleepless in Seattle?*"

"Cute, but no cigar."

"*Runaway Bride?*"

I lowered my voice so only he could hear. "Could be the story of your life, but no."

He made a gun with his thumb and forefinger, cocked it, and mock fired at me.

"*Shall We Dance?*" He smirked.

"No, thanks."

"*You've Got Mail?*"

"Nuh-uh."

"*Two Weeks Notice?*"

"Uh-uh."

"Has to be *Saturday Night Fever.* All those Travolta hip thrusts."

"Loser."

"Tell him this instant!" We both jumped at Anjali's sharp tone, and feeling all of twelve years old, I bowed my head and muttered, "*Dirty Dancing.*"

Rakesh grinned and cupped one hand behind his ear. "Sorry?

What was that? Didn't quite hear you."

Pouting, I crossed my arms. "*Dirty Dancing.* There, satisfied, you big baby?"

"Nobody puts Baby in a corner." His perfect imitation of Patrick Swayze made me smile. Anyone who could quote a line from *Dirty Dancing* was okay in my book.

"What about you?"

By the mischievous glimmer in his dark eyes, I could tell the game was about to start all over again but Anjali put a stop to it.

"Yes, tell us, Rakesh. *Now.*" Anjali frowned and pursed her lips. With her overly made-up face, black-kohled eyes, and orange-coated lips, she looked scarier than the pictures I'd seen of the Indian goddess Kali who had four arms, hair braided with serpents, and a face that could make a grown man quiver.

"It's an oldie," he said, intimidated by Anjali at her most ferocious. I'd have to add lily-livered to the list of attributes I'd given Rita. It wasn't entirely fair, though—I'd be downright terrified if Anjali looked at me like that. "*Casablanca.*"

My eyebrows shot upward. No way. That was Rita's fave film, too. Spooky.

"Of all the gin joints in all the towns in all the world…" Looked like it was one of Anjali's favorites, too, and her expression softened.

"What's yours, Auntie?"

Anjali sighed theatrically, her double chin quivering with intensity. "*An Affair to Remember.* Now that's a movie." She swiped at her eyes and Rakesh lifted a questioning eyebrow in my direction.

I shook my head. My nerves were shot, courtesy of confronting Drew shortly. I wasn't in the mood for Anjali to regale us with whatever tale had elicited those tears.

"Are we there yet?" I changed the subject, glancing out the window on endless barren land, people foraging on the roadside, and an all-pervading dust that covered everything in a red haze.

Rakesh chuckled. "You sure know how to impress a guy. Name-this-movie games, *are we there yet?* conversation, and that sullen pout."

"Who said I'm trying to impress you?"

He blew me a kiss and I couldn't help but smile. "Is that any way to talk to your number one guy? Your betrothed? Your fiancé? The man of your dreams? Your—"

"Okay, okay. I get the picture." *Wiseass*, I mouthed, aware we had to maintain the façade for Buddy—loose lips sink ships and I had no intention of letting Rita's ship go the way of the *Titanic*—and wondering exactly how far I'd have to go before the end of this trip.

"Isn't that Film City now?" Anjali craned her neck and pointed through the dusty windshield, bringing an end to the briefest round two on record when I was getting warmed up for the bout.

"Uh-huh." Rakesh smirked at me and directed Buddy to a back gate, my first glimpse of Mumbai's movie mecca somewhat disappointing.

I'd been to Universal Studios in California once as a kid, and I'd envisioned India's movie-making capital as similar, but on a grander scale. Instead, a nondescript short man wearing a uniform from the Sixties opened a solid wrought iron gate by hand and ushered us through with a brisk wave and a frown.

Once past the gate, my head swiveled every which way, taking in the giant sets, enough electrical equipment to rival Sony's head office, and the mandatory thousand people swarming everywhere, give or take a few hundred.

"Pretty cool, huh?" Rakesh beamed like he owned the joint. Given the home he lived in—paid for by him, a snippet I'd learned courtesy of mommy Anu last night—the casual Armani pants and shirt he wore, and the gold Rolex on his left wrist, he probably did.

Drew had mentioned backing a film in his email and I wondered if that meant the company he ran with Rakesh, or him personally. Either way, these guys were loaded. Not that I cared. Drew didn't impress me despite the whole smart, sexy thing he had going on. The fact I'd noticed his sexiness? Probably some long-suppressed media mogul fantasy. My excuse, and I was sticking to it.

Besides, his high-handedness annoyed the shit out of me, and the only reason I'd come today was to tell him exactly that. And advise him to leave me the hell alone.

Anjali clapped her hands like an excited kid before collapsing back in her seat and clutching her heart. "Isn't that Hrithik Roshan?"

I'd seen my fair share of Bollywood movies while living with Rita the last three months but couldn't remember Hrithik. "Who?"

I followed her line of vision, wondering who had turned her into a swooning, sighing fangirl.

"India's equivalent to Gerard Butler," Rakesh said dryly, rolling his eyes at Anjali's antics but grinning nonetheless.

Gerard Butler's equal? This I had to see.

"Which one is he?"

"The tall one over there trying to beat off those seven girls with a stick."

"Jealous?" Not that he needed to be. From what I could see, he could hold his own against Indian Gerard.

"Of a pretty boy like that? Not bloody likely."

I beamed as Rakesh tugged at his shirt-sleeves and straightened his collar in a fair impression of a guy afraid of the competition.

"It's that extra thumb, you know. Drives the girls wild, apparently."

If he'd said extra inch I could've understood.

Rakesh guffawed at my dumbfounded expression. "Go figure."

Before I got a proper glimpse of Anjali's latest crush, Buddy steered the car down an alley and braked hard as hundreds of dancing women swarmed in front of us, a swirling mass of vibrant topaz, mulberry, magenta, and tangerine as they clapped, stomped, and jumped.

Once the dancers had passed, Buddy edged the car forward, his head swiveling side to side as he stared, goggle-eyed. Several turbaned men brandishing swords gestured at the car to move but Buddy waved at the extras like a celebrity. When one of them tapped on the car's roof, Buddy shook his fist, tooted the horn, and shot forward, sending actors scattering.

"Missy, look. Buddy famous."

I craned my neck and caught sight of a producer giving us the finger for ruining his movie sequence while gesturing with his other hand to move our car.

Anjali reached over the seat to twist Buddy's ear. "Move, you fool, before you get us thrown out. This is my big chance and I won't have you ruin it."

Buddy reversed so fast our necks snapped back, ensuring whiplash all around. Rakesh and I exchanged grins while I pondered Anjali's 'big chance.' Surely she didn't think she'd be discovered on her first trip to Bollywood?

Who needed movie stars to make this day interesting? With Drew's assured prying and Anjali's secret movie star yearnings, I already had my own *masala* movie script playing out right before my eyes. (I love learning the lingo. Bollywood productions are often called masala movies after the Hindi word for spice mixture, *masala*, because they're a mixture of many things. Cool, huh?)

Rakesh pointed to a huge white marquee resembling a giant circus tent. "Pull over there, thanks."

"Oh my." Anjali mopped the perspiration from her brow. "Look at all these men."

I followed Anjali's line of vision and apart from a few guys lolling around, some behind cameras, the rest on giant metal boxes, I couldn't see much to get excited about.

Until Drew stepped into view.

Despite the fact he knew I was a phony and rubbed me the wrong way after one meeting, an irrational, inexplicable, intense, mind-numbing lust stabbed through my veneer of indifference and made me want to fling open the car door and run toward him.

Sheesh, I think the drama of being here was getting to me already.

"There's Drew." Rakesh waved madly, his excitement contagious. His perpetual enthusiasm irritated me a tad but my pretend-fiancé was also endearing. I couldn't wait for Rita to meet him.

While mulling the bizarre night I'd had at the Ramas' welcome party in the wee small hours this morning, I'd come to the conclusion maybe there was such a thing as fate. For others, not me. In my case, fate and the other four-letter F-word were freely interchangeable to describe my life.

What if Rita and Rakesh hit it off and by some weird cosmic twist fell in love? Did stuff like that happen, or were my views of romance tainted by my infatuation with rom-coms? Life wasn't a movie, though I could've debated the fact as I stepped out of the car and into one.

While Anjali gave Buddy instructions to move the car and wait in the parking lot near the entrance, I shifted my weight from foot to foot, my bravado ebbing. Fine and dandy to want a confrontation when I'd received Drew's supercilious email last night, but now I was here, with the man in question striding toward us, focused and formidable, I wish I'd told him where he could stick his summons.

"Glad you could make it." Drew smiled at our group as his gaze met mine in an unmistakable challenge and I resisted the urge to poke out my tongue. "I've taken the liberty of organizing a tour of the studios."

Anjali's eyes lit up like a true movie connoisseur. "Maybe Rakesh could show me the music side of things? His dad and I are old friends."

Pity she couldn't extend the friendship to Anu. I'd get to the bottom of that mystery by the end of this trip if it killed me.

"Fine by me." Rakesh darted a fond glance at Anjali and I respected him all the more. If he knew about her vendetta with his mom, he didn't let on.

"Great." Drew rubbed his hands together like a mastermind before pinning me with a glare that meant business. "Amrita, there's a distant cousin of the Ramas who would love to meet you. Or would you prefer to go with your fiancé?"

I noted the clenched jaw as he said 'Amrita' and 'fiancé,' realizing it must take superhuman effort for a control freak like him not to blurt the truth. Not that the truth would shock anyone in our little foursome.

As for Drew being controlling, call it a gut instinct. Guys like him—mega wealthy, well-put-together, the whole package—thrived on power and his peremptory email summons last night reinforced the fact. Not to mention the tour he'd deliberately organized to get Anjali and Rakesh out of the way.

I'd come to realize one small gesture in this city had a ripple effect: pose as fake fiancée, get blackmailed by guy to meet real fiancée, meet intriguing guy, can't do anything with intriguing guy because of stupid role-playing and the fact I couldn't—and didn't—like him, etc… etc… It went on and on. If I didn't confront him now, the fallout would be disastrous.

I could toy with him and tag along on the tour, but why prolong the inevitable? If he didn't interrogate me here he'd arrange some other time. Best to get it over with.

I rubbed at my temples, not needing to feign the tension squeezing my skull in a vice. "I'm actually feeling a bit light-headed from the heat. Maybe I could have a cup of *chai* and catch up with the tour later?"

Rakesh smirked at my ploy to be alone with Drew. If he only knew. "You sure, honey—"

"She's fine." Anjali slipped her hand through the crook of Rakesh's elbow so fast she almost toppled both of them. "You rest, my dear, we'll see you later."

Anjali dragged Rakesh—who gave a helpless shrug—as they left the marquee and disappeared from view.

Despite the bustle of people moving around us running errands, reading scripts, and toting refreshment trays, risking a glance at Drew only exacerbated my feeling of loneliness. His dour expression, compressed lips, and deep frown made him a formidable adversary.

One I had every intention of taking down.

"If you'd like *chai*, I've got afternoon tea waiting."

"How very civilized," I muttered, trying to pick up the pace when he insisted on sticking to my side like I was a fugitive about to bolt.

Normally, I would've loved having a cute guy cozying up to me but I knew he was after one thing and it wasn't my body—he wanted the truth and I'd be damned if I gave him either.

Not that I should be viewing him as anything other than the enemy. If his resemblance to Brad Stoddard wasn't enough of a warning, the fact I'd been dumped three months ago should boost my immunity against guys, attractive or otherwise.

We reached the refreshment trestle in a corner of the marquee, quiet and far from eavesdropping ears, and I braced for the incoming inquisition.

"I'm surprised you had the guts to stay behind." He handed me a cup of *chai*, his speculative stare sending a jolt of unease through me.

It had been dark on the Ramas' veranda last night so I hadn't noticed the incredible color of his eyes, a startling cross between cobalt and sky, a shade that could never be imitated by artists or technicians or any number of digital experts. I had a thing for blue eyes and Drew's could melt a woman at twenty paces or less, depending how lucky she was in getting close to him.

Blue-schmoo. I was here for one reason and one reason only: get Detective Drew to keep his big mouth shut and keep the heat off Rita in the process.

"I read your email. The old 'we need to talk' line didn't do it for me."

"What does?"

I fought a rising blush and plowed on, ignoring his innuendo and wondering when I'd become such a party-pooper. In my pre-Toad days, I would've lobbed a witty comeback straight at him, continuing the flirtation until one of us capitulated. I hated how Tate had dented my self-confidence, hated how my experience with him had left me wary and suspicious, whereas before I'd confront any situation head-on.

Getting involved with a married guy had been dumb and delusional despite the lies he'd fed me, but the residual self-doubt was what I loathed most. Was my judgment that off? Was I that gullible? The thought alone made my stomach churn, sickening me more than any accusations Drew could hurl my way.

"I've got nothing to say to you."

"But you do, Miss Jones."

"Keep your voice down."

The brazen bastard had the audacity to chuckle at my panic in possibly causing Rita irrefutable shame and condemnation from the Indian community across two continents.

"You're in no position to tell me what to do." He lowered his voice as several bare-chested actors in baggy pants helped themselves to *samosas* and iced tea before moving away. "Listen up. Rakesh is a good friend as well as my business partner. His family is revered around here and I won't let you make a laughingstock out of him. He's engaged to Amrita Muthu and you aren't her. So why don't you tell me exactly what game you're playing?"

The more he pushed for answers, the more I'd clam up. I hated being told what to do. Didn't take a genius to figure out why. Tate had controlled our relationship and when I'd wised up, I took back the power. I liked being in charge and had no intention of kowtowing to anyone, especially some guy who thought he ruled the world along with a movie studio.

"No game." That much was true. Impersonating Rita might have started out as a way to escape my problems back home, but the minute I'd met Rakesh and he'd divulged how this plan could affect Rita if it went awry, I knew I had to protect her.

"Then why are you doing this?"

"I don't owe you any explanations." I tilted my chin up for good measure, trying to stare him down.

Bad move. Boring hazel eyes locked on dazzling blue—and the hazels lost. "I'll tell Rakesh."

I laughed. "*I'll tell Rakesh*," I imitated, enjoying his open-mouthed shock. "*Na-na-na-na-nah. I'm going to tell on you.* Jeez, what are you? A first-grader?"

Emotions warred in his eyes, amusement with anger, frustration with curiosity, and I watched them all, enjoying the show. His high and mighty attitude irked, his supreme confidence rankled, and he was way too good-looking for comfort. But right then I came close to liking this guy for sticking up for his friend, even if he had my motivation all wrong.

I waggled my finger under his nose. "Stay out of my business. This has nothing to do with you."

"This is insane." He backed away from me as if I'd developed a case of leprosy. "Rakesh is one of this country's top businessmen and is known for his intelligence. Why can't he see past you?"

"Because love is blind." I gave a little shrug, grateful when an actress in a stunning chartreuse sari edged between us for a cup, mumbling an apology.

This couldn't go on for much longer. I couldn't keep from laughing at his absolute outrage. He acted like some stuck-up English lord with nothing better to do than harass his poor serfs. I couldn't wait to see his expression when he learned the truth.

The actress moved away, casting us a curious glance, and we waited until she'd rejoined a group at the far end of the marquee before resuming our conversation. I'd been so caught up in our private drama I hadn't noticed the swarming mass moving around the marquee: makeup artists, costume changers, techies, and hangers-on. I'd love to chat to them, get the lowdown on moviemaking Bollywood-style, if I didn't have to deal with an uptight, nosy, know-it-all.

"Love?" He raised an eyebrow in a classic scoff. "You've only just met the guy. How could you possibly love him?"

Biting my inner cheek to keep from laughing, I clasped my hands to my heart. "Don't you believe in love at first sight?"

"Don't be ridiculous."

"Just because it hasn't happened to you doesn't mean it's not real."

"This isn't a movie."

On the contrary, this charade I was perpetuating on behalf of Rita and Rakesh was fast turning into a movie for me. Who would've thought I'd star in my very own rom-com? Sadly, circumstances were heavy on the *com* and not enough *rom*.

"Rakesh is a big boy. He can look after himself. Why don't you butt out and make life easier on all of us?"

He had the penetrating stare down pat, the kind that left me wishing I hadn't had *dhosai* for lunch so my stomach wasn't pushing up against my diaphragm and making me slightly breathless.

In reality, the *dhosai* had digested hours ago and the out-of-breath sensation had everything to do with Drew and little to do with my atrocious diet.

"Easier on you, don't you mean? Isn't that what this is all about? You come here, try to get one of India's richest men to fall for you, and once he's smitten announce you're not his betrothed but you love him anyway?"

"Is that what you think?"

Not a bad plan... if I'd been living in the dark ages. No amount of money would be worth putting up with an arranged marriage, though I guess Drew didn't know that. He lived in a country surrounded by such marriages on a daily basis and though I'd hazard a guess he didn't agree with the concept, he'd obviously grown to accept it as the norm.

How ironic. He thought I was here to marry for money when in fact I was here to break the bind between the betrothed.

He shook his head. "It's the only reason that makes any sense. You're a scam artist. An opportunist who's taken a calculated risk in the hope it pays off. Well, guess what, Miss Jones? To quote your fellow countrymen, it ain't gonna happen."

He did a lousy imitation of a New York accent, sounding like a cross between Big from *Sex and the City* and *The Godfather*. Cute.

I stepped into his personal space in a deliberate taunt. "Seeing as you're so smart, what are you going to do to stop me?"

"Don't push your luck or you'll be sorry." His voice had dropped low and if it hadn't held such menace, I could've really dug its husky timbre.

"Ooh, scary." I covered my eyes with my hands, peeping out from between my fingers, wondering how long I could keep this up before I laughed my ass off.

A faint red stained his cheeks and I felt sorry for the guy. Lame, getting my thrills teasing some guy genuinely concerned for his friend.

"There's a name for women like you."

My amusement faded, replaced by insidious anger, making

my fingers convulse, my manicure digging into my palms. The Toad had used that same line when he dumped me, though the bastard had gone the extra yard and told me exactly what that name was. I'd wanted to kill him for judging me when he'd been the scumbag doing the dirty on his wife. I'd been guilty of naïvete—he'd been guilty of adultery and he'd called me names? Prick.

Having Bollywood Boy echo the Toad's words... not so great if he wanted to walk out of here rather than hobble.

"And there's a name for guys like you, but I'm too polite to use it, so I'll settle for pompous jerk." I jabbed a finger in his direction. "Stop jumping to conclusions and leave me the hell alone."

Shock widened his eyes, vindicating my outburst. I'd matched it with Bollywood Boy and then some.

To his credit, he calmed with effort. "I've got two words for you. Tell him."

"Or what?"

"I will."

"Buzzzzz. Wrong answer. Besides, that's four words."

He muttered under his breath and I'm sure I caught a posh version of 'fuck' but before I could bait him further Rakesh rushed into the marquee.

"Amrita, come quick. You've got to see this."

CHAPTER FIVE

My heart seized at the shock widening his eyes and pinching his lips.

"What's up?"

"It's Anjali." Rakesh grabbed my hand and I barely had a chance to see Drew's reaction to our cozy hand-holding before Rakesh pulled me into the harsh afternoon sunshine. "She's gone stark, raving mad."

Hell, hope she hadn't muscled in on an executive producer's Michelin-starred lunch.

"Where is she — oh."

As we dodged a guy in a cowboy hat and pushed through a throng of people congregating on the outskirts of a set, the crowd parted and I caught a glimpse of Anjali. Not as bad as first thought, though I agreed with Rakesh's earlier assessment of the situation. Anjali *had* gone mad.

She towered over a scrawny old man, yelling 'you know nothing about lost loves and rekindling affairs of the heart, you heathen,' brandishing her fists in his face as a crowd of onlookers gathered around. This wouldn't have been a catastrophe if her sari hadn't loosened and now hung around her waist, on the verge of unraveling completely.

She shrieked, she gestured, and she wobbled, oblivious to her near-naked state and the crowd swelling to movie premiere proportions.

"Quick, do something." Rakesh shoved me none too gently in Anjali's direction and I planted both feet firmly in the dirt.

"And add to the spectacle? No way. She's not my aunt."

"Oh yes, she is," he muttered, with a pointed glare.

"Shit." I had to take care of this debacle? Rita's debt to me was growing by the minute. I chuckled at his horrified expression as his disbelieving stare returned to Anjali. "As my fiancé it's your duty to protect me from scandal, so I think it's *your* job to break up that little melee."

"Melee? It's turning into a circus and about to get worse."

"Why?"

Rakesh cringed. "She just threatened to turn that soothsayer into a eunuch."

"Soothsayer? As in fortune-teller?"

"Yeah."

"What's a fortune-teller doing on a movie set?"

"Damned if I know. Are you going to do something about this or not?"

"Okay, okay. Settle, petal."

Calming an angry Anjali couldn't be any worse than facing the Toad when I'd tried a eunuch trick using my knee. Besides, surrounded by a bunch of people I'd never see again come next week, I didn't care.

I shouldered my way through the onlookers and headed straight for Anjali. "What seems to be the problem, Auntie?"

Anjali turned toward me and I resisted the urge to jump back. With her black eyes blazing, kohl bleeding into the corners, and perspiration rolling down her face, she looked like a deranged asylum escapee.

"Whatever it is, I'm sure we can settle this somewhere more private?" I dropped my voice and used my eyes as an indication to our growing audience, hoping it would work.

"This… this… *charlatan*," she hissed through gritted teeth, "has the audacity to talk about my past and predict my future when he wouldn't know a prophecy from a *paratha!*"

She'd lost it over a lousy prediction? If I got this upset with every horoscope I'd read, especially the ones forecasting riches and TDH—tall, dark, and handsome men—I'd be a basket case. Predictions were hooey. Now I had to convince Anjali.

Before I could open my mouth the toothless old man, who resembled a shrunken monkey, turned his rheumy eyes on me and beckoned with a twisted, arthritic finger.

Great. I didn't need some shriveled guy to predict my future: the TDH man, the fortune, the holiday, the house. Generic crap believed by gullible women the world over, but no longer applied to wised-up me.

"Leave my niece alone, you hypocrite." Anjali latched onto my arm in one of her famous death grips, the same one she'd used when Anu had welcomed me to her house.

"It's okay, I'll handle this." I pried her claw-like fingers off one by one and bent closer to the soothsayer. "I'm sorry, my aunt hasn't been well lately. Please forgive her."

I tried my best dazzling smile, the same one I intended using on Drew when I told him the truth.

The old man's eyes narrowed, his mouth opened, and his hand rose to hover in front of my face, knobbly finger extended.

"You. Be. Famous. Soon. Very soon."

Considering I stood in the lot of one of the world's biggest moviemaking meccas, I guessed this was his standard prediction, like my generic weekly online horoscope forecasting a surprise influx of wealth.

I nodded and maintained the smile. "Thanks, but we really must be going."

"Rich man follow you. Bad man follow you, too."

The rich man was more of the same old, same old. As for the bad man, I thought these guys weren't supposed to elaborate on doom and gloom. Like Anjali said, a real whacko.

"Uh-huh, but—"

"Boss bad man, too. He lie. Make baby with wife. No job for Missy. No house. No life. Missy travel far. Feel better."

My smile slipped and I tried not to physically recoil. How the hell had he known that stuff about Tate? Nobody here knew and I doubt Rita would've informed her aunt. As for Anjali telling this guy, no way.

I backed up, trying not to prompt another scary insight. At least his focus on me had taken the heat off Anjali, and thankfully, she'd quieted. Instead, she stared at me goggle-eyed, her penciled eyebrows raised toward the heavens in a comical WTF.

"Let's go back inside." I linked arms with Anjali and smiled at the crowd, signaling 'show over.'

However, it wasn't over until the skinny man sang—or soothsayed, in this instance.

"Rich man bring joy. Some pain. You decide." His final words wavered before he closed his eyes and his head lolled forward. He sat so still I could barely see his chest moving as he breathed.

"He's not dead, is he?" I muttered to Anjali as we walked away.

"We couldn't be that lucky," she said, belatedly realizing her state of undress as she frantically rewrapped her sari.

"What did he say to get you so wound up? Something about an old boyfriend?"

"Stupid old fool. I don't want to talk about it." She flung the last corner of the sari over her shoulder and sailed ahead of me before coming to an abrupt stop. "Who's this boss that ruined your life?"

"I don't want to talk about it," I fired straight back and waved to Rakesh, skulking by the marquee.

"Cheeky girl. Now, where's that young Drew? I'll have to tell him the tour's off. I need to go home and rest after my ordeal."

"Fine by me."

Better than fine. I'd had enough for one day: interrogations from fake fiancé's friends, real-life drama Anjali-style, and scary soothsaying. I liked watching drama being filmed here. Being a central character, not so much.

"We're leaving," I said as Rakesh materialized by our sides now the throng had dispersed. "No thanks to you."

I sniffed and pretended to ignore him, raising my nose in the air. That lasted all of two seconds when he tweaked it. "Didn't like your fortune, huh?"

"Didn't like the way you wimped out."

"Ouch." He clasped his heart, flashing the boyish smile he used to great effect. Rita had met her match with this one. "I didn't wimp out. I just discovered Kapil the soothsayer is the grandfather of a lead actor and a permanent fixture around here. Been telling fortunes for years."

His smile turned sly. "Besides, I have a reputation to uphold.

It wouldn't be good for me to be seen interfering in women's work."

"*Women's work*? You little worm, you—"

"Gotcha." He had the audacity to wink and I deflated.

Yep, Rita was in for a fine old time with Rollicking Rakesh.

Anjali cleared her throat, suitably shamed as we discussed her escapade. "Why don't I thank Drew for his hospitality and meet you by the car?"

"Good idea." Anything to avoid another confrontation with Bollywood Boy.

As Anjali waddled through the marquee entrance, I turned to Rakesh, now as good a time as any to discuss his friend's suspicions. "Speaking of Drew, we need to talk."

"About your little crush?"

"You're crazy." The same craziness making my heart pitter-patter at the thought of having a crush on a guy like Drew.

"You like him, I can tell." He tweaked my nose again and I swatted him away, annoyed by his intuitiveness. "Just remember you're engaged, otherwise my mother might stone you."

"I'd like to get stoned all right," I muttered, mustering a glare I couldn't maintain when he grinned, a smile between two friends who'd only met recently but clicked anyway.

I hadn't had a male friend before. Boyfriends, yeah. But platonic? Uh-uh. Yet here was a guy from another continent who I'd known for a few days and we'd become buddies. Go figure.

He squeezed my shoulders. "Don't worry. You'll get your chance to make a move on Drew when we're in New York."

"What?"

"Didn't I tell you? This movie he's backing has several New York scenes, so once it's a wrap here, the cast and crew will be heading to the Big Apple for a few weeks. Drew's definitely going, so perhaps you two can get properly *acquainted* there?"

I didn't know whether to kiss Rakesh or slap him. He deserved a kiss for being so astute and a slap for presuming to know more about what I wanted than I did. "Not interested."

Bollywood Boy would be in New York for a few weeks? Big deal. I didn't want a fling, not anymore. Besides, after I revealed the trick I'd played on him, I'd be the last person he'd want to see.

"You're pretty cute when you're in denial," Rakesh said, grabbing my chin and tilting my face from side to side as if studying it.

I elbowed him away. "Now you've had your fun, perhaps you'd like to hear that Drew knows my identity and is giving me grief over it."

"Drew *knows*?" His jaw dropped so far I placed a finger under his chin and guided it shut.

"Uh-huh. And he's becoming a real pain in the ass."

"How?"

"He's giving me a hard time about telling you the truth, implying I'm a gold digger out to fleece you for every rupee, about to ruin your family's reputation, blah, blah, blah."

Rakesh's brows drew together, the frown not detracting from his good looks. "Why didn't you tell him I already know?"

"Um… I didn't think you wanted anyone else in on it."

And I wanted to fool Mr. Hotshot-Know-It-All and have the last laugh.

Maybe it came down to control issues, and having Drew bully me into telling the truth chafed. Maybe I hated being told what to do. But whatever the reasons, I wanted to play this game a little longer. I was suffering Mojito Monday and Rita withdrawal. I had to tolerate Anjali's channel-surfing as she alternated between swooning over Ridge on *Bold and the Beautiful* and lusting after Leno—unfathomable. I'd contemplated flirting with a peeping Tom Lone Ranger look-alike.

I definitely needed another form of entertainment, even if it was an adolescent ruse. It wouldn't hurt to keep him at arm's length either. The guy rattled me. Not in a good way. His accusations and defense of his friend I could handle. The subliminal attraction? Not so much.

I'd come to Mumbai to help Rita, but my trip had been more about nursing my emotional bruises than altruism. Having Drew believe the worst in me was probably good. Last thing I needed was him to pick up on the buzz between us and want to explore it.

Falling for Tate had been dumb. Falling for a guy on the other side of the planet would be monumentally stupid.

Should I feel guilty? Probably. Did I? Hell no.

Rakesh didn't buy my lousy excuse. "But he already knows. He's a good guy, but we'll have to swear him to secrecy. Why didn't you tell—I get it." Rakesh snapped his fingers, his frown clearing, his mouth curving into a smug grin. "You're enjoying baiting him, making him squirm, knowing a secret he doesn't. I bet you're loving every minute of it, you devious woman."

"He's a pompous, arrogant ass who should mind his own business." I folded my arms and pretended to be in a huff when in fact I liked having a friend I could talk to about this. Rakesh knew Drew well, he'd guessed I was interested in the guy, and he'd proven to be an unexpected ally in a short space of time. I liked having him in my corner despite the fact he gave me as much grief as Rita. If the two ever joined forces, I'd be in trouble.

"Listen to yourself. Pompous and arrogant?" Rakesh chuckled

as he led me to the car, softly singing "Drew and Shari sitting in a tree, K.I.S.S.I.N.G."

"Juvenile."

"Flirt."

"Idiot."

"Gorgeous."

"Schmuck."

"Sassy."

"Stop. How can I keep insulting you when you're so damn nice?"

"That's my girl," he said, giving my shoulders an affectionate squeeze as Buddy opened the door for us and I slid inside.

I sagged against the worn leather seats, half listening to Rakesh making idle chatter with Buddy, the soothsayer's words echoing in my head.

Rich man bring joy. Some pain. You decide.

In my exhausted state—I wasn't cut out for all this drama—I didn't like the sound of pain. The rich man? Been there, look how it turned out. The joy I could handle, no problems at all.

As for decision making, I'd been lousy in the past. Time to wise up.

CHAPTER SIX

To: Amrita.M@hotmail.com
From: Shari.J@yahoo.com

Hope you're sitting down, Rita, because this promises to be long.

My first trip to Bollywood didn't quite work out as expected. Your aunt threw a hissy fit over some fortune-teller's prediction. If her voice hadn't attracted a crowd, her impromptu striptease would have.

The list of what you owe me is growing daily: in addition to Leo, the Valentino, Fifth Ave, and the Manolos, add psychotherapy.

Anyway, back to Bollywood. I wasn't discovered, didn't even have a chance to sneak into a scene as an extra, what with

a) fending off Bollywood Boy (hereafter known as BB)'s constant nagging about telling Rakesh the truth—like, duh, he already knows!

b) playacting the devoted fiancée—insert pic of me sticking two fingers down my throat

c) saving your family from utter humiliation if Anjali's sari had unwound all the way.

In other news, I'm still stringing BB along. Rakesh—aka Lover Boy, yours—wants to rub my nose in the fact BB is on my case. LB also thinks I have a 'thing' for BB. As if. I'm supposed to be the devoted fiancée, remember?

I also have to come clean about the charade to BB, and LB is taking me to their offices so I can do it. The only place I can have some privacy with BB without the all-seeing scandalmongers reporting back to Mama Rama (as opposed to Banana Rama). I must be really losing it if I'm making jokes about our all-time fave band of the '80s.

What else? Oh yeah, forgot to mention I'm going to be rich and famous and find true love if I make the right decision. At least I didn't have to pay the fortune-teller. Though if you believe that, you believe LB is your one true love and you'll live happily ever after.

That's about it for now. Not long 'til I'm home, can't wait!

Ship the Manolos to my new apartment (a girl can dream, right?) and have the therapist waiting. Seriously, if I have another day like today, I'm going to need one.

Hugs,
Shari xoxo

After I'd clicked the *send* button later that evening, I wondered if I should email Drew. Wouldn't a quick, impersonal note to tell him the truth be so much easier than a face-to-face meeting?

And miss the priceless look on his face when he discovered I'd been stringing him along for the hell of it? *Nah...*

"Shari, letter for you."

Anjali's voice drifted upstairs, a few octaves lower than usual. Her near brush with nudity in front of the masses had subdued her, and she'd barely spoken a word during dinner.

Padding downstairs, I wondered who'd sent me a letter. Nobody did snail mail these days. Plus, no one knew I was here, apart from Rita, my folks, and U.S. Immigration. Weird.

"Go on, open it." Anjali thrust the large blue envelope at me as I reached the bottom stair. "This is too exciting."

Had I missed something? The way Anjali wrung her hands, receiving a letter ranked right up there with Ridge marrying Brooke for the tenth time on her favorite soap.

"Exciting?" I played dumb, knowing I'd get a verbose explanation one way or the other.

"Yes, yes, very exciting. The young man who delivered it was very handsome, very big, great body, make good husband." She clapped her hands like a hyperactive child while I resisted the urge to clap my hands over her ears in a swift judo chop.

I didn't want a husband, least of all one who delivered letters reeking of Brut 33.

Choosing silence as the best defense against Anjali at her matchmaking worst, I tore open the envelope and reeled back as the overpowering stench shot straight up my nostrils. Even if this guy was Will Shakespeare and Dan Brown rolled into one, I couldn't tolerate longer than a quick scan of his prose before I fainted from the fumes.

"What does it say?" Anjali peered over my shoulder and I took a subtle step away, her resident garlic odor warring with the letter's fragrance in a heady combination equal to chloroform.

To the woman of my dreams,

You haunt me, you impress me, you inspire me.
Seeing you on the big screen was the highlight of my life, until you stepped down from the heavens and entered

our mortal sphere.

I am in awe of your talent and can't wait until we are together, as was written in the stars many moons ago.

Yours forever,

LR

Short, sharp, not so sweet. Freaking great. In a week, I'd managed to capture the interest of some psycho.

"Is it good news?" If Anjali's eyes bulged any further, they'd pop and roll across the cracked ceramic tiles.

"Not really." I wouldn't mind being some guy's inspiration… if I knew who the hell he was. Being the muse of a weirdo who hand-delivered aftershave-drenched letters? No thanks. "What did this guy look like?"

Anjali puffed up with pride, as if seeing my stalker in the flesh was a privilege. "Very big." Her arms spread over a yard wide. "Shoulders this broad. Tall. Nice smile. White teeth."

I hated to disillusion her but so far, her description could've fit countless guys.

"And stylish clothes. Denim never looked so good." She gave me a lewd wink before continuing. "I've always had a thing for cowboys. That Stetson added a real authentic touch."

My blood chilled. I knew this guy. Had to be the one who'd been staring at me the other night.

"Can I read it?"

"Here." I handed her the letter, sneezing five times in succession as my nasal passages did their dandiest to expel the odor from my nose.

A tiny frown appeared between her perfectly sculpted eyebrows. (Despite my admiration, I hadn't braved the string-twirling, hair-pulling beauticians yet. Think I'd stick to wax for now)

"He thinks you're an actress? He must have the wrong woman." Her shoulders sagged with disappointment while I perked up instantly. Perhaps Psycho Guy had made a mistake?

"And what does LR stand for? You'd think he would've used his real name at least." The frown deepened as she shook her head. "Dear, dear, the men of today."

"Probably stands for Loser Rat."

"Maybe Lonely Raj?"

"Lousy Reject."

"How about Lovely Rarity?"

"Living Refuse."

"Naughty girl." She wiggled her finger under my nose and handed me the letter, which I held at arm's length in case my nose rebelled again. "He's probably some lonesome guy who's smitten with you."

Lonesome… lonesome…

Couldn't be. LR… Lone Ranger? Could Psycho Guy possibly be emulating a screen legend? Way too spooky, considering I'd already dubbed him that the other night.

Could my stay get any weirder?

"What should I tell him if he comes again?"

"That I've reported him to the police."

"What nonsense. A nice young man like that?"

"Where I come from, there's a name for nice young men like that. It's 'stalker.'"

Anjali sniffed, affronted. "You girls of today are too picky. In my day if a young man like that came knocking on our door, our parents would've married us off before we could blink."

I refrained from pointing out the obvious, that her parents' choice in grooms seemed dubious at best. "Besides, he's made a harmless mistake. He obviously thinks an actress lives here. I'll set the young man straight if he visits again."

Not wanting to labor the point, I bid Anjali goodnight and climbed the stairs, holding the letter between my fingertips as if it were radioactive.

I didn't think there'd been a mistake, apart from a case of mistaken identity. This guy had been watching me, he knew where I lived, and he'd hand-delivered his fragrant missive. I should be petrified. Instead, a rueful chuckle developed into full-blown hysterics when I reached my room and fell facedown on the bed, getting tangled in the mosquito net and laughing harder.

Taking into consideration what I'd been through the last three months, my life could be scripted for Bollywood Boy's next epic: fired, dumped, evicted, played at fake fiancée, and now stalked.

Yeah, life couldn't get more interesting.

• • •

Testing my interesting life theory the next day, I paid a visit to Eye-on-I, the brainchild of the dynamic duo.

"Glad you could make it, *darling*." Rakesh air-kissed my cheeks like a New York princess, playing the part for Drew, who hovered behind him like the all-pervading wet blanket he was.

"Thanks for sending the limo. It caused quite a stir outside Anjali's place." I'd felt like a celebrity before reality hit and I realized I'd have to fight my way through a crowd ten-deep to reach the car. Thankfully, Anjali's sumo strength came in handy and she'd cut a path through the masses better than Moses.

"Would you like a tour of our humble office?"

Real humble from what I could see in the marble and chrome

foyer, complete with forty-yard atrium, giant plasma screen, and cascading waterfall.

"Drew has to tag along as chaperone but you don't mind, do you?"

I bit back a grin as Rakesh winked. What were the odds he conveniently found a way to leave me stranded with Drew? Not that I'd object. I'd be heading home at the end of next week and though nothing would ever come of my teensy-weensy interest in the gorgeous Brit, it was time to 'fess up.

"That'd be great." I gazed at Rakesh with faux adoration, enjoying the sight of Drew glowering at my fakeness over his friend's shoulder. "Lead the way."

To Drew's credit he maintained a polite façade as we toured the impressive offices of India's number one IT company. Until Rakesh left us alone in the lavish conference room, citing an urgent phone call as his excuse.

I waited until the door clicked shut before turning to Drew. "I need to tell—"

"—Rakesh the truth. Which you haven't done yet and it makes me sick." He stalked across the plush Persian carpet and flung himself into a sleek leather chair at the head of the table.

I tried to work up a temper at his pretentious behavior but failed miserably, what with admiring the way the Hugo Boss suit clung to his back and moved over his butt as he'd strode to his desk. "You're wrong about me."

I followed at a more sedate pace, making sure I worked it as I strolled toward him, and for a split second I glimpsed something akin to desire in his surly glare.

"Wrong? The only thing wrong is this fiasco you're making of Rakesh's life. Your lies, your acting, your—"

"Shut the hell up for one second." I had the satisfaction of seeing his jaw clench as I leaned over him. "He knows, you big British geek. He's known from the start, he's happy with it, and the only person who has a problem with any of this is *you*. So how about you shrug that big chip off your shoulders and get down on your knees and start groveling. I won't accept anything less than a full apology."

"He knows?"

I tried not to feel sorry for him as his mouth opened and closed like a sideshow clown at Central Park during a recent carnival.

"Yeah, apparently you IT guys are one step ahead of the rest of us, though you never did tell me how you found out I'm not Rita. Anyway, Rakesh is one of the good guys, unlike present company, and didn't want to shame her family so he decided to keep his mouth shut."

Drew shook his head, mussing his hair, my fingers tingling with the urge to smooth it back. "I don't get this. Any of it."

"Rita doesn't want a husband, especially one hand-picked by her parents, so she sent me to ditch him." I slid into the seat next to Drew. "We look alike, we thought Rakesh hadn't seen her pic, seemed harmless enough. Her folks are strict Hindu and she can't overtly go against their wishes, hence the subterfuge."

"Some ruse."

"Rakesh had investigated his betrothed and knew I was an imposter from the start. Upshot is, he likes what he sees in Rita so he agreed to perpetuate our charade in exchange for a meeting with the real thing in New York."

He eyeballed me with blatant skepticism. "I take it you're telling the truth this time and not having a laugh at my expense?"

"Been there, done that." My cheeky smile aimed to infuriate. "Joke's on you, Bollywood Boy."

"Bollywood Boy?"

Oops, I'd been having so much fun, the last part slipped out.

"*Bollywood Boy.*" This time, he said it quieter, slower, as if rolling it over his tongue to check the fit. To my amazement he laughed, startling in its volume and unexpectedness, with a sexy depth that had me clenching my thighs together before I did something crazy, like spread them.

"You're an amazing woman, Miss Jones." If his laughter had shocked me, it had nothing on the hundred-watt smile making me wish I had a protective force field.

"Thanks." I batted my eyelashes, slipping into flirt mode, something I'd wanted to do since I first set eyes on the guy. Kudos to Rakesh for having the foresight to arrange this private meeting, bless his scheming heart.

"Let me get this straight. Rakesh has known from day one you're a phony and he's going along with it to protect their families and meet the real Amrita?"

"Yep."

"And you've let me make a fool of myself since we met by harassing you to tell him the truth?"

"Yep, wasn't too difficult." My grin broadened. "Letting you make a fool of yourself, that is."

To give him credit, his smile didn't slip. Instead, his eyes took on a predatory glint and I knew I'd pushed once too often. "You've got a smart mouth. And I think it's time you put it to good use."

Huh? This time, I did the jaw-dropping routine as he closed the gap between us.

Ohmigod.

He was going to kiss me.

In the split second realization hit, I ran my tongue quickly over my teeth, wished I'd flossed that morning, and hoped my technique hadn't slipped, considering it had been a while since I'd lip-locked anybody.

I held my breath as he paused, his face inches from mine. He tipped my chin up with a finger. "Let's see exactly how good you are."

My mind raced frantically as I searched for something witty to say. Sadly, all I could come up with was, "Very good."

"In that case, let's hear it."

Hear what? I knew I was out of practice but last time I checked, kissing involved mouths and lips and tongues — not ears. Unless the guy was very, very good and let his tongue wander to my ear, one of my hot spots.

"Your apology, of course," he said, almost a whisper, his mint-fresh breath wafting over me and begging me to taste. "Sometime this century would be nice." His smug smile grated, but he was right. Besides, the sooner he got his damn apology, the sooner I could break this almost-kiss hold he had over me.

"Sorry."

"Come on, you can do better than that." His fingertip wandered, tracing a lazy path along the tender skin under my chin, and I desperately tried to hang onto my self-control.

Kiss him… kiss him… kiss him… flashed through my mind, an insistent echo like a booming announcement at a Yankees game.

"I'm waiting."

Damn him. How could two innocent words sound like a seductive purr?

"Sorry for stringing you along and wasting your time," I blurted, managing to sit up straighter, dislodge his finger, and put some valuable distance between our faces at the same time.

"Better, though your delivery needs some work." He didn't make a big deal out of my chicken act (this from a woman who'd never backed down from a challenge in her life). The cozy atmosphere he'd created had vanished, though his smile didn't cool my hormones, not one bit.

"Take it or leave it. It's the only apology you'll get out of me."

"Fine. Now you've had your fun at my expense, why don't you tell me what you think of India so far?"

Interesting change of subject. Though I'd rather pursue what he thought of *me*, I'd play along for now. "Chaotic, crazy, and totally mesmerizing. How long have you lived here?"

His eyes lit up with enthusiasm and I irrationally wished he would look at me that way.

"Five years, give or take. I'm mainly based in London, but spend several months a year here from choice, not necessity."

"You like it that much?"

He nodded, enthusiasm sparking his eyes, making my 'kiss-him' mantra rev up again. "From the first minute I set foot here I loved everything about it. The contrasts, the people, the food, the vibrancy. It's magic."

"Are all you English this eloquent or is Shakespeare a long lost uncle?"

"Are you Yanks this brash all the time?"

I squared my shoulders. "Nothing wrong with blunt honesty."

"Fine. Are you attracted to me?"

Shit. I mentally flapped my wings and squawked in a fair chicken impersonation. "Let's get back to our cultural discussion. How did you get involved in the movies?"

He let me off the hook. By the gleam in his eyes I knew it

was only a reprieve. "I've loved them since I was a kid. When Rakesh took me out to Film City one day to see his dad, I was hooked. Bollywood's like the rest of this place. Big, bold, larger than life. Who wouldn't get sucked in?"

"Must admit, I wish I'd had more time to explore yesterday. I'm a bit of a film fanatic."

He grinned, obviously remembering what made me flee. "Anjali's something else. Kapil doles out fortunes to anyone foolish enough to listen. Most people laugh it off so I'd hazard a guess he's never had a half-naked woman attempting to strangle him before."

"She didn't strangle him. She just wanted to beat him around the head a little." I joined in his laughter. This laid-back, comfortable warmth is how I felt with Rakesh, but with Drew, it had an underlying sexual sizzle I knew would combust given kindling and a spark.

"Would you like to visit again? This time, I promise to keep Kapil out of your way."

"Thanks, I'd love to," I said, strangely shy all of a sudden.

Detective Drew had been gruff, rude, and irritatingly condescending and I could handle him without blinking.

Disarming Drew crept under my guard, bamboozling me with charm, and handling him would be way too tempting.

Dreamy Drew was interesting, fun, and sexy, and I knew I couldn't handle him if my life depended on it.

"Good, that's settled. Now, about that other question, about the attraction thing—"

"Hey, you two, sort everything out?" Rakesh poked his head around the door, saw our proximity, and winked.

I'd never been so glad to see anyone in my life.

"Yep." I bolted from my chair and rushed to the door. "Drew

has offered another visit to Film City. Isn't that great? Can't wait. This time I'll get to see everything. You know how I love movies." I babbled like a bimbo, but was grateful for any sound to fill the void left by Drew's hanging question—and the answer reverberating through my head, a deafening, resounding "YES!"

Rakesh led me back to the table, his cocky smile saying he knew exactly why I had a severe case of verbal diarrhea. Turning a chair backward, he sat opposite Drew and leaned on his elbows. "I hear you've been harassing my fiancée."

"Fiancée, my butt," Drew said, sending Rakesh a mock furious glare. "Why didn't you tell me you knew she wasn't Amrita?"

I slid quietly into a chair between the two guys facing off, an eager spectator now the heat was off me.

Rakesh shrugged, his broad shoulders straining against the white business shirt he wore so well, the sleeves casually rolled up to reveal muscled forearms. "I didn't want to make a big deal. How did you find out anyway?"

For an Englishman, Drew had a tanned complexion rather than the pale pastiness evident in his countrymen—no one could defy the Indian sun for long—and to my surprise a faint pink stained his cheeks, adding to my amusement. "Remember the Thornton deal and the all-nighter to secure it?"

Rakesh snapped his fingers. "You must've seen the info I'd pulled on Amrita when I dashed out of the room to head off the raging CEO. Slick."

He nodded. "It got caught up in a few files, and I unintentionally read it. How'd you discover enough to know Shari wasn't Amrita?"

Rakesh's turn to look bashful. "I used the company's PIs."

"Ah." Drew grinned, the two cohorts proud of themselves.

Typical smug males. Like I'd let them off that easily. "How did you know my name that night at the party?"

Two pairs of eyes swiveled toward me, one a warm chocolate brown, the other a startling blue with the potential to make me melt.

"I mean, you knew I wasn't Rita but how did you know my real identity?"

The pink in Drew's cheeks deepened to crimson. "When you were mingling I took a photo of you with my cell, checked it against our search engines, and had the info I needed in less than five minutes."

"Perk of the job, huh? Spying, invading a person's privacy, being an inquisitive English ass?"

"I was looking out for my friend's interests."

"You were sticking your nose in business that didn't concern you."

"And you treated me like an idiot instead of telling me the truth from the start."

"Children, children." Rakesh tut-tutted and made a T sign with his hands. "Time out. Now everyone here knows everyone else's business, what say we keep our lips zipped and continue as before?"

"And go back to him being an uptight, pretentious know-it-all?"

A tad harsh. Once Drew learned the truth he'd lightened to the point where he'd turned flirtatious and I'd loved every second. However, I had a reputation to uphold—my don't-be-stupid-where-guys-are-concerned reputation—and I couldn't let a little healthy flirtation get in the way of my new smarter self.

"And go back to her being a lying, devious diva?"

We deadlocked in a staring competition, challenging the other to look away first. *Bad luck, Bollywood Boy.* I'd been my middle school's staring comp queen three years running and no way would I capitulate.

But he didn't play fair. The longer I stared into his eyes the more I noticed the tiniest green and gold flecks dotted around the irises, overshadowed by that powerful, too-good-to-be-true blue.

I sensed rather than saw the corners of his mouth tilting as if he was laughing at me, and my resolve unwound as fast as Anjali's sari in front of Kapil yesterday.

I caved.

I let out a loud whoop and he joined in while Rakesh shook his head like a proud papa watching his two favorite kids.

"Diva, huh? I like it." I cocked my hip in a sassy 'bring it on.'

Drew's gaze drifted to my hip before slowly sweeping upward to my face, heating every inch he'd visually skimmed. "Guess I need to brush up on my insults."

"Hey, before you get into round two, I need Drew to sign off on a deal," Rakesh interrupted, surprisingly brisk and businesslike. "Time for you to head home, *wife-to-be.*"

"In your dreams."

"In my nightmares," Rakesh said, and I flipped him a rude sign before making a dignified exit.

As dignified as can be expected considering I stumbled when my three-inch heel caught the edge of the Persian rug and threatened to land me on my expanding butt. Damn Anjali and those *ladoos.*

I heard a stifled snort and turned quickly, glaring at both men. "The least one of you bozos could do is escort me to the door."

Drew shrugged and smirked. "Sorry. You'd accuse me of being a know-it-all again and I can't have that. My fragile English ego can't handle it."

Ignoring him, I glared at Rakesh. "And what's your story, Lover Boy?"

"He gets Lover Boy and I get Bollywood Boy? Nice." Drew's eyes glittered with mischief and I fought the urge to run over, wrap my arms around him, and consummate the kiss we'd almost had.

Rakesh scrambled to his feet and crossed the room in two seconds flat, taking my hand and placing it in the crook of his elbow. "I was going to invent some lame excuse but after you've pumped up my ego, how could I be so ungallant?" He lowered his voice to a loud stage whisper. "Bollywood Boy? Good one."

"I thought you said we had to get back to business, Rama? So once you escort the lady to the limo, I'll see you in my office."

"Nice seeing you again, Drew." I sent him a saucy wave over my shoulder, wondering when I'd last had this much fun. Sad, because all we'd done was trade verbal banter, the odd insult, and flirted a little. Yet suddenly my world looked like a brighter place to be.

In all honesty, my life had improved since I'd arrived in this crazy, hot, melting pot of human intrigue, and I hoped my new positive karma carried over when I returned home.

"You too, Miss Jones. Look forward to seeing a lot more of you." His low, seductive chuckle left me in little doubt he wasn't just talking about my physical presence.

Damn, he was good. But I was better.

"The feeling's entirely mutual, Mr. Lansford. Though remember, divas only expect the best."

I licked my top lip in a sexy move I'd seen on TV, savoring

his surprise and flare of heat as he checked me out with a silent promise of more to come.

CHAPTER SEVEN

To: Shari.J@yahoo.com
From: Amrita.M@hotmail.com

Hey Shari,

Only someone as confident as you could lob into a strange city, pull off the impersonation of all time (I hear Anu is a clever cow and if she believes you're me, you deserve the lead in the next Bollywood extravaganza), and find romance with some hot English dude.

He's hot, isn't he? All I hear is you dissing him and complaining, which tells me you have it bad! Uh-oh, let me guess. He's a Hugh look-alike?

Repeat after me: "I am not Julia Roberts. I am not Andie MacDowell. I am not living a film role. Hugh Grant is a sap."

Okay, maybe he's a cute sap but nevertheless, even if this English guy doesn't look like you-know-Hugh, don't get into a thing with a guy who lives on the other side of the world. You're only asking for more heartache, girlfriend, and you've had your fair share thanks to that lowlife scum Tate. (Please forgive slip in using the T-word.)

Lover Boy, huh? If the Boy Rama is anything like the Indian guys I've met, I won't give him a second look, your recommendation notwithstanding. I don't need a master, hot bod or not, and unfortunately that's what these guys want—some docile slave to pander to their every whim while they grow fat on wifey's cooking. No way, no how.

(Note my bravado when voicing my strong opinions to you but discussing my cultural cynicism with my folks? So not happening. Wish I could make them understand I'm as Hindu as they are and respect all that stands for, but I'm a New Yorker, too, and I crave freedom of choice as much as they crave an Indian son-in-law.)

Anyway, that's me for now.

Love you,

Rita xx

(PS. Sorry I've been incommunicado. Been dodging Mom's questions about wedding plans—yeah, all the way from the Grand Canyon!—and busy number-crunching at Berg's. You know how it is... Later.)

I reread the email, searching for a clue to substantiate the suspicious niggle I had that something wasn't right. It had taken Rita two days to respond to my email when we usually spoke/emailed/texted every day. The text messages from NYC to Mumbai had been something along the lines of "R U OK 2DAY?" but at least it'd been contact. Yesterday, there'd been nada.

While I couldn't find anything untoward in the email, I couldn't shake the feeling Rita had something stewing.

"Shari, you ready? The car's here."

"Coming, Auntie." I added an extra slick of gloss and

puckered up at the mirror. Sad, I know, but it was the closest I'd get to a kiss this trip—fantasies about Bollywood Boy notwithstanding.

Drew had sent the limo for our return trip to the studio, and by the height of Anjali's nose stuck in the air, she loved every minute of it. Her smugness as she simpered at the driver, who held the door open for us, was in stark contrast to Buddy's sourness as he hovered in the background, ostensibly polishing the old Beamer while casting malevolent glares at the limo. He hadn't taken too kindly to being demoted from his driving duties for a day.

Taking pity on him, I waved and smiled, his mutinous expression brightening for a second. Buddy could rival the Lone Ranger to head up my Indian fan club. He'd been particularly attentive since the crash'n'bang duty-free incident, trying to make up for it.

As if. I liked having a man in the house to do my bidding, but if I had a choice between Buddy and a mojito right now? No contest.

The driver edged the limo through the crowd outside Anjali's gate and as he turned onto the street, I caught a glimpse of a Stetson.

I grabbed Anjali's arm. "Hey, is that the guy who delivered the letter?"

"Where?" She craned her neck and squinted at where I pointed.

"Standing behind your gawking neighbors."

"Can't see a thing." Not that she was looking all that hard, considering she waved and nodded at the onlookers like the queen from her royal carriage. "Besides, I'm sure he's harmless."

"If I get abducted by some Stetson psycho, I'll remember

that."

She guffawed and settled back in her seat as the limo headed up the street. Despite scanning the crowd in our wake, I couldn't see the hat. Maybe I imagined it? Or maybe some crazy cowboy *was* stalking me? Just what I needed, further intrigue.

Anjali prattled for the entire trip and I listened with half an ear, nodding and ahh-ing in the appropriate places. Drew wouldn't be at Film City today, and while my head said this was a good thing, my heart wouldn't have minded another jump-start from his skilled flirting.

As the studio gates came into sight, the memory of our previous embarrassment had me fixing Anjali with a don't-mess-with-me glare. "Today you stick with me. No wandering off on your own, no interfering, and most of all, no approaching Kapil for a repeat performance."

Anjali's kohl-rimmed eyes widened in a pathetic attempt at innocence. "I'm not a child, you know."

"Then don't throw a tantrum like you did last time and I'll believe you."

"Who, me?" She batted her eyelashes in exaggerated faux innocence, and I experienced a surge of affection for this warm, funny woman who had taken me into her home and protected me from what this bizarre city could throw at me.

Reaching over, I squeezed her hand. "Yes, you. No outbursts today, right?"

"Right." She grinned like a naughty kid and I knew I'd need to keep an eye on her.

However, I didn't have time once we arrived. In Drew's absence he'd entrusted us to his deputy, Desiree, a striking Eurasian woman of indeterminate age, who guided us through the extensive grounds.

We skirted around the mayhem on two sets—a fight scene and a chase scene complete with galloping horses and cowboys, my latent paranoia kicking in as I surreptitiously checked for authentic Stetsons and sniffed the air for Brut. Unable to tell the cowboys apart, I was nonetheless relieved when we stopped at another set, this one featuring a huge fountain as a centerpiece. Fake Roman columns surrounded it, with a covered walkway leading to a gazebo, where a harem of women wearing buttercup, amaranth, and lilac saris spilled down the steps in riotous abandon.

They clapped and twirled and cast coy glances at the male chorus, resplendent in burgundy turbans. My head spun with the noise and color and sheer numbers of extras involved.

Watching a scene shot live would change the way I viewed Bollywood films forever, the vibrancy and animation astounding. The fantastic blur of color and music mesmerized me as I tapped my foot in time with the catchy *tabla* rhythm, wishing I could demonstrate the same *joie de vivre* of the actors. I was particularly impressed with the stunning sari-clad women dancing *chakkars* (pirouettes) and *dhak dhaks* (a dance step involving loads of titillating breast jerks), their grace and liveliness inspiring.

Apparently, most male movie fans loved the *dhak dhak*. Not surprising, considering onscreen kisses were rare, and nudity nonexistent, so the odd breast shimmy—often in the rain for a little extra attention—was about as raunchy as it got. Movie audiences would have a group coronary if Stanley Kubrick produced here.

As the music picked up tempo and the dancers whirled in compelling color, I didn't know where to look first, like a kid on a trip to Disneyland.

"You'll like this, child. Holi is the Hindu festival of color and often used in film sequences. Look." Anjali grabbed my arm in excitement and I followed her line of vision.

"Wow." I stared as a cast of hundreds threw bright powders and sprayed water on one another, dancing and singing and leaping in an astonishing kaleidoscope of color. Peacock blue mingled with emerald, ruby with sunshine yellow, a gorgeous mayhem free-for-all like a bunch of hyperactive preschoolers let loose with finger paints. I yearned to play.

"Watch the heroine," Anjali said, giggling at my goggle-eyed surprise. "More titty action."

Sure enough, the beautiful heroine with exotic almond-shaped green eyes and thick black hair falling to her waist in a sleek curtain emerged from the writhing masses, drenched from head to foot. Color speckled her sheer white chiffon sari and clung to her voluptuous body.

Anjali shook her head. "Men are perverts."

I watched the heroine's graceful movements, perfect body, and gorgeous smile, not blaming guys for a second.

"If you've got it, flaunt it," I said, a small part of me wishing I had one-tenth of the va-va-va-voom the actress had.

"Girls of today have no shame," Anjali said as the heroine flounced off with the handsome hero hot on her heels.

I switched to watching another scene, where a group of women wearing micro-minis and crop tops was trying to entice a tall, leather-clad guy—the hero—away from a demure village girl, the love of his life by the way she made sickening goo-goo eyes at him.

"The vamps in these films always wear scandalous Western clothes," Anjali said, her frowning glance flicking over my own tight white bootleg jeans and flowing pink peasant top as if assessing my vamp factor.

I must've passed the test because she returned to watching the action, including *barsaat* (rain) and wet saris, *jhatkas* (the jerks and *dhak dhaks* of many choreographed songs) and shy glances from the Queen Bee, the industry's top heroine at the time. I'd never seen anything like the constant whir of motion, the frenetic pace, or the mind-boggling spectacle that went into making a Bollywood film.

When the action wound down half an hour later and the director called 'cut,' sweat trickled down my back in rivulets from standing too long and I jumped at Desiree's offer of a drink.

We wound our way between giant sound stages and trucks filled with electronic equipment to a small refreshment tent teeming with actors. Desiree parted the crowd and we bustled to the front, organizing our tea before I gratefully sunk into a canvas chair.

I sipped my *chai,* half-listening to Anjali and Desiree gush, debating the assets of megastar hotties Shah Rukh Khan, Salman Khan, and Akshay Kumar while ogling some seriously prime beefcake. If I didn't live half a world away and had sworn off guys, I could've easily fallen in lust with any number of the buffed guys strutting around the tent.

When we'd finished, Desiree took us behind the scenes of another film, an epic featuring star-crossed lovers, a murdered father, a vengeful son, and a ghost, making my taste in rom-coms seem decidedly tame.

We watched a dazzling dance sequence; a huge cast of whirring, gyrating, hand-thrusting demons dressed in rainbow-colored saris bounced around in the scorching heat. They maintained smiles during the high-octane performance, until the cameras stopped rolling and they flopped onto the nearest crate/chair/piece of ground to moan about the bastard producer and the lousy pay.

The *chai* revived me because I could've sat and watched Bollywood at its best forever. Every aspect fascinated me. When the scene wound down, we moved indoors to a vast area where musicians dubbed the score for the films.

Anjali glanced around. "Is Senthil Rama here today?"

"He sure is," Desiree said, with a beaming smile for the first time today. "He's the best tabla player in Mumbai and we're lucky he works here. Do you know him?"

Anjali shrugged. "We're old friends."

"Then you must say hello."

"Just a quick one. I'm sure he's busy." Anjali appeared disinterested but I couldn't figure why she wanted to say hi to Senthil. It wasn't like she had to impress the guy on my behalf considering I wouldn't see him again once I headed back to NYC. And Anu wasn't around, so it couldn't be to aggravate her. Unless her deviousness extended to hoping Senthil would report back to Anu? Considering her loathing for the woman, I wouldn't put it past Anjali. Or maybe the mystique in Rita's plan was getting to me and I was searching for clues that weren't there.

Desiree nodded. "Yes, he's in great demand."

I didn't feel like greeting my pretend father-in-law. In fact, I'd been extremely lucky so far, only seeing the Ramas at their house once. Though I knew my luck wouldn't hold, as Rakesh had mumbled something about a farewell dinner when I'd left Eye-on-I yesterday.

A dinner party with Mama Rama ranked right up there with my annual gyno visit: things we have to do but hate.

I waved them away. "Go ahead. I'll rest here while you say hello."

"We won't be long." Desiree and Anjali chattered about their favorite Bollywood films as they went in search of the Tabla King.

I sat on the nearest director's chair, wondering whose famous butt graced the canvas before mine. Hoping Senthil's groupies wouldn't be long, I slouched into it, the combination of a full stomach and the heavy afternoon heat acting like a sleeping drug. As my eyelids drooped, I caught a strong waft of Brut as someone sat next to me and I registered their feet before I dozed.

Nice boots.

My eyelids drooped.

Fancy cowboy boots.

I needed matchsticks to pry open my eyelids, they were that heavy.

Shit.

My eyes sprung open as I registered where I'd seen a pair of these great boots recently. And the psycho they were attached to.

Faking a yawn, I sat up straighter and reached for my bag, rummaging in it for any weapon I could find. My choices were limited: stab him with a Sky High Curl mascara wand, clamp him with an eyelash curler, or gloss him with Glam Shine.

Fight wasn't an option so I prepared for flight, not that my heels had anything on the Nikes I kept in storage back home. Before I could spring/leap/dash like I'd seen Cameron Diaz do in *Charlie's Angels*, I sensed movement and braced for the Lone Ranger's lasso.

"Excuse me, but I had to tell you I'm your greatest fan, Miss Rai. I know you must hear this all the time but your work far surpasses anyone else's and your screen presence alone brings joy to my heart."

A polite stalker. Who would've thought?

Ready to settle this confusion once and for all, I deliberately voided any expression from my face and turned toward him.

Yep, it was the guy who'd stared at my window that night and probably the same one who'd delivered the stinky note. The Lone Ranger in the flesh, complete with Stetson shading his face.

Though his body could've rivaled Mr. Universe, his face was nothing to rave about: average brown eyes, average nose, and thin lips. In fact, everything about his face read average, which probably helped in his line of work: Stalking 101.

"Sorry, there's been a mistake. I'm not who you think I am. I'm not an actress. Never have been, unless you count my pathetic rendition of Sandi from *Grease* in high school and—"

I came to an abrupt stop, realizing I was babbling and the Ranger's eyes gleamed now that his supposed idol had deemed to talk to him. Not that I wasn't the teensiest bit flattered. He thought I was Aishwarya Rai Bachan, a former Miss Universe and stunning screen star. If he had to confuse me with someone, she was a glamorous start.

His lips stretched into a scary smile, underscoring the fanatical glint in his eyes. "You don't have to pretend with me. The minute I spotted you at the airport, I knew who you were. I saw that you've left your husband and are staying with some relative, doing your best to act poor, but I've seen you've reverted to taking limos, as you should. You deserve the best and hopefully, someday soon, you'll realize I can give you that."

The guy was seriously loco, and, worse, he'd been watching me. At the airport, at Anjali's place. I knew I'd seen him when I'd entered the limo. And what about the other times I'd glimpsed that hat… yikes! I remembered: the guy who'd bumped into me near the terminal when I'd first arrived, then again when I'd visited Film City first time around and rushed to Anjali's aid.

Shit, the guy had Stalking 101 down pat. A thousand bizarre scenarios ranging from kidnapping to chloroform flashed through my mind, and I knew I had to end this right here, right now.

"Listen, buster. You're way off base. I'm not Aishwarya Rai *Bachan*." I stressed the star's married name, which he'd probably deleted deliberately in his delusional state. "And if you want proof, hang around 'til my aunt gets back. She'll set you straight."

Knowing Anjali, she'd probably take one look at the Lone Ranger's body and start interviewing him as prospective husband material.

For the first time since we'd started talking, his dazed, starstruck expression gave way to fear mingled with admiration. "I saw what she did to Kapil. She's quite a woman."

My panic bordered on hysteria and I calmed my voice with effort. "You were stalking me the other day, too?"

"Stalking? This isn't stalking. This is destiny." He drew out the last word, the apparent fear at what Anjali might do to him replaced by a hopeful expression.

"Destiny my ass," I muttered, tired, grumpy, and craving New York like I never had. At least the psychos there settled for mugging you, not pledging their undying love. "Does Miss Rai star in films made here?"

I used her well-known single name so I wouldn't rile him unnecessarily.

"Yes, you do. I've worshipped you from afar for too long so when fate intervened and I saw you at the airport without that stupid husband of yours, I knew I had to make my declaration. Being so close to you, yet not having contact, has acted like an arrow through my heart."

Nice. He was taking the Western theme to poetic extremes now. *Being so close… uh-oh*. "You work here?"

Didn't places like this have screening tests for psychos?

He nodded, puffing out his pecs with pride. "I'm an extra. I play bad guys because of my body. I'm very good."

Risking a quick glance at his broad chest, I took his word for it.

Inspiration struck. "I'm filming today?"

He looked at me like I'd sprouted horns. "Of course, that's why you're here. Luckily, I'm in the same sequence, too, and we get to be onscreen together for the first time. Told you it was destiny."

I had two options. Wait for Anjali and Desiree to return and go through the rigmarole of convincing him I wasn't Aishwarya—which he probably wouldn't believe because he thought Anjali was in on the hide-my-identity thing—or go with him to the set and show him the real actress.

No-brainer.

"Speaking of filming, you better hurry," he said. "You need to get into costume. I'd be honored if you accompanied me to the set."

Nodding, I stood before he could offer me a hand and tried not to look too indecisive. Knowing the Ranger's one-track mind, he'd probably take it as another red herring I was throwing to my adoring public.

Thankfully, the set wasn't far and we reached it without incident. This guy must be seriously blind not to realize I wasn't the stunning actress. Apart from the occasional smile from people who passed, no one fell at my feet, thrust an autograph book in my face, or begged for a photo.

"It has been a privilege."

Before I could react, he'd taken hold of my hand and bowed over it, the rim of his Stetson colliding with my fake

Fendi, which I hung onto for grim death. If nothing inside it was weapon-worthy, the gold clasp might prove useful to take out an eye if swung in the right trajectory.

With further protests wasted, I waited for him to release my hand, then spied a woman exit a nearby tent, followed by an entourage that would've done the president proud. I couldn't see her face, cloaked in a chiffon veil. Or her body covered in a billowing cerise sari. But the phalanx of foot soldiers around her was a dead giveaway.

I turned to the Lone Ranger. "You still think I'm Ms. Rai?"

He nodded, his guilty expression indicating he was tiring fast of me refusing to acknowledge the truth. I'd give him the freaking truth.

"Then who's that?"

He followed my line of vision and, thank you God, his eyes bulged as he registered his object of lust and computed it wasn't me. "B-but—but—"

"Butt is right," I muttered. Butthead. "Now do you believe me?"

Eyes wide and stricken, he stared at the movie star and her entourage disappearing onto a set. "I've made a terrible mistake. Sorry. Please don't report me. I'll atone for my mistake. I'll offer up many prayers. Please, I beg you."

I should've kicked his sorry ass to the studio gates for being an obsessive weirdo, but I knew what it was like to lust after someone only to have the veil ripped from your eyes. I frowned, putting on my best disgruntled face. "Next time a woman tells you something, believe her. As for Ms. Rai, quit stalking her. She'd be less forgiving than me and have you arrested, capish?"

He nodded, his mouth downturned, and as I walked away I'm sure I heard him mutter, "Destiny is dead."

• • •

Only one thing could distract me from my brush with a lunatic. Retail therapy.

In the car on the way to Crawford Market, I listened to Anjali rave about the music scores she'd been privy to for the latest blockbuster thanks to Senthil. She loved showbiz and I waited a while for a lull in conversation to tell her about my stalker.

When she took a breath, I said, "Remember that hand-delivered letter?"

"From the handsome young man?" She held her arms a yard apart. "With shoulders this big?"

I nodded. "That's the one. Turns out he was stalking me. Thought I was Aishwarya Rai Bachan."

She laughed so hard, kohl streaked her cheeks.

I narrowed my eyes. "Glad some crazy guy following me is so amusing."

She patted my hand, the odd chortle escaping. "Men are so stupid."

"Why? Because he mistook me for a gorgeous movie star?"

She shook her head. "No, because if he liked you, why not approach you directly rather than skulk around?"

Not appeased, I mock frowned. "But you laughed at the case of mistaken identity."

She sighed. "Shari, dear, any fool would know you're not Aishwarya. You're living in my house, you're driving around in a battered Beamer, and there's no sign of Aishwarya's gorgeous husband anywhere."

I forgave her for the raucous laughter, considering she hadn't mentioned I was nowhere near as beautiful as the stunning

Aishwarya Rai Bachan.

She made odd clucking noises with her tongue. "Shame, though, he could've been good husband material for you—"

"Is that the market?" Happy for the distraction as Buddy stopped the car, I pointed at the huge building, which looked like it'd been transported from Paris to Mumbai.

Anjali nodded. "Not what you were expecting?"

Stunned, I noted the artistic blend of Norman and Flemish architectural styles, the clock tower adorned with beautiful Victorian carvings, and the impressive frieze over the main entrance depicting peasants in wheat fields.

"Wow," I mouthed, as we stepped from the car and Anjali took my elbow, her proud strut making me smile.

As we entered the main pavilion, a heady wave of aromas washed over me. Pungent, freshly ground spices—cumin, coriander and garam masala—interspersed with tangy lime and succulent mango and petite Lady Finger bananas.

I inhaled and my stomach grumbled. Looked like I'd caught Anjali's ravenous disease.

Demonstrating an uncanny ability to read food thoughts, Anjali tugged my arm. "This way. You must try the *falooda*."

For once she'd get no protest from me. I barely had time to glance at the hundreds of stalls piled high with fresh fruit and vegetables, cheeses and chocolates, plastic flowers, electrical appliances, kitchenware, crockery, and every knickknack known to man before we stopped at a stall and she ordered the sweet drink.

"Do they sell clothes here?"

She looked me up and down. "Not the kind you'd wear. We'll head to Fashion Street and a few malls later."

Unsure whether she'd insulted or praised me, I accepted my

soda fountain glass and gratefully drank. The smooth rosewater-flavored milk, tapioca balls, and rose jelly slid over my tastebuds. Delicious.

After I'd spooned the last scrumptious morsel into my mouth, I glanced up to find Anjali staring at me with a wide grin. "What?"

"You're starting to enjoy your food, it's good to see." She patted my cheek, her affection wrapping around me like a cozy duvet. I loved her blunt honesty, her forthrightness, her lust for food. Anjali was genuinely enchanting and I'd miss her when I returned home. "Ready to shop 'til you drop?"

I nodded. "Clothes, shoes, and jewelry are on my hit list."

That little financial problem I had considering my unemployed status? I'd deal with it back in New York. Time enough for a dose of reality. For now, had credit card, would travel. Thankfully, Mumbai loved Visa as much as I did.

A woman after my own heart, Anjali took me to three malls, gushing over my choices and exchanging sizes without complaint.

She didn't question my frenetic pace or my dithering over patent leather or suede. She held up scarves and earrings, pronouncing royal blue to be my color and that lemon leeched my glow. She approved my conservative choices and frowned at skimpy.

Best of all, she complied with a smile, as if her endorphins were flowing as freely as mine. Because that was the real reason behind my shopping frenzy. I needed to do something comforting, something familiar, in the lead-up to my final confrontation with Mama Rama.

In New York, I would've fortified with a mojito or two. Here, I settled for shopping to calm my frazzled nerves.

Three hours later, weighed down by countless bags, we staggered into the house, our feet aching, our souls replenished. Nothing soothed like retail therapy.

And nothing intimidated me more than an upcoming encounter with Anu. My post-shopping glow faded at the thought of facing off Mama Rama one last time.

. . .

"Do I have to do this?" I whined the next evening as the Rama house came into view and Buddy drove up to the front door.

"You've done your best by Rita and Rakesh. Kept her reputation intact while agreeing to a chance meeting between the two." Anjali smiled and patted my hand. "After this farewell dinner you're home free. You can wave the cow good-bye, secure in the knowledge you've pulled the hay over her eyes and the grass out from under her feet."

"If I make it out of the paddock." I shuddered, managing to smile at Anjali's metaphors. "Last time I could hide among a hundred guests. A dinner party with only family present? She'll eat me alive."

"I won't let her." Anjali waved away my concern, her eyes assuming a battle gleam. "You're family to me and I couldn't be prouder. Amrita's lucky to have a friend like you."

"And an aunt like you." I meant it. If it hadn't been for Anjali we could never have pulled off this scam, though it helped having the jilted fiancé in on it, too.

"Sweet girl. Ready?"

Buddy opened the door and I took a deep breath as I stepped out, bracing for the onslaught ahead. "Ready as I'll ever be."

Anu waddled out onto the veranda and herded us inside, gushing over me while ignoring Anjali. Moo…

The same welcoming cast had assembled: Senthil beaming, Pooh wiping crumbs from her mouth, Diva studying her lacquered fingernails in boredom, Shrew assessing me before I'd said a word.

I had Anjali protecting my right and Rakesh flanking my left as we headed into the dining room, an elaborate red and gold affair that wouldn't have looked out of place at Buckingham Palace. (I'd seen the pics.)

The moment Mama Rama had issued her invitation, Rakesh, Anjali, and I had made contingency plans to protect me. I had a feeling as the evening progressed I'd need those plans to kick in.

Over a starter of sautéed frogs' legs in garlic and chili, Anu tried to interrogate me about my views on children. Rakesh deftly deflected with a rousing rendition of "Twinkle, Twinkle, Little Star," his favorite nursery rhyme he planned on singing to his kids every night.

Mama Rama smiled indulgently at her only son and resumed eating.

Strike one. Take that, Anu.

Over main dishes including snake gourd (a long, thin vegetable), *aloo gobi* (spicy potatoes), *bhindi masala* (spicy okra), *saag bhaji* (spinach), *chole* (chickpeas), *parippu* (lentils), *gajar matar* (spiced peas and carrots), and enough *parathas* to feed the starving people lining Mumbai's streets, Anu tried another attack.

"You'll live with us once you're married, of course." She pronounced it as a fact while I tried not to choke on my mango *lassi*, a delicious yogurt drink that eased the fire from the chili-rich food.

Senthil frowned, his subtle head shake in Anu's direction

ignored.

"This isn't the Nineties, mother. We'll live in our own house, wherever we want," Rakesh said, ignoring Anu's apoplectic face and sending me a surreptitious wink.

Strike two.

The meal progressed to dessert, and though I'd barely swallowed more than a mouthful of each course thanks to the fearful lump lodged in my throat, I made a big show of oohing and ahhing over the food weighing down the table: *kulfi* (pistachio and rosewater-flavored ice cream), *barfi* (an almond halwa), *Mysore pak* (roasted gram and ghee dessert that melted on the tongue), *rasgulla* (milk curd sponge soaked in syrup), and a myriad of other delicacies.

Almost home free, one more course.

Good-bye Mumbai, hello New York.

"The wedding will be here and I'll arrange the whole thing." Anu slipped that one in with a fake smile tinged with venom as she shoveled another *ladoo* or ten onto my plate.

My hands fisted under the table as I tried to get a grip on my rising temper. I'd like nothing better than to tell this meddling cow to shut up but I couldn't disgrace Amrita. Not when I'd come this far. Not when I wanted to preserve the relationship with Rakesh now I knew him and wanted Rita to as well. Besides, if by some miracle Rakesh and Rita hit it off, they'd hate me for alienating Anu before their relationship had begun.

While I took calming breaths, Anjali stepped up to the plate and took a swing. "It's customary for the bride's family to prepare the wedding, as I'm sure you know, Anu, being a stickler for tradition."

I could almost see Mama Rama biting her tongue in frustration and I quickly munched the calorie-laden balls to avoid bursting out laughing.

Strike three. Anu's out.

The rest was a cinch, coffee and farewells tame in comparison to the onslaught I'd faced over dinner. I'd done it. Pulled off the scam of the century. I hadn't alienated anyone, a la my first goal, but I'd achieved my second: continue the fake engagement so Rakesh could meet Rita. Win-win all around. I'd survived, Rakesh would get his wish, and Rita could give him the brush-off she wanted in person. Relieved, I slipped into the old Beamer, wishing Buddy would hurry up and finish his cigarette by the front gate so we could get the hell out of here.

Rakesh stuck his head through the window, grinning like a fellow escapee from the gallows. "There's a new bar in town and the Westerners from work are going. Want to check it out?"

My brain honed in on *work crowd*. Pity I had to act the decorous fiancée to the end.

"You listening? Or did my mother's interrogation hypnotize you?" Rakesh waved a hand in front of my eyes and I blinked, erasing the wishful fantasy of me giving Drew a good-bye kiss he'd never forget.

"She wasn't that bad."

Mama Rama had nothing on my mom when I flew down to Florida to visit. *Any men on the horizon? Are you dating? Anyone special in your life? My neighbor's son is a nice young man. He's a doctor, you know…* Little wonder I hadn't visited the folks in almost a year.

Rakesh grinned. "You in?"

"I've got packing to do." Lousy excuse but I didn't want to botch things on my last night, a definite possibility if I bumped into Drew.

"Drew will be there." Rakesh's corny wink did little to settle my churning gut.

"That's why I'm packing."

"Surely you owe him a good-bye after the grief you gave him?"

"I don't owe him anything."

"Suit yourself." Rakesh shrugged and straightened. "Bet you'll regret your decision all the way home. Just think, hour after hour, bored with in-flight movies, refusing the drivel they serve up as cuisine, wishing you'd done the right thing—"

"Okay, wiseass, I'll come. Sheesh, you're a pain in the butt. I can't wait for Rita to plant a kick right there."

"Amrita's going to love me." He'd perfected his hand-skimming-hair move just like John Travolta in *Grease*. I laughed.

"You really like movies as much as I do?"

"Ehhh… " This time, he stuck two thumbs up like the Fonz.

"*Happy Days* was a TV show, not a movie, you dolt."

He grinned. "I love it when you call me names."

Chuckling at his antics, I opened the door. "Get in. Anjali should be out any second."

"Once she's finished making eyes at my dad, you mean."

"What?"

He tapped my nose. "You were too nervous in there to notice anything but I reckon I caught Anjali mooning over my dad a few times."

"Really?"

He shrugged. "Just an observation."

"She's not a fan of your mom so she probably did it to make her jealous."

Rakesh raised an eyebrow. "Or she has a thing for him."

"Nah…" Anjali had said she hated Anu because she'd stolen something, nothing to do with Senthil whatsoever. But once

Rakesh planted the idea and it took root, I couldn't dismiss it. An unrequited crush would certainly make sense of her vitriol towards Anu and cast her casual hellos at Film City in a new light.

"'Course she does, what with her practically drooling whenever he looks at her and how much she hates my mom. It's cute."

"Crazy, more like it." Then again, who was I to judge? Since when had I done anything sane recently?

Rakesh slid onto the front seat and turned to face me. "We all have a crush on someone. It's healthy."

"Unless it turns into an obsession." I snapped my fingers, remembering the Lone Ranger episode. "By the way, this crazy cowboy, who turned out to be pretty harmless, was stalking me because he thought I was Aishwarya Rai Bachan. I got rid of him."

Incredulous, his eyebrows shot heavenward. "He thought you were her?"

Of all possible responses I'd imagined coming from him, that hadn't been one of them. No "are you okay?" or "you were being stalked?" or "how did you get rid of him?"

Uh-uh. His incredulity was that a guy could mistake me for India's former Miss Universe.

"Your concern overwhelms me," I said, shaking my head in disgust, enjoying the soft tinkle of drop gold earrings, a present to myself from yesterday's shopping trip for surviving this fiasco.

One of many presents, including embroidered peasant tops, sequined shoes, the softest buttery leather jacket, and an assortment of silk scarves that would jazz up old outfits. Maybe I'd gone overboard, with my money fast running out, but I wanted tangible reminders of this place, items I could wrap up in and feel as good as I had in mystical Mumbai the last few weeks.

"You look fine to me." Rakesh blew me a kiss. "Besides, the stalker has great taste in women, going after you and Aishwarya."

My mock frown failed when the corners of my mouth curved. "Too late for flattery. You should've shown your concern the moment I told you."

He grinned. "You're here, you said he was harmless. And let's face it, what you put up with in there from my mother had to be ten times scarier than surviving an encounter with a second-rate stalker."

Good point.

"You owe me."

To my surprise, his smile waned. "Listen, you're a good friend to do this for Amrita. Not many people would've come here, not knowing what to expect and put up with me and my family. And you had Drew on your case as well. I think you're pretty special, Shari Jones."

His genuine warmth reached out and wrapped me in a soft embrace. There could've been worse things than having Rakesh Rama as an ally in this farce.

"And don't you forget it."

Anjali's arrival at the car ended our bonding moment. With Rakesh's supposition about her crush on Senthil, I was dying to interrogate her but couldn't, considering our audience. Ten minutes later she said good night as Buddy deposited us at the nearby bar.

Pondering Anjali's love life distracted me for a few seconds until I followed Rakesh into the dimly lit bar, which wouldn't have looked out of place in New York, and I saw the one man I'd hoped/feared would be there.

His assessing stare homed in on me and I froze. My breathing didn't kick in again until Rakesh placed a hand on the small of my back and propelled me forward.

"I know having the crowd act as chaperones is a pain in the ass for you and Drew, but you'll have him all to yourself in New York soon." Rakesh broke the spell. "Be good."

He pecked my cheek like an attentive fiancé and pushed me in Drew's direction.

"Hey," I said, aiming for nonchalance as I struggled not to reach out and see if Drew felt as good as he looked. A navy V-neck tee accentuated his tan and brought out the vivid blue of his eyes, while dark Calvin Klein denim made a mockery of every male model that had ever worn them.

"Glad you made it." He gestured to the empty seat beside him. "Would you like a drink?"

Hell yeah. However, I swallowed before I dribbled and shook my head, trying not to stare at the array of alcohol lining the top shelf behind the chrome bar.

"A Perrier would be nice."

He followed my wistful gaze. "Bet it's a pain Amrita's Hindu."

I nodded. "I'd kill for a mojito."

Considering his potent stare, I'd rather get intoxicated on him. "Rain check? When I get to New York, we meet up for a drink and I'll buy you that mojito?"

"Is that your subtle way of asking me on a date?"

His lips curved into a sexy smile. "If you want to call it that."

Something inexplicable gripped my heart. *Other side of the world. Unavailable guy. Hello?* Surely I'd learned from my mistake with Tate.

Unable to resist, I leaned closer. "What would you call it?"

"Two people meeting over a drink, starting off on the right foot this time."

I tapped my bottom lip, pretending to ponder. "Sounds interesting."

It sounded better than interesting; it sounded fan-freaking-tastic.

He chuckled at my poor attempt at reticence. "I take it that's a yes."

I wanted to say no. I should have said no. I nodded instead. "You're switched on, Bollywood Boy. I like that."

"Turned on, more like it," he said, his low voice rippling over me like a caress before he headed for the bar, leaving me stunned and yearning and hopeful.

Stunned by his irresistibility when he turned on the charm.

Yearning for what I couldn't have.

Hopeful I wouldn't read more into this than what it was. A harmless flirtation between two people a world apart.

• • •

Rakesh walked me to the front door, although I wished it'd been Drew, who I'd fare-welled at the bar with a far-too-chaste handshake. Our date in NYC couldn't come quickly enough.

"I have a surprise for you."

I held up my hands. "Please, no more surprises. I've had enough this trip to last me a lifetime."

"Think you'll like this one." He handed me a beige envelope. "This is a thank-you for being such a good sport."

Curious, I ran my finger under the flap and slid out a train and bus ticket. "I don't get it."

He rubbed the back of his neck. "You've been amazing these last few weeks, continuing with the ruse, putting up with my mother, agreeing to let me meet Amrita."

"And?"

His gaze darted away from mine as I wondered what he'd done to look so guilty.

"Remember you told me your birthplace is Arnala? It's only a few hours from here, so I thought you might like to see it before you head home. My treat."

A lump of emotion welled in my throat, making it impossible to speak, as he rushed on. "You deserve this for being so cool about everything. This is your first trip here and I'm not sure if you're interested in seeing where you were born or where your mom was raised but it's a change from Mumbai so I bought you a one-way ticket home on a different date and—"

"Thank you." It came out as a squeak and I swallowed, cleared my throat, and tried again. "It's incredibly sweet."

He shrugged, endearingly bashful. "I didn't know if you'd accept or berate me for interfering."

I dabbed at the corners of my eyes with my pinkies. "Would I do that?"

He laughed and slung his arm across my shoulders. "Hell yeah."

My head leaned on his shoulder for a moment, my heart filled with warmth for this genuinely nice guy. "Rita's a lucky girl."

He squeezed my shoulders. "If you can convince her of that I'll be eternally grateful."

I chuckled and elbowed him away. "Sorry, you're on your own, buddy. I'll arrange a meeting, that's it."

"Fair enough." He bundled me into his arms for a quick hug before setting me back. "See you in New York."

"You bet."

I watched him stride down the cracked path toward his car, crossing my fingers Rita would fall for him. She deserved someone like Rakesh—she just didn't know it yet.

As the driver pulled away from the curb, Rakesh waved and I waved back, strangely nostalgic my stint as a stand-in fiancée had come to an end. Not that I'd want to repeat the craziness but it'd been fun, in a stressful, lunatic kind of way.

The tickets weighed in my palm and I squinted at them, filled with a mix of curiosity and optimism, intrigued by what I may find in my birthplace and hopeful it would stand me in good stead for what was still to come.

• • •

A day later, after a two-hour train and bus trip, I arrived in Arnala, my mom's hometown and the place I popped into the world, kicking and screaming by all accounts.

A small fishing village north of Mumbai, and nestled on the Arabian Sea, Arnala boasted a population of 8,000, about 6,000 of those fishermen and their families. No prizes for guessing where my love of seafood came from.

Mom had regaled me with tales of the town's landlord predecessors, who'd lost their land to farmers after Independence, but the stories had meant nothing. Until now. The weirdest thing? The moment I stepped off the bus and a bunch of locals sitting under a huge banyan tree checking out the new arrivals ogled me, I felt at home.

Inherently corny, but I was grasping at something, anything, to fill the void inside me, an emptiness that had blossomed over the last three months with every failed job interview, with every night I lay in the boxlike spare room in Rita's apartment, with every crying jag over my stupidity at falling for some loser's lies.

I'd traveled halfway across the world to participate in a crazy scheme for my best friend's benefit, yet it was this day trip that had me more excited than I'd been in a long time.

Since Rakesh had given me the tickets and a map with directions to my mom's house courtesy of his online PIs, I'd been mulling my past, particularly the last three months. While my heart had healed I still harbored deep resentment. Toward Tate for his duplicity and toward myself for being stupidly naïve.

I needed to move forward, and I'd pinned my hopes on this side trip bringing me some sense of wholeness, a sense of completion that would propel me forward, allow me to release any residual bitterness, and embrace what the future held.

Philosophical bullshit? Maybe. Whatever it was, stepping onto the dusty path that led to my mom's old home felt right.

I strolled through the town, unsure where to look first, surprised to find it exactly how Mom used to describe it: three grocery shops, two small restaurants, several tailors, a pharmacy, and a few *paan-wallas*, the Indian equivalent of a tobacco shop. A huge Catholic church dominated the scenery, as did a nearby lighthouse, and I wished I could remember the first three years of my life that I'd spent here.

I couldn't recall a snippet, and I trudged along the narrow road, wide enough to allow one bus max, hoping that seeing my ancestral home would give me half the pleasure I'd anticipated.

My first glimpse of the house blew me away.

Two stories, pale-lemon, with blue-trimmed windows, a balcony on the second floor, and a veranda on the ground leading to a duck-egg blue double door. A door I could imagine opening to welcome visitors, a door closing to secure its occupants.

I struggled to remember, rubbing my temples, closing my eyes... but when I reopened them, the house remained the same, my memories of time spent here as a toddler long gone.

I glanced past the house, set amidst two acres of coconut and mango plantations, the humid air heavy with the fragrant jasmine growing in wild abundance.

The house, the plantation, the flowers overloaded my senses as pride, nostalgia, and regret warred within me.

Proud this was part of my heritage.

Reminiscent over the stories Mom had told about this place, this village, this country.

Regret I hadn't visited sooner.

I might be a New Yorker and proud of it, but standing in front of this house, taking in the pineapple and jackfruit trees, the garden overflowing with sunflowers, Duke of Tuscany, and an old-fashioned well, was incredibly humbling.

Being here shamed me. I should've embraced my heritage long before this but I'd snubbed it, preferring to immerse myself in a multicultural USA without a thought for where I'd come from or what it meant. Yeah, Mom was Indian and yeah, my best friend was Indian, but basically, Indian in New York meant take-out and Bollywood DVD rentals to me. Sad but true. Thankfully, coming here had changed all that.

I stared at the house a few moments longer, trying to picture a small child with long, black, plaited hair running among the mango trees, playing hide and seek with the *ayah*. Mom told me that had been my favorite game, but the harder I tried to conjure up the memory, the more my eyes blurred.

Blaming the stinking heat and the omnipresent dust for the tears, I dashed a hand across my eyes and walked another 200 yards to the beach. Rather than the deserted, tranquil stretch of black sand Mom had described, progress had hit with a vengeance as hordes of Mumbai-ians on day-trips crowded the sand, buying food from hawkers and littering the beach with plastic.

Ignoring the messy crowd, I slipped off my sandals and strolled across the hot sand, focusing on the fort rising majestically out of the ocean like a watchful landlord casting an eye over proceedings. It sat on an island a few miles out to sea, with a mosque and a temple peacefully co-existing inside.

I'd have to take a ferry to check it out. Mom had told me a weird story about the community of fishermen who lived inside and I'd never forgotten it. Despite being surrounded by ocean, the fort had a large hexagonal freshwater reservoir inside. No one could explain how or why this freshwater never diminished over the centuries despite minimal rain and no source. Probably another of her tall tales, but India was the land of mystery. While I was here I'd learned to open my mind to a world of possibilities.

When Mom had first told me I'd thought the tale ranked right up there with wearing black bangles to ward off the evil eye, but after Kapil's stint at telling my fortune and his uncanny accuracy so far, I reserved my judgment.

What were the old coot's words? Something about a rich man and me making decisions? Harmless at the time, or so I'd thought. Yet here I was, contemplating my future and doing just that.

Would anything happen with Drew? Would I ever trust a guy enough to let him close to my heart again? Would I ever have the HEA I'd always hoped for?

Damned if I knew, but somehow, standing near the place I was born seemed to infuse me with calm and clarity of purpose I never dreamed possible.

Being here felt right. Fated.

Perhaps all I had to do was believe in myself again and let the cosmos deal me the next karmic hand.

I hoped to return sometime in the future. There was something seductive in the chaos. India charmed me with its boldness and excitement and energy, and tempted me to see more of this intriguing country.

Mom would be thrilled when I told her my plan to save money and tour her homeland. Added incentive to find my next job when I returned to NYC. Maybe I could try something new, something utilizing my legal secretary skills. I enjoyed preparing, proofing, and editing documents. Excelled at it, according to my last HR performance review. Something in publishing, perhaps? An intern position to get me started? Something fresh and new that paid enough for me to get back here ASAP.

I'd been going through the motions job-searching the last three months, trying to heal emotionally while surviving physically. No more. No more bumming on Rita and staying in her apartment, no more lackadaisical interviews. When I got back, I'd nail a job and start saving. Whatever I ended up doing, I had this country to thank for my renewed enthusiasm.

For now, time to head home. Ol' Blue Eyes (Frankie, not Drew) couldn't have summed it up any better when he crooned about wanting to be a part of it. I'd found a new lease on life in Mumbai and discovered inner resilience... but New York was definitely where I was at.

CHAPTER EIGHT

"Can't believe I've come home to this." I spun a 360 as Rita opened the blinds, late afternoon sunlight spilling into the loft apartment and bathing it in a welcoming glow.

"Believe it. My cuz won't need it for six months, you've come up with the rent, it's yours."

I absentmindedly rubbed my third finger, where Tate's ruby had once resided. Thanks to that ring and the rest of the expensive trinkets he'd bought me, I'd been able to pawn it all and make rent on this place for the coming months. Another step in purging the past and embracing my future. It felt good. What would feel even better? Not having to rely on my amazing best friend to keep coming through for me. Rita's help had been invaluable but now I was back, I was more determined than ever to find a job and regain my independence.

Rita threw her arms wide. "Did I come through for you or what?"

"You sure did." I embraced her and we squealed, jumping around and around like a couple of teenagers until we fell down laughing.

When we'd picked ourselves up, I gestured at the polished floor-boards, the exposed brick walls, the floor-to-ceiling windows, and stainless steel steps leading upstairs. "Is this what you were busy organizing all those days you didn't email me?"

Looking deservedly smug, Rita folded her arms. "Yep. Had to convince my cousin not to sublet to a stranger when I had the perfect tenant just waiting to move in."

I blew her a kiss. "I owe you."

I plopped into the nearest chair—yeah, the place came fully furnished—and pinched myself. "Ow! Yep, this isn't a dream. I get home from Mumbai, my best friend's lined up a downtown apartment, and helps me arrange my finances."

"All the girls at work go to that pawnbroker when their engagements break up and they make a quick thirty grand on their Tiffany rings." She tapped the side of her nose. "Apparently he's the best."

Considering what I'd gotten for the ruby alone, I had to agree. I'd been foolish, hanging onto a trinket from sentiment. Considering my bulked-up bank account, I should've done it sooner.

"After what you've been through, you deserved a break." Rita sat in a chair opposite me, slipped off her mules, and tucked her legs under her. "Now start at the beginning and tell me everything."

"Aren't you forgetting something?" I pointed at the mojito jug and glasses I'd glimpsed in the breakfast nook during my tour of the apartment. "It's Monday, right?"

Not that the day would make a difference. I'd been craving a mojito like Anjali craves *ladoos*.

"Coming right up." Rita bustled around the nook, grabbing

ingredients while I relaxed in *my* apartment. How good did that sound? I grinned like an idiot as Rita placed mint leaves in the bottom of the jug, added crushed ice, rum, sugar, lime juice and soda water, stirring it with a cocktail stick before pouring into highball glasses and garnishing with mint.

"Here, get this into you." Rita handed me a huge glass filled to the brim and I tried not to drool as a hint of mint and rum hit my nostrils, the tempting scent triggering an instant image of Drew and his invitation to buy me a mojito in NYC. We hadn't made definite plans that night at the bar, because soon after he'd delivered my Perrier he'd taken a call on his cell, which turned out to be urgent business from London. I hoped his regretful expression as he shook my hand and headed out the door was for my impending departure and not some deal that had hit a snag.

Rita tapped her glass to mine. "Start talking. By your emails, you've got plenty to tell."

I could've skirted around the issue of Drew and made it sound inconsequential that I'd dipped my toes in the guy wading pool. Or in my case, the quagmire. But I'd missed Rita, missed our chats, our teasing, our soul-searching. If anyone could put some perspective on the crazy two weeks I'd spent in Mumbai, she could.

Taking a healthy mojito slurp, I savored every drop as my taste buds did a happy dance. "Okay. Remember I mentioned Drew?"

She smirked. "Bollywood Boy, the Hugh Grant look-alike?"

I nodded. "We clicked after I came clean about my part in your charade. If I hadn't been posing as you, I could've seriously gone for him."

I dunked the mint leaves floating on the top of my drink.

Seeing them go under made me hope I wouldn't do the same. Under threat and under fire of falling for Drew's charms, underwhelmed by my vehement self-protestations it wouldn't go beyond a mild flirtation.

Rita's eyes widened. "Clicked in an *I'm-hot-for-you-babe* way, or clicked in an *I-want-more-than-your-body* way?"

"The first, of course. What do you take me for, a moron?"

Moron… moron… moron… my voice of reason chanted.

At my age, eligible, sexy guys were sized up for more than their bodies and I was definitely lying by telling Rita my interest in Drew was purely horn-bag.

"You're not telling me everything."

My best friend, astute as ever.

"He's backing a film and it's shooting a couple of scenes in New York, so we may catch up for a drink when he's here. That's all." Deep down, I knew that wouldn't be all. If Drew and I ever met for a drink *sans* the chaperones that had followed our every move in Mumbai, I'd jump him, no doubt.

Rita placed her half-empty mojito glass on the coffee table and leaned forward. "This guy is hot, travels the world, looks like Hugh Grant, you dig him, and you're trying to tell me *that's all*?"

"Yeah."

She held up her hands in surrender. "Hey, I'm just calling it as I see it, and what I see is my best friend acting way too casual about a guy who means more than she's letting on. Bet you didn't know those weird green spots in your eyes change color when you're talking about your passions?"

"Like cheesecake?"

She snorted. "Distract me all you want but I'm looking forward to meeting Bollywood Boy. Don't forget, I'm your new yardstick when it comes to guys. No one gets past me without the stamp of approval first."

"When did I say that?"

"After the second jug of mojitos the night you found out about the Toad becoming a daddy."

"Oh." I had a vague recollection of stuffing half a choc-chip cheese-cake and pouring copious mojitos down my throat before sobbing for hours while Rita passed me tissues, topped off my drink, and hugged me. She was the best.

"I guess you can play watchdog. Just take it easy on this one. I want his bone all to myself."

Rita shrieked and clapped her hands. "I've missed you. Now, tell me about the imbecile my parents had me married off to and how I can wriggle out of this meeting you've scheduled."

I couldn't wait for Rita to catch a glimpse of her *imbecile*. She'd deliberately not looked at the photo her parents had pressed on her, tossing it in the trash the moment they'd left the first night they'd announced the betrothal. I'd been curious but she'd refused to let me sneak it out of the trash, citing bad karma. Maybe if she'd snuck a peek at Rakesh's pic, would've saved us both a lot of angst. But then I never would've traveled to Mumbai, never would've met Drew...

"You can't get out of this. Rakesh did the right thing by us in Mumbai and you owe him. Besides, how bad can it be?"

"You tell me." She picked up her glass and took a healthy slurp. "You've met the guy. From what you said in your emails, he sounded almost human, so he wouldn't want an arranged marriage any more than I do. He's seen the lengths I'd go to get out of it, he went along with the charade, yet wants to meet up? It's totally bogus."

"Been watching *Bill and Ted's Excellent Adventure*, have we?"

"It *is* bogus. I don't trust him. What if he's coming out here to blackmail me into marrying him? Or worse, meeting his mother?"

An image of Anu bearing down on me, screeching about being my new mommy, popped into my head and I struggled not to cringe. Maybe Rita had a point. "He's a good guy. He's seen your picture, he's interested. That's it. Honestly? I think you'll like him. Funny, smart, good-looking, the works."

A flicker of interest lit Rita's eyes but she quickly masked it by lowering her lashes. "Bod?"

"TDF."

"To die for? That good?"

"That good."

She shrugged and semi-turned away but not before I'd glimpsed a smile. "Guess it won't hurt to say hi to the guy. When's he arriving?"

"Next week. He'll email me the details. And one more thing."

"What?"

"You're picking him up from the airport."

She leaped to her feet. "*What?*"

"One of his stipulations. Sorry."

It was my turn to shrug and act nonchalant.

Rakesh hadn't made that little stipulation—I had, considering Drew would be accompanying him on the same flight. Excited as I was to see if there was anything more than a mild flirtation between us, showing up to JFK as he stepped off the plane would be too much. Appearing eager was one thing, looking like I was ready to lie down and spread my legs another.

"Anything else I should know?"

"Not that I can think of. Want to see what I brought you?"

The perfect diversionary tactic, and Rita bought it as we

dragged my suitcases into the bedroom and popped the locks. In all honestly, there was a lot more Rita should know, like how eager Rakesh was to meet her, how great a guy he really was, and how my instincts screamed they were perfect for each other.

Then again, since when had I turned into a Kapil? She'd find out soon enough and I'd be the first one to dance at her wedding, arranged or otherwise.

As for me, Rita had helped sort out the homeless part of my life and I'd make a start on the jobless part first thing in the morning.

After another mojito.

God, it was good to be home.

•••

"No way." Rita gripped my arm in a stranglehold and turned frantic eyes to me. "That's *him*? The gorgeous one in black Gucci?"

"Not bad, huh?" I pried her fingers loose, trying not to crane my neck to scan the crowd in search of Rakesh's traveling companion.

Rakesh's email had confirmed Drew and his crew would be traveling on the same flight but I couldn't see him. Technically I shouldn't be here, but when Rita had begged me to accompany her to the airport, reminding me of the great apartment I now lived in courtesy of her, how could I refuse?

I had a strong suspicion she'd use the apartment card a lot over the next six months. Then again, it was worth every favor she asked for to wake up in that loft every morning, take a stroll down to Murray's for fresh bagels, and know I didn't have to put out to live there.

And the best thing? Added incentive to turn a temporary

apartment into a permanent one; an apartment of my own.

Jeez, what had I been thinking, tolerating the Toad situation?

Rita tugged at her sleeves and her earrings, shifting her weight from one foot to the other. "Not bad? Omigod. He's fucking unbelievable!"

"Language, Miss He's-an-imbecile." I bumped her with my hip. "Told you to trust me."

She stopped fidgeting and stiffened. "Shit. Here he comes. How do I look? What should I say? Help me, goddamn you."

I glanced at Rita's envy-inducing curves encased in an amethyst suit and the most drool-worthy pair of matching strappy Christian Louboutins. Her thick black hair hung in a sleek drop down her back, her make-up immaculate courtesy of a visit to the Red Door that morning. Rakesh didn't stand a chance. "You look amazing, so stop freaking out. Be yourself. Besides, what do you care? He's just an *imbecile.*"

"Ssh. Here he comes." With an impressive transformation she switched from dithering mess to coolly elegant, welcoming smile in place as she stepped forward to meet her fiancé.

Technically her ex-fiancé if her plan had worked, but by the way they were staring at each other, I knew there'd be nothing 'ex' about these two. I could hear the band striking up the wedding march, or whatever the Hindu equivalent was.

To give Rakesh credit, he didn't falter as he strode toward us, though I noted his stunned expression as he caught sight of Rita.

"Quick, tell me what to say. My mind's blank," Rita hissed, her smile wobbling the closer he got.

In a flash, I knew the perfect opening. Time to have a little fun.

"He's a huge *Dirty Dancing* fan. Why don't you say Baby's first line when she meets Johnny? He'll go for that in a big way."

"I can't—"

"Hi, Shari. Great to see you again." Rakesh dropped a quick peck on my cheek and held out his hand to Rita, visibly rattled as she shook it. "This must be the beautiful Amrita. Pleased to meet you."

"I brought you a watermelon," she blurted and I stared in amazement, shocked on several counts.

She hated my favorite movie and didn't have the faintest idea whenever I quoted lines at her, which was why I'd jokingly suggested the quote, not expecting her to know it, let alone say it. Secondly, the Rita I knew was polished, elegant, confident, and could twist guys around her little finger without blinking. So who was this shy, nervous woman glaring at me?

Rakesh hadn't lost his smarts or his sense of humor. "Another *Dirty Dancing* fan, huh? Great. I thought Shari was the only one on the planet."

"She is. I hate that film. Her way of playing a trick on us." Another scathing glare directed at me before she turned her smiling attention to Rakesh. "She's sick, posing as me, traveling all the way to India."

"We should discuss the state of your friend's mental health." Rakesh held out his arm and Rita slipped her hand through it, smiling up at him like she'd been handed George Clooney on a plate. Naked.

Yeah, I'd turned into a regular Kapil. If only I could predict my own future as well.

"Drew should be out any second. He's rounding up the crew. Problem with a drunk producer," Rakesh said, his attention never leaving Rita. "We'll be at baggage collection."

I managed a distracted nod in the happy couple's direction as I spotted Drew weaving among the weary masses spewing from economy class, his trademark light brown hair flopping over his forehead as he impatiently pushed it back.

My stomach churned the same way it had in Mumbai and I swiped my clammy palms against the side of my jeans, wishing my pulse pounding in my ears would quiet. I froze the moment he saw me, heat streaking through my body, his sinful smile vindicating my choice of tight skinny jeans and long-sleeved teal tee.

Trying not to launch at him like a depraved fiend, I shifted my weight side to side, waiting until he stood before me, six-feet-plus of corruptibly hot English male, complete with Burberry coat and loafers.

"We meet again, Miss Jones."

That voice. Rich and warm, like hot honey spreading through my veins and sweetening every inch of me.

I'd mentally rehearsed a thousand witty, casual remarks to demonstrate my sophistication and how my presence here meant nothing other than as support for Rita. Predictably, I couldn't think of one as his smile sparked his eyes until all I could focus on was endless, gorgeous blue.

"Don't I get a greeting?"

"Welcome to New York." I sounded like a tour guide—a lousy one at that—and I inwardly cringed.

"Not bad, but I was thinking something more along the lines of this." His intent registered a microsecond before he lowered his head toward me, a waft of Davidoff's Cool Water enveloping me an instant before his arms did, around the same time his lips made contact with mine.

My stomach plummeted as his tongue swept along my bottom lip, teasing me, taunting my mouth open. I didn't hesitate and he deepened the kiss, matching my urgent, demanding need to test the spark between us.

Heat streaked through me, firing every nerve ending, making me tingle all over. Oblivious to passengers streaming the concourse, I clung to him, embarrassingly weak-kneed.

As I angled my head he moaned, a raw, guttural reaction that tugged at something primitive deep within. I didn't dare question it, didn't want to rationalize my visceral response, didn't want to deliberate what it might mean.

As his hands skimmed my waist and slid around my torso, his fingertips skated across the miniscule gap of skin between my top and jeans, sending a jolt equal to fifty volts through me. My heart revved like a prelaunch rocket and I gave in to the luxury of having his arms wrapped around me for the first time.

All too soon he pulled away, amusement crinkling the corners of his eyes. "Now that's a greeting."

Stunned by the force of my feelings urging me to step into his arms for round two, I jammed my hands into my pockets. "New Yorkers are a friendly bunch. We aim to please."

"Is that right?"

I didn't do flustered as a rule but right then, I had no idea what to say. Usually, I would've flirted and continued the wordplay, seeing how far this could go. Instead, my insides had moved on from churning and were currently somewhere between tied up in knots and somersaulting, landing in huge, embarrassing belly flops. "Let's go see what Rakesh and Rita are up to. Looks like they hit it off."

"Sure." He slung his coat over his shoulder, a model for rumpled chic with his day-old designer stubble, slightly crumpled ivory Lauren shirt, and mussed hair.

As he fell into step beside me, I breathed a sigh of relief. He'd bought my change of subject.

"By the way, we're still on for that drink." He touched my arm and a lick of sizzle zapped me again. "If you think I'll let you off the hook like I did back there, you're seriously deluded."

So much for relief.

Ignoring my rampaging pulse, I nodded. "A drink's fine. As for the flirting, I'm over it."

"Liar," he whispered, echoing my thought exactly.

Rakesh and Rita saved me from saying anything else incriminating and as introductions flew, stories were exchanged, and baggage claimed, I had a chance to study Drew.

His air of confidence, his body, and his charm all added up to one thing: trouble.

Looked like I had a movie-trailer full of it heading my way.

CHAPTER NINE

A few days later, I sat across from my best friend at our favorite bar. "When's the wedding?"

I expected Rita to blush, swear, and protest, citing every reason why she'd never consider marrying Rakesh. Instead, she absentmindedly stirred her drink with the little green umbrella stuck on the side, her brows furrowed. If the absence of abuse and the brooding expression hadn't been enough of a clue, the fact she'd ordered a grasshopper—blah—rather than a mojito would've confirmed something was wrong.

"He's just so... so... "

"Smart? Successful? Rich? Gorgeous?"

"It's more than that. He's—"

"Sweet? Funny? Perfect for you?"

She sighed, a glimmer of tears slamming my teasing.

"Hey, I was kidding," I said, torn between wanting to hug her and slap her silly for letting a guy get to her like this.

After the Toad debacle, we'd made a pact: no guy was worth our tears unless it was our engagement, wedding day, or the birth of our firstborn. Rakesh must have sideswiped Rita for her to turn on the waterworks over gentle ribbing.

"It's not you, it's me." Rita dabbed at the underside of her eyes, leaving a smear of mascara that accentuated her vulnerability and made a mockery of her usual immaculate makeup. If she hadn't coated her lashes in waterproof mascara this morning she must be in a bad way.

"Are you breaking up with me?" I deadpanned, relieved at the hint of a smile shimmering through her tears.

"Ha-ha," she said, scrunching the tissue to pulp, taking a healthy slurp of her grasshopper, and grimacing. "I'm pathetic. Stupidly, utterly, pathetic."

"We're talking about your love life not mine."

"Love being the operative word." She polished off her grasshopper and gestured to the cute waiter behind the bar for another. "After everything I put you and Anjali through, all the planning, all the info I made you memorize, I fall in love with the guy anyway."

"You *love* him? As in 'til-death-do-us-part love?"

I knew things had heated up between the happy unarranged couple but I had no idea my cool, level-headed accountant friend would fall so quickly. Sure, Rakesh was a great guy and I'd foreseen them connecting… but *love?*

"Yep. Head over heels. Crazy, huh?"

The irony of the situation struck and I laughed so hard tears ran down my cheeks.

"You think it's funny I'm a loser?"

Wiping my eyes, I sucked in a few breaths to quell the chuckles. "Maybe your parents and the Banana-Ramas knew what they were doing all along. Fate, kismet, and all that."

"All that crap, you mean. My stupid feelings complicate

everything."

"How?"

"If his mom's as scary as you said, she'll kill me."

I waved away her fears. "Rakesh has that part figured out. He's going to blame me, say I was your jealous best friend wanting to snag him for myself."

Admiration softened her expression. "Ingenious."

"Yeah, and I'll never have to see her again unless you two crazy kids march up the aisle and by then she'd be so happy to get her golden boy married off she will have forgiven me." I snapped my fingers in front of her face. "So what's stopping you from going for it if you love him?"

Rita rolled her eyes, managing a pert smile for the waiter as he deposited her drink. "Simple lesson in geography. I don't live in India. I don't *want* to live in India."

"So? Get Lover Boy to move here."

She shook her head, sleek black hair billowing around her shoulders. I'd kill to have Pantene-perfect hair like that. "He can't. His business is everything to him."

"Make him choose. You or Eye."

"I won't do that. Besides, he's Indian. The chances of him cutting Mommy's apron strings for New York are zilch. Less than zilch."

"You're making this way too complicated. If a trip up the aisle is what you both want—and don't forget I told you so the minute I saw him—nothing will stand in your way. You're lucky to have found someone."

Unlike me, I thought, though I wisely kept that particular gem to myself. I'd copped enough flack over Drew from Rita and Rakesh since the Bombay Bobbsey twins had arrived. I'd hardly seen Drew since our earth-shattering lip-lock at the airport, but that didn't stop Rita and Rakesh from teasing me incessantly.

"You're right, but it seems too hard."

"I bet it does," I purred, sliding my fingers up and down my mojito glass in a lewd gesture.

"Stop that. You're getting the waiter horny."

"He's not the one I want to feel like that." Right then, I caught a glimpse of Drew pushing his way through the twenty-deep crowd behind us, typical for a Manhattan Monday at Michu's.

"God, he's gorgeous." Rita sighed and I glanced at her in surprise, until I followed her line of vision and saw Rakesh four steps behind Drew, his face lighting up like fireworks during Diwali as he locked onto Rita.

"You don't mind if we split up? My man and I have some things to discuss."

I nodded, glad to see her determination. At least love hadn't rendered her catatonic or stupid like it had me with the Toad. Though looking back, I'd never been in love. Lust, initially. Security in the middle. Pain at the end. Heartbreaking pain, most of it for my trampled pride and loss of benefits like a job, an apartment, and regular sex with someone who wasn't a psycho or into S&M.

I'd settled. Settled for a posh lifestyle, but I'd given up my self-worth in the process and I'd be damned if I ever fell into the same trap again.

"Go ahead, Drew and I'll be fine."

More than fine if I had anything to do with it.

I'd had days to think about this. Long, boring days between job hunting spent cocooned in my apartment, drinking *masala chai,* subduing the odd *ladoo* craving, and daydreaming about Drew.

So we hit it off? Didn't mean anything. He'd invited me for a drink, nothing more, nothing less. We'd make small-talk, flirt a little. Good, clean, harmless fun. I didn't have any cause to be nervous. A date I could do. A decision about my future phony Kapil had predicted? No way.

I liked Drew but I didn't want a fling; I wanted something real, something tangible, something I could believe in. A relationship with substance this time, not the farce I'd had with Tate.

Was I chasing a dream? Maybe. Shame about the economical and logistical obstacles between us. He was mega-wealthy and lived in India, I was embarrassingly poor and entrenched in NYC. Otherwise I would've had a ball exploring the attraction between us.

"How are the two most beautiful girls in New York tonight?" Rakesh gave us each a peck on the cheek, though his hand slid around Rita's waist and stayed there, a possessive gesture that brought a lump to my throat.

I'd never been part of a couple in public with Tate. He'd been a big shot in the corporate world and so image-conscious he never risked our relationship being discovered. He'd cited the firm's reputation as being the main reason behind his reticence, saying his wife wouldn't have cared one way or the other.

I'd believed him. I didn't like it but I'd bought it, an ostrich in designer shoes, happy to stick my head in the sand as long as the fantasy world I'd created spun in its correct orbit. Monumental idiot.

Rita leaned into Rakesh, snuggling like a confident woman sure of her man, and I couldn't be happier for her. Sure, I'd teased her about our anti-love pact, but we both knew the score. Our lives as sassy New York City girls were filled with mojitos, Bergdorf cosmetics (God bless Rita's staff discount), and fashionista frenzies, but there was more to life than that.

Give us the security of a stable relationship with a great guy, a guy who could deliver on promises, and we'd be in heaven. By Rita's glow, one of us had earned our angel wings.

I winked. "We're fine, now the two hottest guys in New York have shown up."

Lame, but Rakesh had started it with his corny *two most beautiful girls in NY* line.

Rakesh laughed. "Later," and almost tripped in his haste to get Rita all to himself. She wiggled her fingers in a jaunty wave and followed at a similar breakneck speed.

Drew propped a foot on the rung of my barstool, cool and casual and confident. "Looks like one hot guy and one beautiful girl left. Those odds okay with you?"

"Perfect." Longing rippled through me, a reckless craving that had me wanting more from him. Like the two of us naked.

The guy knew how to dress. Charcoal pinstripe pants teamed with a crisp white shirt, dressy yet casual, all class. He leaned forward, his signature scent washing over me, tempting me to do uncharacteristic things like ditch the drinking part of our date and go for broke. "I promised you a drink. What would you like?"

"Surprise me."

"A spontaneous woman. I never would've guessed." His wry smile had a kick like a mule and I resisted the urge to rub the area directly over my heart. "I still can't believe you managed to pull off that charade in Mumbai."

"Sheer talent."

"Quite the little actress." He called the waiter over. "We're employing extras while shooting here. Maybe you should audition."

"Yeah, right."

He chuckled, leaned over the bar, and spoke quietly to the waiter, placing our orders before turning back to me with a speculative gleam in his eyes. "Ever done any acting?"

"Tons." Aside from my impersonating gig in Mumbai, I'd been the epitome of the perfect legal secretary for a year when all the time I'd been bonking buddies with the boss. No one had guessed, so that must've taken considerable acting talent on my part.

While flirting with Drew, the unthinkable happened. As if a single unwelcome thought about the Toad had the power to conjure him up, he appeared before me, weaving his way through the crowd with his telltale smirk.

"Shit," I muttered, darting frantic glances around for an escape route.

I didn't want to face him, not here, not now, not ever. Tonight was about moving on, taking the first step to boosting my immunity against heartbreak and investing in my self-confidence.

He'd always had shitty timing.

"Hey, I was kidding about the acting gig." Drew's warm, intimate smile should've had my heart doing cartwheels. Instead, it did a triple backflip with full pike at the sight of the guy who'd broken it without trying.

I managed a feeble chuckle before grabbing his arm. "Do you want to get out of here?"

"Already?" Confusion creased his brow as I silently cursed and struggled to untangle my bag strap snagged on the leg of the barstool.

"I'll explain later." I had no intention of adhering to that particular promise. I might've been stupid in the past but this was the new me, the improved me, the—

"Hi, Shari."

The totally busted me.

While I'd been disentangling my bag and fumbling for my favorite jacket—vermillion faux fur—the Toad must've barged through the crowd to reach me in record time.

I gritted my teeth to stop the expletive hovering on the tip of my tongue when I looked into his smarmy face.

"Hi." Short, sharp, frosty, and one syllable more than the bastard deserved.

Drew frowned at the lack of introductions. He probably looked at the Toad and saw what everyone else saw: Armani suit (his trademark, he never wore anything else), dirty-blond hair styled a la Jude Law, intelligent green eyes, phony smile.

My stomach roiled as I resigned myself to the inevitable. Not introducing Bollywood Boy to the Toad would make me look like a bitch and as much as I wanted to:

a) throw a drink in the Toad's face;

b) wiggle my little finger to indicate the size of his dick and smirk knowingly;

c) saunter away;

d) all of the above.

I took the wuss option:

e) when in doubt, put your best Manolo forward and hope it crushes the loser beneath it.

Sliding my hand around Drew's arm, I managed a smile as fake as the Toad's. "Drew, this is Tate Embley. He's a liar—oops, I mean lawyer. Silly me."

The Toad's smile slipped and his eyes took on a hardened edge, adding ugliness I'd never recognized until we broke up. He stuck out his hand. "Pleased to meet you."

Despite my death grip on Drew's arm, he managed to reach out and shake the Toad's hand. He performed the fastest handshake in history, releasing Tate's hand after a split-second grasp. "Likewise."

By Drew's studied indifference, I knew he was far from pleased. Join the club.

Tate's spurious grin returned. "English, huh? Bit far from the Motherland, aren't you?"

I cringed, digging my fingers deeper into Drew's arm without thinking. How could the guy I'd thought I loved be such a patronizing, arrogant jerk? I'd been blind and stupid.

"Actually, I own houses in New York, London, Lucerne, Mumbai, and Tokyo, so my Motherland is wherever my Lear lands these days. I'm sure you know how it is, Tate, being a Yankee businessman." Drew prolonged the last word in a shocking imitation of a Southern accent and I bit the inside of my cheek to prevent laughing out loud. If my accidental-on-purpose gaff had annoyed Tate, he radiated anger now. Another thing I hated about him: his colossal ego demanding he had to top everyone.

Drew had summed up the situation in a second and had handled it with class, as opposed to the Toad acting the ass. As for his houses around the world and a private jet, I didn't know if it was true but the fact he'd one-upped the Toad made me want to high-five him.

In true Toad-like fashion, Tate ignored the guy who had bigger toys (and probably balls) and refocused on me. "What're you doing these days?"

"This 'n' that." I flashed a fabulous smile at Drew, gazing into his eyes as if he'd bestowed one of his international mansions to me, hoping the Toad would get the message. *F-off.*

"The office isn't the same without you." He lowered his voice, trying to suck me in with one of his old tricks, the smooth-as-caramel-latte tone, the one that had worked on me countless times before. Before I'd woken up and moved onto espresso.

"You worked with this... guy?" Drew's incredulity, combined with the slight pause, led me to believe he'd been about to say something more accurate like 'loser, cretin, jerk, bastard, moron, scum.'

I managed a mute nod while the Toad leapt in to fill the gap.

"Shari's the best. We had a good thing going for a while. You know how it is, being a businessman and all." He leered, his low voice heavy with innuendo, leaving little doubt as to our previous *business* relationship.

Bastard.

My hand fisted as I itched to slug the sneer off his face and tears burned the back of my eyes. Tears of humiliation, tears of rage, and I'd be damned if I stood there and gave the prick the satisfaction of seeing me cry.

While I floundered for the perfect exit line before my eyes spouted fountains, Drew took control again. "I doubt you and I have much in common. I wouldn't be stupid enough to let an amazing woman like Shari go. *Business-wise*, of course."

I could've kissed him, every protective inch of righteous indignation.

Ignoring the Toad, his face now a satisfying puce, Drew slipped on my coat and hugged me to his side. "The limo's waiting, ready to go? The crowd here isn't as classy as I thought."

I blinked back my tears as I eyeballed the Toad. "You're so right."

But I couldn't leave. Not yet. That's the thing about closure. Whenever the opportunity presented, you had to take it.

Touching Drew's arm, I murmured in his ear. "Could you give me a minute?"

Drew glared at Tate and nodded. "Sure, I'll wait for you outside."

He ran a hand over my hair in a purely possessive gesture not lost on Tate, whose upper lip snarled. Yeah, like he had the right to care, the jerk.

The moment Drew left, Tate made a move to touch me and I blocked his reach with my forearm, shoving him away. Shock widened his eyes a second before they narrowed in distaste. "Didn't take you long to shack up with another rich guy."

His sneer made my fingers curl with the urge to slug him. I didn't condone diva behavior but his smarmy expression deserved a knuckle rap.

"What I do with my life now is no concern to you."

"You didn't always feel like that."

"Screw you."

"Done that too, babe." Before I could knee him he ran a fingertip down my arm and I reacted without thinking, grabbing his finger and bending it until he winced.

"Listen up, you lying bastard." I bent his finger further, enjoying his pain when he paled, knowing he wouldn't make a scene because of his precious ego. "Don't ever come near me again."

I flung his hand away in disgust, my skin crawling with the contact. "Take your cheesy grin and fake charm and snide insults and stick it up your ass."

He gaped and I hustled through the crowd without a backward glance.

Not too bad as an exit line. Tate was a Grade A loser, always had been, always would be, and while I'd had my dubious honor defended by an absolute sweetheart, it felt freaking fantastic to tell him to shove it myself. Totally empowering.

Hoping the evening hadn't turned into a total fiasco, I stepped outside as Drew's cell rang. After a few short 'uh-huhs,' he snapped it shut and slid the slimline into his pocket. "Sorry, something's come up."

"Not to worry."

"We never got to have that drink." His eyes deepened to midnight in the reflected light from the neon signs and I hoped it wasn't disinterest, or worse, disgust at what he'd seen back there. It didn't take an Einstein to work out I'd been involved with Tate thanks to his sleazy innuendos, and as much as I'd enjoyed Drew defending me I was embarrassed. Embarrassed I knew a poser like that, embarrassed I'd put up with his crap, and embarrassed Drew now knew it, too.

"We don't have to reschedule. You're a busy guy, you're not in town for long, I get it."

"Do you get this?" He captured my face between his hands, not giving me room to move, and lowered his head. My heart jackknifed as he edged closer, hovering an inch from my mouth, tension crackling between us like a live wire.

I yearned to close the gap, craving the heady, addictive optimism that accompanied kissing a hot, new guy. I strained toward him, his breath tickling a moment before he touched his lips to mine.

The world tilted in an earth-shattering explosion of heat and desperation as his lips grazed mine, once, twice, taunting and provocative and incredibly tantalizing.

He deepened the pressure until I sagged against him, boneless, mindless, each long, hot, French kiss surpassing every erotic fantasy I'd ever had. That scintillating greeting at the airport? A prelude to this cataclysmic, indescribable sexual attraction combusting whenever we touched.

When his lips reluctantly eased from mine, he left me gasping for air.

Stunned and disoriented, I gaped like a love-struck fool.

His tender smile jabbed at my heart. "Raincheck on our drink date?"

I managed a mute nod.

"Great. Need a lift?"

I hoped my mouth and brain would work in sync. "You really have a limo waiting?"

"Of course. Would I lie to you?"

Probably. It was a design fault in the entire male species on the planet but after he'd played the knight-in-shining-armor to perfection, I owed it to him to cushion his ego a tad.

"After seeing the way that jerk treated you in there, perhaps I should rephrase that."

Was he fishing for info? I needed to tell him something even if it was only a fraction of the ugly truth.

"About Tate—"

"You don't owe me an explanation. I was merely making an observation."

"An accurate one. The guy's a jerk and, unfortunately, it took me a while to realize it."

"How long?"

"A year."

"Ouch."

Saying it out loud made the truth seem more ludicrous. Had I really put up with him for twelve months, listening to his empty promises to leave his wife, storing away our infrequent happy interludes like a starving squirrel hoarding its nuts? *I* was nuts for being so gullible.

I waved my hand in the air as if getting rid of a nasty odor. "Thanks for the sympathy vote but I don't deserve it. I was stupid. Live and learn, I guess. Now, how about that ride?"

Drew opened his mouth as if wanting to say more before he closed it, nodded, and guided me to the sleek black limo parked around the corner.

I liked his style. He could've prodded me for more info, made some droll remark not remotely funny, or generally agreed with my astute observation that I'd been stupid in giving my heart to the Toad. Instead, he handed me into the limo's plush interior, gave the driver my address, and chatted about New York during the drive.

Grateful for his understanding, I fumbled for my purse as the limo drew to a halt outside my loft. I hated this part of an evening and as short as our 'date' had been, I didn't know whether to leap from the limo, mumble something unintelligible, or plant a quick thank-you peck on his cheek. Thankfully, he took matters out of my indecisive hands.

"I'll call you, Miss Jones," he said, dropping a slightly-longer-than-friendly kiss on my lips.

"You do that, Mr. Lansford." I touched his cheek in a poignant, fleeting gesture that wouldn't have been out of place in one of my favorite rom-coms before bolting, afraid I'd acted like an ass.

I willed myself not to look back in case the rumor about not appearing too eager if you looked back at the person held up. No use jinxing this before it'd begun. I let myself into the building and waited until I got inside the apartment before collapsing in an undignified heap on the couch. I kicked off my shoes, flexed my ankles, and wriggled my toes. Didn't help relax me like it usually did.

I'd been uptight before this evening started and now my neck muscles roped with tension. I needed some stress relief, a hot lavender bath followed by watching a Robbie-singing-swing DVD (the one where he's in a tux, drool, drool).

First, sustenance. I grabbed a tub of Ben & Jerry's Chunky Monkey, ripped off the top, and stuck a dessert spoon into the sticky heaven, shoveling it into my mouth with the desperation of a woman who needs a fix of something sweeter than ice cream but making do anyway.

I didn't want to think about Drew or the way he made me feel: gorgeous, special, and after his Sir Galahad act, protected. I didn't need protection (unless it came in a little foil packet and was ripped open with Bollywood Boy's teeth in the throes of passion).

I didn't need a guy in my life. But wouldn't it be fun to audition Bollywood Boy for the part?

As I happily consumed a pint of ice cream, I ignored the voice of doubt in my head, the voice whispering, *He used the tried-and-true line of Jerks United, "I'll call you."* And he probably wouldn't.

I also ignored the slightly sick feeling in my gut (blaming too much honeycomb) if he didn't.

CHAPTER TEN

After six days, twelve hours, and forty minutes, I acknowledged Drew Lansford was a fully paid-up, participating member of Jerks United.

Not that I waited by the phone. Okay, I admit it, I checked my cell's voice mail and messages rather frequently. Sad but true.

Between job interviews—and there'd been many—I'd turned into a partial recluse, heading out for essentials only: pints of Ben & Jerry's, Doritos, and Moonlight Mojito Mix, a weird premixed concoction that tasted like 7UP with zip. Gorging on comfort food wouldn't help my mood, but I needed something familiar in my topsy-turvy world.

Adding a top coat to my nails, I wiggled my toes, facing facts. Despite pawning almost everything and dipping into my nest egg—the size of a sparrow's—I'd nearly blown it all on living expenses. I needed a job pronto before my funds ran out.

Twelve interviews and two call-backs in the last week, not terribly inspiring considering I'd broadened my job search criteria. Along with the usual executive assistant applications,

I'd taken the plunge and applied for a few publishing positions. Copyeditors mostly, but considering the publishers' lack of enthusiasm, Subway sandwich artist was starting to look good. I'd pinned my hopes on the call-backs. If they didn't work out, better get out my knife and loaf and start toasting.

The buzzer rang and my heart did a weird flip-flop, wishing Drew would drop by, before reality set in. If a guy didn't call for almost a week, the possibility of him visiting unannounced was as likely as Bergdorf's throwing out their Hermes bags at cost.

It pealed out again and I waddled to the intercom, not wanting to smudge my nails.

Rabidly antisocial, I stabbed at the intercom button. "Yeah?"

"Let me in, the wind out here would freeze the *cojones* off a brass monkey." Rita added a chimp imitation for good measure, earning a reluctant smile.

"Come on up."

I pressed the button to let Rita in, though my grouchiness hadn't improved at the sound of her voice. As much as I loved her I wasn't in the mood to hear about her budding relationship with Romeo Rama. She'd been trying to get me out all week, inviting me to join them for dinner at Nobu, drinks at Michu, skating at Central Park.

Politely declining, I'd cited a tummy bug, a migraine, and a twisted ankle. Guess she hadn't bought the last excuse when I'd used kickboxing with Jackie Chan as the reason. After I'd OD'd on rom-coms, action flicks were my change of pace. Besides, if I saw a hint of Hugh on the screen, I might throw the remote.

Zipping up my pink hoodie to hide a chocolate stain on the front of my grey T-shirt underneath, I opened the door.

"Hey. What brings you by?"

Rita's contemptuous glance flicked from the top of my lank

hair to the bottoms of my frayed yoga pants before settling on my face, devoid of M.A.C. or Bobbi Brown all week.

"You look like shit," she said, breezing past me, leaving a cloud of Chanel No. 5 in her wake.

"Wish I could say the same." I tried not to turn Kermit-green as I noted a new ebony Prada suit with a cherry silk shell underneath, four-inch black Jimmy Choo pumps, and matching handbag. She looked incredible, glowing from the inside out, while I resembled washed-out slop.

Note to self: Rule number one in acting like all is right with the world: get dressed, wash hair, wear makeup. And no lies about kickboxing Jackie Chan.

Rita swept a pile of *Inside Styles* off the couch and wrinkled her nose at the two empty ice cream containers on the coffee table before perching precariously on the edge of the cushions as if she'd pick up couch cooties by getting comfy.

"What's going on with you?" She pinned me with a determined stare and before I could open my mouth to lie, she continued, "And save the bullshit. The truth, this time."

I wandered around the room, swiping at not-so-imaginary dust and tidying a stack of DVDs on the TV.

Rule number two: don't blow off best friend with lousy excuses. She only gets madder and swears at you.

"And sit down. That fiddling's driving me nuts."

Taking a deep breath, I plopped into a chair. "Nothing's wrong. I'm exhausted, what with the breakup—"

"That was four months ago."

I continued like she'd hadn't spoken, "—and flying halfway across the world to save your butt, then job-hunting like a maniac. It's caught up with me. I'm taking a break, having a little 'me' time."

By her doubtful expression, she didn't buy my excuses for a second. We'd been best friends too long. "It's got nothing to do with Drew?"

"'Course not." I thanked God for my olive complexion. A blush at this point would incriminate.

A triumphant glint lit her eyes. "Good. In that case, you're coming with me to Central Park."

Rule number three: be wary of clever accountant friends who are way smarter than stupid ex legal secretaries who consistently make wrong choices, especially concerning guys in their lives.

"Central Park?" I acted dumb—maybe the acting part wasn't so hard—knowing the park would be the last place I'd want to be if Drew was there.

"They're filming a few scenes. Should be a blast."

I shrugged, trying not to look triumphant. Getting out of this would be too easy. "Thanks, but I've already seen the real thing, remember? I saw them shooting in Bollywood and as interesting as it is I'm all 'filmed' out. But you go, you'll have a ball."

That should get rid of Miss Goody-Two-Choos.

"It wasn't an invitation, it's an order. You're coming. Be ready by two. I'll swing by and pick you up then."

Rule number four: smugness is not a good thing, particularly if victory isn't assured.

"But—"

"Talk to this," she said, holding up her hand as she waltzed out the door, spouting another of her talk-show sayings she knew I hated. At least this one sounded like an Ellen, marginally better than a Dr. Phil.

Cursing under my breath, I checked the time: 12:51. Great, I had just over an hour to do a major grease and overhaul. Who did Rita think I was, a Kardashian?

I didn't have a hair stylist, makeup artist, and clothes consultant on staff. I had a Remington ceramic straightener, an eclectic mix of Lancôme, Lauder, M.A.C., L'Oreal, and Maybelline cosmetics, and a half-decent designer wardrobe, most residing in plastic suit bags because I'd been too lazy to get off my ass and unpack them.

As I bolted for the shower, I glanced at my watch. 12:52

Rule number five in acting like all is right with the world: when in doubt, improvise. They'll never know the difference.

By my skanky reflection in the bathroom mirror as I peeled off my day-old clothes—yeah, I'd slept in them, gross—I was about to pull off one hell of an improvisation.

• • •

"Have you ever seen anything like this?" Rita grabbed my arm, her face lighting with excitement as her head swiveled from the sixty-odd sari-clad dancers twirling in rhythm to the mock fistfight taking place a few paces away.

"Yeah, in Mumbai. Remember?"

As much as I pretended Rita bringing me here was a drag, I couldn't help but join in her enthusiasm. The minute I'd seen the dancers and inhaled the fragrant mix of greasepaint, sweat, and curry powder, I'd been instantly transported back to India and an unexpected wave of nostalgia swept over me.

Rita ignored my pithy tone. "It's so colorful. I watch these movies all the time but they run way too long and skip the sex. Bor-ing."

She'd said the same as we'd watched them almost nightly when I'd crashed at her place for three months. Raiding her stack of old Bollywood DVDs had been fun and a good distraction from my relationship woes. She would've rather grabbed the latest films from Netflix but I'd pulled the 'recently brokenhearted' excuse and she'd capitulated. Her cynical commentary had been annoying but I'd tuned out, captured by the glamour and performance. Nothing had diminished my enjoyment. I'd been virtually glued to the screen, hooked on the drama and tension and spectacle.

"Wait for the simulated rain. That gets the guys going."

She rolled her eyes. "Don't you think it's time Bollywood moved into the twenty-first century? No kissing, no bonking, just lots of fierce hugging and bees flying into flowers and spurting waterfalls. Real symbolic. Not."

I chuckled. "You obviously haven't seen some of the latest flicks—they're hot. Personally, I think there's nothing wrong with a bit of mystery. It's cute they're not so explicit. Hails back to the good old days of Hollywood."

"You're sounding more Indian than my mom. Mumbai made quite an impression on you."

Trust Rita to home in on my feelings. What was she, the New York version of Kapil?

I shrugged. "I guess."

She didn't buy my nonchalance for a second. "I'm your best friend, not some bimbo you can give the runaround to. You've changed."

I blinked back the sting of tears, knowing this wasn't the time or place to try and explain something I could hardly put into words myself.

Even though I'd taken steps to erase the past and secure my future, I couldn't help but feel a tad lost. I lived in a low-rent apartment, I job-searched. I should be happy. Why the persistent nagging I was missing out on something?

"I'm doing the best I can, okay? Lay off."

Rita's eyes widened in horror as she registered my tears. "Sorry, hun, didn't mean to—"

"You!"

Rita's words were cut off by a guy in a white *salwar kameez* bustling between us, his hands outstretched toward me, joined at the tips of his thumbs with fingers spread as he framed my face.

"You're perfect."

At last. A guy who recognized my true worth.

"Butt out, bozo," Rita said, her scathing glare capable of withering any guy, let alone one with corny opening lines.

He ignored her, his hands moving around my face while his head tilted from side to side, assessing all angles. "You'll do nicely."

His hand shot out and he grabbed my arm. "You'll bc in my movie, yes? Come, get into costume. Stand in back row. Smile. Look perfect."

I should've shaken off his hand and given his skinny ass a swift kick, but he sounded serious. Plus he kept saying I was perfect.

"Where are my manners?" He released my arm to smack himself in the head in true dramatic Bollywood fashion. I wouldn't need to take part in his film if he kept up these theatrics—he could do it himself. "Let me introduce myself. I'm Pravin, the producer."

Rita snorted. "Of what? Phony lines to get women to notice you?"

Once again, he ignored Rita, who made stirring the pot signs behind his back. She may be trying to bait Pravin but he wasn't biting. Instead, he kept staring at me like he'd discovered the Indian equivalent of Jennifer Aniston, and I found it unnerving. Very unnerving, considering his head tilted every which way to get a look at my jawline, cheekbones, and side profile.

"I'm the biggest producer of Bollywood films in India. My credentials are impeccable. You want proof, yes?"

"That won't be necessary," I said, as Rita simultaneously blurted, "Yes."

He waved Rita away as if shooing a pesky fly. "What's your name?"

"Shari Jones."

The longer Pravin continued staring, the easier it was for me to imagine my name up in lights, twice as large as the Hollywood sign in California, and just as impressive. Chalk up another one to Kapil. Maybe his fame prediction wasn't far off?

Pravin nodded. "You'll be in my movie, Shari Jones. I speak to the boss man, he vouch for me, you sign contract, everything B-OK, as they say in New York?"

"I think he means A-OK," Rita said, a hint of a smile playing about her mouth. "And I think you've just been discovered."

"This is crazy," I muttered, torn between wanting to send Pravin packing and flattered he thought me movie material. As if my life wasn't strange enough.

Pravin took my hesitation as a sign of approval as he clapped his hands twice. "Good, good, all settled. You leave number, boss man contact you, everything A-OK."

He strode away, the white cotton hanging loosely on his lanky frame and pooling around his ankles, doing little to enhance his image as India's number one producer. Indian clothes tended to flatter but in Pravin's case he needed to eat a few more *parathas* or his tailor needed a new measuring tape.

Shaking my head, I glanced at Rita, whose smile could've been a shining ad for Colgate. "Aren't you going to say something?"

Chuckling, she slipped an arm around my shoulders and

hugged me tight. "Welcome to show biz."

• • •

I expected Pravin's boss man to be some high-falooting executive producer who had the final say on newly discovered Bollywood stars and I assumed I'd never hear from him. I had that effect on guys, the standard "I'll call you" that never eventuated. Besides, how many people get discovered? Claudia Schiffer, maybe. Me? Like hell.

After a quick stop at the corner store where I bought fruit, veggies, and dairy to balance out the Moonlight Mix and ice cream, I headed home. Rakesh had waylaid Rita in Central Park and I'd been happy to leave the lovebirds alone, though I had to promise to have dinner with them tomorrow night before they let me go.

I'd put the groceries away when the buzzer sounded.

I pressed the intercom button. "Who is it?"

"Drew. Can I come up?"

I released the button as if it'd stung. What did he want? To waltz in here like not calling me had been an oversight?

I pressed the button again. "This isn't a good time."

"I know it's rude to drop around without calling first, but I really need to see you."

I nibbled on my bottom lip, torn between wanting to let him in and hear what he had to say and busting Bollywood Boy's balls.

The moment he'd showed up, the decision had been a no-brainer. Not that I'd make it easy for him.

"Shari, it's important."

I jumped as if he'd stepped into the room and crept up on me. "I'm busy."

"Let me guess. Reading a good book, washing your hair, or have a headache coming on?"

Damn his sense of humor. Along with the accent, the voice, the bod, the face, and every other goddamn thing that made him so irresistible.

"Not even close. But you better come up before someone mugs you." I hit the door button and waited until it stopped buzzing before bolting to the bathroom to check my makeup. Yeah, yeah, totally pathetic, but if I was going to do some serious ball-breaking I needed to look my best.

Happy I hadn't changed when I got home — and exceedingly grateful Rita had hauled me out of my sweats in the first place — I ran fingers through my tousled hair and checked to make sure I hadn't spilled anything on my new chartreuse linen dress.

Not bad. If Drew had to come up and see me sometime, now was as good a time as any.

I opened the door and tried not to stagger at the sight of him, extremely doable in denim, a casual white shirt, and a black leather jacket.

"Thanks for letting me up, what with all the book-reading and hair-washing you have to do." He smiled, to add to the torture of wanting something I couldn't have.

"Muggers would've attacked for sure if I'd left you down there one minute longer with those banal lines."

His mouth kicked into a grin. "Can I come in?"

I'd been leaning on the door, trying not to drool. Stepping aside, I gestured him in.

"Nice place," he said, shrugging out of his jacket as I tried — and failed — to avert my eyes riveted to his broad chest as the shirt stretched across it.

"It's not mine. I'm subletting from a cousin of Rita's. Want a drink?" I had to do something, anything, to take my mind off how unsteady this guy made me feel.

"I'd kill for a cup of tea."

"Take the boy out of England but you can't take England out of the boy. *I'd kill for a cup of tea*," I imitated, complete with plum-in-the-mouth accent that turned me on so much.

I ducked down to dishwasher level and opened the cabinet below the oven, dithering over good china or chipped.

"Are you making fun of me, Miss Jones?"

Rummaging for cups and saucers, I almost slammed my head as his voice came from somewhere on my left. Somewhere very close on my left. His radiant heat made my skin prickle.

Get a grip.

Withdrawing my head from the cabinet after locating the cups brought me up close and personal with the guy I wanted to *get a grip on* as he squatted down beside me.

"Here, let me take those."

Damn the rattling cups in my shaking hands. Dead giveaway to how I reacted with him near.

"Would you like *masala chai*? Anjali showed me how to make it. I love the blend of cinnamon, cloves, cardamom, and tea. It's delicious." I inwardly cringed at my jabber, flicking the kettle switch on and bustling around the kitchen like Martha freaking Stewart.

"Sounds good." He leaned against the island bench, way too comfortable. "Sorry for not calling this week, I've been busy."

My golden opportunity to do some ball-breaking. I stopped fussing and looked him straight in the eye. "Is that the guy's equivalent of hair-washing and headaches?"

"No, that's the truth. I've had a lot on my plate, both business and family stuff."

"Don't tell me you've got a wife and kids?" I joked, my stomach somersaulting and landing with a sickening splat.

We hadn't talked about our families. Actually, we hadn't talked much at all. In Mumbai he'd been too busy accusing me of being a gold digger and when he'd learned the truth, all we'd done was flirt. Here in New York, we'd barely skimmed the surface when the Toad had shown up and our evening had ended shortly afterward, courtesy of Drew's business.

Funny business, more likely; I sure as hell wasn't laughing.

"Worse. My mother." He rolled his eyes in the universal God-help-me sign most kids used at some point in their lives. "She discovered I was in town despite my efforts to hide the fact and hasn't stopped hassling me since."

I giggled, an inane, relieved laugh. "Sounds serious."

"She hangs out at The Plaza for a few weeks a year, and this time her trip happens to coincide with my visit." He pinched the bridge of his nose. "I couldn't lie to her when she asked where I was so now I'm facing the usual 'when are you coming home to England? When are you getting married? When are you reproducing?' Mundane stuff like that."

"I get the same from my mom, apart from the England bit."

"Maybe you should get yourself a fake fiancé? Throw her off track." He grinned, the heat notching up in the kitchen having nothing to do with the steaming kettle.

"Touché." I busied myself with the tea, the indecipherable shadows in his eyes disconcerting.

We'd flirted a little and he'd kissed me. That didn't mean his hormones were going crazy like mine or he was harboring the same wicked thoughts I was.

"I almost forgot." He pulled a buff envelope from his back pocket. "This is why I dropped by."

"Oh."

So it wasn't to indulge in wild, climb-the-walls sex? Shame.

He handed it to me. "I'd expect a little more excitement from Pravin's latest discovery."

"*You're* the boss man?"

"Apparently so. I sign the checks, I approve new inclusions, and Pravin raved about you, so you're in."

I ripped open the envelope, pulled out a thick document, and quickly scanned the contract. "I thought he must've been joking."

"Pravin's a Bollywood hotshot. Produced hundreds of films, grossing billions of dollars. He's big and if he wants you in his film, you should be flattered."

"Yeah, right," I said, speed-reading the fine print until a figure leapt off the page and made my eyes bulge. "Ohmigod. This has to be a mistake."

"The contract's standard so I doubt mistakes have been made."

I blinked, reopened my eyes, but the figure remained the same. "You want to pay me a thousand dollars for a bit part? That's insane. I thought extras earned a pittance?"

"Not on Pravin's films. I don't write the contracts, I hand out the cash."

"Then you're insane."

A thousand dollars could buy me an extra month's rent. Or kick off my savings for the trip around India I'd been craving since I returned. Either way, looked like I would make my acting debut.

"There aren't too many things in this world I'm crazy about but when I find them, I'm pretty single-minded."

Something in his voice made me look up. Maybe it was an inflection or a slight change in the timbre but once our eyes met I couldn't look away. I knew exactly how the cobras on Chowpatty Beach Anjali had told me about felt—trapped, unable to move, swaying in time to a turbaned guy playing some kind of flute.

Although I couldn't move he had no such problems, crossing the kitchen in three strides, crowding my personal space and making my hormones haywire. I shouldn't provoke him, I really shouldn't. Then again, when had I ever listened to my voice of reason?

"Tell me what you're crazy about." I aimed for soft and breathy, ended up sounding strangled and desperate.

"Spicy food. Fine shiraz. Anything Indian."

I'd be lying if I didn't admit I hoped he'd add 'you' to that list.

I should've come back with something witty, something to diffuse the tension buzzing between us. Instead, I said the first thing that popped into my head. "I'm half-Indian."

I snapped my jaws shut to prevent blurting 'does that count?'

His eyes sparked and my heart flipped in response. "I wondered, but didn't want to pry."

"Mom's Indian, Dad's American."

Pry away, I wanted to add. *Ask me anything and I'll tell you no lies, like how much I want you.*

He wouldn't. His British stiff upper lip kicked in at the most inopportune times, reminding me of the yawning gap between our cultures. "A great combination considering the result."

Not bad for a backhand compliment. "Little ol' me?"

"You're stunning." He touched my arm, the barest of caresses, his fingers sliding along my skin raising goose bumps, and the gap I'd imagined between us evaporated in a second. "And yeah, I could get crazy about you."

He had me.

My ball-breaking intentions wavered. Not that I'd let him off lightly.

"Really? Because not calling for a week? Doesn't do you any favors."

"Thought I already explained that." He took a step forward, invading my personal space and I held my breath.

Didn't take much to ignite my latent longing, and having him this close put a serious dent in my plans to toughen up. "Doesn't mean I bought your excuses."

"You're a hard woman to impress, Miss Jones."

"Maybe you're not trying hard enough?" I enjoyed our sparring as much as having him stare at me with a glint of excitement.

He tapped his temple, pretending to think. "Let's see. If words don't convince you, what else can I do?"

"Show me," I dared him before he second-guessed his decision to add me to his list of things to get crazy about.

"My pleasure," he said, his lips brushing mine once, twice, lingering, increasing pressure with every glancing touch.

I shivered in expectation as his fingertip grazed the tender skin under my jaw, edged across to the sensitive spot beneath my ear, before slowly trailing across my collarbone, lingering in the hollow at the base of my throat. He traced lazy circles, his touch feather-light and incredibly erotic.

I swayed, lost in sensation, lost in him. I placed my palm flat against his chest, and his searing heat matched mine, palpable through the thin cotton. I was burning from the inside out, revved beyond belief. I held my breath. The taut silence stretched until I couldn't wait another moment. My hand snaked around his neck and guided his head down.

When his lips touched mine, my panties almost shucked off.

He tasted of cloves and cinnamon and passion, and I couldn't get enough. As he deepened the kiss to the point of no return, I writhed against him, shameless and wanton and yearning.

His hands were everywhere, caressing my breasts, molding my waist, flaring over my hips, cupping my butt, setting every inch of me alight with an intense, overwhelming craving to have him inside me, now.

Frantic, we tore at each other's clothes and stumbled to the bedroom, unaware of the wan afternoon sunshine spilling through the slat blinds, unaware of my lingerie draped over the backs of chairs to dry, unaware of everything but the mind-numbing, toe-curling desire consuming us.

The back of his knees hit the edge of the bed and he stalled, his lips trailing down my neck and up again to linger near my ear. "You sure?"

His whisper fanned the sensitive skin beneath my ear and I shivered.

"Does this answer your question?" I pushed him onto the bed, straddled him, and pinned his shoulders with my hands, letting my hair drape across his chest in a teasing sweep.

"Have it your way." His sexy grin sent my heart slamming against my ribcage as he flipped me over in one, smooth move, fumbled for his jeans on the floor, and grabbed a condom out of his wallet.

"Extra large?" I plucked the gold foil packet out of his hand, excitement making mine shake. After all the crazy shit I'd dealt with over the last year, the karma fairy had finally gotten something right.

"Scared?"

"Impressed, more like it."

And hopeful. Very hopeful.

"English humor." He grinned, took the packet out of my hand, and ripped it open with his teeth. "They only come in one size over there."

"So it's not true?"

I tried to keep the disappointment out of my voice; by the amused gleam in his eyes, I failed.

"You tell me."

He set about proving it. Once by bringing me to a screaming orgasm with his mouth and fingers before initiating me into the joys of positions I'd never imagined, let alone tried. Twice, by doing it in the shower. Three times, by christening every room in the apartment as a sultry New York afternoon eased into a beautiful evening.

His hand slid across my belly, exploring my skin in delicious detail, inching downward, toying with me, coherent speech impossible as he took the meaning of foreplay to a new level. Again. "What's the verdict?"

My breath hitched and I arched off the bed as his fingers delved and probed. I wished this day would never end. "Size does matter."

"And?"

"English condom manufacturers don't lie," I managed to grit out as he sent me spiraling into another cataclysmic climax.

"You sure about that?"

He kissed the tender spot at the base of my neck, right above my collarbone, the spot that made me weak and fuzzy—if he hadn't already done that with his masterful fingers.

"I'm sure. *Ooh...* "

He moved lower, sucking a nipple into his mouth, nibbling it, before moving across to the other one. "Maybe we should test another just to make sure?"

"I like the way you think," I whispered, as his hands and mouth played me like an instrument. A well-used, much-practiced, finely tuned instrument that sang the more he played.

I sang—boy, did I sing. Beyonce, Pink, and Lady Gaga had nothing on me.

Drew had me coming back for encore after encore.

All night long.

CHAPTER ELEVEN

Twenty-four hours later, I'd cooked my first Indian meal. From scratch.

Me, the takeout queen, the girl most likely to eat soup from a can rather than cook, the woman who adored eating but didn't go in for the preparation.

I could've asked Mom for recipes, but she would've wanted to know why the sky was falling in—translated: why I was cooking—and Rita would've ribbed me endlessly, so I settled for trusty Google instead. I'd spent the morning raiding a local spice mart and the afternoon slaving over a hot stove. If this didn't impress Drew, nothing would.

Interestingly, I'd enjoyed the methodical process: sourcing ingredients, preparing them, following a recipe, testing the end result. I'd hated the detail-oriented aspect of being a legal secretary, the mundane dotting of every *i* and crossing every *t*, and while I might have been good at it, now I'd had some time away (read: no one wanted to hire me) I could see I'd been going through the motions, paying the bills, funding my lifestyle, not deriving fulfillment.

Surveying the table and the results of my culinary efforts, maybe I should start job-searching for master chef positions. Not so far-fetched considering my other job yearnings. While scouring the publishing vacancies earlier I'd spied an ad for a new travel/food magazine columnist. Way out of my league, but it had seriously piqued my interest and I'd been crazy enough to email my resume before I changed my mind.

Somehow, I didn't think writing copy for legal newsletters was quite in the same league as a magazine column but hey, worth a try. Besides, they'd wanted an international flavor so I'd hammed up my Indian background, citing my recent trip to Mumbai and a long list of Indian dishes I'd written about. In emails to Mom. That was on a strict need-to-know basis.

The intercom buzzed and the bundle of nerves in my stomach bunched. Taking a deep breath and blowing it out, I hit the button to let Drew up. After whipping off my makeshift apron I smoothed my halter top down and checked my lipstick in the mirror. If cooking a feast hadn't been enough of an indication I was seriously into this guy, the fact I hadn't eaten a thing all day confirmed it. I had to eat. Low blood sugar. My excuse, I was sticking to it.

He knocked, I took a deep breath and counted to ten, before opening it and ruining my cool impression by gawking like a teenager. Faded taupe T-shirt, dark denim, stubble, come-get-me smile. Oh boy.

"Something smells great." He ducked his head to nuzzle my neck on the way in and I refrained from tearing his clothes off. Barely.

"You said you liked spicy and Indian."

He stopped in front of the dining table, dumbfounded.

"You cooked all this?"

"Don't sound so surprised. I'm a woman of many talents."

His awe vindicated my chapped hands and sliced fingers—who knew stupid knives could be so sharp? "I can see that." He lifted the lid on the first dish and inhaled, eyes closed, blissed out. "Mmm... tamarind, cumin, coriander, peppercorns. I love mulligatawny."

"*Rasam* to you." I bumped him gently with my hip and he slid his arm around my waist, resting it there like the most natural thing in the world.

"Can I peek at the rest?" His fingers toyed with the edge of my top and I bit back my first retort. He could peek at any damn thing he pleased.

"Why don't we eat? I'll dish up the rice, you pour the wine."

He released me and I immediately regretted it. "Deal."

I bustled around the kitchen, piled *pappadums* on a platter, slid *raita* out of the fridge, and ladled steaming basmati rice into a serving dish, aiming for efficiency, but ending up hot and flustered.

"Let me help." He stepped into the kitchen and took dishes out of my hand, passing a glass of wine with the other. "You shouldn't have gone to all this trouble," he said, brushing a kiss across my lips, his adoration making me glad I did.

I could've replied with a trite "no trouble," but I didn't want lies to taint this relationship. "I wanted to impress you."

His expression softened. "It worked."

I followed him into the dining area, where we placed the dishes on the table before he raised his glass to mine.

"Though you didn't have to cook to impress me. You did that with your fake fiancée impersonation the moment we met."

I winced. "Don't remind me."

His mouth eased into a lazy grin. "Should've seen your face when I busted you."

"You were such an ass."

He laughed and clinked his glass to mine. "Here's to leaving Bollywood behind and moving on to a new script."

One involving less drama, more sex, I hoped.

He pulled out my seat and I preened at his manners, whipping the lids off dishes in an effort to disguise my growing need to devour him.

"*Aloo gobi, avail, murgh masala, dhansak,* and *rasam.*"

"I'm in heaven." He clutched his stomach as he sat. "Want me to serve you?"

"Please, a little of everything." I sipped at my wine as he dished spicy potato, mixed vegetable curry made from coconut and yogurt, and chicken in a tomato, ginger, and spicy sauce. He added lamb cooked with *dahl* and a dollop of rice, spooning *rasam* over the rice. I could get used to being served. Serviced. Whatever.

"Here you go." He placed my plate in front of me before piling food on his own, his appetite for Indian food more than a match for his appetite in the bedroom if last night had been any indication.

Remembering last night—the decadence, the delight, the debauchery—made me want to skip dinner and head straight for Sexy Town. I forked morsels into my mouth, barely tasting the food I'd taken great pains to prepare, while he polished off his and went back for seconds.

"Not hungry?"

I mumbled a noncommittal answer, pushing my food around before surrendering and nudging the plate away. I couldn't pinpoint why I was so nervous about a repeat of our bedroom antics. Until I glanced across the table at his casually mussed hair, his too-blue-to-be-true eyes, his sensual lips perpetually quirked at the corners, and I knew. Knew a repeat of last night would solidify the relentless yearning hammering my common sense into submission, insisting it'd be okay to fall for him.

"That was amazing." He sat back and patted his stomach before reaching across the table and snagging my hand, his thumb brushing the back of it in slow, rhythmic circles. "I could get used to this."

Me too, but the serious glint in his eyes scared me as much as my growing feelings for a guy I hardly knew, a guy I had nothing to offer, a guy so far out of my league we were on different playing fields.

Drew was a keeper.

But what if I wasn't enough to keep him?

"What's up? You've hardly said a word."

I gestured toward the dishes. "I had no idea cooking would wear me out."

"Not too tired, I hope?" He wiggled his eyebrows suggestively.

I laughed. "Why? What did you have in mind?"

"Let me show you." He stood, held out his hand, and when I placed mine in his, he tugged me to my feet flush against him.

We swayed for what seemed like an eternity, savoring the contact, the heat, the growing tension.

I closed my eyes, laid my cheek on his chest, and breathed in a heady combination of Cool Water, freshly laundered cotton, and pure Drew.

We moved to an imaginary song, our feet gliding toward the bedroom.

Lucky I'd bought the *kulfi* and hadn't slaved over the ice cream.

We never made it to dessert.

• • •

Drew and I went for long walks jostling alongside frenetic New Yorkers with things to do and places to be, drank *chai* lattes at Starbucks, ordered in spicy Indian (I conserved my energy for more important activities), and had amazing sex whenever we could.

We curled up on the couch and watched *Seinfeld* and *Friends* reruns. We visited trendy jazz clubs and ate late-night deli suppers. We took decadently long baths and slept in most mornings and couldn't get enough of each other.

I existed in some weird fantasy-reality sphere, like being caught in the Matrix but better. Bolder, sexier, and scarier. The rotten thing about living a fantasy is you know it'll unravel eventually.

"Wow, you look amazing." Rita held me at arm's length. "That shade of fuchsia highlights your hair perfectly."

I twirled and struck a Vogue pose. "You like?"

"You're like a glam Indian *babe*. That *salwar kameez* looks fab on you."

"This old thing?" I smoothed the crystal-embroidered chiffon over my belly, enjoying the silky slide beneath my fingertips. If this was an extra's costume I'd love to slip into a star's outfit.

"You're going to knock 'em dead." She fussed around me, fluffing my hair, adjusting the neckline, fiddling with my earrings, and straightening my billowy sleeves straight out of a harem. "And if you don't, who cares? You've made an easy grand."

"This isn't about the money," I deadpanned for two seconds before joining in her raucous laughter.

Thankful the makeup artist on set prescribed to Maybelline's promise of waterproof mascara I dabbed under my eyes and checked my fingertips for telltale black. "Where's Rakesh? You two are inseparable."

"He had a business lunch with Drew and some corporate bigwigs. Said they'd swing by later."

A sliver of anticipation shimmied through me. "Drew's coming?"

Rita patted my cheek. "This is me you're talking to. Of course he'll be here for your auspicious debut."

"He didn't mention it."

Drew hadn't mentioned much of anything to me the last day or two, appearing distracted the few times we'd caught up. Or been caught up between the sheets, more to the point. As much as I loved the incredible sex, I knew this wouldn't last forever. But I couldn't help craving a little intimacy.

Late twenties, single, female. Do the math.

Flirty flings were fabulous until you hit the big three-O, all downhill from there. Biological clocks started ticking like time bombs waiting to detonate, gravity exerted more force on your life than your mom, and suddenly, the dog-ugliest creep looked like Jake Gyllenhaal.

I nibbled the cuticle of my thumbnail, putting my lipstick to a quick budge-proof test. If I hadn't been nervous about my acting debut before, thoughts of my impending thirties set me positively trembling.

"He probably wanted to surprise you and I've spoiled it," Rita said, averting her eyes but not before I glimpsed a flash of concern.

"Drew and I aren't serious so don't worry about it. If he shows up, he shows up. If not, no biggie." I could've almost believed my nonchalant act if I didn't feel so empty at the thought of him not being here today. He'd teased me about being Pravin's protégée, about using my looks to get ahead, making light of something that secretly meant a whole lot to me.

Pravin had seen something in me I rarely saw myself, my inner Indian.

Rita didn't push for answers on my relationship with Drew. She didn't have to, considering the man in question crept up on me and placed his hands over my eyes. "Guess who?"

Resisting the urge to swing around, jump into his arms, and wrap my legs around his waist, I paused. "By the feel of those strong, masterful hands, I'd say Amitabh Bachchan."

Rita rolled her eyes and made a beeline for Rakesh near the back entrance.

"Hey!" Drew dropped his hands and swung me around, resting them lightly on my shoulders. "You've met the great man already? And if so, how do you know his hands are strong and masterful?"

I bit back a grin. "Sadly, I haven't had the privilege. Pravin's been extolling his virtues."

"Pravin knows his stuff. A BBC poll recently voted him the biggest star of the millennium, surpassing guys like Tom Cruise. Now, tell me more about his hands."

I couldn't think straight with Drew's hands slipping from my shoulders and tracing my curves in delicious slowness, coming to rest on my hips.

"Just teasing. Can't a girl have a little fun?" I bit back a groan as his thumb stroked through the thin chiffon.

"Sure. I can think of plenty more ways." He dropped a soft, lingering kiss on my lips and I leaned into him, grateful for the privacy of the extras' tent, surprisingly empty at this time of day.

I guess the devoted extras were practicing stuff like posing and preening and looking suitably glamorous with the hope of being promoted to a walk-on role or, better yet, a speaking part.

Breaking the kiss with regret—ten minutes until showtime by the clock on the wall—I blinked to dispel the erotic fog that enveloped me whenever this guy got within a foot, and registered Rita and Rakesh were in a clinch of their own.

"Nervous?" Drew cuddled me close and I lapped up the attention, blissfully calm within the circle of his arms.

Until a horrendous, ear-splitting shriek pierced my ears and I glimpsed the horrified face of Mama Rama over Drew's right shoulder.

"What the—" Drew turned as three things happened simultaneously: I shrugged out of his embrace, Rakesh nudged Rita behind him to shield her, and the incensed Mama Rama launched herself in my direction, landing a hard slap on my cheek before I could duck.

"Ow!"

"Bloody hell." Drew tucked me under the protection of his arm. "Enough."

"Take it easy, Mom." Rakesh grabbed the old cow and spun her around to face him while screening my stunned best friend.

Rita had the sense not to speak. No point alienating her future mother-in-law for a small case of mistaken identity, though she did mouth 'fuckity-fuck' over Rakesh's shoulder at me.

"Let me go." Mama Rama wrenched free of Rakesh's grasp and straightened like a cobra ready to strike—with the same amount of venom in her eyes, directed at me.

"How could you do this to my son? He's a good boy, a respectful boy." A bony finger jabbed at my face and Drew cuddled me closer. "You've brought shame on our family and yours, you ungrateful girl. And you, Mr. Drew."

She shook her head in a sorrowful gesture though her glare lost none of its poison. "What have you done?"

Mama Rama collapsed at our feet, beating her chest and setting up a wail that could rival the loudest NYPD siren.

"Shit," I muttered, while Rakesh, stunned, stared at his mother prostrate in front of us.

Senthil, who I'd only just noticed in the background alongside Pooh, Diva, and Shrew, stepped forward simultaneously with Rakesh and drew Mama to her feet.

"Mom, this isn't what you think." Rakesh shot me an apologetic glance. It soothed my conscience at perpetuating this lie but didn't do much for my stinging cheek. "Let me explain."

"No. I don't want to hear." Mama waved him away, clutching onto Senthil like a New York princess latches onto the last Birkin. "This is too much. She has brought disgrace on our family. I knew we shouldn't have come."

Her dramatic sob bordered on staged. "We traveled all this way to meet Amrita's parents and what do we find? Debauchery." The sobs increased. "Disgusting."

She clung to Senthil, darting deadly glares at me as he held her close, murmuring platitudes.

"Mom, listen to me — "

"Who are you?" Mama ignored Rakesh and turned her attention to Rita, her puzzled frown deepening. "And why were you kissing my son? Chi, chi, chi," she clucked in disgust, her horrified gaze swinging among the four of us.

I held my breath as Rita stepped forward, placed her hands together, and gave a deferential little bow. "I'm Amrita Muthu, *Mathaji*. I've lied to you and it's no fault of my friend's. I'm sorry for all this trouble. It's my doing and I'd like a chance to explain and beg your forgiveness."

Beg? Since when did the sassy Rita I know beg? Or call the cow Mom?

To give her credit, she'd hit the right subservient note because Mama deflated.

"What's this nonsense?" Mama glared at me like I was the bad guy while risking uncertain glances in Rita's direction.

"Mom, she's right." Rakesh stepped forward and draped an arm around Rita's shoulders. "Though I'm not going to let her take the blame for this. It's my fault for not telling you the truth."

Rita stared at Rakesh with adoration and I was seriously impressed he wanted to be the fall guy for her scheme. Must be love.

Drew cleared his throat with a discreet cough. "Why don't we sit down, have a cup of tea, and sort this out?"

Freaking British. Thinking they could solve the world's problems with a cup of tea. In this case, I happened to agree with him. We could all do with a calming brew.

"Good idea." I stayed clear of Mama's hard hand as I led the way to the trestle in a corner of the marquee.

The motley crew in our very own Bollywood drama followed, though I could hear Mama's furious mutterings disparaging all Indian kids in general, and her daughters' low buzz as they assimilated the news.

"Why don't you leave this to Rita and Rakesh to clear up?" Drew pulled me aside as we reached the food. "You're due on set in five minutes."

Damn. I'd been so swept up in the drama I'd forgotten my film debut and a chance at the easiest grand I'd ever get. I glanced at the clock, torn between wanting to flee or stick around and watch the fun.

The latter won out.

"I've got eight minutes and, realistically, round two between Mama versus the world isn't going to last long. By the feral gleam in her eye, a TKO is on the cards."

Drew chuckled as he arranged cups and saucers. "Who's going to wear the technical knockout? You, Rita, or her golden boy son?"

"We're all going down, though I'll be damned if I lay on the canvas. I'm going out swinging."

"Shari—"

I ignored Drew's warning and swung back to face the maddening crowd, pasting a confident smile on my face. "Anyone for *chai?*"

The Rama clan had discovered the truth earlier than expected and in less than ideal circumstances, considering Drew had been all over me and their son had been playing tonsil hockey with a girl they didn't know. However, there was an upside. Rakesh and Rita had been coasting along, not making any tough decisions about their future, and this would change all that. Mama would see to it—and how.

"I don't want *chai*, I want the truth." Mama stopped in front of Rakesh, who hadn't released a shell-shocked Rita. "And I want it now."

I caught a quick flash of fear in Rita's eyes. Not that I could blame her, considering Mama's fighting stance: rigid neck, folded arms, feet apart, braced for confrontation, an angry Sumo ready for action.

As Rakesh opened his mouth to respond, Rita placed a finger over his lips and shook her head. "I need to do this. Please."

I'd never seen a guy melt but Rakesh did, his tall frame

softening and all the tension seeping out of him at one, simple touch. That, combined with Rita's absolute devotion told me these guys would make it. Love, marriage, kids, the works. A lump formed in my throat as I blinked back tears.

Dammit, I wished they'd get this over with. I had a film to star in—who said being an extra had gone to my head?—and I didn't have time for a makeup repair job beforehand.

"I'm sorry, *Mathaji*. It's my fault. I didn't want to marry your son so I sent my friend, Shari, to India in my place. I wanted her to break off the engagement and sever all ties with your family. However, once she met you all, she couldn't go through with it. You're such a loving family and Rakesh impressed her so much she knew I had to meet him."

I gawked at Rita but she refused to look my way. Lucky, considering we would split our sides at the bullshit she was shoveling. Not that her lie was too far off the mark—the bit about Rakesh was spot-on. As for the Banana-Ramas being a loving family, I'd rather be raised in a nest of vipers than surrounded by Mama and her three cohorts.

"I'm sorry for my deception. I need you to forgive me because I love your son very much and—"

"You love me?" Rakesh gripped Rita's arms and swung her to face him. "You mean it?"

"You know I do." Rita's whispered response had everyone leaning forward to hear it.

The happy couple fell into each other's arms and sealed their love with a scorching kiss. Drew, Papa, and I clapped (guess the movie buffs in this crowd? Suckers for a happy ending every time), Mama's expression softened, and the girls smiled.

Drew tapped his Rolex in front of my face. "Four minutes."

"Thanks." With determination I ignored the butterflies free-falling in my stomach as I fiddled with the sleeves of my *salwar kameez*. "Do I look okay?"

"You're gorgeous." He dropped a lingering kiss on my lips. "Now go break a leg. I'll be out in a second."

Casting one last look at the Rama drama, I waved and dashed out of the marquee, heading for Pravin and my date with film destiny.

· · ·

My screen presence dazzled Pravin so much he plucked me from the forty extras in his Central Park sequence and thrust me into the limelight, pledging to make me a superstar.

In my dreams.

Instead, my film debut—and encore performance, as I didn't see many job opportunities for an inexperienced extra in Indian films in New York—was anticlimactic as I waited for an hour, watching the *masterji* (dance master) put his lead charges through their paces. He bellowed orders, flapped his arms, and performed too many obscene hip-thrusting moves, a bad cross between Elvis and JLO.

As I waited for my shot at stardom, I watched a scene being filmed. Things became interesting when the hero did a bit of *chamcha*—which literally means tablespoon—and 'tablespooned' himself quite snugly around another gorgeous heroine. I guess she didn't like what he'd had for lunch because the closer he got, the more she shrugged, elbowed, and shoved him away. Probably exes. Or maybe he attended the Anjali school of curry consumption where garlic seemed to be the primary ingredient.

When it was my turn, I hid in the last row of a large, clapping chorus that cheered as the hero and heroine rode off in a horse-drawn carriage. The scene shot in five takes, nice and quick according to the dancer next to me (an expert in these matters, considering this was her tenth extra's role—she'd slept with the cameraman).

Rita, Rakesh, and the Ramas hadn't waited around, not that I'd expected them to, and as I came off set Drew welcomed me with open arms.

"You were brilliant."

I snuggled into him, thrilled he'd shown up and stuck around until the end, knowing I shouldn't feel this good wrapped in his arms. Yet going with the flow regardless. This was the new, improved Shari, remember? My resolve faded into oblivion the minute his lips brushed mine.

"That good, huh?"

"Better." He draped an arm around my shoulders and led me toward the makeshift dressing room. "Have I told you how sexy you look in that Indian getup?"

"No." I batted my eyelashes, loving the falsies the makeup artist had pasted between my own. They'd fall off in the next few weeks but in the meantime I intended on making the most of the only enhanced part of my body. "You have a thing for Indian girls, huh?"

"I've lived in the country on and off for the last five years, so you tell me."

"I'm only half-Indian, remember? That still turn you on?"

His lips nuzzled the tender skin beneath my ear and I shuddered with expectation.

And fear. Deeply-submerged, soul-destroying fear that watching Drew walk away would tear me apart.

It shouldn't feel like this. I'd known what I was getting into at the start: liking a guy who traveled extensively but was based in Mumbai and London, two cities that couldn't be farther from NYC if they tried. It should've been easy: having fun, growing closer, saying good-bye.

I'd known the fantasy would end in the next few weeks. So why did the thought of losing Drew leave me absolutely petrified?

"Everything about you turns me on, Miss Jones. How about we head back to my place and I show you exactly how much?"

His eyes, the exact color of the clear Manhattan sky today, gleamed with wicked intent and I smiled.

"You're on." I slipped my hand into his, quashing my fears, eradicating my doubts, focusing on the moment. "And if you're really lucky I'll keep this outfit on just for you."

He growled. "Don't expect to keep it on for long."

I laughed. "Let's go."

We strolled through the park hand-in-hand, two people with loads in common, living worlds apart.

Life sucked.

Big time.

• • •

We headed to Drew's *place*, the penthouse suite at The Plaza.

I sure knew how to pick them; I just couldn't hold onto them.

In the week since we'd started sleeping together—not that you could call what we did during nocturnal hours sleeping—I'd stayed over once, only to be freaked out by the butler ironing all my clothes (lingerie included) and blown away by room service, which managed to find us authentic *samosas* and *ladoos* at two a.m.

We'd barely made it to the suite clothes intact when a call

came through for Drew. Considering how often his damn cell had interrupted us, the timing of being an IT/media mogul/high-flyer left a lot to be desired.

He winced and covered the phone with his hand. "Sorry, have to take this. Conference call between CEOs in London, Mumbai, and here."

"How long will it take?" I pretend pouted while toying with the neckline of my top, enjoying the carnal gleam in his eyes as they riveted to my breasts beneath.

"I'll make it snappy." He winked and headed into the office off the main room while I sat on an elegant chaise longue and flipped through the latest edition of *Vogue*, trying to ignore the irrational niggle of worry I would never be a priority in this guy's life.

I turned a few pages when the doorbell rang and I hoped it wasn't Bert the butler returning to iron more panties. When the door didn't open via Bert's key card, I crossed the floor to answer it. "May I help you?"

Drew's visitor didn't respond. She gawked at my outfit, not liking what she saw if the tiny wrinkles on the bridge of her aristocratic nose were any indication.

I placed her in her mid-seventies, with an arrogant air that came with old money. Her powder-blue suit with cream lace inlay screamed Chanel and the gorgeous matching bag and shoes were Prada—I'd drooled over them in the window the other day. With her coiffed pale blonde hair, powdered face, and disapproving frown, she looked like a cross between the queen and Barbara Walters.

"Do you have the right room?" I prompted, secretly relieved Queenie had knocked on the door and not some tall, voluptuous blonde. If Drew had to have visitors, I'd prefer old and wrinkly to young and perky any day.

"Is Drew Lansford in?" Her toff English accent sounded a hundred times more stuck-up than Drew's, and she tilted her nose higher and clutched her purse tighter as if I were a bag-snatcher.

Queenie thought I was scum? Two could play this game.

"He might be. Who should I say is calling?" My imitation of a posh accent was lousy at best and Queenie didn't seem impressed.

"His mother."

Oh shit.

His mother. Two words guaranteed to strike fear into any girl's heart, especially if aforementioned girl was bonking buddies with the uptight mother's son. And if aforementioned girl had just tried to rip off Mother's posh accent.

Shit, shit, shit.

"Please come in." I tried my best apologetic smile and threw the door open, stepping aside to let Her Majesty in.

Drew's mother—I couldn't think of her as a mom because "mom" implied warm and friendly, two things this woman definitely wasn't—sailed across the threshold without a backward glance, leaving a powerful waft of Christian Dior's Dune behind her.

She surveyed the room, ascertained Drew wasn't hiding behind the plush velvet drapes, and turned back to me. "Where's my son?"

"Taking a business call. He shouldn't be long."

"Oh."

How Queenie could instill so much disapproval into one tiny syllable I'd never know.

"Would you care for some tea?" I said, sounding like the

subservient serf she obviously thought I was.

"No, thank you."

So much for the universal English icebreaker.

"Please sit down and make yourself comfortable."

Ignoring my forced smile, she perched on the edge of the couch, clutching her bag and eyeing me with barely concealed contempt.

Jeez, and I'd thought posing as Rita for Mama Rama had been tough.

"It's a pleasure to meet you, Mrs. Lansford. I'm Shari Jones, a friend of Drew's." I lied about the pleasure bit but I had to say something to fill the uncomfortable silence. As for introductions, Queenie didn't seem too thrilled to have anything to do with me but I needed to be polite if only for Drew's sake. No point alienating another member of his fan club.

"It's Lady Lansford," she said, disapproval radiating from blue eyes so much like her son's.

Lady? As in a real, honest-to-God title?

Holy-schmoly… did that mean Drew was a lord?

My mind reeled with the implications while my heart ached.

I'd opened up to Drew like I never had with any other guy. Sadly, he hadn't reciprocated.

How could he withhold something so important from me? And what other secrets was he harboring?

With my opinion of Drew shredded, I stood rigid, not daring to move for fear of cracking the emotional shell I'd quickly constructed to show his mom nothing she said surprised me.

"Why are you dressed like that? By your accent, you're American, and Shari Jones doesn't sound Indian."

It was the longest speech she'd made to date and I should've been pleased. Instead, her tone dripped icicles and I suppressed a shiver.

"My mother's Indian, my father American." I cast furtive glances at the closed office door, silently praying Drew would appear any moment. "My outfit's a costume from a movie I was in today."

Hopefully that would impress the old bat. Having to justify what I was wearing to someone I'd just met, Drew's mother or not, sucked.

"A movie?" The wrinkles on her nose increased as if I'd divulged my occupation as brothel madam.

"Yes, one of Drew's, actually."

"That explains it." She crossed her arms tighter over her bag, glaring at me like I'd stolen the Crown jewels.

"Explains what?" I shouldn't have asked, I really shouldn't have, but something behind Queenie's eyes, a cunning, knowing glint, prompted me to do it.

"Your presence here. I've heard you movie people will sleep with anyone to get ahead and obviously you see my son as a meal ticket."

Blood roared through my ears and I saw red. Spiteful cow. Where did she get off accusing me of something like that? She didn't even know me. While I hadn't heard any rumors at work, I'd wondered if people had whispered the same thing about me while I'd been with Tate. Even if they had I probably would've ignored it, content in my self-delusion I deserved an apartment, designer stuff, and a cushy job. I would've justified it with any number of excuses: it was none of their business; they didn't understand our relationship, they were jealous. When in reality I knew how it must've looked: that I'd been sleeping my way to a free ride, and having my reputation tarnished irked as much as the lies he'd told.

It drove me every day, the urge to stand on my own feet, to re-establish my life and take control on *my* terms. This acting gig had been the first step and she'd just defiled it.

"His dalliance with you means nothing. It's a man's instinct to dabble in the exotic before he settles down."

"What if Drew wants to *settle down* with me?"

Drew and I hadn't contemplated getting serious but I needed to wipe away Queenie's smug expression—before I throttled her.

She laughed, a brittle, empty tinkle that made the hair on my nape stand on end. "Don't be ridiculous. As if he would settle for a jumped-up, trashy, half-caste like you."

Hurt, swift and unexpected, stabbed through my deliberate indifference, and I gritted my teeth until they ached rather than let her see how her blatant racism shocked me. I might've been gobsmacked but there was no way I'd let the prejudiced bitch know.

Aware calmness would rile her further, I aimed for demure. "Maybe you don't know your son as well as you think you do."

Her frosty glare warned I hadn't dented her confidence, while mine reeled from her rudeness. "On the contrary, it's you who don't know him very well. This...thing"—she waved her hand at me and made an unattractive little moue with her mouth—"you have with my son will finish soon, make no mistake."

"What makes you so sure?"

"The fact Drew is marrying Amelia Grayhart."

Triumph glittered in her cold blue eyes as I gripped the back of the chair for support. "Amelia's English and a woman of Drew's class."

Drew's engaged.

Shock swept through me, blurring my vision, making my insides churn and my body shake. I wanted to hate him. I wanted to castrate him. Until I dragged in a deep breath and clarity returned.

Jumping to conclusions was exactly what this bigot wanted and I'd be damned if I gave up on Drew without giving him a chance to explain. I'd given Tate the same courtesy and while he hadn't deserved it, as it turned out, Drew did.

They were nothing alike. I hoped.

"Make no mistake, Amelia and Drew are marrying. Soon. Why do you think he's still in town?"

"For work, the movie he's backing."

"You're deluded. He finances movies. He never stays around for the filming." Her mouth twisted into a bitter smile. "Amelia's in town, has been for weeks. That's the reason he's in New York—the *only* reason."

I wanted to give Drew the benefit of the doubt. I wanted to trust my new and improved instincts. But old habits died hard, and his xenophobic mom had unerringly arrowed in on every latent insecurity I'd ever had about this relationship.

I'd secretly worried I wasn't good enough for Drew. Discovering he had a title only exacerbated those feelings of unworthiness.

But what really cut deep was the fact he hadn't told me.

If he'd lied about that, surely an impending engagement to some uppity bitch could be a possibility?

Sick to my stomach, I stood there, torn between wanting to flee and confronting him the moment he stepped into the room.

She glared at my outfit through narrowed eyes, her obvious distaste making me bristle. "You mean nothing to him. My son has an unnatural fascination for India, and you're another tacky plaything he acquired from there. A used, soon to be discarded, tacky plaything."

I could've thrown the Ming vase near my right hand or pummeled her with a Versace cushion lying plump and ready on the chair in front of me. Instead, she made my decision to leave or stay easier.

I straightened my shoulders, walked stiffly to the door and opened it, blinking back furious tears. The classy thing to do would be to march out, slam the door, and never look back. However, Queenie had tarred me with a *tacky* brush, why not live up to it?

I eyeballed her, three words I never would've dreamed saying to anyone older than me, let alone Drew's mother, rolling off my tongue.

"Racist old bitch."

I slammed the door on the way out.

CHAPTER TWELVE

"You called her a racist old bitch? Way to go." Rita lolled on the couch like an ad for all things spicy in her cerise sari, gold flashing at her ears, neck, and wrists as she dipped a Chili Dorito into jalapeño salsa.

After I'd sent out an SOS call she'd headed straight for my place following a successful dinner with her mother-out-law and the rest of the Banana-Ramas.

"I'm guessing that's not what has you this upset?"

I shook my head, bile rising at the thought of Drew's deception. What was the attraction for me with lying, cheating scum?

"Drew's engaged." Saying it out loud made it more final, more hurtful, more *everything*.

"What?" Rita's hand hovered halfway to her mouth, a perfect surprised O.

"You heard me." I pointed to a jalapeño about to land unceremoniously in her lap and she quickly shoved the Dorito and salsa chip sandwich she'd made into her mouth without spilling a drop.

She chewed quickly, her eyes bulging with a shock mirroring mine.

"Guess his mom was right. I was his foray into multiculturalism before going for the pure thing."

"Don't." Rita jabbed a Revlon-tipped finger at me. "Don't you dare go down that path. His mom was talking through her ass and if you buy into it, she wins."

"This isn't a competition," I said, picking up the nearest cushion and hugging it to my chest. Pitiful protection for my shattered heart. "If it were, I'd walk around with a big fat L tattooed on my forehead and be done with it."

"I'm not joining your pity party. Give me all the facts about this so-called engagement. Who's the lucky lady?"

"Amelia Greyhart."

"*The* Amelia Greyhart?" Rita's sculpted brows shot skyward as I sagged farther at the news she'd heard of her.

"Freaking great. You know Amelia?"

Rita laughed and clapped her hands like a three-year-old sculling red soda for an entire afternoon. "You could say that. I manage her account at the store and boy, does that woman know how to shop. Do you know, she spends more on—"

"As riveting as I find the bimbo's spending habits, could you save it for someone who cares?"

Rita continued to laugh. "Hang on, I haven't got to the good bit yet. You know who she regularly shops with and is almost engaged to?"

I screwed up my eyes, tapped my temple, and slapped the side of my head. "Uh, wild guess, Drew Lansford, greatest British prick of all time?"

Rita shook her head, the soft tinkling of gold at her ears

reminding me of the one time I'd worn similar earrings—impersonating her—and the first fateful meeting that night at the Rama welcoming party in Mumbai. Maybe Kapil the soothsayer had a point? I'd had a decision to make and boy, had I botched it big-time.

"It's not Drew. Amelia has bigger fish to fry."

Staring at Rita's smug face, I wondered if I'd done the right thing in calling her. Maybe I should've buried my head in a tub of ice cream for the next few hours before taking a Valium or three.

My best 'I'm not in the mood to play' glare must've worked because she sobered up fast. "Amelia and some Bieber clone?" She entwined her index and middle finger. "Like this."

Disbelief shot through me as I sat bolt upright and dropped the cushion. "If this is your way of cheering me up, forget it."

Justin Bieber was a *teenager,* so it stood to reason some wannabe would be young. As if Amelia freaking Greyhart, Lady Muck's choice of bride for her son, would have a boy toy. Or be remotely serious about him.

"It's true. Everyone at Bergdorf's sees them shopping together whenever they're in town. They're all over each other. And Kelly in cosmetics told Krista in perfumes she'd overheard them discussing carats for an engagement ring. How much more proof do you need?" Rita made a clawing action with both hands and mouthed, "Cougar."

I wanted to laugh but even if Rita's far-fetched tale had a semblance of truth to it, the fiasco with Drew's mom had given me a much-needed wake-up call. She'd mistaken me for some wannabe starlet sleeping her way to the top and had tried to drive me away. A typical overprotective mom I could understand. I could even dismiss the engagement as being wishful thinking on her interfering part. But the fact he had a title and he hadn't told me? Uh-uh. Unacceptable.

He'd lied about his identity and after Tate I'd had a gutful of dishonesty. Besides, according to Lady Muck, a high-and-mighty Lord would marry someone of his class. Someone worlds away from me.

Not that I'd contemplated marriage, but hey, I'm a single gal approaching thirty and I had, very briefly, linked Shari and Lansford together to see how the names sounded. It didn't mean anything. Every female over the age of five did it with any guy she liked.

"If that's true, how come I haven't read about it? I've never heard of her."

"Trust me on this. Drew isn't engaged. Rakesh would've told me." Rita blushed at the mention of Lover Boy and I silently applauded. At least one of us had the happily-ever-after we'd always scoffed at.

"He tells you everything?"

Her blush deepened. "Yeah, he does."

"Lucky you." I swallowed my bitterness, remembering the sweet things Drew had done—serving me dinner, protecting my back as we walked through peak-hour crowds, opening doors. Little things that added up to make him the wonderful guy I thought he was. I'd assumed we were developing the type of connection that invited confidences. Sadly, the small things and the closeness I'd treasured had been a sham.

Rita moved to sit next to me, draped an arm over my shoulders, and gave me a hug. "Rakesh likes you. Says you're one of the few women he knows he can call a friend and if Drew was contemplating an engagement, he wouldn't have let him within two feet of you. You know that."

I managed a mute nod, recognizing a glimmer of truth behind what Rita said. Rakesh was one of the good guys and I felt the same way about him. But Drew was his business partner and best buddy—did guys share confidences the way girls did? Doubtful.

Rita released me, a deep frown slashing her brow as she glared, bearing a strong family resemblance to Anjali at her scariest.

"There's only one way to clear up this mess—"

"I'm not talking to Drew."

Rita might be right, but the way I was feeling, facing the guy I'd grown way too attached to wasn't an option. I needed some time to gather my thoughts, plan my approach, and steel my nerve to make a clean, swift break.

Rita squeezed my hand. "You need to confront him."

Perfectly logical advice. Shame I'd lost rational reason around the time I'd succumbed to Bollywood Boy's first kiss.

"You're right but I need time. Get myself together. Think up a suitable apology for calling Lady Muck a bitch."

"Don't you dare apologize for that." She puffed up like an outraged peacock and I loved her for it. "From your description of her views, I'm surprised Drew loves India so much."

"Do you agree with your parents' view on arranged marriages?"

"Point taken," she said, gnawing at her bottom lip at the mention of marriage.

"What's with the coyness?"

She glanced away, but there was no hiding her dopey grin. "I was going to tell you but maybe now isn't the right time?"

"Tell me what?" I leaned forward, eager to latch onto any news to take my mind off my own misery. Besides, I had an inkling. Kapil, eat your heart out.

"Rakesh and I are getting married."

I screamed and grabbed Rita, hugging the life out of her as we alternated between sobbing, laughing, and squealing. I released her and dabbed at my eyes, gritty as if sandpaper had been rasped across them since I'd walked out of The Plaza two hours ago. "I'm so happy for you."

"Crazy, huh? I send you all the way to India to get me out of the marriage then I take one look at the guy and fall apart."

"Don't say I didn't warn you."

Memories of my time with Rakesh in India flashed through my mind and I smiled, pleased one of my hunches had panned out. As for the other involving Drew and me and a chance at a real relationship… one out of two ain't bad.

"We haven't told our families yet so keep it quiet, okay?"

"I'm guessing the families already know. Wasn't it their idea in the first place?"

"Ha, bloody, ha."

Rita reached for a Dorito and crunched it, a flicker of doubt shadowing her eyes before she blinked.

"What aren't you telling me?"

She sighed. "We want it to happen quickly, in a few weeks, and we want it here. No big Indian wedding, no hordes lingering over days of celebration—just a simple Hindu affair with my parents, his family, and you."

And Drew. Though Rita didn't say it, I knew Rakesh would invite his business partner, especially to a small intimate affair in a foreign city. Which meant I had to see him to clear the air before the wedding. So much for a clean break. Seeing him again had the potential to get messy.

The least I could do for my best friend who'd stood by

me through the traumatic months post-Toad. "So what's the problem?"

A tiny crease appeared between Rita's brows, doing little to mar her beauty. "You've met Mama Rama and you know my mom. Do you seriously think they're going to agree to a no-fuss wedding? Months have gone into the arranging, so do you think they're going to settle for a quickie at the Town Hall followed by a low-key reception at The Russian Tea Room?"

I remembered the force behind Mama Rama's slap all too clearly and I'd hate to think what she'd do to Rita if deprived of a chance to show off as mother of the groom. "Good point."

"We have a plan, though it's risky at best."

"Tell me." At least the intrigue had snapped me out of my funk. I'd stepped back into another Bollywood extravaganza, though thankfully I wouldn't have the lead role this time.

"My folks are due home any day and the Ramas are heading back to Mumbai. Both families want us to get married and Mama Rama is sucking up, thinking I'll get cold feet and ditch her son again. So we thought we'd give them an ultimatum. Either it happens our way now, or it doesn't happen at all."

"Think they'll go for it?" Doubt spiraled through me. Anyone who'd seen Rakesh and Rita together could see how crazy they were for each other. To believe they wouldn't get married at some point in the future would require a serious suspension of belief. Then again, both families were fixated with Bollywood films so it might not be such a big leap for them to make.

Rita quirked an eyebrow and struck a pose. "You think you're the only one with acting talent around here? Wait 'til you see me give Rakesh the cold shoulder and watch Mama Rama fold like a deck of cards."

I chuckled, the sound of my laughter a welcome surprise. When I'd left Drew's suite I felt like I'd never laugh again. "If you need anything, let me know."

Rita's smile waned. "There is one thing."

"What?"

"Mama Rama needs a pedicure before the wedding and I told her you'd be perfect for the job."

"Bitch." I grabbed a handful of Doritos and pelted her as we tussled, laughing until our sides ached.

• • •

Drew called.

Eight times, to be precise.

Four on the home phone, four on my cell.

Very even, very precise, very British. His messages ranged from polite and cool to annoyed and deranged, the last one something like this: *"Shari. This is insane. You cut out on me because my mother drops in for a visit? I know the battle-axe comes across a bit strong but I thought we had something. Surely you can tolerate her for a little while? Anyway, call me."*

He thought I should *tolerate* the old bag? See? Deranged.

When I didn't return his calls that night, he arrived around midnight, ringing the buzzer like a man possessed. I could've let him up but what would be the point? I hadn't formulated what I wanted to say, let alone mentally rehearsed it, and I knew the minute I saw him my hormones would go crazy and start ruling my head again.

I needed space. Space to let my head start talking sense to the rest of my traitorous body and I prayed it made a damn good argument.

Even if the Amelia engagement farce was a ruse Lady Muck

used to get rid of me, Drew had lied to me. He was a Lord. A real, honest-to-goodness, ten-foot-up-himself Lord, and no matter how close we got, how far this relationship went, I couldn't see Lady Muck welcoming a half-caste Lady Lansford into the family.

Half-caste.

Racist old bitch.

I cringed in the darkness as the buzzer eventually silenced, wondering if Lady Muck told Drew about our fond farewell. Being raised to respect my elders, I wasn't proud of my departing line. Then again, who said I had to take shit from a stuck-up meow like her?

I'd take a day or two, marshal my thoughts, set a plan of action, and stick to it.

Then why the sinking feeling in my belly that going through with this plan might be the hardest thing I'd ever have to do? "Plan" being the operative word as, lying on my bed with the blinds pulled up and moonlight spilling through the sheer chiffon drapes and speckling the ceiling, I had no idea what this so-called grand plan would entail. If Rita was right and the engagement thing wasn't true, he deserved a chance to explain the title. It's the least I could do.

My cell beeped.

I ignored the text message for two seconds before curiosity got the better of me. Eight calls, a personal visit — which must've damaged the buzzer by persistence — and a text. Not bad.

Rolling over, I grabbed the cell off the bedside table and checked the message.

U & I NEED 2 TALK.
PLEZ CALL.

BB 4 MJ.
MA.B. 4 EVER?

I scrolled through the message several times, having no control over my easily pleased heart that leaped at his cuteness. The 'Bollywood Boy for Miss Jones, maybe forever?' struck hard.

Guys didn't talk about tomorrow, let alone the future, yet here was my lying lord tugging on my heartstrings with inferences about forever.

What did forever mean to him? I'd be forever available whenever he lobbed into town? I'd be forever waiting for something more, something he couldn't give? Waiting was for suckers. For women without confidence. For women with low self-esteem and high expectations who ended up middle-aged and still waiting.

That wasn't me. Not anymore.

I should call him.

Don't you dare! screamed my voice of reason.

He's been pretty persistent.

So? Let him sweat.

He's sweet to be this concerned.

You think he's sweet on you? Forget it. He's after one thing while he's in town. That forever crap is B.S. Remember when Mom said 'why buy the cow when you can get the milk for free?'

"Shut the hell up," I said, tired of arguing with my voice of reason. I rolled onto my side, clutching the cell like a lucky talisman and toying with the touchpad.

Technically, sending a reply text wouldn't count as calling.

Emotionally, what happened to time-out and my grand plan?

Logically, I owed him some kind of explanation for my lunatic dash, seeing as Mommy Dearest hadn't enlightened him.

Mentally, I didn't have a hope of getting any sleep if I didn't do something right now to bridge the wide chasm between us, even if it was only to kick him hard and swiftly up the ass.

Mind made up, I punched in a reply before I chickened out.

GIVE ME A FEW DAYS.
C U THEN.
BTW, 4 EVER 2 LONG.

Stabbing the *send* button, the text whizzed through cyberspace—or wherever the bizarre little letters ended up flying through—before crash-landing on Drew's screen. My message might not have the same punch as his but at least I'd been honest.

The new and improved Shari had starred in a Bollywood film (starred being a slight exaggeration, but Pravin said I'd struck a very evocative pose in the rear chorus), been stalked for my beauty (so the Lone Ranger needed his eyes checked; nice sentiment all the same), and done the horizontal mambo with Hugh (tragic to fantasize about doing it with a movie star but I swear it only happened once and Drew looked so much like Hugh right at THE moment I couldn't help myself).

The new me was a vast improvement on the old Toad-trampled mess I'd been before India.

The cell buzzed in my hand and I swore this would be the last time I'd check it before switching off. If I didn't want to talk to Drew, I sure as hell didn't want to waste time texting him like an adolescent.

W/OUT U 2 LONG.
CALL ME.
I'LL W8.

Short and sweet.

I hit the cell's *off* button, wondering if he would wait. Did he truly believe forever was too long without me? Or did he want another fix of milk before he dumped the cow and returned to greener pastures?

I closed my eyes, willing sleep. Nada. Why the heck was Drew talking about forever? Especially when I'd run out on him like a madwoman and refused to take his calls? Could he really feel something for me?

May be plausible, but the image of Lady Muck's distaste as she surveyed me from head to foot burned into my retinas. She knew nothing about me but on first appearances, I wasn't good enough for her lordly son. Judgmental, narrow-minded and bigoted? Hell yeah. But the fact I still hadn't found a job and was living in a short-term apartment rankled.

Drew might not care about those things but his mom did, and if we moved past this, what hope did I have for a long-term future without more to offer?

With an exasperated grunt, I rolled onto my stomach, grabbed my netbook from the bedside table, and flipped it open. I'd bookmarked countless job application sites and had enlisted with several job agencies. The call-backs kept coming, but no offers. Right now, that Subway sandwich artist position looked tempting.

I giggled at the thought of Lady Muck's expression if her precious boy dated a bread-butterer, scanning my inbox in the vain hope I'd landed an executive assistant position with Donald Trump. I scrolled down, past spam for million-dollar Nigerian lottery winnings and penis enlargements before spying the subject header JOB APPLICATION. Nothing extraordinary considering I'd emailed a ton of them, but what set this one apart was the sender.

Viand Magazine. Newly launched glossy travel mag focusing on food and featuring real-life reports from travelers roaming the world. A magazine I'd had a call-back interview for, an interview I'd bluffed my way through with countless tales of my Mumbai adventures and Indian recipes I'd cohesively blended together in my first official article.

My finger cramped over the mouse pad and I flexed it a few times before opening the email.

Dear Ms. Jones,

Following your successful interviews and well-formatted article, we're pleased to offer you a trial position as a contributor to Viand Magazine. We were particularly impressed with the food angle of your piece and would like that to be the focus of your articles during the two-week trial period.

While this is not an offer of permanent work, we will be happy to reevaluate the situation at the end of your trial with the hope to extend your contract.

Please present to human resources next Monday, where your trial will be discussed in greater detail.

All the best,
Jorg Lundgren, Editor-in-Chief, *Viand Magazine*

I reread the email three times before leaping off the bed and doing a hip-swaying, shoulder-shimmying, happy dance.

I'd done it. Landed a trial at a hip magazine, one I had every intention of nailing. The highlight? It was an occupation out of my comfort zone, away from boring legal dissertations, and encapsulating two of my new favorite things: travel and food.

I pinched myself, registered pain, and didn't give a shit.

I had a potential new career.

A freaking fantastic potential new profession.

Might not be much of a step up from Lady Muck's wannabe starlet but to me it was a giant leap. Today, fledgling magazine contributor, tomorrow J.K. Rowling.

Okay, so the euphoria had gone to my head but come Monday, my first day on trial, I intended on kicking some serious literary ass. If one considered travel ramblings and recipes literary.

Regardless, I'd be there. Polishing my prose. Reciting recipes. Kowtowing to the editor-in-chief. Doing whatever it took to get this job and be able to confront Drew with my head held high.

• • •

"Shari, my girl."

I staggered back as Anjali, her arms laden with Punjab Sweet Shop boxes, bowled into the apartment two days later, the familiar garlic/curry powder odor hitting me like a blast straight from Mumbai.

She deposited the boxes on the hallway table and turned to face me with a wide grin. "You're way too skinny again, like when you first arrived in India. You need flesh on your bones and I have just the thing."

She ripped the seal off the top box and offered me a piece of cashew *halwa*, guaranteed to add a pound or three with the first bite. "I brought *ladoos* and *barfi* and *gulub jamuns*, plus all your favorites."

She thrust the box under my nose—which trembled at the decadently sweet smell like a rabbit scenting a juicy carrot—and I took the smallest piece to pacify her. I hadn't said a word since opening the door but she hadn't noticed, keeping up a steady stream as always.

"Isn't it wonderful news about Amrita and Rakesh? I'm thrilled they flew me out for the wedding. It's going to be something special." Her eyes misted as she stuffed a piece of *halwa* into her mouth, licking crumbs off her fingers.

I had to agree with her about the wedding. The happy couple had pulled off the coup of the century. They'd convinced their parents the wedding would take place in New York. The wedding would be a small, intimate affair. And soon—much to the horror of Mama Rama, who'd thrown a classic hissy fit before ungraciously capitulating.

I was thrilled for the lovebirds and looking forward to attending my first Hindu wedding.

"What about you, Shari dear? Have you and young Drew got it on yet?"

Anjali grinned like a benevolent god and sat on the couch as I choked on the last bite of *halwa*, shocked that:

a) she knew I had a thing for Drew and it had been obvious in Mumbai, and

b) she knew a phrase like 'get it on.'

Tossing the end of her ochre sari over one shoulder, she fired a glare that meant business. "You thought I didn't notice the way you two looked at each other? I may be old but I'm not blind. I remember that feeling. The spark, the electricity... "

I had to interject before I got the unabridged version of *Anjali Does Mumbai*.

"Have you been talking to Rita?"

Her shifty sideways glance was a dead giveaway she'd probably heard the entire sorry tale from my best friend and wanted to voice her opinion. "No."

"It's complicated," I said, a small part of me admiring

Drew's patience in waiting until I contacted him, impressed he'd respected my wishes. While the rest of me wavered between being downright peeved he hadn't continued to bombard me with calls and convinced his mom had been correct. About everything.

"What a load of nonsense. When a handsome young man is chasing you, why hold him at bay? A week is long enough to make him sweat."

"How'd you know it was a week?"

Anjali rolled her eyes. "Maybe some of that charlatan soothsayer's powers rubbed off on me."

"You said he was phony, so how could he have powers?"

"Stop being so pedantic." She tsk-tsked. "If this is your attitude, no wonder you're having problems with Mr. Drew."

"Lord Drew," I corrected, instantly wanting to slice out my tongue as Anjali leaned so far forward she almost toppled off the couch.

"He's a *Lord*? Like Lord Louis Mountbatten?"

"Louis who?"

"The royal photographer. Loved India. Amazing man." Her eyes glazed for a second, lost in a golden memory before clearing and refocusing on me. She clapped her hands, her excitement almost infectious. "You're going to be a Lady!"

"Drew and I are friends, and that's as far as it goes, so quit it. You're as bad as Rita. And do you actually know the meaning of 'get it on'?"

"I'm not some hick from Mumbai." Anjali tilted her nose in the air as if affronted, and I grinned.

I'd missed this more than I thought; Anjali's consistently one-sided chats, her unwavering focus on guys, our banter. We'd connected in India like a real niece and aunt, something I didn't have, considering both my folks were only kids.

"Furthermore, you're going to listen to me." She took a deep breath, puffing out her chest like the cocky bantam rooster that used to wander into her yard every morning and scratch around for scraps. "You young people of today are clueless. You waste your time pretending not to like each other, trying to get out of relationships as hard as you try to get into them, dancing around the truth, and then complaining when it all falls apart."

"That's not true. Drew and I—"

"Let me finish." She made a zipping motion across her lips. Yeah, like that'd shut me up. "In my day, it wasn't so different. I wasted my one opportunity at true happiness and spent the rest of my life wishing I'd done things differently. Anu might be a bitch but she's smart, and in matters of the heart being nice gets you nowhere."

Confused by her backhanded reference to Anu's intelligence, I waited for her to elaborate. When she didn't and popped another piece of *halwa* into her mouth, I decided to confront the Anu mystery head on.

"What is it with you and Anu?"

Anjali's lips clamped tighter as she chewed.

Undeterred, I plowed on. "You said she stole from you?"

Halwa gone, Anjali sighed and nodded. "She stole the man I loved with her conniving lies and I'll never forgive her for it."

Definite grounds for an ongoing vendetta: broken heart, two women fighting over some stud. Another scene straight out of Bollywood.

"I loved Senthil with all my heart."

Senthil? Jeez, Rakesh had been right. Anjali had a thing for his dad. Wow. And I'd thought the flirting and studio visits had been innocent. Looked like I'd stepped into Act One, Scene Two of another drama. At least it took my mind off my personal production unfolding like a Cannes winner.

"What happened?"

Anjali leaned forward and for a second I thought I'd get to hear every last juicy detail. Instead, her lips compressed in a thin, angry line and she shook her head. "That bitch lied, cheated, and wormed her way into Senthil's family. She knew I loved him but it didn't matter. She became Mrs. Senthil Rama and I got the booby prize."

I'd seen photos of Anjali's husband hidden behind a plethora of framed pictures of Rita and her folks back at her place in Mumbai and had to agree. The guy had greasy black hair in a comb-over, crooked teeth, and a nose rivaling the Concorde. Poor Anjali. Senthil's handlebar moustache and expressive eyes would shape up well next to that.

"I already told you we were incompatible in every way. Then he ups and dies six years into our marriage, leaving me widowed and childless."

"I'm so sorry." Trite but true. Anjali deserved better, but before I could comfort her, she snapped her fingers. "If you love Mr. Drew, go out there, grab him with both hands, and don't let go. You do love him, don't you?"

Did I love him? I had no idea. What was love, apart from some nebulous emotion touted by romance writers and exploited by greeting card companies?

I'd thought I loved the Toad. I'd been wrong.

I'd had a few boyfriends, but love would be too strong to describe the attraction-waning-to-like-turning-to-blah of those relationships.

If love involved stomach-churning desire, losing my appetite, and feeling like part of me was missing when he wasn't around then yeah, I guess I was partway to being in love with Drew.

"Well, child? Are you in love with him?"

"I don't know."

Anjali wouldn't settle for blunt honesty. I could tell by the matchmaking gleam in her eyes. "You won't know if you keep ignoring him. Why don't you two talk? You'll see him at the wedding anyway, so the least you can do is clear the air before Amrita's big day. You never know, maybe a bit of matrimonial happiness might rub off on you."

"Not likely." I needed to distract Anjali before she had Drew and me halfway up the aisle. "Do you have any almond *barfi*? I'd kill for a piece."

Nodding, Anjali pulled out the second box from the bottom and ripped off the sealed wrapper before I could say *flee the ghee*.

I took a piece and nibbled on the ghee-laden delicacy while Anjali mumbled something sounding suspiciously like 'ring Drew, good husband material' as she tut-tutted under her breath. I pretended not to understand, smiling and nodding as if she spoke Hindi rather than English.

Anjali was right about one thing. I'd have to face Drew at the wedding next week and had scheduled a meeting for tomorrow. He'd be busy brokering a deal until then and I'd be busy plucking up courage for the confrontation.

We were from different worlds, different socioeconomic backgrounds, and as much as I'd like to think my cultural background didn't mean anything, in Drew's world it would. Not immediately, but what if I were to really fall, to love him unequivocally, only to find it meant more to him than me?

I couldn't do it. I wouldn't do it.

In a way, hearing about Anjali's failed romance with Senthil only exacerbated my feeling of inevitability. If their grand passion, arranged or otherwise, had failed, what hope did I have of succeeding with so many obstacles?

Maybe I was latching onto excuses to end it, maybe I was giving up without a fight, but I couldn't get in any deeper.

I had to make a clean break, do the 'let's be friends' speech, and act like it wasn't the hardest thing I'd had to do in a long time.

As if reading my mind, Anjali frowned mid-bite. "Call him."

"I will. Now, tell me about the wedding."

Predictably, she launched into an elaborate regaling of Rita's wedding plans as I listened with half an ear, nodding in all the right places, smiling and encouraging, while I mentally rehearsed what the hell I'd say to Drew.

CHAPTER THIRTEEN

I'd used up my bravado quota in organizing to meet Drew eight days after the Lady Muck showdown but had taken the wuss way out in arranging to rendezvous at the local Starbucks, of all places.

Brave? No.

Immature? Yes.

Hoping the caffeine would give me more of a buzz than seeing him again? Maybe.

I'd chosen neutral meeting ground for several reasons:

    a) The apartment held too many memories, most of them involving stripping and canoodling and doing it every which way, and I didn't need a reminder of how hot the guy was when he'd be right in front of me looking way too doable.

    b) A public forum was a safer option in case he wanted to shout at me for calling Lady Muck nasty names.

    c) I'd be less inclined to cry in public, a distinct possibility if he started spouting all that forever nonsense again.

d) I had intense cravings for Starbucks *chai*, a new addiction ranking alongside mojitos and cheesecake (extremely serious).

I sipped at my *chai* and snuggled into an oversized armchair nearest to the cake counter, people-watching. Students with their book-laden arms and bright-eyed enthusiasm, frazzled moms downing giant cappuccinos in record time while repeatedly glancing at their watches and talking in too-loud voices about lack of sleep and diaper brands, and businessmen sneaking away from the office, hiding behind newspapers, trying to look important but spoiling the effect by reading the funnies rather than the financial news.

Through this melting pot of New York Starbucks culture strode Drew, looking ten times better than I remembered. As he drew closer, his suit fitting like a well-made glove, his blue eyes so much brighter and sharper, his lopsided, uncertain grin made the *chai* slop sickeningly in my stomach. Make that a hundred times better.

Oh God. I still had it bad.

All my Oprah-like self talk, all the Dr Phil-isms to confront him, demand the truth, do what was right for me, etc.… would mean nothing in the face of Drew's inherent, natural ability to charm the pants off me. Literally.

Dragging in a deep breath, I squared my shoulders. I had to stand strong. I had to do this. For me.

"Thanks for coming," I rushed in, awkward and gauche and out of my depth as he leaned forward and brushed the faintest of kisses on my cheek.

The awkwardness vanished the moment his lips touched my skin, replaced by a surge of lust/like/affection (a startling combination of all three) that blindsided me quicker than Mama Rama's slap.

"You look great," he said, slipping into the armchair opposite—deliberately placed there by *moi*, not wanting to chance a stray encounter with his thigh brushing mine or his hand touching my arm as we talked.

"Thanks." Mortified, I felt the heat surging up my neck, burning my cheeks, a blazing signal to my utter sappiness when it came to this guy.

I'd aimed for a casual 'I don't care anymore and I'm not trying to impress you' look but pride had prompted me to wear my taupe Stella McCartney ensemble, the one Rita said made me look like a goddess. If I was going out in a blaze of glory, better show the guy what he'd be missing out on.

"Would you like another *chai*?" He pushed a spike of hair off his forehead in a familiar gesture, making my breath catch and my lungs seize.

Damn, this was going to be tough.

"That'd be great."

He smiled, no doubt amused by my scintillating conversation, which had consisted of 'thanks' and 'great' up to that point. I'd known this'd be hard but seeing Drew in his sexy, slightly mussed glory packed a powerful punch that had me staggering on the ropes.

While I struggled not to check out his butt as he ordered at the counter—and lost—I marshaled my thoughts. I should've been angrier, more confrontational from the get-go. Maybe the weeklong break hadn't been a good idea. All the anger and self-righteous indignation had leeched out of me.

"Here you go." He placed a cup of steaming, fragrant *chai* in front of me and pulled his chair around next to mine, undoing my carefully constructed no-physical-contact arrangement. Crap.

I smiled my thanks and picked up the tea, hoping to hide behind the cup while thinking of something fabulously witty or clever to say.

"Now we've got past the awkward stage, how about you tell me what the hell is going on?" His words didn't hold rancor and his expression appeared calm, though the shadows shifting and darkening his eyes made me wish I'd stuck to texting for this entire conversation.

"We're past the awkward stage? Could've fooled me."

"This doesn't have to be awkward." He sat back, his relaxed posture belied by the steely glint in his glare.

"You lied to me—"

"You ran out—"

We both stopped and I cringed at the all-around uneasiness. It wasn't getting any better. It would never get any better until I took the plunge and leapt in.

"You first," he said, sipping his Earl Grey. Pity tea, the British panacea for all ills, couldn't fix this situation.

"You lied to me. You're not just an IT magnate, you're a lord."

He didn't blink, didn't flinch, his coolness infuriating. "My title has nothing to do with my everyday life. I've never used it, probably never will unless I retire to Yorkshire and live out my days in a dilapidated old castle."

His attempt at honesty-cum-humor didn't help.

"You own a *castle*?"

"More like a decrepit pile of rocks that's been in my family for generations. Anyway, what's this got to do with us? We were having a good time, and the next thing I know Mother shows up and you won't speak to me."

I accepted his logic about the title, but I still didn't like the fact he was a lord and I'd never live up to familial expectations that went with it. Technically, he hadn't lied to me, he'd omitted to tell me everything about himself, not a crime as he knew next to nothing about me. Apart from vital things like how I liked my eggs in the morning—scrambled (and unfertilized), my addiction to *chai*, my love of films, my awakening interest in India and its mouth-watering cuisine. Trivial stuff, inconsequential stuff, stuff you didn't base a future on.

Then I remembered the way he'd rub my feet exactly how I liked it—firm pressure, no tickles—how he passed the condiments tray without my having to ask, how he soaped my back and washed my hair with tenderness in the shower, how we'd talk into the wee small hours, cuddled on the sofa, dissecting an old movie before agreeing to disagree.

I was deluding myself. He knew me, knew things about me no other man had, including Tate. That's why I'd been so pissed at the thought of him lying to me. I'd opened up, given him a part of myself, and he'd withheld. Not fair.

I deserved better.

"Did your mother tell you what we talked about?"

His lips thinned, drawing my attention to his mouth, reminding me of how damn good those lips were at navigating their way around my body. "She was pretty pissed, that's all I know." He grabbed my hand. Bad move. Catastrophic move, but I couldn't slip out of his grip no matter how hard I tugged. "Forget whatever she said."

"*Forget*?" My voice—along with my blood pressure—shot up like steam toward the ceiling from the nearby espresso machine and I snatched my hand out of his. "It's natural you'd defend her but you could at least hear me out."

Several people glanced our way and I calmed with effort,

digging my fingernails into the chair's leather to get a grip on my temper.

"I didn't mean to make light of the situation. I just want to put this behind us and move on."

"Move on to what? You're heading back to India soon. Or is it England, to marry your *fiancée*?"

"So that's what this is about." He took another infuriatingly slow sip of tea. "Let me guess. Mother mentioned her dream about me marrying Amelia and you jumped to all the wrong conclusions and have wasted a week of our time together because of it."

"Like you didn't know." Theoretically, I accepted Rita's logical explanation. Emotionally, it still bugged the crap out of me I hadn't heard the truth from him.

"I *didn't* know," he said, staring me in the eye, willing me to believe, yet I couldn't give in that easily.

"Then why haven't you pushed to tell me? You'd have to know I'd be upset to run out on you, yet you've been happy for me to call the shots, to wait around to hear why I was upset, to meet me *here* to do it?"

My irrational accusations should've got a reaction out of him. Instead, he shook his head like I'd disappointed him in some way. Better now than later.

"You're trying to pick a fight. I'm not buying into it. You're a grown woman capable of making her own decisions. You chose not to see me, I respected that. Yeah, I knew something major had pissed you off. Yeah, I knew my mother had a hand in it. I called you countless times, I texted you, and you wanted time out. I gave you that because I like you. A lot. Or are you so caught up in living out your own little melodrama you can't see what's right in front of you?"

Feeling smaller than a sugar granule stuck on my teaspoon, I released my death grip on the chair. "What's that?"

"A guy who's crazy about you."

My heart flip-flopped and tumbled and danced for joy but I wouldn't be distracted. This could only end one way. "A guy who lives on the other side of the planet."

He leaned forward and braced his elbows on his knees. "A guy who's mobile and who owns his own plane." Not a trace of smugness or ego, making him all the more appealing.

His knee brushed mine, unsettling and distracting. "A guy who's expected to marry and produce a castle full of little Lord Fontleroys."

He smiled. "A guy who has no intention of getting married anytime soon and if he did, he'd probably chat with you about it first."

What did he mean by that? I'd be the first to know he'd be tying the knot with some Amelia-clone or I'd be the one he had in mind? Damn, he was good at this.

My eyes narrowed. "A guy who's not into commitment?"

"A guy who's willing to discuss what it means with the right woman." His stare bore into me, loaded, unwavering.

"A guy who hints at forever and doesn't follow through?" I held my breath after delivering the last one. Forever was a long time and the way I saw it, the F-word didn't belong in the same sentence as Shari and Drew.

"A guy who wants to explore all the possibilities that forever may entail."

Not a bad response.

"With *you*." He laid a hand on my knee and gave a gentle squeeze, his reassurance making my heart roll over.

Great response. Freaking fantastic response. A response

that pretty much shelved my ditch-him-now-before-the-bastard-ditches-you plan.

However, I couldn't ignore one of Mom's many mismatched clichés: 'where's there's smoke, there's a raging inferno.' Lady Muck must've had some reason to imply Drew was almost engaged to the Greyhart bimbo and I had to know more.

"Why did your mom tell me you and Amelia are engaged?" I scooted back a fraction and he removed his hand. Worse luck. I sipped at my *chai*, feigning nonchalance, as if I didn't care about his answer.

By the knowing glint in his eyes, I guess my acting skills weren't as impressive as I'd hoped. "Amelia and I grew up together. Our families are friends, we're the same age, so we hung out. As we got older we used each other as last-minute dates for social functions and I guess Mother read too much into it."

His quick look away alerted me to the fact there was more to this convenient buddy-buddy story.

"And?"

"And what?" His sheepish half-grin would've melted my heart in the past. Not anymore. Shari the Sap had taken a permanent vacation and Shari the Ball-breaker was back in town.

"What aren't you telling me?" I set my mug down on the coffee table, reluctant to hang onto anything that could be used as a weapon in the next few seconds, depending what he divulged.

He sighed but didn't look nervous or remorseful or guilty as I'd expected. He sat back, way too comfortable, way too cute, before looking me straight in the eyes. "I might've fueled Mother's assumptions about marrying Amelia one day."

"I see." Where was that mug when I needed it? A heavy piece of china would've made a great flying missile to knock some sense into him.

"Amelia and I used to joke around in front of our folks if we were single by the time we were forty, we'd get married. Because Mother believed it, she stopped hassling me. So whenever Amelia and I get together in her presence, we play up the 'we're going to the chapel and we're going to get married' charade. It means nothing and it keeps Mother off my back. That's it."

The irony wasn't lost on me. "Like what I was doing with Rakesh to keep Rita's mom appeased?"

"Exactly."

I searched for some hint of duplicity, some glimmer of a lie, some indication he was trying to dupe me. In reality, I was looking for any excuse to end it and get the hell away from this guy who had the power to melt me like the Wicked Witch of the West beneath a deluge of water.

He took hold of my hand, intertwining his fingers between mine, and I enjoyed the contact for a moment. I'd missed him, missed this, the simple pleasure of holding hands with a special guy. "I bet you're thinking it's immature behavior from a grown man but you don't know my mother."

"Actually, I think I do." I eased my hand out of his, missing his comforting touch no matter how brief it'd been.

He frowned, staring at his hand, as if not quite believing I'd have the audacity to release it when he was practically down on his knees begging forgiveness. "What did she say to you exactly? I questioned her at length but a pack of mules has nothing on Mother when she's in one of her moods."

"You really want to know?"

He nodded, that damn lock of hair falling over his forehead, making my fingers itch to reach out and smooth it back.

I shrugged, knowing the truth wouldn't make or break us. He had a right to know Mommy Dearest deserved the names

I'd called her and more. "Trashy, half-caste slut was the main gist of it."

"Fuck." Drew paled, his lips compressed in a hard, thin line and a deep frown furrowing his brow. "I had no idea it was that bad."

"Now you know." I picked at a loose thread on the armchair's seat cushion, wondering why I didn't feel better after showing up his mother for what she was. I'd been so furious when I'd stormed out of The Plaza I could've easily driven a stake through the old vampire's heart. Yet outing Lady Muck to her son didn't bring the peace I'd hoped for. In fact, it made me churlish, like a little girl tattling on the school bully.

"I'm so sorry." He reached out, his thumb brushing my hairline and sending delightful shivers skittering down my spine.

I allowed myself the luxury of savoring his caress, wondering where I'd find the strength to end this. "I'm a big girl; I can take it."

"You shouldn't have to put up with that prejudiced bullshit."

"I didn't." In favor of full disclosure, I came clean. "I called her a racist old bitch."

His brows shot heavenward, the corners of his mouth curving with amusement. "So that's what had her so pissed. She would've hated being called old."

I winced at his lame joke. "I'm not proud of what I said."

"Considering the load of bollocks she heaped on you?" He cringed. "I'm ashamed of her."

My shoulders slumped with the added guilt of coming between him and Lady Muck. "She's a mom. She's overprotective."

"Still doesn't give her the right to treat you like that." He shook his head. "I meant what I said earlier, about exploring forever with you."

Wow. I could've melted into his arms but the new, improved, Shari-with-a-backbone wouldn't fall for charming words or smooth lines anymore. Drew had said all the right things but could I really trust him? Despite being more upstanding than most, he was a member of the belly-crawling species.

I needed to think, something I'd been lousy at on the spur of the moment. I usually came up with a killer comeback or smart idea hours later. But in that instant it came to me: a way to see how serious he was about a future. "Forever's a long time."

"Try me."

I quirked an eyebrow, an impudent move Rita had down pat but probably looked like a caterpillar break-dancing on my forehead. "Fine, I will."

"How?" A spark of interest lit his eyes. I wondered how long it'd stay when he heard my proposition.

"A meeting. You, me, and your mother. A chance to clear the air." And for him to prove to the old bat that I'm not the fling she thinks I am.

He blinked once, twice, before a slow grin spread across his face. "I'm not sure whether to admire your bravado or have you certified insane."

I tossed my head, grateful for the lathering of conditioner I'd used earlier that morning. "I get it. You're prepared to talk forever as long as Mommy Dearest doesn't hear about it. Maybe she's right. Maybe I am your last exotic dabble before settling down with someone of your own class."

"Don't be ridiculous." He flushed an angry crimson, the added color accentuating his good looks rather than detracting. "You need a meeting for me to prove I'm not bullshitting you? Fine. I'll set it up."

His jaw clenched, his mouth set in a grim line, and his eyes glittered with cold, hard challenge, leaving me craving his sexy smile and that special something that lit his face when he glanced my way.

I'd wanted proof of his feelings, but at what cost? Time to backpedal a tad.

"I've been a bitch."

His face softened. "No, you're a woman who needs proof she's not being had."

I pouted and folded my arms. "I'm not insecure." Well, maybe a little… But hey, being called trashy and a last-ditch fling did that to a girl.

"That diva behavior turns me on."

A sliver of heat shot through me. I turned him on? The feeling was entirely mutual, but I wouldn't give in that easily, not after I'd gone to such lengths to test his feelings.

"Keep talking." I tried a mock frown and failed miserably.

His lips curved upward at the corners. "Does that mean I'm forgiven?"

"Maybe."

"Maybe means you'll consider adjourning this meeting to your place or mine?"

"Maybe means you're pushing your luck."

Though the thought of running the short distance back to the apartment dragging Drew behind me with the promise of mind-blowing sex didn't seem like pushing luck. It seemed like an abundance of good luck to me.

The fact was, I'd already forgiven him where it counted, deep in my heart. He'd been completely honest with me—about everything—and that said a lot after what I'd been through with Tate. I couldn't abide lies, not anymore, and having Drew divulge the truth was the sealer for our burgeoning relationship.

"I missed you," he said, stroking my cheek with a slow, deliberate sweep in a tender move straight out of a film, one of those special, tearjerking moments when the hero lets the girl know exactly how special she is with one simple action and a few well-chosen words.

I melted. No other word to describe the warm, fuzzy buzz flowing from my head to my toes, sparking everywhere in between. I might not be able to recognize true love but at that moment I sure as hell came close.

"You're okay for a lord," I mumbled, taking hold of his hand and drawing him to his feet. "How about I take you back to my castle and we play some old-fashioned fencing games?"

"Fencing games?" He pretended not to understand, though I saw the naughty gleam in his eyes the second my entendre registered.

"If you expect me to say how mighty your sword is, forget it."

"Just once?" He pulled me flush against his body—that amazing, hot, hard body—before snatching my breath with a kiss that left me staggering and grabbing onto his jacket lapels for support.

"Sword. Mighty. Let's go." I clung to his hand as we bolted out of Starbucks and up the street like a couple of lunatics. A couple of horny lunatics.

To think, I'd wanted to ditch this guy over a title, a racist mom, and a faux engagement.

"Can't you take those things off?" He glared at my three-inch stilettos, hampering my running speed.

My first response of 'no' died on my lips at the heat blazing in his eyes so I did the only thing a sassy New York girl would do: slipped off my shoes, swung them over my shoulder, and jumped into his arms.

"If you say one word about my weight, the fencing games are off," I said, inhaling a lungful of Cool Water and trying not to swoon in ecstasy.

Drew was a smart guy. He smiled, dropped a brief yet scorching kiss on my lips, and proceeded to march up the street, dodging passersby, head held high while murmuring exactly what he was going to do to every inch of my body when we reached the apartment.

I held him to each and every one of his decadently wicked promises.

CHAPTER FOURTEEN

Like the rest of the female population of New York, I valued first impressions. If the gorgeous black Donna Karan number wasn't just right, if the Choos and handbag didn't match, and if the makeup channeled Alice Cooper more than Sarah Jessica, forget it. I wasn't walking out of my front door.

Thankfully, I'd outdone myself today. As I strode toward Drew's penthouse suite and my second home (like The Plaza staff would give me the time of day after Drew left town) I knew there was at least one area Lady Muck couldn't fault me in: if clothes maketh the woman, I was dressed to kill and then some. Black pencil skirt, baby pink cashmere twinset, moderate-heeled black pumps, and a cute little clutch complementing my demure look perfectly.

Not that I was trying to impress the old witch or anything. Given half a chance, I would've donned one of Rita's saris for a stir but what would that achieve? I wanted to prove a point at this meeting, not alienate the one guy who rocked my world.

My outfit wasn't the only thing making me feel good today.

Before I'd left the apartment, I'd learned my first article had been accepted at *Viand*. Not bad for a trial employee and a much-needed confidence boost before I faced Her Ladyship.

Clearing my throat and squaring my shoulders, I rang the bell, annoyed when my finger shook. Nothing to be nervous about. Just because I'd called my boyfriend's mother a racist old bitch the first time we met didn't mean anything. Water under the bridge and all those other common English clichés.

My fake smile waned as the door opened.

Shit, you're not Drew.

"Lady Lansford." I inclined my head with a cool, polite nod that would've given Her Majesty a run for her money.

"Won't you come in?" Pure, frigid ice dripped from every word, a perfect match for her Arctic-bleak expression.

"Thanks." I entered and suppressed a shiver. I swear the cold radiating from every pore in her well-preserved body was palpable. Where the hell was Drew?

"Drew will be here shortly," she said, eerily answering my thoughts. "Urgent business."

She shut the door with a resounding thud, clasping her hands so tight her knuckles stood out beneath translucent skin, her contemptuous glance flicking me from head to foot.

Urgent business, my ass.

I'd kill him. Why hadn't he called? Warned me he'd be late? Daniel walking into the lions' den had nothing on this.

"He said he tried to call but you didn't answer." She made it sound like I'd ignored a royal summons and I silently cursed my last minute dash to the corner store for mints. A group of teenagers had entered around the same time, complete with blaring stereo, which is when I must've missed Drew's call. Bad timing.

Lady Luck as well as Lady Muck had it in for me.

"Would you like something to drink?"

A mojito, straight up.

"No thanks, I'm fine."

Like being stuck between a rampant Anu and jealous Anjali. Truly shudder-inducing.

"I see you're looking more respectable today." She waved toward a chair as she perched on the edge of the sofa, and while I looked longingly at the door and considered making a run for it, I gritted my teeth and sat.

"I'm sure a continent of Indian women would dare you to say they're not respectable in their elegant clothes," I said, deriving satisfaction when two spots of color appeared on her high cheeks.

Rather than backing down, the high priestess of anti-India went on the attack. "I don't know what you hope to achieve by coming here today. My son said you wanted to meet. Why?"

I stifled a triumphant grin. She was playing right into my hands and though Drew wasn't around to hear this I couldn't let the opportunity pass to score a few early points. "I feel we got off on the wrong foot last time. Considering I'm part of Drew's life, it seems only fair that we clear the air and get to know each other better."

That sounded truly barf-worthy, but hey, it had the desired effect as her mouth opened and shut like a goldfish. However, you couldn't keep a bad woman down for long and she came back fighting. "You may think you're part of Drew's life, but we've already established it's only temporary."

She actually sniffed—how she managed to make it sound condescending I'll never know—and dabbed delicately at her upturned nose with a lace-edged handkerchief pulled from her sleeve.

"You think he's sowing his royal oats," I said, knowing I'd heard a similar line in an Eddie Murphy movie once, racking my brains to place it before *Coming to America* flashed into my head. I doubted Lady Muck would be a movie buff or appreciate Eddie's humor.

She did a mean, malevolent glare. "Exactly."

"You're wrong." I smiled, a self-satisfied smirk that screamed "I know something you don't," mentally counting the minutes until Drew returned to set the old cow straight.

"I'm never wrong." She pushed the *New York Post* across the exquisite marble coffee table between us and opened it to Page Six. "If you won't listen to me, see for yourself."

Unwilling to buy into her games, I glanced at the paper, not particularly caring what I'd find. Until I saw Drew and a gorgeous blonde with their heads close, her bejeweled hand resting possessively on his forearm.

I cared. Way too much to be good for me.

"Lovely couple, aren't they?"

I ignored her, my eyes drawn to the small print beneath the boxed pic.

Man about town—or should that read the world?—Lord Drew Lansford is seen here in New York with his regular girlfriend, Amelia Greyhart, heiress to Greyhart Industries. The two looked particularly cozy at the Waldorf Astoria, a favorite hotel of the Greyharts. What we want to know is when will Amelia become Lady Lansford? The two are regular companions in London and it looks like their global love affair is heading into new territory with the stunning pair spending time in New York. Perhaps the Big Apple will be the chosen venue for pending nuptials? Stay tuned.

I could've labeled the article a load of speculative crap except for two things: the date under the picture, and Amelia's blatant adoration as she gazed at him with wide eyes and smiling mouth. You couldn't fake that look, and my blood chilled as I realized the cool blonde WASP princess, every bit as stunning as I expected, had bought into the soon-to-be-engaged scenario Drew had conjured up for his mother's benefit.

I could've excused him. He couldn't control the Ice Princess' feelings. However, he could control who he spent his time with and where, and if my memory served me correctly, the date printed under that pretty picture correlated perfectly with our first drink date.

My gut twisted as I remembered not having that drink and why: the phone call on Drew's cell, his smooth 'something's come up' and taking a rain check.

Jealousy, vile and potent, strangled every well-thought-out reason why I'd demanded this meeting. I'd wanted to make nice with Lady Muck because I cared for Drew. But what if Drew didn't reciprocate? Was he that fickle he'd set up a date with one woman only to ditch her for another?

I didn't have any right to be possessive over what had been a first date but we'd come a long way and this irked. I blinked, willing away the image of Amelia touching Drew, and inhaled sharply, needing air to alleviate my sudden breathlessness.

"You're seeing sense."

I clenched my hands at Lady Muck's audible triumph and bit back a host of retorts, most of them involving the F-word I rarely used, and schooled my face into an impassive mask with effort.

With effort? Who was I trying to kid? It took a miraculous contortion of hundreds of tiny muscles not to look like Satan on speed and even then, a constipated grimace would've looked elegant compared with my rigor-mortis expression.

"I never would've guessed you'd read *trashy* gossip columns," I said, scoring a direct hit by the flash of fire in her eyes but unable to derive comfort from it.

"Everyone needs their fix of trash now and then." Lady Muck's pointed stare left me in little doubt where she thought her son was getting his fix.

Stupid, pointless tears burned the back of my eyes and I blinked rapidly, not wanting to give her the satisfaction of seeing me cry. The newspaper photo rankled, but not half as much as having my boyfriend's mother treat me like doggy-doo she'd stepped in with her fancy shoes.

Her derision took the gloss off my earlier confidence and shattered any illusions I'd held of smoothing things over between us for Drew's sake. She made me feel worthless in a way being homeless and jobless never had. And it hurt, dammit, more than it should.

I wanted her to like me, to accept me, to acknowledge me.

That's when the stunning realization detonated. Why I'd really come here today, why her opinion mattered.

I loved Drew.

Somewhere between taunting him in Mumbai and flaunting him in New York, I'd fallen for him. Hard.

We'd dealt with a faux engagement—his, not mine—and a very real title, so that newspaper article? Not worth the print it was written on. The newspaper had fallen for the same scenario I initially had without knowing the facts. They'd printed a load of speculative crap and while the date that picture was taken still needled, I wouldn't buy into Lady Muck's games.

She hadn't driven me away first time around so she was still trying, using anything to make me walk away.

Try again, lady.

Realistically, I didn't want her to try. I wanted her to accept me. Something that would never happen going by her disgusted moue.

"You should leave." She rattled the newspaper in my face. "You'll never belong in my son's world, not like Amelia."

Damn her. Damn me for caring about her opinion so much.

Her imperious gaze swept over the outfit I'd chosen with such care. "Play dress-up all you like but you can't fool me. I know your type."

By the taunting tilt of her lips, she wanted me to ask 'what type's that?' but I wouldn't give her the satisfaction. Besides, I couldn't speak even if I wanted to. Sadness tightened my throat, making swallowing painful.

The sting of tears burned but I didn't look away, daring her to finish what she'd started.

She folded the paper precisely, creating a perfect frame for the picture of Drew and Amelia. "You'll never compete with that. Class above ass, I always say."

She held the picture in front of my face and I swatted it away, losing my battle to subdue the tears as the door opened and Drew strode into the room, more agitated than I'd ever seen him: tie askance, suit rumpled, hair virtually standing on end.

"Sorry I'm late." Horror dawned as he registered the tears. Crossing the room in three short strides, he laid a protective arm across my shoulder. "What the hell's going on here, Mother?"

"Nothing, dear. And don't swear, it doesn't become you." Lady Muck stood, cool, calm, confident, and unflappable.

"I'll do and say whatever I damn well please." Drew never raised his voice, unless you count the times I baited him in India, and seeing him angry and masterful impressed me.

"Shari's crying and I'd like to know why. What did you do?"

My "I'm not crying," and Lady Muck's "Nothing" overlapped and Drew shook his head, ready to throttle both of us.

"Shari, what's going on?"

"Your mom seems to think this is significant." I pointed at the newspaper clutched in her hand.

He snatched it and glanced at the photo before throwing it back on the table. "I've already explained all this. Amelia's a friend, nothing more."

"How can you say that?" Lady Muck's hands fluttered in the vicinity of her heart and for a moment I wondered if she was going into cardiac arrest.

Impossible. The battle-ax had to have a heart for it to arrest.

Weary to the bone, I eyeballed him. "I believe you, but you have to admit ditching a drink date with me for a cozy sojourn in a posh hotel with her is poor form."

His mother smothered a delighted snort and his tolerant expression shifted to furious in a second.

"Sit down, Mother, and don't say another bloody word until I tell you."

He pointed to the sofa and Queenie sat, honing her goldfish impersonations, when he turned to me. "I didn't know about the picture; otherwise, I would've explained it when I told you the truth at Starbucks, remember?"

I remembered. I'd demanded answers, he'd explained, and the make-up sex had been memorable. Heat seeped into my cheeks at the scorching recollection.

"That night I was with you when something came up? My assistant called, saying I had urgent business to attend to at the office so I dropped you off and headed there. The *urgent business* happened to be the interfering old biddy sitting on that sofa over there. Of course, Mother didn't tell me Amelia was in town or she'd been conveniently invited in another blatant attempt to push us up the aisle, so I spent a polite hour in their company before heading back here."

He held up a finger when his mom opened her mouth to respond. "Mother arranged for us to have supper at the Waldorf. I'd already taken a raincheck on our date so I went along. I hadn't seen Amelia in months and haven't seen her since. That's it. No cozy meeting, no secret liaison, no pre-planning. Isn't that right, Mother?"

He swung to face Lady Muck, his face thunderous. If Dashing Drew was seriously suave, Dastardly Drew was scarily sexy.

His mom lifted her head and I knew she wouldn't back down without a fight. "You're blind, dear." She stabbed a finger at the picture in the newspaper. "You can't deny Amelia's feelings for you. Look at her expression. She's smitten. Surely you return the sentiment—"

"Amelia's smitten all right." Drew touched my hand and winked. I didn't need the reassurance. Looked like Rita's wild theory had been right and Drew wasn't the object of Amelia's affections. "Here's a heads up, Mother. Amelia is dating some guy half her age. He's all she talks about. That look in the photo? Probably waxing lyrical about her toy boy while you visited the Ladies. Satisfied?"

I stifled a grin at the strangled "Yes" from Lady Muck's mouth.

"Now that's out of the way, it's time to get a few things clear, Mother." Drew glowered as he slid an arm around my shoulders. I straightened, proud to be by his side, part of me never wanting to leave. "Firstly, Amelia and I played a role around you all these years to keep you off my back. Secondly, Shari is the special woman in my life and you owe her an apology. And thirdly, you tell me right now what the hell is behind this bizarre vendetta of yours. You've never been racist in your life and I want to know what's gotten into you."

"Leave me alone, I'm tired," she said, her hands waving ineffectually in front of her, fluttering in helpless circles before coming to rest in her lap. In that instant, I almost felt sorry for her—almost, but not quite—as her stately frame crumpled before our eyes, turning her from an elegant older woman to a wizened crone sinking into the corner of the sofa.

Helpless, Drew glanced at me and I gave him a gentle push in her direction.

I was a feisty New York City girl, able to leap tall buildings and guys in a single bound, while my nemesis lay huddled in a pathetic heap. I could be gallant in the face of her humiliating defeat. Besides, I knew what it felt like to be down and out, and, at that moment, his mom's pathetic slump surpassed me at my lowest.

"Mother, tell me." Drew spoke softly, as if to a child, and my heart clenched at the myriad of emotions playing across his face: anger warring with disappointment, fear with concern.

I hoped she wasn't faking, because if she was I'd never forgive the old witch for putting the guy I cared for through that.

"Your father had a mistress, a half-caste woman, part African, part Spanish, a gorgeous coffee-skinned thing that stole his heart and effectively ended our marriage."

Drew's stunned expression mirrored mine and I plopped into the chair I'd vacated earlier, knowing I shouldn't be privy to this but unable to look away, like a horror-struck passerby at an accident.

"But you and Dad were married for forty years before he died," Drew said, laying a tentative hand over his mother's.

By his fleeting guilt, I could swear he wasn't as surprised by the news of his dad's mistress as he first made out. Perhaps his stunned expression was more about his mother knowing and how she'd kept it secret all these years.

"A sham, all of it. A cold, lifeless marriage for the sake of appearances. That woman had your father's love and I had nothing. I hated her." Her voice hitched and I froze, trying not to squirm when she raised accusing eyes to me. "I didn't want the same thing happening to Amelia. That's why I said those horrible things. To get rid of you before the damage was done. But I've made a mistake."

Unsure whether I should respond, I settled for an imperceptible nod and deferred to Drew, who took hold of her hands and squeezed. "Yes, you have. I'm sorry about Dad and your marriage but it doesn't excuse what you put Shari through. Isn't there something else you'd like to say?"

I would never know if she would've stooped so low as to apologize to me without Drew's prompting but I didn't care. She had demons of her own to conquer, that was punishment enough.

She released Drew's hands and stood, circumnavigating the coffee table to stand in front of me with hand outstretched. "I'm sorry, dear. I was very rude and you didn't deserve it. I hope you can forgive me. Considering our mutual regard for my son, we may have more in common than I first thought."

She glanced fondly at Drew, who watched us with bemusement, as if he expected me to give his mother a hug before throwing her over my shoulder in a mock Chan move.

I stood and shook Lady Lansford's hand. (Abrupt change in title but I couldn't keep calling her sarcastic pet names, even in my own head, after her apology. Didn't seem right.)

If the regal old duck could apologize, I had to do a bit of groveling myself. "And I'm sorry for calling you names."

To my surprise, a glimmer of amusement sparked her eyes. "You know, I was most insulted by you calling me old."

"Drew said as much." I smiled as our hands dropped, wondering if the astute gleam in her eyes was that of a woman who'd manipulated a situation to her advantage or that of a woman who'd come to her senses. I'd probably never know and I didn't care.

"Mother, I need a moment alone with Shari if you don't mind."

I watched Lady Lansford's mouth tighten, expecting her to say 'actually I do' in that posh accent. Instead, she inclined her head toward me in a polite nod, waved to Drew, and headed into the suite's den, shutting the door.

"Sorry you had to hear all that stuff about your dad." My apology ran deep, because seeing his mom's obvious pain rammed home what I'd been doing with Tate. I'd been the other woman. I'd believed his lies about his supposedly rotten marriage, letting my sympathy for him assuage my guilt. Guilt that now flooded back, seeing the devastation it had wreaked on Drew's mom.

Had Tate's wife known about his infidelity or had she been blinded by his lies, too? For her sake, I hoped she lived in ignorant bliss because the ramifications of the role I'd played in that marriage was something I had to live with every day.

"You knew, didn't you?"

He nodded, grimaced. "I suspected."

"Why didn't you tell her?"

"Timing, I guess." He dragged a hand through his hair, rumpling it. "I only discovered the affair a year or so before he died."

"Did you confront him?"

"Yeah. The old bastard had the audacity to paint Mother in a bad light. Said she drove him to it, he'd never been happy, sought affection elsewhere because he got none at home." His fists clenched at his sides and his mouth twisted. "I blamed him, sure, but what kind of woman puts up with some cheating fool using her? Mortifyingly stupid."

My guilt coalesced into a hard, indigestible ball stuck in my chest, suffocating.

"What's wrong?"

I paced a few steps, dragged air into my lungs, shaking out my arms like a prizefighter about to enter the ring.

"You're scaring me." He touched my arm and I stopped, knowing I'd have to tell the truth if we were to have any chance at a future, but hating what it could do to us. He was so moral, so upstanding, so fair. What would he think of me once he learned the truth?

I inhaled and blew out a long, slow breath. "I was mortifyingly stupid."

A deep groove slashed his brow and I longed to smooth it away.

"That jerk we ran into at the bar? Married."

I couldn't bear to see the censure in his eyes so I stared at the gold light fixture over his left shoulder. "I knew but it didn't matter because I bought his sob story. The usual 'wife doesn't understand me, love me, come near me, our marriage is platonic for appearances' bullshit. I bought it because I thought I loved him and we were happy together and my life was easier being with him. We practically lived together, we worked together, and I had no reason not to believe him."

"What happened?"

"His wife got pregnant."

He swore and I reiterated the sentiment. "Yeah, he took advantage of me but I let him. I believed him. And I was selfish for not thinking about his wife."

I dredged up the courage to eyeball him, not surprised by the condemnation I glimpsed. "I'm not proud of what I did and seeing your mom's pain reinforced what an idiot I was, putting up with Tate's toxic shit and not caring about anyone else."

The stern lines bracketing his mouth faded as I dared to hope. "Is it too late to take back the mortifyingly stupid comment?"

"Why? I deserved it."

He shook his head. "You deserved a guy who respected you enough to tell you the truth."

I opened my mouth to self-flagellate further but he silenced me with a finger against my lips.

"That bastard used you. Are you guilty by association? Probably. But you could only go on what he told you and if those were a bunch of lies, that's his fault, not yours."

"So you don't think I'm a bad person?"

His expression softened as he cupped my cheek. "I think you're a great person."

I fell in love with him a little bit more at that moment.

Maybe a lot.

He hadn't judged me or berated me; he'd accepted me, faults and all.

This one was a keeper.

Only problem was, how to keep him when he'd be flitting back to India shortly? Needing to change the subject before I blurted my feelings, I jerked my thumb toward the door. "Will your mom be okay? Perhaps you should go comfort her."

"You're rather magnanimous."

I chuckled. "She wasn't that bad once she started groveling."

"A rare sight, believe me." He smiled. "I'll leave her for a bit. Besides, I wouldn't put it past her to pull the sympathy act just to look good out of all this. For all I know, she might've been onto the sly codger for years and is using this as an excuse for the shabby way she treated you. She's pretty headstrong, and hates being wrong."

"I kind of got that impression."

He pointed at the newspaper and the den door, encompassing the dramas of the last half hour. "Sorry you had to put up with all that."

"You're forgiven," I said, snuggling into his arms and letting his scent infuse my senses and calm me better than a shot of valerian. Calm was good. Calm would keep me grounded when he left. Calm would fortify me in the lonely months to come, when I rehashed every reason why we couldn't be together and how I shouldn't have fallen for him in the first place.

"Prove it."

I kissed him without hesitation. Not surprisingly, the kiss quickly escalated to a hot meshing of lips and tongues, notching up my temperature, feeding my desperation to ease the burning ache I'd never experienced until this guy.

"What'll Mommy Dearest think?" I managed to gasp out when we came up for air, my fingers bunching his shirt, wishing I could pop the buttons in one, swift rip.

"Don't know, don't care." He tunneled his fingers through my hair, making me shiver with the sensual pleasure of it. "Where were we?"

"About to head to my place if you think your mom's fine? And only if you're interested—"

"She's fine. She probably has her ear pressed to the door and if she wasn't fine we'd hear about it."

He released me long enough to cup his hands around his mouth. "Mother, I'm taking Shari home. See you later."

Much later, if I had a say.

· · ·

"Want to know a secret?"

I braced for the worst. Secret fiancée? Secret family? Secret fetish? If Drew divulged anything less dramatic, I could deal with it.

Considering we'd discussed the fake fiancée, I scratched that off my list and waited.

"You'll tell me eventually."

He laughed and hugged me. If I were any closer I'd be on his lap rather than the limo seat next to him. "You're no fun. I expected you to pester me."

I shrugged, nonchalant on the outside, dying of curiosity on the inside.

"Fine, I won't tell you."

I elbowed him.

He laughed. "I'll *show* you."

He tapped the partition, waiting until it lowered before telling the driver to take the next left. I hadn't been noting the surroundings, what with the serious make-out session in the back seat since we'd left The Plaza, and as I glanced around I didn't have a clue where we were.

"You're not abducting me? Whisking me away to have your nefarious way with me? Making me take a Pilates class with

Amelia—"

As a silencing technique, his kiss effectively shut me up and wiped my mind.

The limo slowed, preventing us from picking up where we'd left off and I craned my neck, confused by the dingy street, mollified by the sidewalks teeming with people carrying takeout bags.

"Where are we?"

"Best Indian snack shop in NYC."

He had me at *Indian snack shop*.

"Want to come in or wait here?"

My stomach rumbled. "What do you think?"

He chucked me under the chin. "I love a woman with a good appetite."

I leaned into him and nuzzled his neck. "We're talking about food, right?"

"For now." His lips brushed mine and I forgot to breathe.

"If we stock up quick, we can satisfy both those insatiable appetites of yours," he whispered against the side of my mouth and I almost skipped the Indian snacks. Almost.

"Come on, I'm starving."

He held the door open for me and gripped my hand as I stepped onto the sidewalk. Immediately jostled by the bustling hordes, the rustle of plastic bags banging against my legs, stray elbows, and curry powder aroma heavy in the air instantly transported me back to Mumbai.

"Can't believe you've never been to Sassoon's," he said, tugging me toward the nearest doorway, leading into a brightly lit shop.

"I can't believe it either," I said, stepping into the shop and feeling like I'd come home.

The aromas hit me first and I inhaled deeply, the heady mix of cumin and mustard seeds and *garam masala* making me salivate. Food covered every surface, from the *samosa*-filled platters on the spotless stainless steel counters to the layered shelves in glass cabinets lining every wall. I didn't know where to look first: the tiffin snacks, the street vendor food, or the sweets, arranged in towering pyramids that made my waist as well as my eyes bulge by looking.

"What do you fancy?"

"Apart from you?"

He squeezed my hand. "I love a good comeback. But right this minute, I want you to make a fast choice so we can head to your place, where I'm going to—"

He ducked down and whispered in my ear exactly what he was going to do. In exquisite, erotic detail.

I gulped, the heat from ghee sizzling in *kadai*s nothing to the heat surging through me.

"Choose. Quickly."

I didn't have to be told twice. I'd made my choices by the time we reached the counter a *long* five minutes later.

"You choose savory, I'll grab sweets, my treat," he said, giving my hand a squeeze before he released it and moved down the counter, looking delightfully out of place in his suit, tall and commanding and utterly gorgeous.

My stomach flipped—not from hunger—as he sensed my stare and half-turned, his lop-sided smile making me want to shove aside the people separating us and fling myself into his arms.

I was in over my head with this one.

Floundering and yearning and craving a happily-ever-after that probably wasn't feasible.

With a wistful sigh I swiveled toward the counter and ordered *singharas* (Bengali version of a samosa), *masala vada* (deep-fried spicy lentil snacks), *vegetable bhaji* (vegetables mixed with chickpea flour and fried), *shrimp pakoras* (same as bhaji but with shrimp), *kachoris* (fried flat bread stuffed with spicy dahl), and *aloo tikki* (potato patties).

Enough food to keep us fed for ages. Enough food to keep us locked away in my apartment without having to venture out.

My shoulders sagged as I snagged the heavy bags a second before Drew joined me.

I eyed the boxes of sweets stacked in his arms and laughed. "A man after my own heart."

He shrugged. "Didn't want to leave the apartment for a while."

I jiggled the bags. "Same here."

His eyes darkened with passion and my body buzzed in anticipation. "Let's go."

I'd wanted to memorize the route from the shop to my apartment so I could revisit but the fifteen-minute limo ride passed in a blur of unbridled tension and loaded glances and whispered promises.

By the time we made it back to my brownstone I could barely stand, my knees wobbling with the thought of what was to come. Admirably chivalrous, Drew managed to hold the bags, juggle the sweet boxes, and hold my hand as we stumbled up the steps, through the main door, and into the elevator.

We didn't speak. The air between us crackled with expectation, and when the elevator doors slid open we tumbled out in our haste. My hand shook as I juggled the key, once, twice, before sliding it home. Flinging open the door, we bustled in.

Drew dropped the bags and boxes on a nearby hall table.

I dropped my handbag.

We dropped all pretenses at taking this slow as we reached for each other.

Hands clawed at clothes. Fingers fumbled with buttons. Bodies strained.

We stripped in record time, the tearing of expensive cotton and the satisfying pop of buttons not bothering us as he protected himself and slid into me on a long, drawn out moan.

My back hit the nearest wall and he supported my butt as I hooked my legs around his waist, taking him in deeper, taking him all the way.

With every thrust my muscles clenched.

With every caress my skin hummed.

With every exquisitely torturous grind of his hips against mine, I lost myself in the out-of-control, pinwheeling, escalating eroticism.

Our mouths found their way to each other, a desperate fusion of lips and tongues, hot, long, wet kisses lasting forever. He shifted a fraction, changing the angle and within three thrusts I shattered, bit down on his shoulder, swept away in the throes of a mind-blowing orgasm.

He came a moment later, yelling my name, the sweetest, most satisfying sound I'd ever heard. He cradled me, supporting my weight, and in that moment, as heat from our sweat-slicked bodies enveloped us in an intimate cocoon, the soul-destroying realization hit.

How could I let him walk away?

• • •

Drew walked away the next day.

Urgent business in Chicago, massive IT deal worth billions.

Put my trial at the magazine into perspective. Which I still hadn't told him about for several reasons: I didn't want to jinx it and I didn't want to look like a failure if a permanent job didn't eventuate. Being unemployed was bad enough. Not being good enough to secure a job after a trial? Loser. Hopefully, I could wow him with my new job if/when I impressed *Viand* enough.

Stupid thing was, I'd been willing to accept our differences until that run-in with his mom. I may have forgiven her vileness but I couldn't forget. She'd been right in a way. Dress this relationship up any way I liked but when I stripped away the newness and romance and international glamour of our meeting and consequential hook-up now, Drew and I were worlds apart.

While I had potential, a work-in-progress the editor-in-chief would say, Drew was the real deal. He'd achieved so much, had done so much, it made my life to date pale in comparison.

Sure, I may have exciting things to look forward to—my trial ended today and I'd checked my cell every five seconds, beyond nervous I wouldn't get this job and be back where I started—was that enough to offer him? A city girl finding her feet falling for a worldly guy taking constant giant leaps?

My cell pinged and my heart stopped. I fumbled it out of my hoodie pocket and glanced at the screen, nerves warring with excitement, almost relieved when Rita's name popped up above the message.

Hey S, any news?

My thumb flew over the tiny alphabetical keys, tapping a quick response.

No & stop asking me. Will let u know ASAP.

MM at the ready. Call me!

I smiled. Any excuse for a Mojito Monday. I typed *Gr8, S x* and received a super-fast *xoxo* in response.

Rita's support meant a lot but I knew who I'd rather be getting those kisses and hugs from.

Drew said he'd probably be too busy to call. That didn't stop me wishing he would.

Falling in love with a mogul sucked. Especially when he'd be heading back to Mumbai the day after the wedding.

The front door intercom buzzed and I jumped, the part of me prone to fantasy wishing that was Drew lobbing on my doorstep. Crazy? Hell yeah, but he'd done it once before.

I jabbed at the button. "Yes?"

"Delivery for Miss Jones."

"Come on up." I let the guy in downstairs, checked my cell one last time, and gave it a little shake—like that would speed up news of my job.

The delivery guy knocked and when I opened the door, the first thing to hit me was the smell. A heady, tempting aroma of spices. Cinnamon, cardamom, star anise, turmeric—I could distinguish between each, considering I'd consumed enough of them since my love of Indian food had kicked in, and my mouth watered.

"Here you go." He handed me two bulging bags and I placed them on the floor before signing his electronic device and tipping him.

He saluted. "Freelance couriers usually deliver parcels and flowers." He pointed at the bags. "First time I've ever wanted to eat whatever's in there before I got here."

I smiled and shut the door, grabbing the bags and heading

into the lounge. I knew that smell. Could name each individual item sealed in the bags: *samosas, bondas, vada, pakoras*. My favorites. Known by a certain person.

I ripped open the first bag and inhaled, the *masala* blend bringing back instant memories of Mumbai—and Drew. We'd shared these delectable morsels in this very apartment. In bed.

Heat lit my cheeks at the recollection as I spied a note wedged between Sassoon's cartons.

Flowers are passé. I've heard Indian is in.

See you soon.

Drew x

Like a love-struck heroine in a rom-com, I clutched the note to my chest, grinning inanely. I loved the fact my guy didn't do flowers. I loved the fact my guy knew the way to my heart was through my stomach. I loved my guy. Period.

I popped a potato *bonda* into my mouth and sighed. Heavenly.

That's the moment my cell buzzed with an incoming message and I leapt off the sofa, food forgotten, scrambling to grab it.My palms were so clammy it almost slipped out of my hands but I managed to hold it long enough to read:

Congrats, Shari. Your last article on beach food vendors in Mumbai blew us away. Your trial at Viand has been a success. We're thrilled to offer you a permanent position. See you next week.

No signature. Fairly indicative of my lowly position and paltry salary. Didn't matter, since I'd inputted Jorg, the editor-in-chief's number, into my cell the first day we'd met and he'd raved about my *'highly original take on Indian food.'*

I squealed, threw my arms in the air, and did a wicked hula. Until one of my hips clunked and I fell onto the sofa in a giggling heap, staring at the cell until the letters blurred.

I'd done it. Impressed them enough to employ me. Hot damn.

Knowing Rita would be watching her cell as obsessively as I'd been, I quickly tapped a text.

Got it!

Her answer came so fast I barely had time to pop a *pakora* in my mouth.

Yay! U. Me. MM. Celebr8 big time xx

I could hardly wait.

@ 8 2nite, my place. Squeee! x

My thumb hovered over the keypad. I wanted to send a text to Drew about my job but the teeny part of me deep down that still harbored insecurities wanted to see his reaction when I told him. So I settled for:

Thx for snacks, u know me well. Don't work 2 hard. MJ x

I always signed my texts to him Miss Jones. He seemed to get a kick out of it and it reminded me of our first momentous meeting. I'd toyed with writing *miss you* before deciding it sounded too needy. And that wasn't me. Not when I had a kick-ass job. Woo-hoo!

I might not be the born and bred lady his mom wanted me to be but the way my life was coming together, maybe I had something to offer her son after all.

• • •

I entered Rita's hotel room, took one look at the bride decked out in her finery, and glanced down at my dress, wondering how I could feel like faded wallpaper in Valentino.

"You look amazing." I spoke barely above a whisper, in awe of my beautiful friend, who was doing a fair statue impersonation, unmoving, unblinking.

Uh-oh. Maybe Mama Rama had slipped something into her *chai* to prevent this wedding going ahead. Wouldn't put anything past the domineering cow.

"I feel sick." Rita raised stricken eyes, the only sign of movement in her rigid body. "How could you let me do something like this?"

Smiling, I hugged Rita and air-kissed both cheeks, not wanting to spoil the exquisite makeup job by one of Sarah Jessica Parker's entourage (a friend of a friend of a work acquaintance at Bergdorf's came through for Rita in a big way).

"What's with the nerves? It's not like you're a blushing bride or anything. You and Romeo have been getting it on since his plane touched down at JFK."

"Rakesh… " Rita breathed his name on the softest sigh, her eyes losing focus, lost in a memory. A damn good one by the smug smile lifting the corners of her plumped and glossed mouth.

"Yeah, Rakesh. The guy you're marrying. For life. The ball and chain, the anchor around your neck, always looking over your shoulder, forever and ever and ever."

I grinned as she slapped my arm.

In comparison to Mama Rama's stinging slap when she first

caught us out at Central Park? A gentle love tap.

"You're right. Nerves are a waste of time." Rita shook her head in characteristic defiance, setting off a cute melody from the tiny bells dangling from an elaborate head scarf. Combined with the rest of the gold hanging from various parts of her body, she glittered and twinkled like a Christmas bauble.

"To think, you wanted me to blow him off."

She quirked an eyebrow and thrust out a hip, looking every inch a woman who had the love of a good man. "'Til I realized if there's any blowing to be done, that'll be done by me and me only, thank you very much."

I made barf noises. "Too much information. Now, do a twirl and let me see this amazing outfit."

Rita obliged, my fashion-plate partner-in-crime only too happy to show off her bridal splendor. Decked out in a vibrant red sari edged in gold embroidered *jeri* work, the traditional garb of a Hindu bride, she looked more Indian than I'd ever seen her. Yet somehow it suited her better than all the D&G, Prada, and Gucci she usually favored.

"Think the folks and out-laws will approve?"

I nodded, knowing Rita didn't give a damn what anyone but Rakesh thought, as it should be. "Your mum'll be fine, and hopefully Mama Rama won't do a regular *rona dhona*. For this anyway," I added as an afterthought, knowing it wouldn't take much for Mama Rama to throw in a theatrical weeping and wailing scene.

Rita chuckled. "You really picked up the Bollywood lingo, didn't you?"

I studied my French manicure at arm's length, doing a good impersonation of a bored starlet. "Being the best extra in the business, it pays to listen."

"If you're that good, be careful Pravin doesn't cast you as the next *item* girl."

I did a little shimmy, shaking my boobs like a true item girl, the hot actress chosen to do the essential song in modern Bollywood films. This actress might not appear in the rest of the film but she always performed the *dhak dhak*, the dance step I'd seen several times now where jerky, perky, bouncy boobs guaranteed to get the guys titillated.

As for Mama Rama's possible theatrics, I could definitely see her throwing a full-on *rona dhona* and ruining Rita's big day.

"Lucky I don't have to worry about acting anymore, considering my *new job*." I fist-pumped the air, stoked I'd stepped out of my comfort zone and landed a job that challenged as well as satisfied.

"I'm so proud of how you've got your shit together since Tate." Rita grabbed my hands, gripping them so tightly her knuckles stood out. "It's been one hell of a ride these last few months."

Images of Mumbai, the Ramas' compound, Film City, my room at Anjali's, The Plaza, Central Park, Drew's mother, Starbucks, Sassoon's, my fab new career, and Drew, mostly Drew, flashed through my mind. "Sure has."

"You know what you're doing?"

I laughed and tried to slip out of Rita's death grip but she wouldn't let go. "I'm supposed to be asking you that. Besides, I'm not the one marrying some guy she barely knows."

Predictably, Rita wouldn't accept my brush-off. We hadn't had a chance to talk much since I'd patched things up with Drew but she knew the basics: I'd accepted his explanations, I'd forgiven Mommy Dearest, and we'd been going at it like two people who'd been celibate for a decade (not true, but a fitting analogy if you took a peek into our boudoir activities).

"Tell me Drew isn't going to break your heart."

"Drew isn't going to break my heart," I said in a flat monotone, managing a cocky grin designed to allay Rita's concerns while masking my own.

Of course he'd break my heart, considering I'd served it up to him on a silver platter complete with knife to plunge into it when he jet-setted back to India. I'd accepted the inevitability and was making the most of every moment we had together, storing away the memories to dredge out on freezing winter evenings when I'd be curled indoors, sculling *chai* and stuffing *ladoos* in my mouth. I could see many days of comfort eating ahead. Sassoon's better brace for a heartbroken regular.

"I worry about you." Rita tugged on my hands until I had no option but to fall into her Chanel No. 5-infused embrace.

"Save your worry for when you tell Mama Rama the good news that you're dragging her golden boy away from Mumbai for six months of the year."

Rita stiffened, and I used the opportunity to slip out of her bear hug. Don't get me wrong, I liked hugging my best friend, but I didn't need reminding of my upcoming heartache, not today, when I wanted to focus on happiness.

"Kali forbid. Do you think she'd dare slap her new daughter-in-law?"

Rubbing my cheek in memory of Mama's fury, I screwed up my nose. "For your sake, I sure as hell hope not."

"Crap. I hope I'm doing the right thing."

I didn't like the quiver in Rita's whisper or the deep groove between her eyebrows.

"Listen up. You're marrying the guy of your dreams, he's

agreed to live half the year in your home city, and vice versa. You've made major decisions, you've faced your overbearing families, and you've planned a life together. Not to mention survived Mama Rama in the flesh. You *are* doing the right thing. Don't doubt it for a second."

Fear warred with self-belief in Rita's ebony eyes and, thankfully, self-belief won out.

"You're right. Screw these pre-wedding jitters."

"Good girl." I tapped my watch. "We've got a ceremony to attend."

I fussed around her, smoothing the folds of her stunning silk sari and arranging the fall of her head scarf.

"Shari?"

"Yeah?" Satisfied, I stood back to survey my handiwork. Not that I'd done much apart from last-minute tweaks. I couldn't improve on Rita's perfection. I'd never seen a more stunning bride.

"Be happy."

"You too," I said as we air-kissed, fervently hoping we got our wish.

CHAPTER FIFTEEN

I'd never been to a Hindu wedding, and the traditions enthralled me: Rita and Rakesh tied together by their scarves and walking seven times around a fire, Rakesh placing a black and gold necklace around Rita's neck and putting red powder in her hair parting. Intriguing stuff.

I would've enjoyed it more if I'd understood a word of what the priest said, but the hour-long ceremony was conducted in Sanskrit. The enchanting, important mantras went straight over my head. The bride and groom radiated a happy glow; no translation necessary.

Rakesh made a maroon *kurta*, the guy's version of a *salwaar kameez*, hot, though the top ended mid-calf and made him look like an elegant Aladdin. After the ceremony Rita changed into a stunning red *sharara* for the reception, a sexy *salwaar kameez* edged in gold *jeri* like her sari. Guess it'd be difficult to party hard wearing yards of fabric with the potential to unravel around your body. Ask Anjali, or the unfortunate Kapil.

The party couldn't officially start until Rita's parents had welcomed Rakesh, Mama Rama, and Senthil at the door by washing their feet and waving a lamp around them to drive away evil spirits. In my opinion, Mama Rama should've vanished on the spot if that were the case, but she remained entrenched as the gloating mother of the groom.

Once the reception started I joined in the festivities with gusto, taking center stage on the parquet floor and dancing the *dhak dhak* my way. Not pretty, but Drew's eyes lit up, all the incentive I needed to flaunt.

After I'd finished my best Bollywood dance impersonations, Anjali managed to grab a dance with Senthil, despite Mama Rama's evil eye casting a shadow on the surprisingly light-footed pair. I watched with a hint of maudlin creeping through my romantic soul.

What if Anjali had gotten her man? Would her life have been different?

I sighed. "Don't they look cute together?"

Drew, remarkably debonair in a tux, grabbed champagne from a passing waiter and handed it to me. "Anjali and Senthil? Not sure about cute. Makeover material for *Dancing with the Stars* maybe?"

"They're cute." I stamped my foot for emphasis, belatedly hoping I hadn't popped a sequin, my latent acting genes simultaneously bubbling to the surface just like the fizzy bubbles in my Moet-filled flute. "If it hadn't been for Anu they'd be a couple. It's sad when true love doesn't run smoothly."

"Sometimes sadder when it does," he said, dropping a quick peck on my cheek to take the sting out of his cryptic words.

Was he referring to us? Our ill-fated, soon-to-end love affair?

Not that he'd said the L-word or anything remotely like it,

but we'd been spending all our free time together and I'd never felt so comfortable with a guy.

I loved him. Wish I knew if he returned the sentiment. Not that it should matter. He'd be jetting back to Mumbai tomorrow. End of story.

"What's that supposed to mean?"

He quirked a brow at my snarky tone. "Exactly that. Some relationships start out grand love affairs and end up a war zone."

"Personal experience?"

He shrugged, the action annoying me as much as his studied nonchalance. "More an observation."

"So now you're an anthropologist?" I abhorred the latent insecurity making me do this. "As well as jet-setting tycoon, moviemaker, IT specialist, and the rest."

"What's with the attitude?" He frowned and laid a steadying hand on my shoulder. "Is this about me leaving tomorrow?"

He'd honed in on the motivation behind my unexpected irritability, and that riled me further. He knew me so well in such a short space of time, we connected on so many levels, and even when I was behaving like a moody cow he stood there, cool and unflappable.

It made me want to slug him. For the simple fact that the best thing to ever happen to me would be walking out of my life and there wasn't one damn thing I could do about it.

"Not everything's about you, hotshot." I hated doing this, my fear of losing him bubbling to the surface at the worst possible time.

"Let's take this outside." His fingers dug into my shoulder.

"Just because we've slept together a few dozen times doesn't give you the right to boss me around."

He recoiled and a part of me broke. I knew what I was doing.

Deliberately sabotaging us, giving him an excuse to walk away before I begged him to stay. Or stupidly tossed in my dream job to be with him.

"What the hell's gotten into you?"

"Nothing!"

Where there'd been chatter and laughter and music a second ago, the room quieted into an eerie silence and my back prickled with the daggers of many stares.

Shoving his hand off, I bolted.

Ashamed I'd made a scene at my best friend's wedding, I didn't dare make eye contact with anyone, so I stared at the floor as I moved toward the door. I'd almost made it when a phalanx of spangly, bejeweled feet blocked my exit.

A large, bloated pair in lurid gold sandals, the straps biting into swollen flesh.

A slim pair in gaudy sequined wedge flip-flops, passable in a red light district.

A chubby pair squashed into garish red court shoes, which went out with the Ark.

A small pair in dainty, spangled, open-toe espadrilles, gold toe rings adorning each pinkie.

I knew who the musketeers were before I reluctantly raised my eyes: Mama Rama, Diva, Pooh, and Shrew, their appalling taste in footwear the least of my problems.

"How dare you make a scene at my son's wedding?" Flecks of spit flew from Mama Rama's mouth as she wobbled with rage and I inched back, eager to put as much distance between her hand and my face as possible. "You've brought nothing but disgrace on my family since the moment you set foot in our house. Shame on you."

"Why don't we calm—"

"Stay out of this, Mr. Drew." Mama's venomous glare swung his way. "This is between the ladies."

I didn't see any ladies present.

"Sorry." I injected subservience into my tone when I wanted to place my thumb on my nose and wiggle my fingers.

Poor Rita. She had to cop what this harridan dished out when she lived in Mumbai for six months every year. Damn, how had my sassy, street-smart friend agreed to that? Sure, Rakesh seemed like a modern guy but he was Indian and Rita had told me when this fiasco started about their mommy's boy tendencies. Lord help Rita.

"She's not sorry, Ma. Look at her eyes. Evil."

I turned my evil eye on Diva, she of the hooker flip-flops, and struggled to keep a straight face. She wasn't even looking at me when she spoke, her adoring goo-eyes on Drew. Ah... so that's how it was.

"You shouldn't have made a scene," Pooh chimed in, her chastisement losing sting with pastry crumbs from a *samosa* glued around her lipstick-smeared mouth.

"I agree with my sisters and mother." Shrew's narrowed eyes swung between her mom and siblings, watching, assessing.

"Leave." Mama Rama pointed at the door, her black brows drawn together so closely they formed a unibrow. "Now."

She took a menacing step toward me and I swear I saw her hand clench into a fist. Before I could react Drew edged between us, living up to his dashing hero status and making me feel like a bitch for overreacting a few minutes ago.

Wasn't his fault I was head over heels and not handling it well.

"Look, I've already apologized. Maybe it's best for the bridal couple if we forget this and enjoy the festivities?" I tried my best suck-up smile.

It didn't work. Mama Rama's frown deepened, if anything.

"The mother of the groom must have more important things to worry about than a little altercation between friends." Drew's modulated, acquiescent tone would've melted a saint. It did little for me, considering he didn't even stumble over the word 'friends.'

"Let's move on, please?" I hated to beg but I did it for Rita. Least I could do after all she'd done for me.

Firing a malevolent glare in my direction, Mama Rama straightened. "Very well. Mr. Drew's a good friend to Rakesh and for my son's sake I'll overlook your behavior. Girls, come."

She clapped her hands like a queen calling her subjects to heel and the girls followed, Diva casting a final longing look in Drew's direction, Pooh's attention already snagged by the buffet, and Shrew shrugging in resignation as she made up the procession's tail.

"Thanks. Better get back to the party—"

"Not so fast." He grabbed my hand and pulled me out the door as I frantically searched my brain for some excuse for my behavior back there, one that didn't involve telling him the truth.

We maneuvered into a small space between the elevators and a huge potted palm, leaving me little room to move. Releasing my hand, he placed his arms on either side of me, boxing me in, blocking my escape. "Start talking."

"Nice weather we're having."

He didn't smile. "What happened back there? One minute we're joking around, the next you're a banshee."

"Would you believe PMS?"

"No."

"Worth a shot." I sagged against the wall, grateful for the support as weariness seeped through me. I was tired of putting on a front, tired of pretending, tired of being the one left holding the bouquet—figuratively.

"You're leaving tomorrow," I blurted, making it sound like he had an STD.

"Thought that might be it." He traced my cheek with a fingertip, a slow, tender gesture that almost undid me completely. "This doesn't have to end."

My heart leaped before logic slapped it down. I didn't want to be some guy's standby anymore. I wanted to be prime and center in his life, wanted a guy like Drew to come home to, to snuggle with, to wake up to every morning.

It'd taken me a while to realize I deserved someone special. Sadly, I was looking straight at him, and he lived on another continent.

Emotionally, ending this relationship sucked. Logically, I had few other options. "I found a job."

If my slight deviation in topic surprised him he didn't let on. "That's great. Doing what?"

"Writing articles for a new travel/foodie magazine."

"Impressive." He touched my arm. "Maybe you should do some firsthand research in Mumbai?"

I wished. "Don't think the mag's entertainment AMEX extends to overseas jaunts."

"Too bad." The warmth in his eyes faded, replaced by caution. A smart guy like him would've picked up on my reluctance to joke about this. I couldn't, not with my heart aching from what I was about to do.

His hand slid up and down my arm, every stroke reinforcing how much I'd miss this contact, how much I'd miss *him*, when he left. "There are ways for us to be together."

"You want a relationship?" I dared to hope despite the obstacles between us.

Something indefinable flickered in his eyes. Regret? Relief? Damned if I knew.

He nodded. "I'm willing to give it a shot if you are."

I should've run up and down the corridor doing backflips that an amazing guy like Drew wanted to do more than bonk me. Instead, I couldn't get past the stumbling blocks: the distance, the differences between us, the insecurities I buried deep, the main one being what a guy like him saw in a girl like me.

I might've wised up since Tate but I had a way to go before my self-confidence was fully restored. My new job would help, followed by a place of my own. Maybe then I'd feel like I could enter this relationship as semi-equals.

"Long distance sucks."

He laughed but I saw the tightness around his mouth, the slightly clenched jaw. "You've tried it?"

"No, but—"

"I travel a lot. We could spend time together whenever I'm in New York."

No freaking way.

I'd been at the Toad's beck and call, waiting for him whenever he had a free afternoon or evening or weekend, taking whatever scraps of time he could give me. I'd sworn I'd never do that again.

Drew was nothing like the Toad but I couldn't be the part-time girlfriend he wanted. I wouldn't. I wanted more. I wanted it all.

Commitment, marriage, the works.

But the timing was off.

I'd just landed a fab job, was working toward living in a place of my own rather than a borrowed apartment, and had a vague idea of what I wanted to do with my life. Something a together-guy like him would never understand.

I laid my hand against his cheek, loving the slight rasp of stubble under my palm even though he'd shaved a few hours ago, knowing I'd miss everything about him. "I care about you. A lot. But I'm not ready to jump into a long-distance relationship. I need more than that."

"Like what?" He reached for me but I held up my hands to ward him off and he flinched at my rejection. "Tell me what you need."

His deep voice held a hint of desperation and I had a sudden flash of insight of how great it would be to have this guy love me, want me, need me forever.

"I need you to understand."

"Understand what?"

"Me." I stood on tiptoes and planted a soft, lingering kiss on his mouth, resisting the urge to prolong the sweet contact for as long as possible.

"You're asking the impossible," he said, his breath fanning my cheek as he hugged me tight, holding on like he never wanted to let go. "You're the most complex, intriguing, infuriating woman I've ever met."

I eased out of his arms but he wouldn't release me, his hands anchored on my waist. "We can make this work, Shari, I know we can."

My heart ached with the inevitability of our breakup. My head insisted I was doing the right thing. What did I have to offer? How long would he be content with long distance? Who'd have to compromise if the relationship turned serious? Considering my job didn't pay nearly as well as Drew's, I'd have to capitulate and move to be with him, and I'd be right back where I started, making compromises for the guy I loved, losing my self-respect in the process.

"I'm not leaving 'til you tell me the truth." His fingers dug into my hips and hauled me closer. "Tell me why you won't give us a chance."

Trapped in the desperation of his stare, I had to give him something, anything, so he'd release me and let me go before I blubbered all over his tux. "I don't have anything to give."

He let rip an expletive. "What the—"

"When I asked you to understand me, this is what I meant." I grabbed his lapels, wishing I could shake sense into him. "You're so together, probably the most successful person I know, and I'm… a work in progress."

He opened his mouth to protest and I rushed on. "I live in a temporary low-rent apartment, I have a job that pays as much in a year as you make in a day, and my assets fit into twenty shoe boxes. That's it. That's me. And until I'm back on my feet and feeling good about myself again, I have nothing to offer you."

"Fuck." He rested his forehead against mine and I hoped half of what I was thinking would magically transfer by osmosis. "You really feel like that?"

I sighed, wanting to kiss him so badly it hurt.

Easing away, I nodded. "Our time together has been incredible. But until I have my shit together, I can't be with you."

Light from a wall sconce cast shadows across his face, highlighting his sharp cheekbones, accentuating his strong jaw, emphasizing his compassion as he struggled to understand. "You need time."

The ever-expanding lump in my throat grew and I swallowed twice before I could speak. "I don't know how long—"

He tipped up my chin, studying my face as if memorizing it. "When you're ready to revisit this, we'll talk."

"I can't make any promises—"

"I'm not asking for any." He kissed me, a frantic clash of lips as we surged together, desperate to prolong the contact and banish the prospect of good-bye.

The elevator pinged, discharging waiters pushing food carts, and we tore apart, chests heaving, breaths ragged. He waited until the last waiter had stopped ogling and entered the reception hall before cupping my face and looking me in the eye. "Just so you know, I'm willing to wait, but I can't wait forever."

A lone tear seeped out of the corner of my eye and trickled down my cheek. He kissed it away and I placed my hands on his chest to stop this from going further.

Drew giving me time to sort myself out had only complicated matters. Knowing he was patiently waiting on the other side of the world, even if it was only for another few months, was a powerful incentive for me to head back. Maybe explore what we'd started here? Fall deeper? But then what? Go through the heartache of parting all over again? Him staying in India, me based in NYC?

A clean break would've been better. No loose ends. No false hope. No wishing for the impossible.

Giving my shattered heart time to heal.

• • •

Some girls cry at weddings, others do the best man, and most get rip-roaring drunk to drown their sorrows at being one of the few remaining desperadoes left to catch the bouquet.

Me? I went one better.

I broke up with my boyfriend.

Mama Rama and her crones ignored me for the rest of the reception. Drew never left my side. We slow danced to corny Shania Twain ballads and boogied to an ancient Elvis medley. We ate more *julabis* and *barfi* and *kulfi* than humanly possible, then worked it off later with frantic sex for twelve hours straight while we did our best to ignore his impending departure. I might have broken up with him in my head at the wedding, but my heart and body needed a proper good-bye, something our decadent day in bed provided.

He flew out the night after the wedding, leaving me lonelier than I'd ever been in my entire life.

After work the following Monday I spent the evening doing stupid things like wandering into Starbucks and having four cups of *chai*, remembering the way we'd bolted from there back to my apartment. Walking through Central Park, reminiscing about my Bollywood debut, and the way it all happened. I even took a stroll past The Plaza, where Phil the doorman pretended not to know me now that Drew had checked out. Pathetic, I know, but I needed closure and by taking a sprint down memory lane I hoped to put the whole rip-roaring adventure behind me.

Adventure? Who was I trying to kid? Being with Drew had been an exhilarating thrill and I'd never forget the rush of feeling freaking wonderful.

Anjali left for Mumbai the day after Drew, but not before extracting a promise from me to come and visit. I wished. Rita and Rakesh were due to leave on a three-month honeymoon to Europe tonight, but not before we shared a final mojito.

"You're still moping."

My finger stilled where I'd been tracing circles in the condensation on my glass. "Guess the manic pace at work is getting me down."

Rita snorted. "Yeah, like a steep learning curve has you losing five pounds in a few days."

An incriminating blush crept into my cheeks.

"Have you spoken to him?"

"He's called." I glanced at my cell phone. I'd sat on my sofa for an hour this afternoon, replaying Drew's messages, wishing things could be different.

"And?"

"I've been busy—"

"Bullshit. You're screening and you're scared."

I gulped the rest of my mojito rather than answer.

"What are you so frightened of? Being happy? Being with a guy who adores you?"

I'd never seen her so fierce and my protestations of 'butt out' died on my lips.

"He lives on the other side of the world—"

"Then go be with him." She made it sound so easy and for a moment I imagined packing, booking a ticket, and jumping on the next plane out to surprise him.

Before reality set in.

Kapil had been dead accurate. The rich man had brought me joy. But the pain of not having him around the last few days, I could do without.

You decide. Easy for Kapil to soothsay. He wasn't the one feeling lost and confused and craving a guy with the potential to break my heart.

"What are you waiting for?" Rita glowered, her drink forgotten, and I knew I'd have to give her something for her to let this go.

"You know this new job means a lot to me. I'm finally starting to stand on my own two feet."

"But?" Trust my best friend to keep probing.

"But I still feel like I have nothing to offer him."

Her eyes widened. "Don't you get it? He doesn't want anything but you."

"It's not that simple—"

"Yeah, it is." She leaped off the sofa and started pacing, her heels clacking against the floorboards, before she halted in front of me, her frown ominous. "You're in the best position to follow your heart. Not having a permanent lease is a bonus. You couldn't up and leave if you had one." She swept her arm wide. "You've paid up on this place so no stress here."

"New job? *Hello*?"

She tapped her bottom lip, thinking. "You said the magazine's expanding its online version, right?"

"Yeah."

She snapped her fingers. "Easy. You give them a big spiel about writing extra copy direct from the source. Tell them your long-lost aunt owns a culinary school in Mumbai and has offered you an apprenticeship. Or maybe she's writing a cookbook and needs your input and you'll give the magazine exclusive excerpts. Or maybe—"

Laughing at her enthusiasm, I shook my head. "I can't lie like that."

She grabbed my arms and gave me a little shake. "And you can't pass up an opportunity like this. Just go."

She made it sound so tempting, so easy.

One of her suggestions had sparked an idea. The editor-in-chief had asked me for more articles for the magazine's online version but there were only so many visits to Sassoon's and phone calls to Mom begging recipes before I ran out of ideas.

If I'd had the luck to land this job in the first place through sheer bluffing and padding my qualifications, I could probably come up with a pitch to wow him into letting me submit from Mumbai.

A little elaborating here, a little expanding there, and I could convince him to send me on a special assignment. Though it was more likely I'd have to pay my own way and still adhere to deadlines.

Hating how I was wavering, I shrugged. "No money."

She pointed at my TAG watch. "Sell that."

I covered the watch with my other hand, protective. I hadn't sold it when I'd pawned the rest of Tate's trinkets because it didn't count as a gift from him. I'd paid for it. As I reluctantly slid my hand away and uncovered the mother of pearl face, I knew I was lying to myself.

The watch might not have been a gift from Tate, but when I checked the time it proved that period in my life hadn't been all about him, that I had been able to support myself, that I didn't always need him. It made what I'd done more bearable and I'd been hanging onto it out of stubborn sentimentality.

Rita sat next to me and squeezed my arm. "You've got nothing holding you here. Why don't you go to India, give it a shot with Drew? What have you got to lose?"

Everything.

CHAPTER SIXTEEN

Mumbai hadn't lost any of its charm the second time around. (Charm could easily be interchanged with shock-value, chaos, or bedlam).

Thankfully, Jorg had loved my pitch and thought attending an Indian culinary school for a few months would be excellent article fodder. (Okay, so I'd used Rita's lie. I preferred to call it *stretching the truth*.) On the downside, he refused to fund the trip so I'd worked my ass off the last two months, writing as many articles as I could and saving every cent. Along with the proceeds from selling the TAG, I'd finally made it back here.

My folks were intrigued I intended on spending several months in India for work. I hadn't told them the real motivation behind my wanderlust. Time enough for that if everything worked out as I hoped.

Starting now.

Drew cared about me. He'd consistently called. He'd waited for me. I owed him more than the hasty brush-off farewell we'd had in New York. So here I was, with a death grip on a worn vinyl seat as a taxi veered through the chaotic streets of Mumbai, coming to a screeching halt in front of the Eye-on-I building.

Thankful I'd arrived in one piece, and tipping the driver way too many rupees because of it, I hoisted my backpack onto one shoulder and strode into the building.

I checked in with security, who eyed my backpack with a frown, until I mentioned the boss man's name. Instantly, he directed me to wait on an ebony leather sofa while he called upstairs before gesturing me toward the elevator.

If I had any doubt Drew wouldn't like a surprise visitor, he dispelled it by meeting me as I stepped out of the elevator, lifting me off my feet and hugging the life out of me.

"What are you doing here?" He held me at arm's length for a moment, his expression a mix of disbelief and awe, before kissing me on the lips in full view of his secretary, who stared with blatant curiosity at our non-Bollywood-like greeting.

"I was in the neighborhood. Thought I'd drop by."

My casual tone didn't fool him for a second as he slipped my backpack off my shoulder, hoisted it onto his, and held my hand in a tight 'this time I'm not letting you get away' grip.

I could live in hope.

"Come in," he said, the deep timbre of his voice making my insides clench in remembrance. The way he'd laugh, the way he'd playfully called me Miss Jones, the way he'd moan my name in the throes of passion.

"Guess you're surprised, huh?" Not my best opening line but standing here brought back a flood of memories that had me yearning to fling myself into his arms and forget explanations.

"Nothing about you surprises me." He smiled, the same sexy grin that made his eyes crinkle, the same grin that rendered me witless. "I'd like to think you missed me like hell the last few months and that's why you're here. But considering you rarely return my calls, I'm doubtful."

I perched on the end of his desk. "I needed to see you, to explain why I'm kafutzing around."

He grinned. "Kafutzing?"

"My version of making a mess of everything."

Drew didn't speak, wisely giving me time, and I took a deep breath, a waft of Cool Water enveloping me in a familiarity that snatched my breath. If this were a rom-com I'd ignore my reasons for making this trip, drag his head down to mine, and kiss him senseless before delivering some upbeat line to cue the closing credits and HEA. Sadly, I had no idea if I was destined for the fated happily ever after.

"I botched our good-bye in New York—"

"You don't need to do this," he said, placing a finger against my lips while I resisted the urge to nibble it. "I got the message, it's okay."

I shook my head. "No, it's not. I used my insecurities to push you away. When in reality, I'm terrified."

Concerned creases bracketed his mouth, all the encouragement I needed to take a deep breath and lay my heart on the line.

"Terrified of giving us a chance only to lose you in the end." I swallowed the lump welling in my throat. "You mean too much to me, despite the ridiculous circumstances of how we met, the misunderstandings and roadblocks, and the too-good-to-be-true fairytale romance we had in New York."

I gasped for air at the end of my spiel, deserving of a prize like all those years ago when I'd recited the McDonald's two-all-beef-patties jingle better than any other kid in my class.

I had my prize, staring straight at me with confusion in his beautiful blue eyes.

"You mean a lot to me, too—"

I held up my hand, needing to finish. "I didn't return many of your calls these last few months because I knew what would happen if I did."

Smart guy, he didn't butt in and risk talking to the hand again.

"Hearing your voice would've made me jump on the first plane out here and I didn't want to be that person anymore."

"I'm not following." He rubbed the back of his neck, bewilderment slashing his brows.

"Bear with me for a bit longer." I slipped off the desk and slid my hand into his, threading our fingers together. "I'm impulsive. I jump into situations, hoping they'll work out in the end."

He squeezed my hand in encouragement. "Like agreeing to impersonate your best friend to break her engagement?"

"Exactly like that." I managed a weak smile. "Considering how that worked out, it wasn't all bad. But rash decisions I've made in the past have been disastrous."

"You're talking about the jerk that did a number on you?"

I nodded. "I wasted a year of my life on him, and he didn't mean—"

He placed a fingertip under my chin and tilted it up. "Mean what?"

"Mean half as much as you do."

His lips kicked into a proud grin and I exhaled in relief. So far so good.

"I've come back because I want to give us a chance. I want to get to know you without the surrealism of sleeping over at The Plaza and making snack runs to Sassoon's and doing the romantic touristy stuff like walking through Central Park and sharing hot dogs on street corners."

I glimpsed excitement and hope and something indefinable in his eyes.

"I don't want to rush into this. I want us to take our time, get to really know each other, develop our friendship, and see where this relationship takes us. You in?"

"I'm all in." Three little words that may not pack the same punch as 'I love you' but based on how I felt at that moment, they came pretty damn close.

"I'm planning on hanging around a few months. You okay with that?"

He froze, and my heart stalled. Jamming a hand through his hair, he muttered a curse. "You turning up, saying what I've been dying to hear, distracted me."

I tried to quell my rising panic and failed. "From?"

He pointed at his desk. "Major acquisition deal in the UK. We're in a position to buy an Internet provider, and Rakesh is on his honeymoon, so I'm booked to fly out there tomorrow."

Okay, not so bad. I could hang out with Anjali for a few days. "For how long?"

"Six weeks."

Shit.

So much for getting to know each other. What could I say? Don't go? I'd busted my ass to be here, juggling my work duties—lying, for goodness sake—and the moment I arrive he has to leave. I'd never been a clingy girlfriend and I didn't intend to start now, not when Drew meant more to me than any other guy I'd ever known.

Uncertain, I dithered over a suitable response when he stalked around his desk and jabbed at his keyboard.

"Give me a second." He squinted at the screen, tapped some more, his fingers flying while I fidgeted, rubbing the bare spot on my forearm where my TAG used to reside.

His cell rang and he answered it as he typed one-handed, his frigid tone and escalating volume culminating in an extended argument. He paced, alternating between gesticulating with his free hand to dragging it through his hair, barking orders into the phone.

With "you're in charge" and "you make the deal happen" ringing in my ears, he opened his top drawer, flung the cell into it, and slammed it shut.

Had he just done what I thought he'd done?

His exultant whoop as he vaulted the desk made me jump.

I mentally crossed my fingers. "What's happening—"

"I'm not going anywhere." He picked me up and whirled me around until the room spun, our insane laughter echoing in his cavernous office.

When he put me down, I clung to him, determined to never let go. "But the acquisition? If it's that important—"

"Nothing's as important as you and me." His arms wrapped around my waist, snug and secure. "Business has always been my entire world." He paused, the emotion shadowing his eyes making me hold my breath. "Until I met you."

Don't cry... don't cry...

"I know it's early and we're hell-bent on exploring our connection, but you're the one, Shari Jones."

"The one?" I squeaked before clearing my throat, not daring to imagine what he meant.

He ducked his head to hum the bridal waltz in my ear and whispered, "I love you."

Elated, I buried my face in his chest so he couldn't see my soppy grin and big fat tears.

When we straightened, I laid my palm over his heart, the

consistent, steady beat, indicative of the guy I loved.

"Thanks for being patient with me."

"My pleasure." He kissed me, a soft, understanding kiss filled with promise and hope for our future.

• • •

Technically, I'd never lived with a guy. Tate had dropped by the Park Avenue apartment when it suited but we hadn't spent longer than a weekend together. So cohabitating with Drew for a few months proved to be a good test of our relationship.

We'd wanted to explore beyond the spark we shared, to test the depth of our commitment. Living with someone who snored when he slept on his back, who made odd disapproving noises when he read the newspaper, who didn't like my mess, proved to be challenging and enlightening and encouraging. Thank goodness the guy wasn't perfect.

He even let me pay a measly rent now I could afford it—I'd insisted, complete with a threat to fly back to NYC—but we both knew it was token value. I couldn't have afforded the rent on his amazing apartment on Marine Drive, featuring some of the highest land prices in Mumbai, if I starred in the next Bollywood blockbuster.

While he had his faults and I had mine, we managed to muddle along in some semblance of domestic bliss, and every morning when I woke, warm and cozy with his arm draped over my waist, I couldn't believe how damn lucky I was.

I'd lie there for ten minutes, almost holding my breath not to wake him, so I could watch him sleep. The spiky shadows cast by his eyelashes, the tempting stubble, the strong jaw. I knew every inch of him intimately: the ticklish spot behind his knee, the sensitive patch in the curve of his hipbones, the way he liked his back scratched.

Though it was more than physical. We strolled along Marine Drive every evening, the Arabian Sea stretching like a sparkling slick, talking about anything and everything. We attended work functions and movie premieres and nightclub openings as a couple. He even tolerated being dragged along to every restaurant and street stall I could find, all in the name of research for my column, never doubting our growing bond for a second.

At least, Drew didn't. Me? After two months, with my money running out as the column switched from weekly to monthly and the online version of *Viand* cut back on contributors, I knew the time fast approached where I'd have to make a permanent choice.

I knew what I wanted.

I wanted it all. The guy, the job, the transcontinental thrill.

Ideally, I'd expand my work to include freelancing for other travel magazines while dividing my time between NYC and Mumbai. For research purposes, and other more pleasurable pursuits. Namely, my evolving relationship with one very sexy Brit.

When Drew had to visit Goa for a few days on business, I took the opportunity to head back to Arnala. My birthplace had made a lasting impression during my first, all-too-brief visit. Fitting that I'd be contemplating a momentous decision there.

For a glorious five days I existed on *thali*s (a banana leaf plate covered in small mounds of rice, vegetables, *dahl, raita,* and pickles). I spent my time exploring the town, seeing the sights, absorbing the culture my ancestors took for granted on a daily basis. I took enough photos to fill two memory sticks and wrote continually, filling four journals with recipes and ramblings, all good fodder for work.

I soaked up the serenity of the people and the place, the peace infusing me with clarity.

Yeah, I missed Drew. Would he find the sea view from my dorm-like window enchanting? Would he like to sit under a banyan tree and listen to the lilting singsong accent of the locals swap stories? Would he favor the *sambhar* over the *dahl*?

Everywhere I went, with every new experience I had, it all came back to Drew.

He was my world.

It was as simple as that.

I didn't have to second-guess this decision.

Tate had been a minor aberration in the overall scheme of my life and I'd learned from it (never trust a man who has a designer shoe fetish to match yours). My self-confidence had taken a beating, making me doubt any decision I had to make.

Not anymore.

Living with Drew, trusting Drew, opening my heart to Drew, had restored my faith in myself.

I'd healed, with the help of a vibrant, startling, eye-opening country and the love of an incredible man.

Best of all, I'd done this for *me*. Every step I'd taken, every risk I'd chanced, had been worth it because it led me to this moment. Realizing how far I'd come and how far I was willing to go to secure my future.

Smiling, I hugged my knees to my chest as I sat on Arnala beach.

I wouldn't waste another minute.

I knew what I had to do.

• • •

Anjali helped me prepare.

She loved the intrigue, and I couldn't blame her. While I was terrified he'd think I was a lunatic for doing this, considering we'd only been living together two months, I couldn't wait to see Drew's face.

I hadn't seen Anjali for three weeks, and while she helped me dress, she caught me up on the latest gossip. She'd met someone, another musician (sitar player this time)—groupie!—and had lost twelve pounds. Amazing what a new love interest could do to subdue *ladoo* cravings.

Rita and Rakesh were flitting around Europe and nauseatingly in love. We Skyped them, and by Rakesh's devotion it looked like Mama Rama was out of the picture and he'd walk on hot coals for his new wife. Rita appeared radiant, and we made a pact to continue Mojito Mondays once we were back in New York. Or Mumbai, if I was lucky.

Not much had changed with the Ramas. Anu continued to terrorize Senthil, who in turn spent more time at Film City. Diva had given up her crush on Drew and moved onto someone more attainable, a guy from her local call center. Pooh had hooked up with the owner of a sweetshop. Shrew continued to watch everyone and became so good at it she was a hit at local parties, weeding out crashers.

As Buddy drove me through Mumbai's chaotic streets I forced myself to sit back, relax, and not hold onto the seat for dear life.

Despite the traffic, the pollution, the people, and the food (I patted my expanding waistline and vowed to never allow another *ladoo* to pass my lips) I'd grown to love this place. In a bizarre way, Mumbai rivaled New York City: buzzing, cosmopolitan, with a vibe all its own.

Throw in a few extra billion people, the heat, the congestion, the vile black fumes that hung over everything, the traffic mayhem (I would never curse a New York cabbie again), and a caste system that confused the hell out of anyone who didn't live here, and you get the general idea.

Mumbai dazzled and frazzled and had a unique smell—a mix of diesel fumes, smoke from burning cow patties, and sandalwood—and I'd fallen for the madness in a big way.

When we reached Film City, Buddy dropped me off inside the gates and I headed for the main office, where my man would be after returning from his business trip an hour ago.

My man.

Had a nice ring to it.

Desiree, in on the plan, gave me a thumbs up sign of encouragement as I snuck into the office. I smiled my thanks, turned the knob, and eased the door open.

Drew had his back to me, cell glued to one ear while gesticulating with his free hand, brokering some deal involving megabucks. His ivory business shirt stretched across his shoulders and my fingers tingled with the urge to touch his back as the muscles bunched and shifted beneath the crisp cotton.

I soundlessly shut the door and waited, shifting from side to side, desperate to run across the office and fling myself at him.

My chest constricted when he caught sight of me, his eyes lighting with excitement and pleasure and joy mirroring mine as he hung up mid-sentence.

"I'm glad you're back."

"Me too." He stalked around the desk and my heart flipped. "You're wearing a sari."

I gnawed on my bottom lip, botching Anjali's makeup job. "Uh-huh."

"A red sari."

He took a step.

"Yep."

Another step.

"Edged in gold *jeri*."

"Hmm."

"A bridal sari."

Three more steps, bringing him within touching distance.

"But you're not Hindu."

I whacked him playfully on the chest. "Play along with me."

He smiled. "I love the color."

He picked up my hands, studied them. "Your hands are henna-ed."

"You like?"

"Yeah." He raised my hands to his lips, brushing his lips across my knuckles, kissing each and every one until I almost keeled over. "Let me get this straight. We've been apart less than a week and you can't wait 'til I get home to see me. You're dressed like a bride. Something you're trying to tell me?"

I flung myself into his arms and he hugged me with a fierceness I reciprocated. "These last few months have been amazing. I'm not being impulsive; I've had time to figure this out, and my feelings haven't changed." I took a steadying breath and went for broke. "Scratch that. They have changed. I love you and I want to marry you if you'll have me and—"

"Whoa. Back track a second." He eased away, searching for confirmation I wasn't going crazy on him again. "You love me?"

"Like you didn't know." I patted his chest, my heart skipping a beat at the indescribable elation lighting his eyes. "I thought you were smarter than that, Bollywood Boy."

"I am, Miss Jones." His tender smile almost made me swoon. "I knew we were destined to be together from the moment we met. Took you a while to catch on."

He captured my face, stared into my eyes shimmering with tears. "I love every stubborn, outrageous, independent inch of you, and when you're ready we'll have the biggest wedding both continents have ever seen. What've you got to say about that?"

"Can Sassoon's cater?"

He laughed and wrapped his arms around my waist, lifting me up and swirling me around until I couldn't breathe.

"Put me down, you crazy man." I playfully pummeled his back and he obliged, sliding me down with measured consideration, our bodies in tantalizing full-frontal contact.

"Crazy about you," he said, a second before his lips claimed mine and I surrendered to the addictive pleasure of his kiss. When Drew locked the door and unwound my sari with gradual deliberation, his fingertips grazing my neck, my waist, my hips, lingering, teasing, I gave in to the unparalleled sizzle of starring in a scene not fit for Bollywood consumption.

Cue the music.

Roll the closing credits.

The kicker?

For us, THE END was just the beginning.

ACKNOWLEDGEMENTS

Heartfelt thanks to the following people for helping turn this book into a reality:

Liz Pelletier, Heather Howland, and the dedicated team at Entangled Publishing. Your professionalism, tirelessness, and transparency are a breath of fresh air. Kudos.

My fabulous editor Libby Murphy, for her insight, enthusiasm, and general championing. You rock, Libby!

Lewis Pollak, my publicist, for his dedicated efforts in promoting my book.

My writing allies Natalie Anderson, Fiona Lowe, and Joan Kilby, your support means so much. Whether writing, revising, brainstorming, or cyber chatting, you're always there for me. Huge hugs.

Iris Leach (dear I.I.) for the laughs, cheers, and belief in my books. Thanks from the bottom of my heart.

Serena Tatti, who read this book in its original form many moons ago. Thanks for your keen editorial eye, honest suggestions, and the best choc-mint ice cream cake ever!

Sindhu Venkadesh, for setting me right with names. And for reigniting my taste for rasam!

Ajit & Sulabha Nimbkar, for assisting with Arnala & Hindu wedding research.

My parents, Olly and Millie, for instilling their love of India in me (& for consistently whipping up incredible Indian feasts!).

My husband, Martin, who makes me laugh daily and believes I can achieve anything.

Last but not least, my littlest heroes, Heath and Jude. Thanks for your patience while mummy pounds away on the computer in the midst of Lego & Play-Doh. Your smiles, snuggles, and squishiest hugs are the best. Love you to the moon and back, my gorgeous boys. xx

Lucky
GIRL

CATE LORD

Keep reading for sample chapters of
LUCKY GIRL
by Cate Lord

Jessica Devlin isn't looking for love. Heartbroken after being dumped by her unfaithful ex-fiancé, she's determined to have a fabulous time during her vacation in England where she'll be maid-of-honor at her cousin's wedding. After working overtime as beauty editor of Orlando's *O Tart* magazine, avoiding dating, and putting on ten pounds, Jess is ready to toss her past like an empty lipstick tube and party like a single gal.

But when she steps into the church on her cousin's wedding day, she sees the one man who could sabotage her plan— James-Bond-gorgeous Nick Mondinello. She's never forgotten the London marketing exec who held her in his arms after her beloved grandfather's funeral two years ago. Ambitious, and lusted after by women everywhere, Nick is completely wrong for guarded, Plain Jane Jess.

Could Spy Man Nick ever fall for her? Nope. Not unless Jess is one lucky girl.

CHAPTER ONE

Orlando, Florida
Early June, Present Day

"Hey, Jess. If these two lipsticks were gorgeous guys asking you out on a date, which one would you choose: Mauve Mitchell or Plum Paul?"

I dragged my gaze from my computer screen. As my concentration vanished, the hum of conversation in the open-plan office and clatter of the photocopier flooded into my thoughts. The insightful sentence forming in my mind that would have added soooo much to my half-written article on the latest waterproof mascaras... Gone. Argh!

"What?" I squinted up at redheaded Miranda, my closest friend among my colleagues at *O Tart*, the Orlando-based monthly beauty and fashion magazine. She leaned her hip against the side of my desk — not that slim, fit, work-out-at-the-gym-four-times-a week Miranda had what I'd call hips.

Not compared to mine, anyway.

In her purple-nailed fingers, Miranda held two small plastic bubbles of lipstick attached to information cards. I recognized the testers. They'd landed on my desk last week amidst the deluge of catalogs, invitations, and cosmetic samples I received as the magazine's beauty editor.

I'd passed the shimmery mauve and dark plum testers on to Miranda because I'd already tried enough of that makeup line to write a review for an upcoming issue. And, as evidenced by her sparkly purple eye shadow, purple dress, and purple jewelry, Miranda worshiped purple.

Clearly sensing I hadn't wrapped my brain around her question, she said, "If these two lipstick testers were smokin' hot guys—"

A yawn broke past my lips.

"Oh, forget it," Miranda said with a huff.

"I'm sorry, Mir—"

"No you're not, Jessica Devlin."

I raised my trembling hand in protest. Maybe I shouldn't have downed that fourth humongous cup of coffee to help me stay awake. "I *am* sorry. Really."

Miranda arched a plucked eyebrow—a gesture I recognized as a silent demand for an explanation. She was probably hoping I'd admit to a torrid late-night affair, that I'd divulge all the intimate details about the man who'd kept me busy way past my bedtime. That was so far from my reality, I could cry. The best I could offer her was a more heartfelt apology.

"Look, I didn't get much sleep last night. I was up until three o'clock writing and scheduling posts for the beauty blog. It gets a lot of traffic, and I didn't want it to be neglected while I'm on vacation."

"Mmm," Miranda said, in a faintly distracted tone.

"I still have two articles to finish before I leave today. I need
to do laundry, and I haven't started packing even though my
flight to England is tomorrow afternoon. Oh! And," I glanced
at my watch, "I have a twelve o'clock appointment for the final
fitting of my dress."

"Is that all?" Miranda rolled her eyes, yet I saw a hint of
sympathy in her gaze.

"No, actually. My mom's meeting me at the dress shop. When
I'm done, we're going to lunch. It's my last chance to see her
before I leave. Anyway, after lunch, I'll be right back here, butt
in chair, until all my work is finished." I raised an eyebrow at her.
"Don't let me forget my appointment. Promise?"

"Promise." Miranda's mouth curved into a sly smile. "As long
as you bring me a souvenir from England."

"Sure. I intended to, anyway."

"Yay." Her smile turned wistful then she sighed. "Lucky you.
Leaving for two whole weeks of vacation. No phone calls, boring
staff meetings, impossible deadlines..." She wrinkled her nose.
"I'm so jealous."

"Now you know how I felt when you deserted me last
summer to get married and go on your honeymoon."

Miranda shrugged. "That was different."

"I'm *not* going to feel guilty." I gave her a mock glare. "This
is the first vacation I've had in over two years. I'm going to enjoy
every moment of it."

A deeply buried pain nudged my heart. I looked at my
computer, where five new emails had popped into my inbox. Two
years since I'd had time away from the office. That vacation, too,
had been spent in England, but with my ex-fiancé, Stan.

Hell, I *would* have taken time off long before now, but after
Stan and I had gotten engaged—almost fourteen months ago—

I'd put all ideas of a vacation on hold. I'd hung onto my vacation time, so we could book the same weeks off for our nuptials and lusty honeymoon in the Bahamas.

And then, four months ago, he'd broken my heart.

Correction—crushed it to a bloody pulp, the two-timing bastard.

In the aftermath of his betrayal, I'd wanted to take time off work. But when I'd left the apartment Stan and I had shared, tears streaming down my face, I'd sworn that I was *not* going to waste one vacation day on the anguish he'd caused me.

After moving into a rental house that I decided to buy, there were more bills to pay, plus debts for my not-happening wedding. Now that I was finally in a position to take a vacation, I was going to make the most it.

"You okay?" Miranda asked.

I snapped my gaze back to her and forced a bright smile. "Just tired." I glanced at my watch again. "Forty-two minutes until I need to head out."

"Jess." Her voice softened. "I mean, are you okay with going to your cousin's wedding? I know you had, well, doubts."

The hurt inside me wove deeper. "I did, but I plan to have a good time. A *very* good time, for a gal who's twenty-nine and single."

"Good. You deserve to have some fun. You know—"

A phone bleeped. The sound came from Miranda's desk, a short distance away, next to another cluttered desk where a dark-haired intern leafed through a stack of files. Miranda thrust her finger at me. "I'll be right back." She hurried over and answered the phone.

I swiveled my chair to face my computer. I really should try to add a few more sentences to this article, which seemed to be taking for*ever*. But as I stared at my monitor, waiting for inspiration to return, my gaze slid to the figurine beside my pen holder—an adorable, three-inch-high penguin dressed in a white shirt and tuxedo with tails, holding a bouquet of red roses. Plucky Penguin. A clever spy, and the main character of the old British TV cartoon, *The Adventures of Plucky Penguin*. Twenty-three episodes had aired before the show was canceled.

Smiling, I picked him up and ran my finger over the cool porcelain. Not a single chip—and I intended to keep him that way. How I loved this figurine and the others carefully wrapped and stowed in a box under my bed. Among them was Plucky Penguin's sidekick, Chicky Dee, a perky female spy penguin with coiffed blonde hair.

Plucky Penguin might have flirted with every bird in sight, but Chicky Dee was the only one he loved. Mistress of ingenuity, she'd wiggled her way out of every nerve-racking situation using her nifty spy-girl gadgets, red-lipped smile, and sharp-as-a-broken-fingernail wits—and saved Plucky Penguin's feather-covered ass more than once.

Grandpa George, father of my British-born dad, had introduced me to Plucky Penguin and the collectible figurines when I was twelve. After my parents divorced on terms even worse than nasty, Grandpa had become the most important person in my world. In my wild-child-teenager years, he'd been my foundation in an existence cracked by emptiness and hurt. I still treasured his letters, tucked away with the figurines.

He'd died of a heart attack two years ago, just shy of turning eighty. No way would I have missed his funeral, and Stan had flown with me to England so I could say my final good-byes. Anguish ran through me, and I tightened my hold on the figurine. I'd never forget the pain of my grandfather's death.

The reason for the trip had been heartbreaking, yet it had given me the chance to reconnect with my English cousins. We'd gotten along great, and had kept in touch ever since.

Definitely a trip I'd always remember. Although, I really wish I could forget one part of it. The part that had happened at the pub the day after the funeral—one of *the* most mortifying moments of my entire life.

But there was no point worrying about it, or the gorgeous stranger who'd come to my rescue when Stan was busy guzzling beer. I'd never see that guy again.

If I ever *did* see him again... Oh, my God, I'd simply—

The speaker on my phone beeped, making me jump. "Jess," Miranda said. "Want to get some coffee?"

I spun my chair toward her desk. "You are so lazy. You *could* walk the five steps over to my desk and ask me."

She grinned. "Yeah, but you might say 'no,' and then I'd have to walk the five steps back."

Judging by my shaky hands, I didn't need one more drop of coffee. But another yawn tickled the back of my throat. "You know I'm going to say yes. I have to stay awake. And I have to get some work done, or I'll never be able to go home tonight."

We walked together to the small kitchen with cracked vinyl flooring, a beige refrigerator from the 1980s, a fifteen-year-old microwave, and a plastic table and four chairs.

Natalie, a slender, twenty-something blonde, stood in the kitchen. Formerly in Advertising, she'd transferred to the Editorial Department a few weeks ago. She'd just taken a chilled bottle of spring water and a grapefruit from the fridge.

"Hi, Natalie." I crossed to the coffee maker, poured Miranda a cup, then filled one for myself.

I turned toward the doorway just as my gray-haired boss,

Mr. Stevens, walked by. He wore his familiar slick, black suit with a white shirt. His brooding gaze met mine, and he came to an abrupt stop.

"Jess." He leaned into the doorway. "Those articles. When will you have them to me?"

Ack! "I'll email them to you by the end of the day. I've got graphics to run with the stories too."

"And the blog posts?"

"Done, as promised. I have them scheduled to run while I'm away."

"Good." He smiled at Natalie, who sipped her water, then shifted his attention back to me. "This afternoon, I'd like you to give this lovely young lady here"—he tipped his head toward Natalie—"a quick rundown of your job. She'll be covering for you while you're away—opening your mail, answering your email, taking your phone calls."

A weird chill ran through me. I fought the urge to cast Miranda a what-the-hell glance. "Mr. Stevens, I really don't think that's necessary. I thought we'd agreed—"

"Change of plans. Two weeks is a long time to have a staff member out of the office." He straightened, tugging down his jacket sleeves. "Make sure you set an auto reply on your email with Natalie's contact information. Okay?"

"Yes, sir."

"Oh, and if I don't see you before you leave tonight, have a good time in England."

"Thanks." God, it was hard not to scowl.

Stevens walked away, and I turned my gaze to Natalie. She smiled, her glossy, scarlet-painted mouth too perfect to be real. In fact, everything about her looked model perfect—straight teeth, tailored red suit, white blouse with silver buttons, and shiny black heels.

Thanks to Miss Beauty Pageant, I felt positively... inadequate.

"This afternoon, then," she said. "What's a good time for you, Jess? Shall we say—"

"Two o'clock."

"Perfect. I'll see you then." She strolled out of the kitchen.

Miranda raised her eyebrows, as though about to launch into a hushed discussion about Natalie. I didn't have time to talk. I *had* to get my work done. I was not going to give Stevens one reason to complain about my being away for two weeks— especially when, after eight years at *O Tart*, I was in line to become Managing Editor when the position opened.

I spun on my heel, headed back to my desk, set down my coffee, and dropped into my chair.

With a faint crackle of static, my monitor woke up.

"Waterproof mascara," I said under my breath, focusing on the screen. "Come on, Jess. Write something brilliant."

Just as the words finally began to flow, my cell phone trilled. I fished the phone from my purse and glanced at the number. Recognizing it—and the time displayed on the screen—I groaned.

Crap.

"Appointment," Miranda called from her desk.

"Hi, Mom," I said into the phone. I closed my document, grabbed my purse, and dashed for the door. "Yes, I know. I'm on my way."

• • •

"What do you think?" the seamstress asked.

I stood in front of the shop's three-way mirror, under the glare of bright lights. She adjusted the drape of the shimmering, peach-colored gown that touched the carpeted floor and covered most of blowsy, unfit me.

Ugh.

Regardless of the alterations she'd made to the dress, this tight-bodiced, puffy-sleeved abomination didn't suit me. I doubted it would look good on any twenty-first century gal with a bra size over 36C. It transformed me into a double D. Maybe even an E.

Whoa, mama. Just watch me strut into that English church, boobs first, displaying my busty bounty like a voluptuous, carved goddess on the prow of an old Viking ship.

Not.

Smoothing my hands down over my belly, I turned for a profile view. Gah! How had I let my stomach get so plump? Why, after Stan left me, had I allowed myself to eat whatever I wanted, whenever I craved it? Proof of all those reckless snack fests stared back at me.

"You are unhappy with the fit?" The woman sounded disappointed.

"No, you've done a great job." I couldn't bear to explain that my dissatisfaction had nothing to do with her skill, and everything to do with me.

She reached for a side seam, as if looking for a way to take the dress in another half-inch and thereby make me look slimmer. A sniffling sound came from behind me. My gown rustled as I turned to look at my mom, sitting on a chair beside a long rack of clothes to be altered. The bright lighting accentuated the gray in her honey-colored, shoulder-length bob.

She wiped her eyes then rummaged in her purse.

"Are you okay?" I asked, crossing to her. Although I loved my mother dearly, she could be a bit of a drama queen at times.

However, she'd told me a few weeks ago she was going through menopause—although I'd already guessed—and that she couldn't help her emotional outbursts.

Whatever the reason for her crying, I hated to see her in tears. It stirred up those painful memories of being twelve, and the months after my dad had left us. I'd stood outside her closed bedroom door in the middle of night, listening to her cry. How badly I'd wanted to help her, but hadn't known what to do.

She flicked her hand at me. "I'm fine, honey. Make sure your dress is the way you want it."

Her brisk tone told me she didn't want to discuss what was bothering her. Not here, anyway. Later, at lunch, I'd likely be subjected to every last detail.

As I turned back toward the mirror, my gaze landed on the gauzy, beaded wedding dress lying on a nearby table. Suddenly, I knew why she was upset. If Stan hadn't left me, she and I would still be at the seamstress', only I wouldn't be busting out of a maid-of-honor gown. I'd be wearing my wedding dress.

Pain cut into me. *No.* I would not allow myself to get all teary eyed, too.

I walked back to the mirror, welcoming the anger I saw in my eyes. Anger that had kept me going from the moment I'd found out Stan had screwed one of the receptionists from his office—in our bed, no less—while I was working late to meet a deadline. My wedding dreams had dissolved in a cloud of choking dust.

Even now, I heard his voice, as though he sat on my shoulder and taunted, "Could you blame me? You weren't home. Besides, she's a hell of a lot better in bed than you."

As the hurtful words had poured from his mouth, my fingers had itched to get hold of Chicky Dee's Instant-Ice Zapper gun, to pull the trigger and freeze his mouth along with every other unfaithful part of him—until I'd chosen to unfreeze him.

Which might have been never.

A tug on the back of my gown brought my focus back to the seamstress, cutting a loose thread from the hem. I shoved away all memories of Stan. I had a lot more important things to think about, like finishing my articles so I could finally take my vacation.

The seamstress stood.

"The dress is fine," I said. "If you don't mind, I'm on my lunch break. I need to get back to work as soon as possible."

"Of course. I'll get a garment bag for your gown while you get dressed."

I started toward the fitting room, and Mom came up beside me. "You look very nice, Jess."

No, I didn't. But, being an ever-supportive mother, she offered me the encouragement she thought I needed. For that, I was grateful.

"Thanks, Mom."

Her eyes looked dry now, and the familiar sparkle in them had returned. She guided me toward the fitting room in that no-nonsense, motherly way. "Let's go to that Italian restaurant down the street for lunch. The one that makes that fabulous tiramisu."

My stomach gurgled in appreciation. Tiramisu was one of my top five favorite desserts, as she well knew. It was also loaded with calories. I didn't dare put on one more pound before my vacation.

"Mom, I can't take a long lunch today. I have to—"

"I know, you need to get back to the office. You can't skip lunch, though. That Stevens doesn't expect you to work on an empty stomach, does he?"

CHAPTER TWO

Hertfordshire, England

God, I hate my boobs.

I frowned at my reflection in the gilt-framed mirror hanging above the sinks in the English church bathroom. The mirror looked oh so very elegant paired with the floral-print wallpaper. But then, there was me. I was no pretty English rose like each of my cousins, but a nondescript-looking American gal squeezed into a hideous maid-of-honor gown.

I'd secretly hoped for a miracle during the nine-hour plane flight from Orlando. Maybe, just maybe, I'd arrive in England a slimmer, prettier me. Maybe, just maybe, I'd have grown to adore my dress.

That miracle clearly wasn't happening any time soon.

Trying not to listen to the peeing noise coming from the bathroom stall behind me, I silently pleaded for my cousin Charlotte to hurry up.

Sticking out my tongue at my reflection, I tugged at the

peach silk stretched as tight as plastic wrap over my breasts. My boobs looked like two fat blobs straining against the silk. Thanks to the cool interior of the old stone church—brr, so different from hot, muggy Florida—my nipples made round bumps under the fabric like two olives stuck on top for decoration.

Jess, the giant peach, with bonus pitted olives.

Oh, stop!

Exhaling on a huff, I tugged again. The fabric refused to budge. Not even one teeny, forgiving pucker.

I swallowed a groan and tried to ignore the organ music floating in under the main bathroom door. In a few short minutes, I'd be walking up the aisle in Tilly's fairy-tale wedding. The whole family knew the classic story of how she'd fallen in love with a rich hottie from London, whom she'd met in one of her university courses.

Hurt pierced somewhere in the vicinity of my heart, a stupid, senseless anguish over my own fairy-tale wedding that had never come to be. An icky feeling—like I'd swallowed a foot-long slug—slid down into my stomach.

Had I made the right decision to come to this wedding? It was kind of late to have regrets, but should I have been smart like Chicky Dee? She wouldn't have had a single qualm about calling her English relatives the day of her scheduled flight to say, "You won't believe what happened. I busted my ankle. How? Well, I was leaving the *O Tart* office yesterday when I saw a turtle plodding across the scorching hot parking lot. I dashed off the sidewalk to rescue it, and... *snap*. One broken ankle. I'm sorry, but I just don't think I'm up to flying." Yesss! The perfect excuse to have stayed home, ordered pizza every night, and overindulged in sitcom reruns.

No, Jessica Devlin, an annoying voice inside my head piped up.

You agreed to be the maid of honor because Tilly is a wonderful cousin and she wanted you to be in her wedding party. Plus, you haven't had a vacation in forever. You need to get a life.

Sheesh. Life was pretty sad, indeed, when I agreed with voices inside my head.

Studying my reflection again, I tweaked my blah brown hair, coiled up in a french twist with wispy strands curving down by my cheeks. Under my breath, I recited the mantra I'd invented on the long plane flight to England. "I, Jessica Devlin, will have a fan-damn-tasic vacation. I will *not* wallow in the smelly cow pies of the past."

In those tedious hours of traveling, I'd assigned myself a mission—to become as resourceful as Chicky Dee. To use this vacation to explore beyond my humdrum comfort zone. I'd return home a revitalized, more confident Jess.

Righty-ho.

I smiled at myself in the mirror and did a slow, sassy wink just like Chicky Dee's. At the reception later, I hoped to get a good British kiss—a "snog" as they called it this side of the pond—and any other sensual delights that might lead to.

I let the posh-sounding word roll over my tongue. "SSSnnnooogggg," I said softly to the mirror before pursing my lips in a perfect Chicky Dee imitation. "SSSnnn—"

A loud gurgling noise erupted behind me.

"—ooooggg."

The bolt on the door behind me clicked. My nineteen-year-old cousin, Charlotte, walked out of the stall, smoothing her dress.

She squinted her blue eyes at me. "Did you say something?"

Ack! "No." I rubbed my lips together, pretending to blend the Estée Lauder lipstick Mom had given me out of a gift with purchase because she'd already gotten the shade.

Charlotte was still staring at me. "Are you sure you're all right? You were squishing up your lips."

Double ack! I shoved stray hair back behind my ear. "Just fixing my lipstick."

She giggled. "It looked like you were going to kiss the mirror."

I rolled my eyes, hoping my dramatics would put an end to my cousin's musings. "Why would I do that?"

She shrugged, crossed to the sink, and switched on the hot and cold taps to wash her hands. How pretty she looked, her long blonde hair pinned up, her slim figure outlined by her peach dress. Like an angel from a Victorian painting. Even her name was elegant. I imagined my Aunt Cleo saying "Charlotte" in her posh accent—Shaaahhh-lotte—a verbal mélange of Arabian prince and onion.

Charlotte's lips were tinted with sheer, apricot-colored lip gloss. With her fair coloring, she'd look dynamite in the lipstick sample I'd tested the other week, a claret red called Throb.

But judging by her virginal demeanor, I guessed Charlotte hadn't throbbed a man yet, so maybe that wasn't appropriate. Besides, the shade was better suited for slinky black velvet than peach silk.

"I'm so glad you could be here today," Charlotte said, a lavender scent wafting up from her soapy hands. "It means a lot to Tilly."

"I wouldn't have missed her wedding. I've really looked forward to it." Hell, I didn't even blush. When had I learned to lie so easily?

I was becoming as wily as Stan, the Two-Timing Jerk.

No. Not quite. It was no lie I was a sucker for a good party with lots of gin. Or margaritas. Or piña coladas. Or—

Charlotte turned off the water. "At least you'll have a break from your busy job." She reached for a paper towel, then dried her hands.

"Yes. I had to get my articles for the August issue written before I left, though. My 'Mascara Madness' write-up—"

"Mascara! Oh, thanks. I knew I'd forgotten to fix something." Charlotte squinted at her reflection and swiped at her lower lashes. Then, with a satisfied sigh, she stepped away from the mirror and smiled at me.

"What? Do I have lipstick all over my teeth?" I bared my pearly whites for the mirror.

"No, Cuz. I was just thinking now pretty you look."

"Really?" I didn't mean to sound so astonished.

Charlotte nodded.

Was I the only one who saw how boob-squishingly awful I looked in this gown? A tiny bubble of relief floated up inside me.

Then again, would sweet Charlotte really tell me if I looked hideous?

She blew out a shaky breath. "I'm nervous. Are you?"

"A bit." As in, *yeah, a whole lot.*

"I'm so happy you came to England, Jess. It seems like forever since..." Her voice trailed off to awkward silence, but I knew what she'd planned to say—*since you and Stan visited for Grandpa George's funeral.*

Another memory of the gorgeous stranger who'd comforted me all those years ago teased my thoughts. How dumb, to keep thinking about him. Honestly, what was the point? There had to be a one-in-a-gazillion chance I'd ever see him again. "There was no way I'd miss a favorite cousin's wedding."

"You'll recognize a few blokes in the wedding party. I

remember you met some of Tilly and Andrew's friends last time you were here."

"That's right. Who—"

The main bathroom door flew open, and my Aunt Cleo—wife of my Uncle William and mother of Charlotte, Tilly, and my other cousin, Anna—hurried in. Plumpish and round faced, she looked elegant in her sage green chiffon.

Aunt Cleo was my dad's sister. I saw a shadow of him in her smooth brow and generous mouth, but their resemblance stopped there. My dad didn't have the courtesy to reschedule his two-month trip to South America with his latest bit of fluff, yet Aunt Cleo would never miss a young relative's wedding. I had fully expected her to cross the pond for mine.

Peering into the mirror, she patted her blonde hair streaked with white-gray. "Is my hair all right?"

"Yes," Charlotte and I said in unison.

"Be honest, you two. Has it gone frizzy again?"

"It's perfect," I said. Considering the gallon of hair spray I had spritzed on her updo earlier, it should stay put for a month.

"Thank you." Her cultured, British-accented voice sounded close to panic overload. She glanced at me and Charlotte. "Tilly's arrived. Come on."

My stomach twisted. The big moment loomed.

Taking careful steps in my glitzy sandals with three-inch heels, I followed Charlotte out into the foyer. My uncle helped the ushers—all young, fit, and *GQ* handsome—to direct arriving guests. A little flower girl toyed with the fresh daisies in her basket tied with ribbons, while her mom tweaked her curly ringlets.

The church door stood open. Light spilled in, tingeing the old wood paneling and vases of peach roses with gold. I peered outside. A sleek white car was parked close by, the back door open. Tilly sat inside. Next to her was the third bridesmaid, a friend of Tilly's named Valerie, who looked obscenely pretty in peach silk.

A huge bouquet of white and peach roses lay in Tilly's lap. Her french-manicured hand curled like a flower into the veil gathered around her like a wispy cloud. She looked like a model out of the bridal magazines I'd bought months ago. I'd pored over them, tucking away ideas for my dream wedding, while Stan sprawled, beer in hand, in front of the TV watching football.

A sharply dressed photographer positioned himself close to Tilly and snapped pictures with a digital camera. "That's it," he murmured. "Tilt your head. Chin up a bit, love. Good. Now, if you and Valerie could smile for me..."

Sunshine streamed through the limo's open door, softening Tilly's flawless skin and making her ivory silk gown shimmer. The sequins decorating her train glittered like fairy dust.

She positively glowed, the light shining not only from the outside, but also from within. Tilly loved herself, despite her quirks and flaws. She adored the guy she was about to marry, and he cherished her.

Lucky girl.

Envy curled up within me like poison ivy.

Tilly glanced at the church door as if she felt my gaze. She smiled and waved to me.

I managed a wave back, trying to ignore the torment stabbing through me. It wasn't my fault that I, being the oldest cousin, had always been expected to marry first.

It wasn't my fault that at the ripe old age of twenty-nine, life had thrown a curve ball my way and knocked me on my butt without a man.

Without even a boyfriend, or the prospect of one.

How pathetic.

I suddenly craved the cold, creamy, delicious depravity of Ben & Jerry's Vanilla Heath Bar Crunch ice cream, a staple of my diet for the past several months. Okay, more than a staple— my culinary crutch. Mmm. Right now, I could snarf the whole carton in two minutes, flat. Why not add another pound to the extra ten around my belly and hips?

Knowing my rotten luck, I'd eat two gorgeous mouthfuls and drop the third on my dress. That unattractive, melted smear would be the perfect finishing touch for this nightmare gown.

Yeah, right.

"I, Jessica Devlin, am going to have a great vacation," I said under my breath. "I will *not* wallow in the smelly cow pies of ex-fiancé dumpdom. I will return to Orlando a brand new Chicky Dee Jess."

A burst of activity in the foyer caught my attention. Aunt Cleo hurried out of a side room carrying bouquets of peach and white roses tied with white ribbons. She handed one to Charlotte and my cousin Anna, whose spiky auburn hair and smart-girl glasses made her look way older than twenty-two.

Turning toward me, my aunt rushed over and pushed a slightly larger bouquet into my hands. "Here you are." She patted my arm. "Smile, Jess."

"I just hope I don't mess up." At that moment, more people stepped into the church and, in the flurry of "hellos," she didn't hear me.

I stared down at the pretty, perfect blooms. Oh God, I'd better not screw up. Maybe that's why I felt so weird about this wedding. I was totally unprepared for today's mission, in more ways than one.

My seventy-two-year-old Aunt Prim had picked me up at Gatwick airport—waited well over two hours for me, since my plane had landed late and my suitcase had taken forever to turn up. I'd stayed one night at her quaint London home, then we'd ended up in a six-hour traffic jam on our drive up to Hertfordshire last night. Aunt Prim had gripped the steering wheel and said "Bloody hell, we'll never get there," every thirty seconds. I'd had to pee *sooo* badly.

Aunt Prim had driven me straight to the wedding rehearsal and dinner, but I'd arrived *very* late. I didn't even have a chance for a chin-wag with my aunt, uncle, and cousins to catch up on all their news. The groom and his buddies had already left for a rowdy night of pub-crawling. The priest had walked me back to the church and shown me what to do during the ceremony, but that wasn't quite the same as a bona fide rehearsal.

Ugh. I did *not* want to embarrass Tilly on her day—the special day every woman dreamed of.

Oh, please, please, please. Let my bad luck vanish for the next twelve hours.

A high-pitched ringing noise filled my ears. Chicky Dee had never missed a step no matter how skinny her heels. I, however...

I suddenly imagined myself tripping and sailing into the air, my dress flying up around my face to reveal my white undies. With a loud, undignified shriek, I'd land facedown on the church aisle in a heap of ripped peach silk.

Wouldn't that be lovely? Not!

I would *not* trip. I would *not* fall face first.

A boisterous rendition of Bach's Jesu, Joy of Man's Desiring started up inside the church. I glanced in. The pews were almost filled. I recognized Aunt Prim. She was impossible to miss, even from behind, her curly gray hair poking out from beneath her enormous white hat spattered with fuchsia, yellow, and pink flowers.

The groom, Andrew Castleton, a handsome guy with wavy blond hair, stood with his best man near the altar. Andrew clasped and unclasped his hands as if he couldn't keep them still. Yup, I'd say he was nervous.

Anna and Charlotte moved to my side. When Andrew saw them, relief softened his features. He grinned, and I knew exactly what he was thinking: *Tilly, the woman I love, is here.*My cousins giggled and nodded.

My attention shifted to the best man. Mmm. Tall, broad-shouldered—

Oh. My. God!

My heart jolted like I'd just stuck my pinkie into an electrical outlet.

Nick Mondinello. The man my cousins had whispered about years ago. Sex God. Playboy. Heartbreaker.

Spy Man.

He still looked like a younger version of Pierce Brosnan, the actor who'd starred in a couple of James Bond movies. Nick wore his dark hair shorter now and spiked with gel. He filled out his tailored gray suit very, very nicely.

Memories whooshed through my mind. The day after Grandpa George's funeral. The Creaky Wicket Pub. The potted plant. Heat flooded my face, hotter than if I had yanked open an oven set to broil.

Aaahhh! How could my mind torture me at a time like this?

Nick glanced at me. Vines seemed to have snaked up from the carpet and locked around my ankles. The heels of my sandals felt rooted to the floor. The murmurs and music around me faded into a weird, twilight-zone buzz.

Doo-dee-doo-doo, Doo-dee-doo-doo.

I forced my lips into a stiff, polite smile and adjusted my sweaty-handed hold on my bouquet. It would be just my luck to drop the pretty arrangement on the floor and turn it into a mangled hodgepodge.

Nick looked at someone on the other side of the church, and I exhaled noisily.

Then he looked at me again. He squinted, as though he was trying to place me. Maybe he was wondering why I was blushing so fiercely.

Severe sunburn. Hot flushes. Woman's stuff.

I hadn't blushed like this on my first date.

I held the roses tighter to my chest. Thank goodness the big bouquet would draw attention away from my boobs.

My face burned. Scorched, more like it. Embarrassing now, but not quite as mortifying as what I'd done two years ago.

Glancing away from Nick, I watched one of the ushers escort Aunt Cleo to a front pew, where she sat beside Aunt Prim.

I felt acutely alert, as if I was a taut spring, about to uncoil with a loud *poing* like a jack-in-the-box.

Was Nick still looking at me?

I struggled to quiet the desperate squeak rising in my throat. Maybe I was worrying for nothing. Maybe Nick didn't even remember what had happened.

He'd been drinking that night. We all had. Some of us—specifically *moi*—a lot more than others.

I dared a glance. Nick nodded in response to something Andrew said. A smile curved Nick's mouth.

Hushed voices along with the whisper of silk came from behind me. Valerie, Tilly, and my uncle had entered the church.

My belly squeezed tight. Any moment now, the ceremony

would begin.

Dread shivered through me.

A countdown began ticking in my head.

Ten... nine...

Oh no. In the recessional, I would have to walk arm in arm with Nick. Help!

Seven... six...

Butterflies swooped in my stomach. My hands felt coated in olive oil. The ushers led the last of the guests to their pews.

Three... two...

When the guys returned, the organist paused for a moment then struck up a vibrant march.

The "Wedding March."

Ping. The moment of truth was upon me.

I hadn't prayed in months. But as the ushers began a slow walk up the aisle, I prayed I didn't trip, stumble, or make a fool of myself.

Not in front of Tilly and my relatives.

Not in front of gorgeous Nick Mondinello.

Again.

Anna, Charlotte, and Valerie lined up ahead of me to begin their graceful stroll up the aisle. As I drew a deep breath, Nick's gaze locked with mine.

He was still smiling.

In that moment, I knew without the teeniest bit of doubt.

He remembered.